SILENT THUNDER

ALSO BY IRIS JOHANSEN

QUICKSAND

PANDORA'S DAUGHTER

STALEMATE

AN UNEXPECTED SONG

KILLER DREAMS

ON THE RUN

COUNTDOWN

BLIND ALLEY

FIRESTORM

ALSO BY ROY JOHANSEN

DEADLY VISIONS

BEYOND BELIEF

THE ANSWER MAN

SILENT

IRIS JOHANSEN

THUNDER

AND ROY JOHANSEN

ST. MARTIN'S PRESS ✻ NEW YORK

SILENT THUNDER. Copyright © 2008 by Johansen Publishing, LLP, and Roy Johansen. All rights reserved. Printed in the United States of America. For information, address St. Martin's Press, 175 Fifth Avenue, New York, N.Y. 10010.

www.stmartins.com

Book design by Dylan Rosal Greif

Library of Congress Cataloging-in-Publication Data
Johansen, Iris.
    Silent thunder : Iris Johansen and Roy Johansen.—1st ed.
       p. cm.
    ISBN-13: 978-0-312-36799-2
    ISBN-10: 0-312-36799-6
    1. Naval architects—Fiction.   2. Brothers and sisters—Fiction.   3. Submarines (Ships)—Fiction.   4. Nuclear submarines—Fiction.   I. Johansen, Roy.   II. Title.
    PS3560.O275S55   2008b
    813' .54—dc22   2008010706

First Edition: July 2008

10   9   8   7   6   5   4   3   2   1

For Iva Beatrice Needham

mother and grandmother

celebrating a landmark birthday...
celebrating her eternal place in our hearts

ACKNOWLEDGMENTS

No one knows submarines better than the brave men and women who spend months at (and under the) sea on the vessels, and their input was vital to the story, atmosphere, and very concept of this book. Special thanks to Captain Third Rank Igor Kolosov, former staff officer of the Russian submarine fleet in Vladivostok. His patience and kindness were nothing short of monumental as he shared his years of experience with us.

On the other side of the Cold War, we also owe a debt of gratitude to David H. Stryker, USN (Ret.), former executive officer of the USS *Will Rogers*. A chance meeting in Poland became a valuable resource for the technology—and psychology—of underwater warfare.

SILENT THUNDER

PROLOGUE

Kirov!

No, it couldn't be Kirov, Jennings thought frantically, as he ran down the dock. Kirov was dead. Pavski had given him his word that the stories were all lies. He'd laughed and said that a ghost couldn't kill.

And the person behind him was no ghost. It didn't have to be Kirov. Jennings had made a lot of enemies in his life, and any one of them might be the man behind him.

But there was no one behind him now. A quick glance behind him revealed an empty dock. His heart slowed as he drew a deep, relieved breath. He'd lost him. Maybe it had only been a thief. Yes, that was it. It was a lousy section of town, and the man had just targeted his wallet.

Not his life.

He shouldn't have panicked. But after he'd heard about Lantz's death, his nerves had been on edge. He'd be glad to be done with this business. His pace slowed as he approached the pier where the sub was moored. The *Silent Thunder* lay still and lethal as if crouching, waiting for prey, waiting to take another life.

Prey. He tried to suppress the shiver that went through him. He only had to get on the sub and do what Pavski had asked him to do. Nothing was going to happen. It was no more a death ship than Kirov was a ghost.

But, God, he didn't want to go on that sub, he thought desperately as he reached the end of the block. He should have never listened to Pavski and stayed undercover. No amount of money was worth this—

A leather noose slipped around his neck from behind!

Pain. He struggled wildly to turn his head to see the man who had stepped out of the shadows. He only had an impression of height and broad shoulders as he started to black out. He couldn't breathe . . .

The garrote tightened around his neck.

The sub . . .

He could see the *Silent Thunder* before him, patiently waiting, ready to take him to hell as it had all the others. His vision was fading, and he could see nothing but that monster of a sub. He was going to die, he realized incredulously. No! He struggled harder.

"Stop it." The order was a soft murmur in his ear. "I don't want to kill you yet. They say you might still be useful."

Kirov. My God. Damn you, Pavski. Lies. Lies. Lies.

Kill the bastard. His hand closed on the knife holstered on his left arm.

"Well, actually I do want to kill you now," Kirov said. "Thank you for giving me the excuse."

He twisted the garrote, jerked backward, and broke his victim's neck.

ONE

ROCK BAY HARBOR, MAINE
EIGHT MONTHS LATER

"She's beautiful, isn't she?" Conner parked the van on the dock and leaned back in his seat with a sigh of contentment. "She looks like a panther. Sleek, graceful, and magnificently lethal."

"My God, you're waxing poetic." Hannah chuckled and shook her head as she jumped out of the van. "It's a machine, Conner. A submarine. And she's beautiful only in the way a finely constructed machine is beautiful. It was designed and built by man. It's not as if it's alive."

"You have no soul." Conner got out of the van and moved eagerly toward the edge of the pier. "Do you think Michelangelo's *David* has no beauty because it was carved from stone? This is the same thing."

"You always say that." She followed her brother to the edge of the pier and gazed appraisingly at the black submarine. But she could see why Conner was bubbling with enthusiasm. There was something sleek and elegant about all submarines and this Oscar II was no exception although the hull showed every one of its twenty-two years. Officially named *Kulyenchikov,* the twin-reactor nuclear sub was dubbed *Silent Thunder* by its builders in the Severodvinsk shipyard, and the workers' name stuck. An appropriate moniker, Hannah thought. The *Silent Thunder*'s dark, massive hull seemed to devour all light around it. At more than five hundred feet in length, it was one of the largest submarines in the world.

She glanced back at Conner. "You even thought that submersible I designed for the *Titanic* expedition was beautiful, and it looked like a goggle-eyed frog."

"Frogs can be beautiful." He made a face. "Well, they can be interesting-looking. Did I really say it was beautiful?"

She nodded. "But you were drunk at the time. It was the night we had the party at that bar in Halifax when the expedition was over. You were going home to Cathy and the kids, and you thought everything was beautiful."

"That was the longest time I ever had to be away from them. You had too many damn problems with that submersible."

"But interesting problems. And it performed well in the end."

He lifted a brow. "And that was all that was important to you. All the romance and excitement of the greatest expedition of the century, and you were only concerned with how efficiently your machine worked."

"You can have all the excitement." She took a step closer to the sub. "Satisfaction is enough for me. I did a good job, and it made it possible for all you dreamers to indulge yourselves to your hearts' content."

"Well, thank God this job won't be as all-consuming. Cathy told me she wanted me home in two weeks, or she was filing for divorce."

"Fat chance." Cathy was as practical as Conner was idealistic, and after ten years of marriage it had become second nature to her to act as her husband's guardian as well as his lover. Since Cathy had been a high-powered and very successful aide to Congressman George Preston before the birth of their son, the transition was entirely natural. "But the job shouldn't take more than a couple weeks. All I'm being paid for is doing a second schematic of the sub, checking it out for possible hazards, and suggesting a few tourist-friendly modifications before the museum opens it for exhibition. That's the only reason I took the job. I needed a filler while I waited for them to be ready for me on the Marinth site."

"Oh, no, you couldn't just sit back and rest for a little while. I'm surprised they didn't do that check before they sailed it into this harbor. After all, it's a nuclear submarine."

"The government did check it out for weapons and contamination last year when they discovered it hidden in that bay in Finland."

"That's another weirdo. Why would the Russians want to hide this particular sub?"

"They say they didn't, that they merely lost track of it during the political upheaval when the Soviet Union was breaking apart." She shrugged. "But the State Department thinks they're giving us the usual bullshit. The Russians still don't tell us anything they can keep to themselves. The scuttlebutt is that some Russian bureaucrat pocketed the money that had been appropriated for its dismantling. He paid off the shipyard director in Finland to hide it among the dozens of other ships and subs that the Russian Navy has there awaiting deactivation."

"There are that many?"

She nodded. "It's expensive to scrap a submarine, especially if there are nuclear materials involved. Anyway, Bradworth says they've been very cooperative since the Finns discovered it."

"Bradworth?"

"Dan Bradworth, he's the State Department liaison who negotiated with the Russians for the purchase of the sub for the Maritime Museum. Though not that much negotiation was necessary. Russia is so strapped for cash, they gave the museum a bargain. But the museum didn't want to take any chances on surprises when they brought it here to set up the exhibit. That's why Bradworth tapped us for the job."

"Tapped you," he corrected. "You're the expert. You know it was the *Ariel* that got you the job."

She shrugged. "Maybe." Four years before, she'd designed a new Orca-class U.S. Navy submarine called *Ariel,* and it had marked a bold departure from what had come before. Nuclear-powered submarines had changed little in their first half century of use, and her innovative concepts brought her much attention among naval buffs and marine architects. Although the Orca program was ultimately shelved due to budget cuts, the classified plans found their way into naval magazines and Web sites, where *The Submarine That Never Was* and its young creator had taken on a peculiar mystique. Whenever

Hannah met someone in her profession, the *Ariel* was one of the first topics of conversation.

"No maybe. You're the real star here, and you know it," Conner said. "I just go along for the ride."

"That's not true." She frowned. "You're very good at your job. I wouldn't know what to do without you."

"Hey, I didn't mean to make you feel guilty. I like being your gofer. Where else would I get paid for traveling all over the world and accepting your abuse?" His smile faded when she still looked troubled. "Stop it, Hannah. Do you think I would have worked with you all these years if I hadn't wanted to do it? I love you, but I'm not that self-sacrificing. I've always known you were the smart one in the family. Not only are you a mathematical and mechanical whiz, but you have that quirky memory. I knew from the minute you took one glance and quoted my Boy Scout manual from cover to cover that I was going to be trailing behind you."

"I didn't mean to make you feel—I was just a kid trying to be a smart aleck. You were always making fun of me. It's what brothers do. I guess I wanted you to think I was special."

"And you were special," he said gently. "And I could see it wasn't easy for you. I saw how the other kids teased you. That's why I stopped doing it myself. Being different is always hard. A lot of jealousy. A lot of misunderstanding. I never wanted that burden. I'm no Einstein, but that's okay. I like what I do, and I like who I am." He grinned. "And thank God Cathy likes who I am, too."

She cleared her throat, and said gruffly, "She'd better. You're kind of special."

"Not 'kind of.' Absolutely."

"And you *are* smart."

He chuckled. "I have horse sense, but there's no brilliance lurking in my noggin. I wouldn't want it. It would be too uncomfortable." He gave her a sly glance. "And it might prevent me from enjoying the finer things in life. Look at you. You can't even enjoy the beauty of this submarine. It's a true work of art."

"It was built to kill, Conner. At the time it was in action it was a state-of-the-art nuclear submarine."

"Or to keep killing from happening. It's all how you look at it. *Silent Thunder* was built during the Cold War. The Russians were just as afraid of our doing a first strike as we were of them."

"Now you're waxing philosophic about the Cold War?"

"Sure, why not?" His smile faded as his gaze returned to the submarine. "She's beautiful, but it's going to be strange working on her."

"Why?"

"She's an Oscar II. Ever since I watched the TV coverage of the deaths of those Russian sailors on the *Kursk,* I can't think of Oscar II without remembering them. It's like they're all . . . ghost ships. It makes me sad."

"Not me. It makes me angry." Her lips tightened. "I offered my services to the Russian government to find a way to get those sailors out of that sub, and they were too proud to let me do it."

"I remember. At the time you were so mad you were ready to start World War III."

"They let them die. They didn't do enough. God, I hate politicians. How do you think those sailors felt, trapped and knowing they were going to die?"

"Easy," Conner said. "It's over, Hannah. You did all you could. It wasn't your failure."

"Yes, it was. It was everyone's failure. We should have ignored all that international diplomacy bullshit and gone in and saved them. I wouldn't make that mistake again. They'd have to shoot me out of the water to keep me from trying a rescue."

He gave a low whistle. "All that passion. I seem to have stirred you up a bit. Or maybe you're feeling a little of the same creepiness I am about this submarine."

"Don't be ridiculous."

"What do we know about the crew?"

"Not much yet. Bradworth obtained a complete dossier on them for the museum from the Russians, but I haven't seen it. He's also supposed to give me the complete documentation of the sub from the time it was discovered in Finland until it was sailed into this harbor."

"Then how do you know I'm being ridiculous?"

"Ghost ships?" She stared at him incredulously. "You've got to be kidding. It's just an old sub."

"But maybe it's sending out vibes." He lowered his voice melodramatically. "Concentrate. Do you feel them, Hannah?"

A sudden chill went through her. What the hell? It had to be suggestion, and she'd be damned if she'd let Conner know he'd gotten to her. "I'm too busy concentrating on keeping myself from calling out the booby hatch brigade for you."

He threw back his head and laughed. "I almost had you. I could see it."

"You did not. I'm not that gullible."

"But you seem to be in an uncommonly sensitive mood. It doesn't happen that often, and I thought I'd get you while the getting was good."

"Uncommonly sensitive? I *am* sensitive, you bastard."

"And so delicate in expressing it. Forgive me for doubting you, but you—Ouch."

"Dammit, I'll show you delicate." She punched him again in the arm. "First, you make me feel guilty, and then you tell me I'm a callous bitch."

"I didn't actually say it." He laughed as he backed away from her. "And you shouldn't object if I did. You have to admit that it's not your gentler side that fills you with pride. You're definitely a no-nonsense woman, Hannah. I'm surprised you took offense."

She was a little surprised too. From the time she was ten years old she had known what she wanted of her life. Machines had always fascinated her, and the sea had called her with a power that couldn't be denied. Every college break she had spent on a ship, working and perfecting her knowledge and skills. Even after she had graduated with honors, it still hadn't been an easy road. She had fought her way up the ladder in a man's world by her independence and tough-mindedness. It was odd that little remark by Conner had triggered a sudden rush of guilt. Or maybe not so odd. It could be that she had been worrying about Conner on a subconscious level for a long time. "You know, if you ever want to leave me and get a job in Boston closer to Cathy and the kids, it will be okay with me." She was lying. It wouldn't be okay. They'd been together too long. As children they'd had the usual sibling rivalries, but that had passed, and they'd grown closer and closer over the years. From the time she had brought him on board on her first independent job, he had been her anchor and her friend as well as her brother. She'd be miserably lonely without him.

He grinned mischievously. "I'd consider it, but I'd hate to wreck your career. We both know I'm the only one who'd put up with you. One of my biggest career assets is my ability to smooth down all the assholes you refuse to tolerate. What I lack in brains I make up for in social skills. That's why we're such a good team."

She opened her mouth to defend herself, then closed it again. "Come on, we're supposed to meet Bradworth at the bed-and-breakfast in an hour." She turned away and started back up the pier. "But you're right, I certainly don't know what I'd do without you."

"My, my, sensitivity again? I was expecting you to give me a verbal knockout punch. What's gotten into you?"

She smiled at him over her shoulder. "Maybe you're rubbing off on me. Next, I'll be comparing that damn sub to a sunset or a tropical flower." She glanced at the submarine lying still and dark in the water like a sleek shark waiting to attack its prey. Another chill went through her, and she quickly looked away. "But somehow I don't think so."

Bradworth rocked slowly back and forth in the rocking chair on the porch of Richardson's Bed-and-Breakfast, his gaze on the glimpse of sea he could see in the distance. It was nice here, he thought wistfully. Quiet, pleasant, ocean views that made him re-member the house near Myrtle Beach where he'd grown up.

Jesus, he must be getting old if he was already starting to think of the good old days. Nah, the juices were still flowing if he could feel that stir of lust as he watched Hannah Bryson and her brother walk up the street toward him. At least, he assumed it was her brother, Conner. He'd never been introduced to him and had only briefly met Hannah two weeks ago when he and Randolph, the pub-lic relations director for the museum, had gone to her apartment in Boston to offer her the job. They didn't look much alike. Conner Bryson was smaller, built with a lean, wiry muscularity, and his tightly curled dark hair and triangular face gave him a puckish ap-pearance. There was nothing puckish about Hannah. Her features were strong, with high cheekbones, deep-set blue eyes, and chestnut hair that curled wildly and incongruously around that riveting face. According to her dossier she was thirty-five, but she looked younger. No, that wasn't quite right. She was one of those women who ap-peared ageless. She was probably five-foot-nine or -ten with a strong, slim body, long legs, and great shoulders. God, he loved women with straight, broad shoulders. Tits and ass were all very well, but there was something more subtly challenging in the turn-on of those smooth, broad shoulders and that bold carriage. It made a man want to meet that challenge in the most basic sexual way.

Hell, Hannah Bryson was probably going to be a challenge in more ways than the physical. She was exceptionally intelligent. He had recently watched a two-year-old National Geographic special in which Hannah had described her childhood obsession with scuba diving, and her ever-increasing desire to go farther and deeper than her tanks could ever take her. Before she'd even graduated from college, she had made a name for herself with a series of radical yet extremely workable sub designs that instantly catapulted her to the forefront of the traditionally male-dominated profession of marine architecture. She possessed an amazing photographic memory that gave her instant mental access to every sub ever designed, and her skill and creativity enabled her to improve on many of them.

Bradworth ruefully shook his head. Dammit, he would have preferred to have someone a hell of a lot less sharp, but he'd been forced to accept her. He just hoped he could get her through this and—

His phone rang, and he picked up. "Bradworth."

"Is she there?"

He tensed. "Dammit, Kirov, I told you I'd call you after I spoke to her. Stop pressuring me."

"Is she there?"

"She's walking down the street toward me right now."

"She took her time. They were down at the pier looking at the sub an hour ago."

"And you were there watching her. I told you to stay away from that damn sub, Kirov."

"And I told you to go to hell. I'll do what I please." He paused. "I wasn't the only one watching her. There was a small yacht cruising around the bay, and I saw the man on the bridge was using high-powered video binoculars."

"Could have been nothing. A five-hundred-and-fifty-foot Russian submarine is definitely a curiosity in these waters."

"And it could have been Pavski. We'll assume it was until proven otherwise."

Annoyance seared through him. Arrogant bastard. Call him on it? He hesitated. Oh, what the hell. He was tired of pussyfooting around with Kirov. He had to prove to the son of a bitch that he wasn't to be intimidated. "You're sure you're not using Pavski as an excuse?"

Silence. "I beg your pardon?"

The words were spoken softly, but Bradworth felt a chill go down his spine. He smothered it and kept his voice as low and hard as Kirov's. "I've gone to a good deal of trouble to set this up, and I'd be very annoyed if I found out that you have another agenda other than our mutually agreed objective."

"Really? And what would you do?"

"You're not irreplaceable. We created you. We can destroy you."

"Indeed? Try." Kirov's voice was still soft, but the inflection had become icy. "And you didn't create me. I'm my own creation. I started as a skeleton with nothing inside but hate, and I infused that corpse with blood and guts."

"And you don't owe us anything for teaching you, helping you?"

Kirov laughed. "My God, you expect me to be grateful? Hell, yes, I learned from you. And then it wasn't enough and I went to Hong Kong and learned more and then I went to India and had them teach—" He stopped, and then said, "Let's just say, you were only the first step in my education. As for helping me, every time you helped me, you helped yourself. And do you think I haven't looked over my shoulder all the way to make sure you didn't decide I was expendable?

I'm *not* expendable, Bradworth. And if you decide to explore that possibility, you might have to start looking over your shoulder."

"I didn't say we were going to target you. I just wanted to make our position clear." Bradworth was backtracking, he realized with disgust. He hadn't expected to unleash quite this much deadliness in Kirov. He'd only been concerned with his own pride and self-respect. No, he wouldn't have been that unprofessional. He'd also been told that Kirov might have to be reined in. The bastard had been walking too close to the edge lately. "If you're being entirely honest with us, then you have nothing to fear."

"I'm not afraid." Kirov's voice was suddenly weary. "I got rid of that emotion along with other nonessentials a long time ago." His tone changed to brusqueness. "The license number of that yacht is PA 3717 ZW. Check it out and get back to me. Start the Bryson woman working on the sub tomorrow morning. I want her to finish as soon as possible."

"And what if she's not ready to start yet?"

"Persuade her. But I think she'll be ready. According to the dossier you furnished me, she's a dynamo, and she'll want to dive in."

"We would have preferred someone not quite so independent. We could have had one of our Navy engineers do this job, and the report would have been—"

"Not as thorough as Hannah Bryson's. Look, I told you that to put anyone on the sub was like baiting a tiger. You didn't agree and went ahead with it. So as long as it's being done, let's do it right. She's brilliant and the best in her field. Besides, she has a photographic memory, and that will move the project at lightning speed.

She'll take that sub apart and put it back together before she turns in a schematic. I've read her reports in the *Marine Log.*"

"We just wanted to make absolutely sure. She's probably not going to come up with anything more than the team we had go through it in Helsinki."

"Even if she doesn't, Pavski is a little too interested for there not to be something in the wind."

"You can't be that sure that Jennings was working for Pavski in Helsinki. You were too eager to kill the bastard."

"True. And I enjoyed every second of it. But I don't have to be sure. My sources told me that Pavski was finding Jennings a liability. The minute Jennings caught on that he was going to be a target, he would have disappeared from the scene. I couldn't risk that."

"We don't agree with your sources. Maybe he would have told us where to find Pavski."

"Jennings was too low on the totem pole to have direct access to him. You would have drawn a blank."

"You have an answer to everything."

"I don't have all the answers, but I do have instincts. These days my instincts are very sharp where Pavski is concerned. I'm done arguing with you about this, Bradworth. Call me if I'm wrong about Hannah Bryson, and she wants to delay starting work. I'll see if I can do something to nudge her."

"No! Stay away from her, dammit."

"Then persuade her." He hung up the phone.

Christ, he was actually sweating, Bradworth realized as he

pressed the disconnect. Cold sweat. He took a deep breath. Stupid that Kirov had this effect on him. He wasn't without courage, as his record proved. And stupid that he'd forced himself to try to overcome it by confronting the bastard. He should have been more diplomatic and noncommittal.

And Kirov would have seen right through him anyway. Forget it. Forget him. Hannah Bryson had opened the garden gate, and she and her brother were starting up the walk toward the porch. He got to his feet and smiled warmly as he went down the steps toward her. "Good to see you, Ms. Bryson. This is going to be a pleasant job for you. You'll like this inn. It has so many windows facing the sea, it's like cruising on a yacht. I've been sitting here rocking and day-dreaming. It's like being in another century . . ."

Bradworth had surprised him, Kirov thought as he tucked his phone in his jacket pocket and walked to the edge of the cliff overlooking the pier where the *Silent Thunder* was moored. Bradworth was an old-time company man with all the accompanying baggage. He'd tried to convert to the modern mind-set, but he was still stuck in the rut he'd formed when he'd been trained as a young agent. Threats, control, and the American way.

Not that Kirov thought that agenda couldn't be effective. To control and use authority had been bred in him since he was a boy. It was just that adaptation was the key to survival and success, and he *would* succeed.

Would he have to take out Bradworth? The man was afraid of

him, and although he'd used that fear on occasion to get his own way, fear could be dangerous.

Maybe, but not yet. He needed him to guide Hannah Bryson to do what he wanted her to do.

He glanced at the horizon. The yacht was gone, and no other craft seemed to be circling like a buzzard. Yes, the term was apt, he thought grimly. Pavski was a buzzard trying to eat the bones of the sub lying defenseless and stripped of power.

But why?

He had a good idea, but he'd find out. It was only a matter of time.

But he might not have the time. Pavski moved fast, and he'd regard this period as an opportunity. Hannah Bryson had to start work immediately and get one step ahead of him.

Or stand in his way. Either action might be beneficial for Kirov. Not so beneficial for Hannah Bryson. Pavski's usual method of removing obstacles was to destroy them.

Too bad. He liked what he'd heard about the woman. He hoped he could get to Pavski before he killed her.

In the meantime he'd guard that lovely lady lying in the water at the pier. They'd removed *Silent Thunder*'s weapons, but she was still beautiful and powerful and stirring to the senses. He sat down and crossed his legs, his gaze on the sleek hull.

"Come and get her, Pavski. Make your play," he whispered. "I'm waiting."

TWO

"You'll start right away?" Bradworth asked. "I'm sorry to push you, Ms. Bryson, but the museum is eager to start publicity rolling, and they can't do it until you inspect every inch of that sub, draw up your plans, and supervise the modifications that will make it safe for tourists to move through."

"I'm as eager to get started as they are to have me," Hannah said. "I need to wrap this job up in a few weeks." She glanced teasingly at her brother. "Conner's marriage depends on it."

Conner nodded solemnly. "That's true. Of course, it has nothing to do with the fact that Hannah has another job waiting in the wings."

"Oh, that's right. She mentioned that lost underwater city." Bradworth frowned. "But you're not going to sail off before the job's done? I'll need your promise."

Lord, the man was solemn, Hannah thought. And not the most charismatic person she'd ever met. She was glad that she wouldn't be working directly with him. "I don't go back on my word. The museum will get its schematic and report. When can I get access to the sub?"

"Tomorrow. I'll have someone from the naval team who brought it here meet you at the pier at nine."

"Seven."

He smiled. "Seven."

"And isn't it pretty odd not having guards around the sub? The local kids would find it pretty irresistible. Conner and I had no trouble approaching it this afternoon."

"There are guards. You were watched from the time you parked your van on the pier. We're keeping a very low profile with the townspeople. I told my men you'd probably be stopping by and not to interfere with you. The gate that bars the harbor is enough to keep most people out, and the museum asked us to be discreet. They don't want anyone getting in the way of your job or the cleanup. And the less talk about the sub, the better until they can start the publicity." He got up from the chair. "Now may I escort you into dinner? This inn is famous for its great food."

"I'll take your word for it." She glanced at Conner. "I'm going back to the pier. Want to come with me?"

He shook his head. "Dinner and then a call home to Cathy sound a lot better to me than staring at a sub you can't even board yet."

"I can examine the exterior a little more closely. We didn't take much time."

"You have photos."

"I'm going." She turned to Bradworth. "I suppose I'll see you in the morning?"

He hesitated. "I could go with you, and we could have dinner at a restaurant on the dock."

She had no desire to be social right now and certainly not with a government bureaucrat. "That's okay, I'm not hungry." She started down the steps. "And there's no use your going along. I'm not intending to do anything but look at the sub and compare it to my notes." She stopped and turned back. "By the way, do you have a copy of the reports on the crew you got from the Russians? I may want to contact them if I have any questions."

"Of course." He reached into his briefcase and handed her a large, bulky envelope. "Here's the history of *Silent Thunder*'s journey from Finland. Videos and tapes that the museum intends to use in its presentation." He handed her a folder. "And here's the personnel file. But I'm afraid it won't help you much. Captain Vladzar died three years ago and his first mate, Valentin Gregor, is in Chechnya working with the rebels. He's got his hands full just keeping one step ahead of Putin's security forces."

"There may be someone else who can tell me something." She slid the information into her denim satchel. "I don't need much technical info. I'm familiar with the Oscar II, but there are sometimes small variations in design. I just want a backup in case I run into something that I'm not—"

"I'd be glad to come with you and go over the reports. Perhaps I can shed some light on—" He stopped as he saw her shaking her head. "No?"

"She wants to be alone with the sub," Conner said gravely, his lips twitching.

"What?" Bradworth asked blankly.

"She has an empathy with machines. No romanticism, but she's not as hardheaded as you might think. She has a sensitive side. Just ask her."

"I'm going to murder you." Hannah grimaced over her shoulder as she started down the steps. "Or better yet, I'll work you to death checking those schematics." She waved as she moved down the walk. "I don't know when I'll be back. But I'll see you tomorrow. Say hello to Cathy and the kids for me."

The sun was going down when Hannah reached the pier. The twilight softened and masked the age-worn hull of the sub, and *Silent Thunder* seemed young again. Good God, that thought had come out of nowhere and was sickeningly maudlin. Conner would have laughed at her as he'd laughed at her returning to the pier tonight. She couldn't blame him. What the hell was she doing here? She wasn't going to accomplish anything, and she certainly hadn't felt the empathy Conner had teased her about. She was proud of her cool analytical approach to her work.

So the fact that she'd been drawn back here this evening must have been because she wanted to get the right mind-set to start the job.

Maybe.

Oh, screw it. She was tired of questioning her every thought and motive. She was tired, period. It could be that Conner's talk about the sub had sparked her imagination. Or it could be that she hadn't wanted to stick around the inn when she knew Conner would be too busy with his phone calls to keep her company. The first night away from his family was always difficult for them, and he was usually on the phone most of the evening.

Jesus, that sounded selfish. It wasn't as if she begrudged him either the loving relationship or his family. She had no right when she'd deliberately chosen the single life for herself after her divorce from Ken. It was just that sometimes she felt a twinge of wistfulness and loneliness.

Okay, stay here for an hour or so and glance over the crew dossier, then stroll back to the inn. By then it would be time to get ready for bed, and tomorrow she could dive in and start work. That would be exciting and satisfying, and she'd rid herself of this strange emotional jag.

Now think about the sub. Think about the problems of taking the craft's interior apart, inspecting each piece for possible tourist hazards, then putting it seamlessly back together again. This deadly attack sub would soon be hosting scores of curious elementary-schoolers on class field trips. She'd have to make subtle modifications that wouldn't clash with a spartan environment designed for battle-tested sailors. It had sounded a hell of a lot easier when Bradworth had proposed it to her in Boston.

She glanced at the maritime museum that bordered the site. It was a white two-story building fronted by a massive anchor-shaped monument with the names of dozens of seamen who had died in the waters off this port. Mostly fishermen trying to earn a living for their families, Hannah thought. An artificial lagoon was being constructed around the *Silent Thunder,* with suspended concrete ramps that would one day hold the lines of visitors. A pair of large, ugly gates now separated the craft from the ocean, structures Hannah assumed would be replaced with more aesthetically pleasing barriers.

She sat down on the pier and pulled the folder out of her satchel. Captain Sergai Vladzar's dossier was on top. He was bearded and white-haired, had a hook nose and a stern expression. His blue eyes were staring out of the photo with a boldness that was a little intimidating. He definitely looked like a commander of a lethal submarine, she thought. His first mate, Valentin Gregor, appeared to be in his forties, with a round face and an expression that was much less intimidating. Of course, the photos were at least fifteen years old, and the first mate evidently was both older and more dangerous than he looked these days. It seemed strange to think that these two men had lived and worked on this ship when it had been a queen of the seas. It was a little like the feeling she'd had when she was at the *Titanic* site.

It's like they're all ghost ships.

Nonsense. *Silent Thunder* had been a state-of-the-art warship, and tragedies happened to many well-built craft. Just because that horror had occurred didn't have anything to do with this sub.

Yet she had felt a chill when Conner had said those words.

And she was feeling a chill now.

It was as if someone on that sub were staring at her.

No, not the sub. Somewhere else . . .

Her head quickly lifted, and her gaze flew to the cliffs across the harbor.

Nothing.

No, someone was *there.*

Don't panic. She was being stupid. It was probably one of the guards stationed around the area by Bradworth. No reason to be afraid.

If it wasn't her imagination.

It didn't matter. She still wanted to jump to her feet and run back to the dock.

She drew deep breaths, and in a moment her heart steadied. She deliberately focused her gaze on the captain's dossier and tried to concentrate. She was in no mood to scan them now, but she would not give in and leave here until she decided to go back to the inn, dammit. That would be both foolish and a surrender to unreason.

It had to be imagination.

She knew he was there, Kirov realized.

It wasn't only that glance she had cast up at the cliff. Her body language was tense, alert, wary.

He wouldn't have been surprised if instinct had made her turn and scurry away. She perceived a threat, and an unknown threat was always more frightening.

She wasn't running. She was deliberately ignoring that instinct and leafing through the records Bradworth must have given her.

The last rays of the setting sun were touching her, enveloping her with a warm glow. She looked young and alive and, in this moment, a little vulnerable. Yet he could tell she had the same charged strength as the submarine she was studying.

He smiled at the thought. "You probably wouldn't appreciate the comparison," he murmured. "But I can't offer you a greater compliment, Hannah Bryson."

And he found he wanted to keep on looking at her as he always did *Silent Thunder.*

He trained the powerful binoculars on her face, watching the play of expressions.

Yes, I'm here. Yes, I may be a threat. But if you won't run away, then you'll have to accept me, take me . . .

You took long enough. It's almost eleven." Conner hung up the phone and rose from the porch swing. "I thought maybe you'd managed to break into that sub and started the job tonight."

"No, you didn't. You know I wouldn't be that stupid. How's Cathy?" She climbed the steps. "And what are you doing out here? I expected you to be in bed."

He ignored the last question. "Cathy's fine. Ronnie scored two goals in his soccer game this afternoon."

"Great." She opened the screen door. "I'm sorry you weren't there to see it."

"So am I. But that's the breaks."

"If it wasn't past his bedtime, I'd call and congratulate him. I'll do it tomorrow. How is he doing?"

"As usual. Eleven going on thirty. How did I ever produce such a serious offspring? He thinks Donna's nose is out of joint because he's getting so much attention. He told me I should start her in a gymnastic class so that she'd feel good about herself. She's only five, for God's sake."

Hannah smiled. "So when does she start classes?"

He sighed. "When Cathy gets around to it. We can't let Ronnie think he's running our lives."

"He'd be a very benevolent dictator."

"It's probably your fault. I think he takes after you." He changed the subject. "Why are you so late? Anything wrong?"

"No." She wasn't about to tell him she had deliberately stayed at that pier because she refused to give in to an idiotic case of nerves. "It was just a nice night. I didn't know you'd be waiting up like an anxious father."

"Someone has to worry about you. You don't do a very good job of it yourself. I bet you didn't stop and grab a meal, did you?"

She shook her head. "Everything was closed. This little town evidently rolls up the sidewalks when the sun goes down."

"I didn't think so. You probably wouldn't have eaten anyway." He took her elbow and nudged her away from the stairs toward the hall. "That's why I had Mrs. Richardson make up a plate for you to microwave. Homemade biscuits, corn on the cob, and country fried steak."

"Not exactly New England fare." She made a face. "And too heavy to eat this late."

"You can nibble. Do you want to hurt my feelings? Come on, I'll have a glass of milk and give you a blow-by-blow description of Ronnie's game."

"We have to get up early."

"You'll be in the shower in thirty minutes." He turned on the kitchen lights. "That's the wonder of microwave. You should appreciate the efficiency since you're so in love with machines."

She gave in. "I'll have a glass of milk and a biscuit." She sat down at the table. "Did you and Bradworth bond at dinner?"

He shrugged as he opened the refrigerator door. "He's okay. But I don't think we have much in common." He took out the plate and a carton of milk. "Though he tried to convince me we did."

"Really?"

"He tried a little too hard. It didn't ring true." He poured two glasses of milk. "You didn't care much for him either. I could tell."

She took a sip of milk. "I have a problem with any bureaucrat. He's a little too slick for me. But maybe he's not so bad. And neither of us will have to put up with him long." She grinned. "With any luck, you'll be home for Ronnie's next big game."

"If we're not off to Marinth." He held up his hand as she started to speak. "And that's okay with me. But it would be nice to spend a couple of days at home before we get the call." He took her satchel and opened it. "While I heat up your biscuits, get out the paperwork and show me what we have to do." He headed for the microwave. "You said you had the schematics. What's left?"

"I told you." She spread the sheets out on the kitchen table. "We have to make sure they're accurate and no surprises. The U.S. Navy probably did a good job, but I'm sure they were more interested in evaluating the *Silent Thunder* for combat weaknesses and strategic possibilities. It's the first Oscar II they've been able to examine up close, and the Russians still have a few of them in service. Anyway, the museum wants it certified by a civilian company, and they also want my input on how to best display the various sections to visitors who may have never been inside a sub before."

"And the reputation you earned on the *Titanic* expedition won't hurt their publicity campaign."

"Maybe." She shrugged. "I know it's not the kind of project we usually take on, but I was just as curious as the Pentagon brass to go inside an Oscar II."

"And I'm sure that the thought of actually relaxing scared the living hell out of you."

She ignored the comment. "Anyway, we unscrew every hatch, panel, grating, and control plate on the sub to photograph and document. Then we put it back together and call on the nuclear boys to make sure there's nothing lingering behind those panels that might have been missed when the sub was deactivated."

"So where do we start?"

"You start in the control room. I'll do the officers' quarters. The Oscar II has a double hull, and from the schematic I can see that the designers were clever about utilizing the space between hulls. I thought we could check out that area together."

"Sounds good."

"Were you able to round up any of our team?"

He nodded. "We'll have four, maybe five of our guys to help out. The earliest I could get any of them to promise to show up was in three or four days. I gotta tell you, it wasn't easy. They're enjoying the downtime before we head out for our next job. I think you pay them too much."

"It's hard to find good people. They're worth every dime."

He set the biscuits down before her. "Even with the help, it's a lot to do in two weeks."

"We have the government report and schematic as a starting point. It shouldn't be impossible if we work hard and fast."

He chuckled. "If? You don't know any other way to work."

She smiled back at him. "I have a reason to hurry. I want to be at Ronnie's next soccer game too."

"Good. You need to be around real people for a while instead of messing around with gyros and propellers." He paused and looked away from her. "And you need to have a kid of your own instead of spoiling mine."

She stiffened. She hadn't seen this coming. She tried to ward him off. "I like spoiling your kids," she said lightly. "All the fun and none of the responsibility."

"You need a kid of your own," he repeated.

He wasn't going to be evaded. Her smile faded. "Knock it off, Conner."

"Nope." He lifted his gaze to meet her own. "I've been skirting talking to you about Jordan for years. I need to catch you while you have a few of the barriers down. This is a good time."

"The hell it is."

"You lost your baby, and that's a terrible thing. But you're robbing yourself of one of the richest experiences a person can have. God, I love my kids."

"I know you do." She looked down at her plate. "So do I."

"But they're not your kids. I can share them, but I want you to have the whole nine yards."

"I don't want to talk about this now."

"I've backed off too many times. It's been four years. Some of the pain must have gone away."

The pain was no longer fresh, but there were moments that the memory rushed out of nowhere, and it was as if her son's death had happened yesterday. "I don't . . . dwell on it. That would be dumb." She drew a shaky breath. "I know you and Cathy probably wonder why it hit me so hard. My son only lived a few weeks. I didn't have all the joy or the laughter or the experiences that you've had with your children." She stopped to steady her voice. "But I *knew* him. From the time Jordan was conceived, I talked to him, I . . . shared. I planned our life together. Whenever I stayed at an inn like this while I was on a job, I'd think, 'I'll take Jordan here someday.' I wanted to show him the whole damn world. You know my marriage sucked, but he was the light at the end of the tunnel. I loved him, Conner."

"You can still love him and let someone else have a little love too," he said gently. "Have another child, Hannah."

"I'm not good at reining myself in. It wouldn't be a little."

"And you're scared."

"I'm not ready yet."

"You're scared."

33

"Shut up, Conner. Stop pushing." She tried to smile as she looked up and met his eyes. "Don't you find it a little bizarre that you're urging me to have a child when there's no hint of a father on the horizon?"

"Not at all. I'd love you to have what Cathy and I have, but you're such a workaholic you might not have time to develop a relationship. If you don't, we'll try the panda bear way."

"Panda?"

"Artificial insemination. They can't seem to get it on either."

"I am *not* a panda."

"No, they're lazy. You're an Energizer Bunny."

"I'm not a bunny either."

"It's too late for me to think of another animal to compare you to. I guess I'll have to drop the subject for now. But only for now, Hannah." He shoved the biscuits closer to her. "Eat."

She was relieved. She knew he only wanted what was best for her and she loved him all the more for it. But those last few minutes had been too painful. She bit into a biscuit. "Satisfied?"

"When you finish both of them, I will be." He took a drink of his milk. "Why are you taking the officers' quarters first? I'd think you'd want to zero in on the engineering deck. Did you find anything worthy of note in those crew dossiers?"

She shook her head. "Not that I can tell from first glance." She thought about it. "Maybe. Vladzar is kind of interesting."

"Why?"

"I don't know. I guess his photo appealed to me. All bearded and white-haired and leonine. He looked like the kind of man who could handle the responsibility of a nuclear sub. Sort of stern and wise. There aren't many men who would be capable of doing a job like that. He was born in Kiev and went to St. Petersburg Naval Academy. Evidently he was brilliant. He was awarded all kinds of medals and commendation during his years in the service."

"How old was he when he was in command of *Silent Thunder*?"

"Early fifties. That would make him seventysomething when he died. Evidently *Silent Thunder* was his last command. He retired to Arcadia, Odessa, and lived there until he died."

"Maybe he was forced to retire if he was in command when the Russians 'misplaced' the sub."

"That's nonsense. Vladzar wouldn't have had anything—stop laughing, admit it."

"Listen to yourself. You don't know anything about him, and you're leaping to his defense." His eyes were twinkling. "I've always suspected you have a father complex."

"I do not."

"Sure, you do. Dad died when you were only nine, and you've been looking for a father figure ever since."

"Bullshit."

"White hair. Stern. Lionlike," he reminded her. "Sounds pretty fatherly to me."

"I just admire what I read about the man."

"And that's why you're going to check out his quarters first."

"No, blast you." She took another bite. "There will be plenty for both of us to do in the control room. I just want to eliminate the quarters so that I can concentrate on the more important areas." She finished the biscuit and pushed the plate away. "That's all I'm going to eat." She stood up. "And now I'm going to go shower and hit the sack. I suggest you do the same. We want to get this job done and out of the way. We both want to get back home in time for Ronnie's next game."

"Hmm. I don't believe I've ever heard you speak with such fervor." He took the glasses over to the sink and ran water in them. "And I don't think it has anything to do with Ronnie's soccer game. Could it be that you're a little on edge?"

"No, it could not. Why should I be on edge?" She didn't wait for an answer. "Good night, Conner."

"Good night, Hannah. Sleep well."

"Don't worry, I will."

Of course, she wasn't on edge, she thought as she climbed the stairs. She had fought through that weird case of nerves she'd experienced at the pier and now was ready to start the job. If she was eager to have it over, it was only because she wanted Conner to have his quality time with his family before they set off for Marinth.

She stopped at the window at the top of the stairs. Bradworth was right. The views were wonderful from this old house.

She felt a ripple of pain as she remembered what she'd told Conner about planning to show her son all the places she'd visited. Any little boy would love this old house, with all its wide porches and rocking chairs.

She drew a deep breath. It was never going to happen. Stop feeling sorry for yourself. You have a satisfying life and a great job. Tomorrow that job would totally involve her, and this pain would once more recede into the background.

She could see the main street and beyond it the glimmer of water and the end of the pier that led to where the sub lay. She couldn't see the sub itself from this spot. Only a stretch of deserted pier and the moonlight-dappled sea.

But the pier wasn't deserted. Bradworth had assured her it was well guarded, and she had no reason to doubt the claim. And she had certainly been sure there was someone watching her earlier that evening. So stop staring out this damn window and obsessing over nothing and get to bed. She forced herself to turn away and moved determinedly down the hall toward her room.

M s. Bryson? I'm glad to meet you. I'm Lieutenant Mel Cox." The young freckle-faced officer who was standing on the pier was smiling broadly. "Mr. Bradworth told me I'm to make your job as easy as possible. If there's anything you want to know, anything you want done, just ask."

"Thank you." Hannah shook his hand. "This is my brother, Conner. He's my right-hand man and going to be responsible for a great deal of the work."

"Honored, sir." The lieutenant shook his hand. "I hope you'll call on me. May I help you with that equipment, Ms. Bryson?"

"I think I can manage."

"You can help me," Conner said. "I don't have any female hangups about carrying my own weight in a man's world." He shoved a metal chest at Cox. "You can carry the Geiger counters."

Cox stiffened. "You won't need those. This sub is completely free of radioactivity. We made sure of that before we left Finland."

"We?" Hannah looked at him in surprise. "Oh, that's right. You were with the crew who brought the sub here."

"Yes, ma'am. Mr. Bradworth thought you'd prefer someone with experience with *Silent Thunder*. I was an officer under Captain John Samuel, who was in charge from the moment the Russians made the deal with the museum." He frowned. "I assure you, Captain Samuel would never have permitted the sub to have been brought here if there had been any question about there being remaining radioactivity."

Lord, the kid was serious, Hannah thought. But she found his youth and dedication very appealing in this cynical world. "I'm sure your captain did his job. But our job is to make sure when we remove those panels that there are no lingering pockets that might come back to haunt the museum later."

"The captain was very thorough," Cox said. "I'm sure that you won't find—"

"Then my report will reflect how efficiently he did his duty," Hannah said. "Those Geiger counters are here to protect us and any visitors to the exhibit. They're very basic. If we were here to investigate your captain, we'd have brought in a tech team with a truckload of equipment. Doesn't that make sense?"

He was silent a moment. "Yes." He shook his head ruefully. "Sorry. I guess I'm a little defensive."

"Why?"

"Captain Samuel had a few other headaches with this mission.

He had to deal with the Finns, the Russians, and our own environmental protection agency. He doesn't need any more flack."

"He won't get it from me," Hannah said. "All I want is to do my job and get out." She met his eyes. "And I'll take all the help you can give me, Lieutenant. In spite of my brother's idea of a joke, I have no feminist reservations. Even he'll admit I'm fully capable of making you work your buns off."

"Oh, yes," Conner murmured. "You can see I'm a mere shadow of a man."

"With an extremely big mouth." Hannah handed the lieutenant the basket she was carrying. "You take this, and I'll carry my tool chest and satchel. After you show us around the sub, you can go back to the van and get some of the other equipment. Okay?"

"Okay. How much other equipment do you have?"

"Nothing very intimidating. We have to take pictures of everything we do, so we have a complete stock of cameras, tripods, and lights. Books, manuals . . ." She shrugged. "We'll only bring what we need on board, or we'd be tripping over the stuff."

He nodded. "I can see that." He looked down at the basket. "At least this doesn't look like Geiger counters."

"No," she said solemnly as she headed for the sub. "I wouldn't think of compromising your duty to your captain."

"Then what is it?"

She grinned at him over her shoulder. "Lunch."

THREE

Conner sniffed as he followed her down the hatch. "Diesel fumes."

"What did you expect?" Hannah asked as she glanced around the dimly lit engineering deck. "You know that when the nuclear reactor isn't functioning it's common to run the auxiliary diesel engines. I can tell from the design diagrams that the Oscar IIs don't ventilate the exhaust very well."

"I thought this sub was towed across the Atlantic."

"It was, but they piloted it here into its slip under its own power." She turned to the lieutenant. "The captain's quarters?"

He nodded. "This way."

A few minutes later Lieutenant Cox threw open the door of the stateroom. "Not exactly palatial but very comfortable compared to the rest of the officers' cabins."

"It looks pretty sparse to me." Hannah followed him into the cabin and glanced around. The compartment was approximately six by eight feet, featuring the same low ceilings, and dim, recessed lighting as the other living quarters she'd seen on the way. "But no more austere than others I've seen." She glanced in surprise at the shelves over the bed. "Books? Don't tell me the museum has already started to try to add atmosphere to their exhibit?"

"No, these were here when we took it over from the Finns." He wrinkled his nose. "I'm afraid you won't find much to help you in them. The Russians charged in like gangbusters and took all the journals and logs. They wanted to take everything, but the captain got tough. Our deal with Putin was that we got the sub as it was, and they had no right to confiscate anything. Captain Samuel told them the museum might want them to authenticate the exhibit, so they left those books." He turned to Conner. "The control room next? Ready?"

Conner nodded. "I should get started. I have a boss who's demanding as hell." He turned to Hannah. "See you at lunch?"

"Sure," she said absently as she moved toward the shelves. She'd always had a passion for books, and she was curious to see what this Russian captain had found interesting or entertaining. The cabin was so stark and impersonal that the introduction of such a personal note was almost shocking.

"I'll call you when I come to a good stopping place," Conner said. "Then you can come and help me. It shouldn't take you any time at all to document and certify this cabin as safe."

"Yeah," she murmured, her gaze never leaving the books. "No time at all."

Conner chuckled. "Come on, Lieutenant. You'll have to forgive my sister. She's been having an unusual bout of sensitivity since she came in contact with this sub. Maybe it's a hormonal issue."

"Bite me." She took a slender blue volume from the shelf. "Get out of here, Conner."

"Yes, ma'am." He was still chuckling as he followed Cox from the cabin.

"Now let's see who you are, Vladzar." She flipped open the book. Russian. She wasn't going to find out much about the captain from this book, she thought ruefully. It appeared to be a textbook or navigational aid, but she couldn't understand either the language or the weird symbols or equations that appeared fairly frequently. She put the book back on the shelf and reached for a thicker volume next to it. That's better. English. *The World According to Garp.* Not what she would have expected from a good Communist like the man Bradworth had described. Nor was the next volume she picked up. English again. This time three plays by Shakespeare. *Romeo and Juliet, A Midsummer Night's Dream, Julius Caesar.* She sat down on the bunk and opened the book. The pages were well thumbed, and it felt strangely intimate as she tentatively touched one worn corner. The captain had spent hours in this cabin, reading this book and then rereading it. It was almost like touching him . . .

Christ, what was wrong with her? She snapped the book shut and shoved it back on the shelf. She'd never felt like this when she'd handled the *Titanic* artifacts. Conner had claimed that he had felt a kinship with the victims of that disaster, but she had felt only sadness and anger at a useless tragedy. It was bizarre she was having this response to the possessions of a Russian captain who had not even died on this ship.

It must be the memory of the *Kursk* that was triggering all this fascination and emotion. A clear case of substitution. So forget that old man who had died in his bed two years ago far from the glory of his military days. Get to work unscrewing the back of the desk across the room and check it out. Then move on to the head in the adjoining bathroom.

She bent down, opened her tool chest, and stopped. Why should she stop glancing through the books when that was what she wanted to do? They might even tell her something she should know about the sub. It would only take a little while to go through them.

An excuse?

Maybe. The Russians had probably taken everything that would be useful. But she knew she was going to take that time anyway, and she didn't need an excuse. She could do whatever she wanted with this sub, dammit.

She slammed the tool chest shut, stood up, and crossed the cabin again to stand before the shelves. She could feel a tingle of eagerness as she reached for the next book on the shelf. "Okay, Captain, you've got me. Now tell me something that will keep Conner from claiming I'm becoming a nutcase about your damn sub."

"Out," Conner said firmly. "I've called you twice for lunch. Get your booty out of this cabin and out on the pier. It's almost four. We'll eat out there. You need to get a breath of air that's not stale and reeking of the great Soviet past."

"Is it?" She shut the book and scrambled to her feet. "I didn't think it was that late. I guess I was busy." She laid the book carefully on the bed. "How are you coming in the control room?"

"Better than you are here. I've got three panels off and photographed." He glanced around the cabin. "While you appear to have been slacking."

"I'll catch up." She passed him and went toward the stairs. "I'm almost finished going through his books. There's nothing that can help us."

"I don't know why you bothered. Cox told you that they took all the journals and logs. You couldn't expect to find anything."

"I guess not." She glanced at him over her shoulder. "So stop saying I told you so."

"No way. I don't get the chance that often." He grinned as he helped her out of the sub and onto the pier. "I want to rub your nose in it."

"Actually, I did find something in that Shakespearean anthology." She sat down on the pier and took the piece of chicken he handed her. "A photo."

"And?"

"Not helpful. It was a young woman. Blond, very pretty. Probably the captain's daughter."

"Unless he was a sailor who had a woman in every port."

"I don't think so." She made a face. "I guess I don't want to think so. I like to believe anyone entrusted with enough firepower to destroy Washington, D.C., was more stable than that."

"He was a man, Hannah. He was fifty-six, in the prime of life, when he commanded this vessel. Maybe he compartmentalized the different facets of his life. It very well could be the photo of a mistress."

"And it could very well be that he wanted to keep a picture of his daughter close to him."

"Lord, you're stubborn." Conner smiled as he leaned back against a post. "By all means, think the best of him. It's healthy for you."

"Healthy?"

"At least, it hints at emotional involvement. Better an obsession with a dead man than a nuclear reactor."

"I'm not obsessed with him." She took a drink of coffee. "I'm . . . interested. And you're talking as if my sex life was nonexistent."

"How many relationships have you had since you gave Ken his walking papers?"

She was silent. "A few."

"A few rolls in the hay maybe."

"And I didn't give Ken his walking papers. He found someone else."

"And you breathed a sigh of relief that you didn't have to feel guilty about leaving him. The marriage still wouldn't have lasted another six months even if you hadn't walked in and found him sleeping with another woman."

"Possibly." She looked away from him. "I did love him once, Conner."

"You loved the sex. I don't know if you even knew him. He sure as hell didn't seem to know what you were all about. He did every-thing wrong."

"I made mistakes, too. I left him for months at a time when I was off on a job."

"And if he was smart, he'd have known how to keep you home or how to trail along with you."

"He was an advertising executive. He couldn't just hop on a plane whenever I had to go somewhere. And he didn't do everything wrong." She paused. "He gave me Jordan. Even if it was only for a few weeks, he gave me my baby."

"And then flitted off and left you to go through your pregnancy alone."

"Our marriage was over by that time. There's no way I would have wanted him to stick around out of a sense of duty."

"I still think I'd vote for the panda solution over your Ken."

"He's not my—Why am I arguing about this? It's over."

"You have to examine your mistakes so that you don't repeat them."

"My, it must be wonderful to be so knowledgeable about the frailty of human nature."

"Hell, yes." He grinned. "I'm glad you appreciate my expertise."

"Pompous ass."

"I guess that means you want me to stay out of your business? Okay, I'll drop it for now. But don't expect a permanent reprieve. Fixating on a dead man is all right in the short term, but I regard it as my duty to someday guide you into a permanent and enriching relationship."

"Cripes, I may be sick. I can't take any more of this." She stood up. "Now I'm going back to my 'fixation' and finish checking through those books to make sure that I haven't missed anything. Then I'm going to take that cabin apart and put a seal on it. Tomorrow I'll be ready to help you in the control room."

"Then I take it we're going to put in a late night?"

"I am." She packed her cup and plate in the basket. "You can quit early and go back to the inn if you like."

"Since you consider a twelve-hour day as quitting early, I'm not impressed by your generosity." He got to his feet. "So I might as well stay until you're ready to leave. Although I intend to take a break and call Cathy when I'm sure the kids are all home."

"What a surprise."

"Predictability is one of my charms. Solid and steady, and everyone always knows where they are with me. Cathy likes it like that."

"So do I." She smiled. "I wouldn't have you any other way."

"I know." He closed the picnic basket. "It's kind of nice knowing I'm the anchor for two of the most powerful women I've ever met. Makes me feel worthwhile." He started toward the sub. "But you'd better get that cabin done by midnight, or I'll give up on the control room and come down and drag you out."

She's headed back to the inn," Koppel said when Pavski picked up. "She and her brother have been in there since early morning. Cox left around seven this evening, but they stayed on the sub until after midnight."

"Doing what?"

"How should I know? It's a sub. You told me not to get near enough to be seen, and I can't just blunder down the hatch like a—"

"I don't want excuses. I told you what I need. I have to know what's going on in that sub."

Silence. "They may not find anything. We couldn't."

"We didn't have time in Helsinki. They have all the time in the world, and she's an expert."

"It may not even be—"

"We have to know."

"If we get too close, Bradworth's men might see us."

"You know where they're stationed. Use a distraction."

"What if it doesn't work? It may be necessary to get rid of them. Is that okay?"

"No, it's not okay. I don't want Feds all over this harbor because you thought killing those agents is easier. Use your brain, dammit. You don't tip our hand until I tell you it's worthwhile to do it." He hung up the phone.

Christ, Koppel was dense, Pavski thought as he leaned back in his deck chair. It was annoying that he couldn't risk staying close enough to the sub to gather the reins into his own hands. As long as Koppel received detailed instructions, he was efficient enough, but he couldn't think for himself, and that was dangerous in a situation where Kirov might pop up at any moment.

Kirov . . .

His gaze lifted to the horizon, and he felt a tingle of excitement. Kirov was here. He could feel it. Over the years, Kirov had been like a shadow hovering over him. He'd come close a number of times, but he'd chosen other targets.

Now he, Pavski, was the target.

And, by God, Pavski was ready for him. He was almost willing to sacrifice Koppel and the others just for the chance of facing Kirov at last.

Almost.

The stakes were too high, the prize too tempting not to delay that final confrontation, he thought regretfully. There would be time later to kill Kirov very slowly and painfully when he had the leisure to enjoy it. Kirov wouldn't be going anywhere. He'd be waiting like a dark angel, spreading his wings over that sub in hopes of scooping up Pavski. He didn't realize that he was up against a much more formidable foe than those other fools on the committee he had killed so easily.

Yes, Pavski could afford to wait and go after Hannah Bryson first.

Kirov's hands tightened on the infrared binoculars as he saw the movement on the pier.

A man in a black scuba suit pulled himself from the water and was gliding toward the hatch of *Silent Thunder*.

"Okay," he murmured beneath his breath. "First move, Pavski."

The man disappeared down the hatch.

"Yes!" It was what he'd expected, what he'd hoped would happen. He scanned the horizon, but he didn't expect to see anything.

Pavski wouldn't have sent in a scuba operative if he'd intended an all-out assault. His purpose was evident, and it filled Kirov with infinite satisfaction.

Should he call Bradworth? This move would never have been completed if his sentries hadn't been circumvented in some way.

He'd decide later. He and Bradworth were walking different paths right now, and he might want to keep him in ignorance.

Then he had a sudden memory of the strange kinship he'd felt toward Hannah Bryson when he'd watched her sitting on the pier that first evening. He'd thought her vulnerable then, but now that Pavski had made his first foray, her vulnerability had increased a hundredfold. It might be more to his advantage to keep Bradworth in ignorance, but the woman could die if Bradworth wasn't warned.

A calculated risk?

He was very good at calculating risks and was usually coldly efficient at balancing the odds. It was just a little more difficult this time.

He didn't have to make a decision now since Conner and Hannah had already gone back to the inn.

He settled down to wait for the scuba diver to come out of the hatch.

"Come on, Hannah. Tonight you're going to get back to the inn in time for dinner," Conner said firmly. "We haven't left this sub before ten for the last three days. I want a good meal, and I won't enjoy it if I know you're back here working. God knows why."

"Okay." She brushed her hair back from her forehead. Jesus, it was stuffy in here. It gave you an idea what it must have felt like for the crew cooped up for months at a time. "I'm not going to argue. I could use an early night."

"Will wonders never cease?" He smiled. "But I'll believe it when I see you go to bed after dinner and not back to the sub."

"I'm not that much of a workaholic. I can walk away from it." She saw his skeptical look, and amended, "Sometimes." She moved toward the door. "Wait for me on the pier. I want to get something."

"Three minutes," he called after her as he started climbing the ladder. "My stomach is starting to growl."

She jumped down onto the pier only two minutes later. "Let's go."

"What's that?" His gaze was on the small tape recorder she was carrying.

"I found it in the back of the closet in the captain's cabin yesterday. Evidently the Russians didn't find it before Samuel stepped in and booted them out."

"Soviet top secrets?" he hissed melodramatically.

She shook her head. "Music. Nothing but music." She pressed the button and the strains of Rachmaninoff issued from the recorder. "He liked classics, the Beatles, Michael Jackson, and some jazz. He seems to have favored Louis Armstrong."

"And when did you have time to discover all that?"

"I went down to his cabin and listened to the tape yesterday."

"So why didn't you share it with me when I was having lunch?"

"I'm sharing it now."

"But you wanted to listen to it first, didn't you?"

She didn't answer for a moment. He was right, for some reason she'd wanted to experience the intimacy of discovery. Jesus, maybe she *was* getting weird. "Maybe. It's like putting together a puzzle. It's always exciting when you run across a key piece."

"And you were being selfish about sharing your gnarled lion of a captain."

"He's not gnarled."

"No, he's dead."

"True. And you should be respectful of the departed."

"Who? Me?" His brows lifted. "Surely you're joking."

"What am I thinking?" She shook her head. "You're right, I can't remember the last time you were—" She stopped as Conner's phone rang. "That's got to be Cathy."

"Why? I'm a very popular guy." He pressed the button. "Hi, Cathy." He glanced at Hannah. "Yes, we're on our way back to the inn now. She didn't argue with me." He handed the phone to Hannah. "She wants to talk to you."

She sighed. "Cathy, I should have known you'd try to micromanage. Yes, I'm going to have a good dinner."

"Just doing my job. You shouldn't be skipping meals. If you have a good dinner, so will Conner. Besides, I do have a slight interest in your well-being."

"I can't tell you how cherished that makes me feel," Hannah said dryly. "Is that why you wanted to talk to me?"

"No, I wanted to ask if he's been wearing that damn gray wool sweater."

She glanced at Conner. "Not today. Navy blue."

"Yesterday?"

Hannah thought back. "I think so."

"Well, if you get a chance find a way of tossing that gray sweater into the drink. I was going through a nesting phobia when I was pregnant with Donna, and I tried to learn to knit. It wasn't a good try. Hell, it looks like it was knitted by an elephant. But Conner insisted on keeping that blasted monstrosity ever since."

"Donna is five now. Why are you suddenly so worried about him wearing that sweater?"

"Because I saw him throw it in his duffel before he left. I thought he'd gotten rid of it. He never wears it around me."

"Because you intimidate him?"

"Be for real. He likes to make a show of being henpecked by a bossy wife, but Conner's not lacking in self-confidence. He just doesn't want to make me a laughingstock among our friends. I don't like to do anything badly, and everyone knows it. But I don't want any of those museum people thinking he's less than he is."

"I assure you, we're not hobnobbing with many museum personnel."

"No one is going to laugh at my Conner. If you care for me, get rid of it, Hannah."

She was serious, and Hannah did care for her. Cathy was one of her favorite people. "I'll see what I can do."

"Thanks." Cathy paused. "And maybe I do have more than a slight interest in your well-being."

"I know you do. Otherwise, you wouldn't try to boss me around."

"It's second nature. You should have seen me wheeling and dealing in Washington during my heyday. I was awesome."

"You're still awesome."

"Yeah, I know. I just have to hide my light under a bushel these days, so I don't embarrass the kids." She paused. "I hear you've got a thing going for some dead Russian."

"No, I have not." She gave Conner a dagger glance. "I'm just interested in the man. Conner can't tell the difference."

"It didn't sound like you. But Conner can be pretty sensitive at times. He thinks you've got a father hangup about him."

"Nonsense."

"I agree. You're not looking for a father; you're looking for a man as strong as you are. That's why your marriage with Ken failed."

"You and Conner seem to have all kinds of opinions about my divorce."

"Of course we do. You're family. Conner described this Vladzar, and he sounds a little like Sean Connery in *Hunt for Red October*."

"Oh, for God's sake."

"He doesn't remind you of him?"

"Just because he was the captain of a Russian sub? No, he does not. This isn't a Clancy novel, and I'm not the kind of person who idolizes movie stars."

"I know. But it was one theory to explore." Her tone became brusque as she changed the subject. "Get back to the inn for dinner at least every other evening. That's a compromise. Okay?"

"As long as it doesn't interfere with getting this job done in time for us to get to Ronnie's next ball game."

"You obviously have a fine sense for priorities. I'll give in on that point as long as you get rid of the sweater."

"I said, I'll do what I can. Do you want to talk to Conner?"

"No, he'll call me tonight. He'll want to talk to the kids too. Have a good dinner." She paused. "And give me a call when the fishes are wearing Conner's gray sweater." She hung up.

"Your Cathy is nothing if not determined." She was smiling as she returned the phone to Conner.

He sighed. "The sweater. Right?"

"She wants you to give it to the fishes."

He shook his head. "No way."

"Why not?"

"She knitted it. I remember her sitting there frowning and muttering curses beneath her breath. But she finished it and gave it to me. It brings back a lot of memories." A smile lit his face. He added simply, "And it warms my heart."

She shook her head as she saw the tenderness in his expression. How could she do anything that would take that expression away?

Cathy, my dear, you may have lost this one.

FOUR

"Can you come over here for a minute, Hannah?" Conner crawled out from behind a displaced control panel. "I've found something . . . weird."

"In a minute." She focused her camera and took another shot of the cavity behind the navigation console before she turned and walked toward him. "What is it?"

"There's another metal plate bolted to this surface metal."

"What's it for? Is it on the schematic that the Navy furnished?"

"Hell, no." He frowned. "And I have no idea what it's for. I'm trying to find out. I thought you might know. I've taken out the first three screws. Two more to go." He went back to work. "I'll get this one. You unscrew the other one."

"It could be nothing." She knelt beside him and started to unscrew the bolt. "You know that all Class Oscar IIs aren't absolutely identical."

"But the Russians usually have a logical reason for everything. An extra plate here doesn't make sense."

"You mean three extra plates."

"What do you mean?"

She aimed her flashlight lower. Below the plate were two others, all bolted to the reverse side of the bulkhead in the same fashion. Each plate was a dull brass color and measured approximately two feet by three feet. She grinned at him. "Now let's take these off and see if they're plugging holes to keep this tub afloat."

"Very funny." He carefully removed the top plate. "I'd appreciate a little sober consideration. This is the first thing we've found in the past three days of taking this sub apart that wasn't cut-and-dried and by the book. Isn't that what the museum wanted us to look for?"

"Yep. Sorry, I couldn't resist teasing you. You looked like you'd discovered a hydrogen bomb that Cox's Captain Samuel had left behind." She shined her beam on the detached metal plate. "And I don't think the Russians are as infallible as you might—" She gave a low whistle. "What the hell?"

The reverse side of the plate appeared as if it had been once part of a large industrial food container, now cut and flattened to fit flush against the bulkhead. Conner turned the plate back around. Faint marks were visible on its dull surface. "It looks like hen scratching. Somebody's idea of a joke?"

"It's not hen scratching." She took the tin plate out and laid it on the floor. "And I don't think it was a joke."

In the illumination of the work lights, Hannah could see that the plate was covered with an intricate pattern of symbols and geo-metric shapes.

"Triangles, circles, and squares, oh my," Conner murmured.

"And I thought we were going to get through this job without a *Wizard of Oz* reference from you," Hannah said. Her hand traced the markings. Triangles seemed to be the dominant figure, joined by thin straight lines to the other shapes. There were eight vertical columns of figures, each ending with a single-digit numeral.

"Conner . . ."

As was often the case on their jobs together, it was as if he had read her mind. He had already begun to unfasten the other two plates. "You've seen this kind of stuff before? What is it?"

"I saw something like it in one of the captain's books. I'm not sure if it's the same thing."

"So what do we do with it? Turn it over to the museum?"

She nodded. "It's almost midnight, or I'd call them now. I'll contact them tomorrow morning and ask them if they want it sent to the lab or if they'd rather we just replace it where we found it. Until they decide, we document the discovery, photograph it, and add it to the schematic."

"Got you." He finished detaching the other two plates and placed them on the floor next to the first one. They featured the same distinctive arrangement of numbers and symbols.

Hannah pointed to the second two plates. "Look, the handwrit-ing gets more and more erratic. By the time we get to the bottom of the third plate, the symbols are very difficult to read."

"In this light, *most* of these hen scratchings are impossible to read. The markings are too shallow." He grabbed his camera and took a few shots before shaking his head. "No, I'll need stronger lights. Maybe if I brush some phosphorous powder over the surface and photograph it under an ultraviolet light . . ."

"Then do it." Hannah went to the table where she'd set her laptop. "I'll do the initial journal entry. You can do the entire expanded report later."

"I knew I wasn't going to get off with taking a few photos." Conner sighed. "I think you should have to do the paperwork since I made this historic discovery."

"You called it hen scratchings. Now it's historic?"

"Historic hen scratchings," he said firmly. "And you should do all the paperwork."

"We'll talk about it after I notify the museum." Her gaze returned to the computer screen. "And after you get us some decent photos to accompany the report."

"I'm on it." He propped one of the panels against the chair and studied it in the viewfinder. "Not clear enough. I'll have to go back to the van and get the lights."

"I'll do it." She pressed SAVE and stood up. "I need to call Bradworth and tell him about the find anyway. I can't get good reception on my cell in here."

"Yeah, I know. I always have to go out on the pier to talk to Cathy. Why don't you wait until tomorrow and call Bradworth at the same time you call the museum?"

"He said he was at our disposal day or night, and we might as well take him at his word. Your hen scratchings could be important, if not historic, and I'm shifting the responsibility onto his shoulders."

"Good idea." He took another picture and then changed the position of the plate and backed away from it. "Bring my other camera too."

"That's right, load me up like a pack mule." She headed for the ladder. "You're just trying to punish me for making you do the report."

He grinned at her over his shoulder. "How did you guess? Maybe you could bring the tripod, the heavy one, and the video camera, and a—"

"No way. You want anything more than those lights and you go after them yourself," she said as she opened the hatch. "And if you manage to get the photos without those monster lights before I get back, I'll break your neck."

"Abuse and threats. It's a wonder I put up with you."

"Ditto."

Her smile faded as she jumped down on the pier. The call to Bradworth might be totally unnecessary, but she was uneasy and curious. The plates had clearly been hidden, and the marks on their surface done hurriedly and by hand. Why?

Well, it wasn't her concern. It was an interesting anomaly that she should ignore and get on with her work. After she turned the panels over to Bradworth or the museum, they could do what they wanted with them.

She was dialing Bradworth's number as she walked down the pier. She quickly filled him in as she opened the back door of the van and started to pull the strobe light out. "That's the story. It's up to you whether you want to notify the museum tonight. I'm going back to the sub to finish taking the photos and make the report and you can let me know tomorrow what I should do with—"

"Markings? What kind of markings?"

"Conner calls them hen scratchings, but that's only because they're pretty crude. They could be some kind of formula or maybe navigational code. I saw something like it in one of Captain Vladzar's books."

Silence. "You did? You're sure?"

"I didn't say I was sure. I said it was similar. I can't be certain until I get clear photos and can compare them. And the book was in Russian, so I couldn't really make heads or tails of that either. Are you going to call the museum tonight?" Bradworth didn't answer, and she said impatiently, "Look, I have to get these lights back to the sub. Conner is waiting for them. You do what you want about—"

"No," Bradworth said sharply. "Don't go back to the sub. Get the hell out of there."

She stiffened. "What are you saying?"

"I'm saying you should forget about the damn plates and get— Hold on, my other phone's ringing. Don't hang up. I have to take this call." She heard his muffled voice on the other line. "Yes, she's on the phone now. I'll take care of it. Screw you. I'm doing the best I can." He came back on the line. "Hannah, I'm going to call my agent stationed on the dock and get him down to the submarine on the double."

"Why? What's happening?"

But he was gone, and he was cursing when he came back on the line. "I can't make contact. No response." His words came fast and urgently. "Listen to me. Don't ask questions. I can't waste any more time. I have to call someone else. Get out of there. *Now!*"

"The hell I won't ask questions." Her hand clenched on the phone. "Tell me why I should do what—"

"Because if you don't, you'll be dead." He hung up.

Dead?

Crazy, she thought numbly. Bradworth was nuts, and so was the panic that was starting to soar within her. Yet Bradworth had frightened her because he'd been frightened. His tone had been deadly serious.

Deadly. That word again.

What if he wasn't crazy? What if there was a reason to—

Don't go back to the sub.

But Conner was still in the sub.

Conner!

Kirov didn't answer when Bradworth called him back. Was the bastard making his move?

Bradworth hung up the phone and jumped to his feet.

He had to get down there. No time. He'd have to call the rest of his team while he was on the way.

Damn, he wished Kirov had answered.

Hannah whirled and started to run down the dock toward the pier. Christ, her heart was beating so hard it hurt. Stupid to be so frightened. It had to be a false alarm. It made no sense. There had been no reason to—

She reached the pier.

The hatch of the submarine was closing.

"*No!*"

She tore down the pier. "Conner!"

Why was she screaming? He couldn't hear her.

Get into the sub. Call the police. Call 911. Do something that made sense.

Her hand was shaking as she dialed 911. She made contact with the 911 operator as she reached the sub. "Something's happening. Send someone. Conner—"

Her head exploded as pain tore through it.

Her knees buckled as the world spun around her.

"No . . ." She couldn't fall. Fight the dizziness. She had to get to Conn—

Nothingness.

Water.

In her mouth, in her lungs.

She couldn't breathe.

Fight for air.

No air.

Only water. Choking. Smothering.

"Stop struggling, dammit." A man's voice. A man's arm lifting her head above the surface of the water. "Let me do it."

Do what?

Water. Lungs filling. Drowning.

Conner.

"Stop fighting."

Couldn't stop fighting. Have to get to Conner.

"Very well, have it your way."

Her head jerked back as his fist connected with her chin.

Darkness again.

G et that stretcher down from the dock, dammit. We've got a big enough mess to cover up without her dying on us."

Bradworth's angry voice, she realized vaguely. Close. Above her. But she'd just talked to him on the phone . . .

Get the hell out of there. Don't go back to the sub.

But she'd had to go back.

Conner was there, and she had to—

Conner!

Her lids flew open. "Conner." She sat upright. Dizzy. Hold on. Fight it. "Someone was . . . The hatch was closing."

Bradworth's hands gripped her shoulders. "Lie back down. You've got a nasty head wound. You're soaking wet and suffering from exposure and God knows what else. We've got an ambulance coming to take you to the hospital."

"I'm not going to any hospital. Conner . . ." She struggled to her knees. "I have to get to my brother."

"No, you don't." He looked away from her. "Maybe later."

Something was wrong. Something . . .

"Go to hell." She got to her feet. Don't fall. Get to the hatch. Get to Conner.

"Stay out of the sub." Bradworth was beside her, his hand on her arm. "You don't want to go down there."

Panic surged through her. "Let me go."

His hand tightened. "Do what I tell you. This isn't—"

"Let me go." Her fist lashed out into his stomach with all her strength.

He staggered back, his grip loosening. "Okay, go. What the hell do I care?"

She staggered toward the sub. The hatch was open. Just make it down the ladder.

One step.

Another.

"Conner?"

A man was standing by the control panel with his back to her. Dark blond crew cut, a big man.

Not Conner.

"You shouldn't be here, ma'am," he said over his shoulder.

"My brother . . ."

"You're Ms. Bryson? I'm Agent Ted Freiland." He repeated, "You shouldn't be here. Why don't you turn around and go back to the pier?" He was turning to face her, and as he shifted she saw what he had been looking at.

Blood. Blood everywhere.

And still pouring in a stream from the shattered skull of the small, wiry man lying crumpled on the floor.

No face.

It couldn't be Conner.

No face. His head almost blown off his shoulders.

It couldn't be—

Oh, God. Oh, God. Please, God . . .

"Let me take you up." Freiland was walking toward her. "This is nothing you should see. Hell, it's nothing anyone should see. We'll take care of your brother."

Not her brother. Not that mutilated horror of a— Not Conner.

The digital camera was smashed and shattered to fragments lying by his right hand.

I'll need stronger lights.

His gray wool sweater Cathy had wanted destroyed was now stained with blood and bits of flesh.

Conner . . .

Sweet Jesus.

An agonized scream tore from her throat.

told you that you shouldn't go down there." Bradworth met her as Agent Freiland helped her out of the hatch. "I tried to stop you."

Not very hard, she thought numbly. "What happened to him? His head . . ."

"We believe it was a high-caliber Magnum pistol. Close range."

She shuddered. "Why?"

"We're not sure. An investigation is under way."

"He's dead." Her voice was shaking. "My brother's dead, and there's no reason for it. No reason at all. He was kind and generous and he . . ." She had to stop for a moment. "No one would want to kill Conner."

"I'm sure you're right." Bradworth's gaze shifted to Agent Freiland. "Take her to the hospital and have her checked out. Stay with her."

"I'm not going to the hospital."

"You may think you're okay, but you have a head wound, possibly a concussion. You're wet, cold, and you're in shock."

"And I have a brother I love who was murdered. I have to tell his wife that he's not coming home."

"We can call her," Bradworth said.

"No." She shook her head. "It's my job." She started down the pier. Horrible job. Horrible night. "I'm going back to the inn."

"You can barely walk," Bradworth said impatiently. "You'll be lucky if you don't collapse before you get there. Go with her, Freiland. Stay with her. She's your assignment from now on."

"Right." Ted Freiland caught up with her and put his hand beneath her elbow. "We'll take good care of you, Ms. Bryson. It's going to be okay."

She gazed at him in disbelief. How could it be okay? How could anything be right or normal again? Conner was dead.

"Ms. Bryson."

She looked over her shoulder at Bradworth.

"We need to keep this investigation confidential if we're to find the man who killed your brother. No statements to the press."

"It's all wrong. It shouldn't have happened." Don't cry. Don't break down. Wait until you've done your duty and talked to Cathy. Then you can let go. She swallowed to ease the tightness in her throat. "Damn you, I don't promise anything. It's all wrong, and you know more than you're telling me."

"We'll talk later," Bradworth said. "Go call your sister-in-law."

"You bet we'll talk later. What am I going to tell her? Not enough. Not nearly enough. I need to know why my brother died and who killed him, Bradworth."

"That's what we all want."

We've got a big enough mess to cover up without her dying on us.

His first words she had heard when she had regained consciousness came back to her.

Cover-up.

"Is it?" She didn't wait for an answer as she walked away from him. She didn't know what was going on, but she couldn't sift through it right now. She was hurting too much.

"Here." Freiland was putting his jacket around her shoulders. "You're shaking with cold from that dip you took in the ocean. We need to get you warm and dry."

The chill didn't come from being in the sea, she wanted to tell him. It was bone deep, soul deep, and she felt as if she'd never be warm again. But Freiland seemed to be trying to be kind. "Thank you." She drew the jacket closer. "Who pulled me out of the water?"

"I don't know. This pier was crawling with agents by the time I arrived from my post near the lighthouse. It was probably one of them. You were lying on the pier with Bradworth standing over you when I got here. Maybe it was him."

"No." Bradworth had shown no signs of being in the water, and she vaguely remembered someone had been in the sea with her.

"Then you'll have to ask Bradworth."

"I will." But not now. Not until she could blunder through this haze of pain to think clearly. "You say there were other agents on the pier? I only saw Bradworth and one other man. And I didn't see anyone but you on the sub."

"Jenkins and Bobeck were down in the officers' quarters. I had orders to stay with the body." He saw her flinch, and said quickly, "I mean, your brother. I didn't mean to be insensitive."

"I know." Yet, he was right. That wasn't her brother lying in that control room. It was a bloody, broken body with all the spirit and lovable humor and character that had made Conner what he was torn away.

Shit. Hold on. She was shattering, falling apart, and she couldn't do that yet.

Freiland handed her a handkerchief. "Can you make it?"

It was only then that she realized tears were running down her cheeks. She nodded jerkily as she wiped her eyes. "I'll make it." But that memory of Conner had splintered what little self-control she still had, and she felt as if she were bleeding inside. She didn't know how long she'd be able to keep from breaking down. Her pace quickened. "Come on, I have to get to the inn and call Cathy right away."

C athy arrived at the inn seven hours later.

She entered Hannah's room without knocking. She was small and thin, but no one usually noticed her lack of stature because of her boundless vitality. Today, she looked very fragile. She was haggard, her short, brown hair clinging limply around her pale face, her dark eyes red from weeping. "He's dead. I didn't believe you. But he's really dead."

Hannah got up from her chair and came toward her. "Cathy . . ."

Cathy shook her head and stepped back before Hannah could take her in her arms. "No, don't touch me yet. I can't break down again. I have to ask you some questions first."

"It's no use. I don't have any answers yet."

"Don't *tell* me that. I just saw what used to be my husband in that morgue downtown. I have to have answers."

"Oh, Christ, I told you not to go to see him."

"And I told you, I didn't believe you. I called Bradworth and asked him to meet me at the morgue. I had to see Conner for myself." She drew a deep shaky breath. "I couldn't make any sense of it."

"Neither can I."

"But you must know something. This couldn't have just happened out of the blue." Cathy's voice vibrated with intensity. "*Why?*"

"I'll find out. I promise you." Hannah's voice broke. "Don't you think I'm asking myself the same questions? Cathy, I'd never have brought Conner on board any job that would have endangered him. I loved him."

The tears were suddenly flowing down Cathy's cheeks. "Oh, shit. I know you did." She went into Hannah's arms, and whispered, "I couldn't tell the kids. How could I? When I couldn't believe it myself. What was I to say? Your daddy got his head blown off and won't be home anymore? He won't be there to watch your next game or be proud when you go to your first prom or see you grow up or—" She broke off, sobbing. "I don't know *how* to tell them. I don't know how to make sense out of something that's—"

"We'll figure it out." Hannah's arms tightened around her. "Are they with your mother?"

"Yes, but I'll have to go back and make arrangements for the memorial service. Conner wanted to be cremated, you know."

"Yes." She hesitated. "But they may not release the body if there's an investigation."

"Bradworth said there wouldn't be a problem," Cathy said dully. "He said they had all the evidence they needed. They'll autopsy and check for DNA. It's not as if they're going to have to determine the cause of death." She shuddered. "He said if we wouldn't make any statements to the media, he'd try to keep them in the dark about this monstrosity until later. He even offered to make the arrangements with the crematory."

She stiffened. "Did you agree?"

"Why not? I wanted it over." She wiped her eyes on the back of her hand. "I don't want my kids bothered by reporters, and I didn't want Conner to stay in that . . . place. He hated funeral homes. He wanted his ashes thrown out to sea."

"It's just a surprise that Bradworth would approach you about arrangements at a moment like that."

"He only asked me what I intended to do about—Oh, I don't know. Maybe it was weird. But he's giving me what I want, and that's all that's—I can't talk any more about it, Hannah. Not now."

Hannah didn't want to dwell on those arrangements either. She'd thought she'd gotten control of her emotions in those seven hours of tears and heartache when she'd been waiting for Cathy. But the practicalities were too harsh and made the wounds sting anew. "Then let's not talk at all. Do you want to take a nap? I'll call your mother."

She shook her head. "I can't—" She moistened her lips. "The questions have to be answered, but I can't think any more about them now. I have to get that memory of Conner lying on that slab out of my mind. I don't want to ever remember him like that. I . . . want to talk about *him*. Not his death. Not what they did to him. Can we do that, Hannah?"

Hannah nodded and wiped her own eyes. "I'd like that, too." She pushed Cathy down on the bed and pulled a blanket up around her. Then she curled up in the chair beside the bed. "You're right, we have to remember who he was, the difference he made to our lives."

"You start. I can't seem to stop crying."

Neither could Hannah. "What do you want to—Shall I tell you about Conner when we were children together?"

"Whatever you like."

No, those golden childhood memories would be too poignant for Hannah, and Cathy would not be able to relate to them. Start with something current.

"Do you know what he said when I wanted to take that gray sweater away from him? He said, no way. That it brought back memories and warmed his heart. And then he smiled, and that smile warmed my heart . . ."

FIVE

"He's gone." Cathy gazed into the sea, where she'd poured the ashes. "So quick. I've been dreading this moment, but now I want it back." She turned toward her sister-in-law but Hannah wasn't sure Cathy really saw her. "Isn't that strange?"

"Are you okay?"

Cathy shook her head. "I don't know if I'll ever be okay again." Her voice held a note of wonder. "How can I live without him?"

"Ronnie. Donna."

Cathy nodded, her gaze going to her mother, who was standing with the children across the deck. "I know. They need me. I should be with them now. I want them to remember me holding them when they think back on this. The ship's already heading back to the dock."

"Are you going back to Boston right away?"

She nodded. "My mother has her SUV parked at the dock, and we'll leave as soon as we get off the boat. The sooner I get the kids back to a normal schedule, the healthier for them." She looked down into the water again for a long moment. "It's not really good-bye, Conner," she whispered. "You'll be with me every day of my life. You know that." She straightened her shoulders and turned to look at Hannah again. "I'm being selfish. It's been all about me. You're hurting too."

"Oh, yes. Big-time." She tried to smile. "But you're entitled."

"I'm entitled to something else, too. You promised me answers. I want those answers. And I also want the man who killed my husband to burn in hell." She stared Hannah directly in the eye. "Keep your promise."

"I will."

"Bradworth told me you couldn't remember anything about those plates. Were you telling him the truth?"

"Yes. I can't recall anything connected to that night without going into a mental tailspin. I've told you before that I can't isolate a specific memory. Everything overlaps and runs together. I can't think of the plates without thinking about that last night with Conner." She said unevenly, "And it may be a while before I have the guts to do that. I'm sorry, Cathy."

"Nothing to be sorry about. I doubt if I could do it either. Then we'll just find a way to get Conner's killer without knowing about the plates. I'll help you all I can, but Ronnie and Donna have to come first." She paused. "I trust you, Hannah. Don't let me down." She didn't wait for a reply as she started toward her son and daughter.

Hannah took a step closer to the rail and looked down into the water. A thousand memories of Conner bombarded her.

"I won't let her down, Conner," she murmured. "And I won't let you down. I swear it."

"Aunt Hannah."

She turned around to see Ronnie standing a few feet away from her. Jesus, he looked like Conner, she realized anew with a pang. The same tight, dark curly hair, the angular face, the elfin arch to his eyebrows. Donna was small and vital like Cathy, but Ronnie was all Conner. He looked older than his eleven years in his dark suit and striped tie. Older and pale and hurting. She held out her hand to him. "Hi."

"Hi." His voice was gruff, and he came forward to nestle against her. "I thought I'd come and be with you. You looked lonely."

"I guess we're all lonely today."

"Yeah." He laid his head against her arm. "It's bad . . . isn't it?"

"Terrible." She hugged him close and forced herself to release him. "Maybe you should go back and be with your mom. She needs you."

"It's okay. I told Donna to take care of her."

"She's only five, Ronnie."

"But she's smart . . . sometimes. You just have to nudge her. I think she'll get better in a year or two."

"Oh, she will? I'm glad to hear that."

Eleven going on thirty.

Her eyes stung as she remembered Conner's description of Ronnie.

"Well, I'm glad to have the company, but if you want to go back to your mom, I'll understand."

He shook his head. "Dad would want me here. He worried about you. He told me so."

"Did he? When?"

"A couple years ago. I was just a kid, and I was making a fuss about him leaving to go off with you. He told me that we had to take care of you. That we all had each other, and we had to make sure you knew that we belonged to you too. He didn't want you to be alone." He whispered, "Now he can't take care of you anymore. I have to do it."

She felt as if she were splintering, breaking apart. "I'll be okay," she said unevenly. "It's your mom who—"

He was shaking his head. "He wanted you not to be alone. I have to take his place. I can't do it right now. I'm still a kid, and Mom needs me. But later, when I'm older, maybe I can go away with you and watch out for you like he did."

Dear heaven, she loved him. "Maybe you can." She pressed her lips to his forehead. "We'll talk about it in a year or two. Right now, we just have to get through the next few days."

He nodded, his gaze going to the sea. "It's going to be different. It hurts . . ." His eyes were glittering with tears. "It hurts bad."

What could she say? Offer comfort when there was no comfort to be had? She gave him the only gift she could. "I love you, Ronnie," she whispered. "And I'm very proud of you. Your dad would be proud of you too . . ."

Bradworth was sitting on the porch at the bed-and-breakfast when Hannah got back from the dock. He rose to his feet, and said soberly, "My sympathy. I admit I was surprised you phoned and asked me to come here today. I would have come to the dock, but I understood the service was for family only. I know this is a tough day for you."

"Not as tough as the day Conner died."

He shook his head. "But I hoped I'd made it as easy as I could for you and your sister-in-law."

"You made it almost too easy for Cathy," she said bluntly. "You arranged for the cremation, gave her the name of the captain of a boat here. You made sure that there weren't any newspaper reporters harassing her. My brother's remains disappeared from this earth as if he'd never been here."

"I can understand how you might feel antagonistic. Would you rather there had been a publicity stink that would have hurt the museum and your brother's family?"

"You know damn well I wouldn't. The only reason I didn't step in is that Conner would have wanted Cathy and the kids to have as little emotional upheaval as possible."

"Then I did the right thing."

"But for what reason? Why did you want to erase what happened to Conner?" She stared him in the eye. "And you knew what might happen when I phoned you that night. The minute I told you about those plates we found, you knew. You even warned me not to go back there."

"And doesn't that tell you anything? I wanted to keep you safe. I never wanted this to happen."

"Because it made a mess you had to cover up?" she asked bitterly. "Isn't that what you said when you thought I was unconscious on that pier?"

"You misunderstood. Very understandable considering your condition."

"I didn't misunderstand. Were those plates still in the control room when you found Conner?"

He didn't answer.

"Were they, dammit? *Answer* me."

"No."

"And why would anyone be willing to kill Conner to get them?"

"I have no idea."

"You're lying."

"Think what you will."

"And whoever went after those plates knew about them almost as soon as I did. How?"

He didn't answer.

"How?"

He shrugged. "There was a device planted on the sub to monitor your conversations."

She stared at him in shock. "What? By you?"

"No."

"But you knew about it."

"I was advised when it was planted."

"And you didn't tell me."

"I thought we'd be able to scoop up those bastards before they could do any harm."

"My God, and you used us as bait?"

"I didn't expect them to move that quickly if you found something of interest to them. It would have been smarter of them to avoid killing anyone. I thought they might come back for anything valuable after you'd left the submarine."

"But they didn't, did they? They came in like a SWAT team and blew my brother's head off."

"And I can't tell you how much I regret it."

"Regret? You son of a bitch."

"I'm sorry you became involved in something that had such a tragic end, but your best course of action is to walk away from *Silent Thunder* and forget all about it. In time, I'm sure we'll find the killer of your brother. Trust me."

She stared at him incredulously. "Trust you? You've got to be kidding."

"What are your options? The museum wants to have nothing more to do with you. What happened could be an embarrassment that would taint the opening of their new exhibit. This exhibit could bring big money to this small town, and the local police are being very cooperative and leaving the investigation entirely in our hands."

"They wouldn't do that. There has to be some other reason."

He hesitated, then said, "You're right. Homeland Security called them and told them they had an involvement."

"Homeland Security?"

"They wield an enormous amount of influence these days."

"You're saying terrorists killed Conner?"

"I didn't say that. I said Homeland Security has an involvement. But you don't want to go up against them, Hannah."

"The hell I don't."

"Then go ahead and see how far you get. All it would take would be for Homeland Security to drop a hint in your file that they're interested in your activities. No one would be willing to hire you with that cloud hanging over you." He leaned back in the rocking chair. "Of course, you could go to the newspapers. The press is always ready to leap on any juicy story. It might mean that your brother's widow and children could be hounded unmercifully, but it might be worth it to you."

"You bastard."

"No, I'm one of the good guys."

"The hell you are. You're not with the State Department. You seem to have a good deal of knowledge of Homeland Security. Is that who you work for?"

"No."

"Who?"

He hesitated. "CIA."

"What? You've got to be kidding. Everyone knows CIA isn't supposed to operate inside the U.S."

"This is *our* case. We've been working on it for years overseas. Just because it moved to U.S. soil didn't mean that we were going to be shut out. Since 9/11 the other agencies are giving us a hell of a lot more latitude."

"Shit. And you involved Conner and me in your dirty games?"

He gave her a pained frown. "We thought we had you well protected. You don't understand. Choices have to be made when the stakes are this high."

"You're not talking about choices, you're talking about sacrifices. Not *my* brother. What stakes?"

"I truly wish I could discuss it with you." He got to his feet. "I believe we've said all that can be said. If I can help you, please call on me."

Damn hypocrite. "I'll call on you. I want to go back on that sub."

"You want to make your own search? That's not possible. The museum has severed its ties with you."

"I don't believe the museum has any control over what you do. I want on that sub."

He shook his head. "Go back to Boston and comfort your family. They need you."

"And I need to know why my brother was killed."

His expression hardened. "Let me make this clear. The sub will be under guard, and you won't be permitted even as close as the pier. You're out of this, Hannah."

"No way." She turned and headed for the gate. "I've just started, Bradworth."

radworth hadn't lied. There were two guards standing at the end of the pier.

She didn't even try to get past them. She turned and started back toward the bed-and-breakfast. She doubted if she would have found anything valuable on the sub anyway. What Conner's killers hadn't stolen would have been confiscated by Bradworth if he thought it valuable . . . or incriminating. How *in* the hell did she know what the bastard was doing?

Well, find out. Go around Bradworth. Think. There had to be another path.

She stopped short, turned, and looked back at the pier.

Of course.

There was a path and she already had the map that would take her down it.

t wasn't there, dammit, Hannah realized in frustration.

Maybe she'd put it somewhere else. In the confusion after Conner's death it was possible.

After thirty minutes more of looking, she gave up and called Cathy.

"I'm sorry to bother you. Are you still on the road?"

"Yes. And it's no bother. You sound pissed."

"To put it mildly. Can I talk?"

"Go ahead. The kids and my mom are fast asleep in the backseat of the SUV. I doubt if a three-alarm fire would wake them. They were totally exhausted."

"And you are too. Sorry, but I wanted to fill you in on what I learned. And get you started."

"Started?"

"I need your help. Bradworth wouldn't answer any questions, and he's trying to close me out. He won't let me go on the sub, he got the museum to fire me, and threatened me with Homeland Security if I went to the newspapers."

"Why would he do that?"

"He's CIA. The bastard knew that Conner and I were in danger on that sub. He knew it, and he didn't warn us."

"Shit."

"And when I got back to my room I couldn't find my satchel with all the information Bradworth had given me about *Silent Thunder.*"

"But he must know you'd already gone through them."

"But I didn't study the videos and DVDs of the sub's journey from Finland furnished by the museum. That's what I was going to do when I got back to my room. They made four stops along the way, mostly for publicity purposes. Baltimore, New York, Boston, and Norfolk. I only glanced at them, but I had a vague recollection of a lot of small craft buzzing around the sub at every stop. In fact, on the first day we arrived here, Conner remarked on a launch that kept making passes beyond the harbor gates. It would make sense that someone interested in those plates we found would want to keep an eye on the sub. My guess is there must be something on the video that Bradworth doesn't want me to see."

"Then why would he give them to you?"

"A mistake? The footage was provided by the museum, and maybe a casual glance wouldn't reveal anything suspicious. But I am suspicious, and I was going to go over everything with a microscope. I'm not going to get that chance now. But there has to be other footage, and we have to go after it. No, *you* have to go after it. If we can locate some clear shots of the vessels, I can blow up the photos and get registration numbers. I may not know any White House gurus, but I have marine contacts all over the world. Call your friends in Washington and start to stir up the pot."

"I've been out of the loop for over ten years."

"Are you saying you can't do it?"

"Hell, no. I'm telling you it will take more time than I'd like. I'll get on the line with Congressman Preston first thing in the morning and start that pot boiling." She paused, thinking. "Then I'll call Ross Calvin at the White House and see what he can do for me. Anything else?"

"Yes, *Silent Thunder.* All the information Bradworth gave me is suspect. I need to know everything that you can get on the sub, past and present. Don't take anything for granted. Start fresh and work fast. See if you can find someone who actually served on the sub."

"You don't want much."

"I want everything. Most of all I want to know who killed Conner." She paused. "I don't want to pressure you, Cathy. If you can't do it, let me know, and I'll find someone else."

"Don't you dare." Cathy's tone was fierce. "I'll do it. It will give me something to think about besides Conner lying in that morgue. There's nothing worse than brooding and not being able to take action."

"It's still a long shot. But we have to start with what we have."

"And what will you do if—" Cathy broke off. "One step at a time. I won't stop until I get you what you need, Hannah."

"I know you won't. We're in this together."

"You're damn right we are."

"Then try to sleep if you can't do anything until tomorrow. Good-bye, Cathy."

"Wait. When are you coming back to Boston?"

"I'm packed up and heading for the van in about five minutes. I'll call you from my apartment tomorrow morning and see if you were able to make contact with Preston."

"I'll make contact," Cathy said grimly. "If I have to track him down on a safari in the Congo. Drive safely." She hung up.

Yes, Cathy would find Preston. She had relentless drive, and it would all be focused on getting the information Hannah had asked.

And Hannah had to focus her determination on getting information about those boats that had clustered around *Silent Thunder* like barracudas around a wounded shark. She grabbed her duffel and carried it down to the van.

eautiful." Pavski stepped back and admired the worn, battered metal plates as if they were the work of a Renaissance master. "Simply beautiful."

Koppel snorted. "Beautiful? Only if you like chicken scratches."

Pavski refused to let the moron's cynicism dampen the moment. Koppel was useful to him in many ways and efficient at carrying out orders, but he had no sensitivity. Pavski would not let that bother him. He had come too far and worked too hard. The three plates from *Silent Thunder*'s bulkhead panel stood on tall easels in the miniwarehouse that had served as his headquarters since his arrival in New England. Located thirty miles south of Boston, the five-acre storage facility was deserted save for a few furniture makers and powerboat mechanics who conducted their businesses out of the units.

Koppel's eyes narrowed on the columns of geometric shapes. "Can you make any sense of them?"

"Not yet." Pavski switched on the reflector lights angled toward the plates. The scratches were filled with white powder, making them stand out in stark relief from the dark gray plates. "But they're definitely navigational coordinates."

"Not like any coordinates I've ever seen."

"They're Samsovian."

"I'm not familiar with them. Are you sure?"

"Only a few assorted crackpots used them. An instructor at the St. Petersburg Naval Academy developed the system in the early seventies and taught it to his best students. He probably hoped it would catch on, but it never did. I'm a little familiar with the system but not enough to be able to decode this. But a few officers swore by the system and knew it backward and forward, including most of the officers on the *Silent Thunder* and Captain Heiser."

"Heiser?"

"I'm quite sure Heiser wrote these. He *did* leave a message behind."

"What good is it to us if only a handful of people can read it?"

"We just find the people who can. I'm making arrangements to do that." He frowned. "But this looks pretty scanty to me. I don't think it's complete. Is this all? You're sure you didn't miss any other plates with symbols?"

"I don't think so, but we didn't have the luxury of time. Once we knew they'd found something, we had to move fast."

Pavski nodded. He wanted to blame Koppel, but knew things probably wouldn't have been different if he'd been there himself. They were lucky to have the plates they had. His gaze went back to the plates. These crude scratches could be worth billions, but that wasn't the point. Koppel didn't understand that those scratchings were more precious than mere monetary value. He didn't hear the call. He had no destiny other than to be a drone in the scheme of things. He pointed at a tiny symbol that resembled a cross within a circle on the bottom of the third plate. "And I don't think this is Samsovian."

"You're sure?"

He frowned. "No, not really. It does look familiar . . ." He forced himself to look away from the symbol. "No matter. We may have to find a way to correct any possible omission."

"How?"

"I'll have to contact Moscow and get Danzyl with the GRU to do a little work for me. And I have to confirm that last symbol isn't

Samsovian. I'll get Dananka to check on that. And since Bradworth must be in contact with Kirov, you might try to tap his phone to get any information, including Kirov's number. He probably has relays, but you can never tell." His mind was moving, weighing possibilities. There might be a quicker way to get what he wanted than try to figure out this damn symbol. "You read the report I gave you on Hannah Bryson?"

"Of course."

"Then you realize how valuable she could be to us now."

"The photographic memory? You think she really can do that stuff? It seems . . . weird."

"I believe the possibility exists. It's documented in all her records."

"But we've already got the plates."

"Which very likely may be incomplete. I have to know if she's seen anything else resembling them on that sub. She may not even realize it herself. Even an extraordinary memory can be tricky . . ." But if he had the opportunity, he could make her remember. And if she was of no help to him, then he'd make sure she'd be of no help to anyone else. He'd had her interaction with Bradworth watched closely since the death of her brother, and the CIA man would have been sent scurrying if she'd given him any information about the plates. She'd clearly been traumatized, and that might pass. But it hadn't happened yet, and he still had a chance to stop her from giving anyone the information on those plates. "I have to make sure we're dealing properly with Hannah Bryson, Koppel."

"Properly? I was only waiting for instructions." He pulled out his cell phone. "I'll take care of it."

Bradworth was waiting by Conner's van in the museum parking lot when Hannah reached it. "I don't like the idea of you driving that distance alone. It's not smart."

"Your concern is touching." Hannah loaded an equipment case into the back of the van. "But those scumbags got what they wanted when they killed Conner. There's nothing in this van anyone could want."

Bradworth's jaw tightened. "Your crew stayed for the funeral, didn't they? One of them can drive the van back to Boston. There's no need for you to do it."

"Need has nothing to do with this. This was my brother's van, and I want to take it back myself." She glanced at the "Save Mission Bay" bumper sticker that Conner had lovingly maintained with White-out and Magic Markers long after the original finish had worn off. It was still incredibly hard to believe that she would never see him again. "So don't get in my way, Bradworth." She got into the driver's seat. "Or I'll run you down."

Bradworth watched the van drive out of the parking lot before he reached for his phone.

"She wouldn't listen to me, Kirov. She's driving the van herself."

"I didn't think she'd do anything you asked her to do. If she gets chopped, I'm not going to be pleased with you."

"Screw you. I'm handling it." He hung up the phone.

Let it go, Hannah thought as she pulled onto I-95 and headed south toward Boston. This trip wasn't supposed to be about Bradworth, she reminded herself. It was about Conner.

Since his death, she'd been consumed with logistics, helping Cathy plan his funeral and making the sad calls to his enormous circle of friends. Cathy and the kids had needed her, and she was glad to help. But now it was her turn to remember Conner, and she could think of no better way than to make one last journey in the van they had taken on so many assignments.

Everywhere she looked, Conner was there. In the shell necklace hanging from the rearview mirror. In the picture of Cathy, Ronnie, and Donna clipped to the sun visor. In his collection of reggae compact discs, neatly organized by artist.

He'd liked to torture her with that music, knowing she couldn't stand it any more than his wife and kids could. The bastard.

God, she missed him.

She drove for two hours, and it seemed that every rest stop and roadside diner held some memory of Conner. She'd not only lost a brother but a valued colleague. He had always been so quick to play down his abilities but he was a smart and resourceful partner who encouraged her to trust her instincts and push the envelope even when everyone else was telling her to be cautious. "You don't make history by playing it safe," he'd told her.

He always knew just what to—

A high-pitched shriek erupted from the rear of the van.

"What the hell." It startled her, but she recognized the sound immediately; an alarm from Conner's collection of test equipment. She must have accidentally switched it on while loading up the gear.

The alarm grew louder and more persistent . . . and annoying. She glanced back at the component racks to try to see which device it was coming from.

The minesweeper. Although it wasn't really used to detect mines, it was designed and built by Conner to detect hidden radio beacons on the ocean floor that relayed information about their secret test dives. The beacons were sometimes planted by foreign intelligence agents but just as often were the work of rival contractors who wanted to monitor their progress. It was always on standby, but Conner had made sure the frequency wouldn't let it go off if it detected police radar or a nearby radio station. Why the hell was it going off now?

It didn't matter. She had to get it to stop before it drove her crazy.

She pulled off the road into a gas station whose red-and-white gas pumps and soda-bottle vending machines made it look as if it had been frozen in the fifties.

She jumped out of the van and opened the back door of the van. "Can I help you?"

She turned to see a thin, white-haired station attendant. He looked to be at least seventy, with faded blue eyes and ruddy complexion.

He smiled. "Heck of a racket you're making. I'm a pretty good mechanic, but I don't promise I can fix these newfangled car alarms. I'll give it a try, if you like."

Nice guy. "Thanks. I don't think I'll need any help, Mr.—" She looked at the name on his uniform shirt. Larry Simpson. "Mr. Simpson. If I can find it, I can fix it." She hit the gas cap switch. "Fill it up, please."

She climbed in the van and picked up the minesweeper. The pitch went up by a half octave. She frowned and waved it around the van. The pitch lowered as she moved it toward the rear, then heightened as she waved it toward the front. She shimmied between the two front seats, holding the minesweeper in front of her. The pitch went up another octave. She waved it over the dashboard, listening as the pitch wavered even more in her electronic game of hot and cold.

The passenger-side air-conditioning vent.

What the devil?

Affixed to the vent's top shutter, was a small black cylindrical object. She carefully pulled it out and saw that it was attached to six inches of thin black wire.

She switched off the minesweeper and studied the strange device. It looked familiar to her. Where had she seen—

Kudasi, Turkey. A bug. Not exactly like this one but close enough.

Bradworth?

Anger seared through her. The bastard.

She pulled out her cell phone. No signal. Not surprising in these hills.

"Do you have a pay phone?" she asked the attendant.

He pointed to an early 1960s vintage phone booth at the edge of the gravel parking lot. She strode across the lot and a moment later was sliding the glass door of the phone booth closed behind her.

She picked up the handset and brought up Bradworth's number on her cell directory. Be calm. Just tell the son of a bitch to keep his snooping hands off her privacy and hang up.

A roar of flying gravel.

She glanced out the glass door.

Shit.

A silver-blue utility vehicle was barreling toward her.

She grabbed the worn aluminum handle of the booth door and yanked.

Hurry.

The SUV was heading straight for the booth.

With speed. With purpose.

She leaped through the open booth door, stumbled, then regained her footing.

Gravel kicked up from the tires as the vehicle skidded to a stop. Both front doors flew open, and two men leaped toward her. Before she could react, one of the men pressed a wad of gauze over her mouth. It smelled sickly sweet.

She instinctively held her breath. The one whiff had already made her woozy.

Can't let it happen. Can't let the bastards do this.

The other man wrapped his arms around her legs while the first man pressed the gauze even tighter against her face.

Her eyes watered. Her lungs burned.

A shotgun blast rang out.

"Put her down, boys." The station manager, Simpson, was standing in the doorway of his office. He leveled the shotgun at the men. "Real easy now."

The man holding her feet loosened his grip slightly. "You don't understand, sir. We're U.S. Marshals and we're apprehending a suspect. My name is Jim Dennis and this is Ray Fontaine. Lower your shotgun."

"I never heard of Marshals trying to chloroform a suspect. I think that's a bunch of bull. Let her go."

The men slowly placed Hannah's feet on the gravel parking lot. She staggered a few feet away from them, breathing deep to try to clear her head.

"You're interfering with the law," the man who'd called himself Jim Dennis said. "The woman is under arrest. Put down your weapon."

The old man lowered his gun only a little. "And you talk kinda funny. You're not from around here. Show me your ID."

Thank God for that hint of a Russian accent, Hannah thought.

"Of course," Dennis said. "Right after we secure our suspect."

"They're lying, Mr. Simpson," Hannah said desperately. "I didn't do anything wrong."

"Just take it easy, lady," Simpson said. "No one's going to hurt you. Go on over to your van and let me take care of this."

She started moving across the parking lot. Weapons. There might be a weapon in the van. Jesus, her head was spinning.

"Stop, you bitch." Dennis muttered a helpless curse beneath his breath before he turned back to the station manager. "You're in big trouble, old man. You're aiding the escape of a dangerous felon."

"She don't look so dangerous to me," Simpson said. "Prove it. Show me your ID."

She'd reached the van. The back door was still open and the shelves of equipment were before her. What could she use to—?

"Okay," Dennis said. "I'm reaching for my badge. Don't do anything stupid."

"If you're who you say you are, we don't have a problem."

"Misunderstandings can cost lives." Dennis pulled open his brown leather jacket and slowly reached inside. "I've seen it happen. Just stay calm. If you'd like to come closer, I'll show you all the ID you could want to see."

Hannah saw the almost imperceptible signs of Dennis's hand tightening beneath his jacket.

"No!" she screamed. "Watch out. He's going to—"

Too late.

The pistol was already in Dennis's hand, out, and firing three bullets in rapid succession.

The old man screamed in pain as one bullet hit him in the upper chest. The other two were close misses, and pierced the fuel pump next to him.

The old man crumpled to the ground.

Dead? Hannah wondered frantically. What could she do to—

It was already done. Simpson's shotgun discharged as he fell to the gravel.

And the charge hit Dennis in the face. His head exploded.

Fontaine stared in disbelief at Dennis, but he recovered immediately. He started toward Hannah, the anesthetic-soaked cloth in his hand.

Think fast. Weapon. Find a weapon. What weapon?

The gasoline smell was thick in the air. The gas from the pierced fuel pump was gushing and trickling as it made a trail downhill.

Right toward the van.

Right toward Fontaine, who was now running toward her.

And then she knew what weapon to use.

She dove toward the equipment rack and her hand grasped the handle. She took aim and squeezed the trigger.

The signal flare exploded onto the concrete slab and caught the gasoline. The hot, bluish flame raced for the gunman. In an instant the puddle beneath him ignited. It consumed his clothes and then his hair.

And then his flesh.

He *screamed.*

She closed her eyes, then forced herself to open them. No time for squeamishness. She had to get out of here. This place was going to be a tinderbox in minutes, maybe seconds.

Hannah ran to the station manager. He was conscious, thank God. He was staring in horror at the burning man.

"Can you walk?"

He couldn't seem to take his eyes off the man who was now writhing on the pavement. "Fire . . . need extinguisher."

"No time." She pulled him to his feet and slung his arm over her shoulder. "We need to hurry. Walk with me, okay?"

He shook his head as he looked back at the pumps. "My station . . ."

Hannah half pulled, half dragged the man across the two-lane road.

She heard a deep, low rumbling.

The tanks!

She pushed the old man down and hit the ground on her stomach. The gas station exploded, sending shock waves off the hillside next to her. Fiery debris rained down on them as the blast filled their ears and echoed in the distance.

She opened her eyes. Objects were burning all around them. The station, SUV, and Conner's van were nothing more than black, burning hulks. She leaned toward Simpson and brushed an ember off his back. "Are you okay?"

"I guess so." He stared at a charred object only inches from his face. "What's . . . that?"

She quickly looked away. She felt sick. "I don't know." And, Christ, she didn't want to know. She started unbuttoning his shirt. "It looks like you have an upper-chest wound, but you may have gotten lucky." She hoped to heaven that was true. "You're not bleeding very much. I'll see if I can do some first aid before I try to get you help."

SIX

It was over two hours later, when Hannah saw a familiar silhouette outlined against the flashing lights of the fire engines and paramedic units parked on what was left of the gas station parking lot.

Bradworth.

"Did you hop on a jet to come to my rescue?" she asked bitterly.

"I'd never do that, Hannah. I'm a public official." He shrugged. "I hopped on a helicopter."

"Good one. Who says bureaucrats don't have a sense of humor."

"I have two ex-wives who might say that."

"Would they also say your timing sucks? Some rescue."

"I told you that I didn't want you driving by yourself."

"Because you knew this horror wasn't over. You knew they didn't get everything they wanted."

"There was a chance."

"A damn good chance. They didn't want to kill me. They tried to kidnap me. That means they thought I could give them something they wanted."

"That's reasonable," he said.

"Ever cautious. God, I'm sick of you," she said wearily. "That old man who owns this station was shot and his station destroyed just because I drove in here. He didn't have anything to do with this."

"How is he?"

"They took him to the hospital about an hour ago. The paramedics said he'd be okay." She gazed at the ruin of the station. "I'm not so sure. He told me he opened this station when he came home from fighting World War II. It's been his whole life for over fifty years. Then in the flicker of an eyelash, it's gone."

"Insurance?"

"Yes, but that won't replace the emotional attachment."

"He'll survive. It's probably better he retire anyway." Bradworth changed the subject. "I've been in touch with the local police department, so I'm pretty much up to speed on things. Did the officers here tell you that the SUV's license plates were stolen?"

"No."

"They are. And it appears that the registration numbers have been removed. I'm having it towed to the FBI garage in Boston so they can give it the once-over. You didn't recognize either man?"

"No."

"Then we have to assume that your memory may be your biggest liability right now. Maybe they think you've seen other plates like those on the sub that they might not have been able to carry away. Or maybe they want to be the only ones who have that information on the plates. Are you sure there isn't anything more you can tell us about what you saw on the sub?"

Her fingernails dug into her palms as her fists clenched. "Dammit, there's nothing more to *tell*. There's no way I can remember anything about those plates. It's just a blank. All I can see is Conner lying there, dead."

He shrugged. "Just checking. It might be a good idea if I had a couple agents assigned to you for the next few weeks. For your protection."

"I guess you thought this would be a good idea, too." She pulled out the device she'd found in Conner's car vent.

"What's that?"

"Don't play stupid with me, Bradworth. This thing's government issue all the way. I saw one in Turkey a couple years ago. The U.S. Navy brought me in to recommend modifications to the Turkish submarine fleet, and our hosts were most upset to find one of these in their transports. They determined U.S. Military Intelligence had planted it."

"It doesn't mean I had anything to do with planting this bug."

"You were the only one who knew I was driving Conner's van back." Her eyes narrowed on his face. "But were those men using it to track me? Were you working with them?"

"Christ, no, Hannah. Okay, I did put it in the van. For your protection."

"Yeah, sure."

"It was sending pulses to a GPS satellite. I was worried and wanted to keep tabs on you."

"So you could set me up again."

"Let me take you back to town. We can talk and—"

"I already have a ride. One of the officers will take me back to his precinct. I have a rental car waiting for me there." She got to her feet. "I only want two things from you, Bradworth. One, I don't want Cathy to hear about this. She has enough to worry about. Two, you smooth the way with those insurance people who are going to be cross-examining Larry Simpson. I don't want him suffering any more than he has to because he was unlucky enough to have me stop at his station."

"I'll do my best."

"Do more than your best," she said fiercely. "I'm sick of innocent people getting the shaft because they got in the way of you and your friends' little games."

"I don't regard it as a game. I'm doing my job and—"

"I'm through talking to you. You're either pitifully inefficient or you're crooked as hell." She strode toward the police car. "I'm leaning toward the latter. Just stay away from me, Bradworth."

Hannah Bryson is damn lucky," Kirov said curtly. "Yeah, you were handling it. Why weren't you there when she needed you?"

"I don't have to answer to you."

"The hell you don't."

"And we don't even know that it was Pavski. It could be a new player in the game."

"No, it's Pavski."

"How are you so sure?"

"The attention to detail. The stolen plates, the erased registration numbers. He's always been good at covering his tracks. Do you know what they tried to knock her out with?"

"Not yet. I assumed it was chloroform."

"It wasn't. Pavski has always been partial to midazolam. It works faster and leaves the victim with less of a headache later."

"Considerate guy."

"If he wants information, he'd need her to have a clear head. Midazolam." He paused. "And if he made a move on her, then he doesn't have everything he needs. I'm betting he's still hovering near *Silent Thunder.*"

"We need him alive, Kirov."

"So you've told me."

"We need information. Once we get that, what you do is your own business. Do we have an understanding?"

"Oh, I've always understood you and your 'superiors.' You're the ones who've failed to read me."

"But you'll keep your word?"

"As long as I don't see signs of a double cross. But make no mistake, Bradworth. If, after you have him in custody, you cut Pavski a deal, all bets are off."

"And?"

"I'll still find him and finish him off." He added, "And anyone else who stands in my way. It might be wise to remember that, Bradworth."

Sorry to keep you waiting out in the hall." Congressman George Preston sat behind his mahogany desk and smiled at Hannah and Cathy. "My assistant needed to take her daughter to the doctor, so it's just me here until after lunch. What can I do for you?"

"I appreciate your agreeing to see us. I know you're busy when you come home to Boston," Hannah said. "I promise we won't take much of your time."

"My pleasure." Preston's smile faded. "No, my duty. Cathy has always been my friend as well as my employee, and I have to find a way to help her . . . and you."

"Thank you." Hannah felt a surge of warmth. She had liked Preston the few times she'd met him. He'd gotten his start in politics over two decades before, when, as a high-school civics teacher, he ran for a seat in the U.S. House of Representatives merely as a lesson for his students. The local media picked up the story, his support snowballed, and he eventually won the race by a narrow margin. Hannah glanced at the framed newspaper on his wall, with the headline MR. PRESTON GOES TO WASHINGTON. It said something about him that he identified with that Frank Capra classic.

"Again, I can't tell you how sorry I am about Conner. He was a good man."

"He was an extraordinary man," Cathy said quietly. "Thank you, George."

Preston glanced at Hannah. "When Cathy first called asking for information about the *Silent Thunder,* I didn't know you were involved with the project. I suppose I should have guessed. You and Conner were so close. Anyway, here it is." Preston gestured toward the two large file boxes stacked next to his desk. "Most of this is stuff from the media clipping services. We use them to gauge media reaction to various people or issues, and they compile just about everything said or written about a subject in a designated time span. I doubt there's anything there you don't already know."

"Are there photographs?" Hannah asked.

"Photographs, videos, maybe even compact discs of a news radio story or two."

"This must have been expensive," Cathy said.

"I'm on a committee that has a contract with this particular clipping service. We're not using them for much else right now, so at least this way they earn the money we're already paying them. After you're finished, I'll give all of this material to the maritime museum. I'm sure they'd like to have it for their archives."

Cathy stood up and picked up one of the boxes. "Thank you. We'll take good care of these."

"I know you will." He hesitated. "And you know I'll continue to help you as much as I can." He added gently, "But don't you believe that others are more qualified and working hard to find Conner's murderers?"

Hannah didn't answer directly as she rose and picked up the other box. "We just want to make sure all the bases are covered."

"What makes you think they aren't?"

Cathy said quickly, "This is for me, George. I need to *do* something. Can you understand?"

"Of course. I just want you to be careful. Ronnie and Donna need you now."

"I know." She tried to smile as she turned to leave. "And God knows, I need them."

H annah Bryson and her brother's widow just left Congressman Preston's office," Koppel hung up his phone. "Trouble?"

"I'm sure she's trying to stir up as much trouble as she can," Pavski said. "And probably snooping." He frowned. "Keep the surveillance sharp on her and Cathy Bryson." He sat back in his chair. "This wouldn't have been necessary if your so-called experts hadn't fumbled."

"They were experts," Koppel protested. "Something must have gone wrong."

"They fumbled," Pavski repeated coldly. "That's what went wrong. Now we have to find another way. Contact Carwell and have him check his go-to list. I need a wedge to get under Bryson's guard. Have you transmitted my message to Danzyl in Moscow?"

Koppel nodded. "He's working on it. He'll get it to you soon."

"Soon isn't good enough. I need it now." Keep calm. This trouble with Hannah Bryson was only a small glitch in the scheme of things. Danzyl would give him what he needed, and he could start doing the research to bring him what he wanted. He had several strings to his bow, and one arrow would strike home.

An hour after they left the congressman's office, Hannah and Cathy were walking around Hannah's Back Bay condominium, which had recently become a veritable bulletin board. Every inch of wall space was covered by hundreds of photocopied newspaper and magazine stories, photographs and broadcast transcriptions. A stack of DVDs rested on top of Hannah's television set, which displayed a marathon of television news reports relating to the *Silent Thunder*'s arrival in the U.S.

"These pinholes are going to wreak havoc with your resale value," Cathy said.

Hannah shrugged. "The damage has already been done. I've spent too many nights pacing around here with blueprints for my new submarine designs tacked across every wall, window, and appliance. You wouldn't believe the inspiration that can come while scribbling on a shower door."

"I'll take your word for it." Cathy surveyed the newspaper accounts. "You're featured in at least half these stories. You're more famous than I thought."

Hannah glanced at a few of the clippings. "Conner should have been in them, too."

Cathy shook her head. "No."

Hannah gazed questioningly at her.

"Conner hated the limelight. I know you don't care for it, either, but he absolutely hated it." Cathy smiled. "He was happy to be quietly brilliant, then to come home to his family in blissful anonymity. He said that one star in the family was enough. He was so proud of you."

Hannah felt the tears sting her eyes and looked quickly away. "Thanks for telling me. Do you know, Conner and I talked about this in Rock Bay Harbor, and I was worried that he was feeling cheated. He denied it, but it's good to know that—" She had to stop to clear her throat and checked her watch. "Cathy, if you need to go pick up Ronnie and Donna—"

"It's okay. I still have a few hours. They're with my mother. I think it's a relief for them to spend time with someone who isn't struggling just to hold herself together."

"I've seen you with them. You're doing great."

Cathy gazed at the photo-covered walls. "I'd be doing great if we could find something here we could use."

"There's some good background in this material, but we probably won't find what we need here. We have to find out what was scratched on those bulkhead plates, and to do that, we have to find out more about the *Silent Thunder*'s history."

"Didn't the Russians give you that when they sold the sub to the museum?"

"Not really. We don't even know how many miles it logged. The Russians are notoriously secretive about their submarine fleet. They're constantly renaming and renumbering them to make it hard for other governments to know how many they have in service. They're not about to give us details of its missions."

"So what are you going to do?"

"One of the ships on my first *Titanic* expedition was a Russian scientific vessel. There were some former Soviet Navy officers on the crew, so I've made some calls to see if they can help us out."

Cathy reached into one of the file boxes and pulled out another stack of articles and photographs. "In the meantime, I'll find some place to plaster these up." She turned away. "You say you're partial to the shower door?"

Two and a half hours later, Hannah walked around the condo with a small stack of photographs in her hand. She studied another picture on the wall, then plucked it off and added it to the pile. She repeated the routine several more times as she worked her way from the living room to the kitchen.

"What did you find?" Cathy asked.

Hannah threw down the stack on the dining table and spread out the photos. "Look at these. The four stops that the *Silent Thunder* made before arriving at Rock Bay: Baltimore, New York, Boston, and Norfolk. Notice something in common about all these shots?"

Cathy studied the photos. "Other than the tons of ribbons and streamers littering the water in each of these ports?"

"It's all biodegradable and dissolves in just a few hours. Keep looking."

She gazed a few moments longer, then finally pointed to a craft resting a few hundred yards off shore. "This boat."

"Yes." Hannah shuffled through the photos. "It was at each of the ports. This boat was following the *Silent Thunder*."

Cathy looked at the photo that featured the boat most prominently. It was a small fishing trawler, approximately thirty feet in length, with a single mast and elevated steering platform. The silhouette of a tall, broad-shouldered man could be seen on the platform.

"He could be a submarine buff," Cathy said.

"Possibly. Or a journalist covering the *Silent Thunder*'s final voyage. It's strange how he seems to be keeping his distance, though. The other boats are in position to observe the submarine. He seems to be positioned to watch the other boats. See?"

Cathy nodded. "So what do we do?"

Hannah found a picture that offered a view of the vessel's registration ID and examined it under a magnifying glass. She picked up her phone, punched a number.

"Who are you calling?" Cathy asked.

"Jack Fowler, he's with the Coast Guard."

Fowler picked up on the fifth ring.

"Hi, Jack. Hannah Bryson here."

He was clearly surprised to hear from her. "Hannah . . . Listen, I've been meaning to call you ever since I heard about Conner. I can't tell you how sorry I am."

"Thank you, Jack. It's been a tough time."

"If there's anything I can do, you know—"

"Actually, there is. I need you to run a vessel ID for me."

"Jeez, Hannah. I can direct you to the license office, but—"

"It'll take forever that way. Just a few clicks on that keyboard in front of you will give me everything I need."

"Dammit, I'm the U.S. Coast Guard's legal counsel. It's part of my job to keep our people from doing what you've just asked me to do."

"Tell them to do as you say, not as you do."

"And what do I say when I'm called down on the carpet for giving out sensitive information?"

She hesitated. It had to be done. "Remind them who helped you get the job there. If I hadn't put in a word for you, your expertise in maritime law would probably still be helping the oil companies pollute the oceans."

He paused. "That's below the belt, Hannah."

"I agree, and I'd never do it if I wasn't desperate. Help me, Jack."

"You're a wicked woman, Hannah."

"Please, Jack. BDR 54992 B8 67."

Silence. Then she heard the clicking of a keyboard.

Success.

"Okay, I guess I'm not really giving you anything you couldn't have found out with some paperwork and a bit of time. The vessel belongs to a Captain Henry Danforth."

"Class?"

"Hmm. It's a fishing trawler, but it's licensed for personal/recreational use."

"That's unusual, isn't it?"

"Well, deep-sea fishermen retire, and sometimes they just want a boat they're comfortable with. The boat's hailing port isn't far from you: Gloucester, Massachusetts, probably inner harbor. Are you happy now?"

"Very. Thanks, Jack. I'll remember this."

"I'd just as soon you forget it. It will be safer for me."

"Whatever you say." She hung up and turned to Cathy. "We've *got* him. Gloucester."

Ninety minutes later, Hannah turned left off Route 128 to East Main Street, which would take her past the State Fish Pier and along the inner harbor. Cathy had wanted to come with her, but she'd had to pick up her kids. Hannah was just as happy to go alone. She didn't know what she'd find in Gloucester.

Her cell phone rang, and she glanced at the caller ID screen. Bradworth. She let it go to voice mail. It was the third call from him in the past two hours. He'd probably learned about the clip files she'd obtained from Congressman Preston. No doubt the bastard wanted to warn her off from what she was doing.

No way.

In less than a mile, she turned off East Main and drove toward the water. Gloucester was a charming fishing village that almost seemed at odds with its recent popularity as a tourist destination. The old-timers were resentful of the transition, but the tourist industry had helped take up the slack as the region's commercial fishing industry plummeted.

She drove to the pier, which was lined with scores of fishing boats and pleasure craft. Was the trawler even here now? She knew it could be anywhere on the Eastern Seaboard, and boat owners were notoriously uncooperative when it came to keeping current info on file with the licensing authorities. She parked her car on the street and walked toward the pier.

It was a cool, overcast afternoon, just the sort of day that kept tourists away in droves. She walked along the wharf area, occasionally raising her binoculars to examine the boats.

She stiffened. There it was!

She focused her binoculars on the ID number. Definitely the right one. The trawler was moored between two other fishing boats. Its maroon, barnacle-covered hull was in need of a resurfacing, and the windows were fogged by sea salt. She looked for a name on the stern, but there was none.

She watched the boat for a few minutes longer, looking for any signs of life inside. None visible.

She walked down to the pier and made her way to the trawler, slowing her pace as she drew closer. The wind kicked up, and cold sprinkles of rain pelted her face.

Lights off, hatches closed. It didn't look as if anyone was home.

"Hi." In the boat next to the trawler, a bearded man in his early twenties rolled up a ragged net and glanced up at Hannah. He gave a low appreciative whistle. "You're lost, right?"

She smiled. "Not exactly. I want to talk to the captain of this boat. Know when he'll be back?"

He shook his head. "Nope. If it's a charter you're looking for, I don't think he does that kind of thing."

"Not even for the right price?"

"I don't think so. I've never seen anybody on the boat but him." His gaze slowly studied her up and down. "You look like you're used to a nicer boat anyhow, like maybe a yacht."

"I'll take that as a compliment."

He smiled. "It was. I'm Josh Sarks."

"Hannah. Good to meet you." She stepped closer. "Maybe I'm confusing this man with someone else. What does he look like?"

"Tall, dark hair, late forties or maybe fifty. He talks with an accent."

"What kind of accent?"

"Irish or Scottish, I can never tell the difference."

"See him around here much?"

"Sometimes." Sarks jerked his thumb toward a bar next to the pier entrance. "And I've run into him at the Seagull Saloon. I was there with a girlfriend, and she went dippy over him. I don't know if it's the accent or what." He grimaced. "You wouldn't think a young chick like her would go for an old guy like that."

Forties was old? Christ, this kid was young. "He goes there to pick up women?"

"Nah. As far as I know, he always comes back here alone." He frowned. "You're asking a lot of questions. Are you his wife or something? Have I put my foot in it?"

She smiled. "Hardly. I promise you I've never met the man. I'm here on business, and I appreciate your help. So he lives here on the boat?"

"Yep."

"What does he do for a living?"

He shrugged. "Maybe nothing. He's sure not a fisherman. My dad and I have been moored here for the last three years, and I've never seen him bring in a catch. The boat comes and goes. It'll be here for a few weeks, then goes away."

"Goes where?"

"No idea. I don't think anyone around here knows him very well."

And neither did Josh Sarks. She'd probably found out all she was going to get from him. "Well, he doesn't sound like the man I was looking for. Thanks for your help."

"Maybe we could go up to the Seagull, and I could buy you a drink?" he called after her. "Someone there might be able to tell you something."

"I wish I could. I don't have the time right now." She smiled at him as she started up the pier. "Give me a rain check?"

Ten minutes later, Hannah sat at a window table of the Coffee Dunk 'n' Dine across the street from the Seagull Saloon. She flipped up the lid of her laptop and glanced outside. She could see the trawler, so if the vessel's owner returned, he'd be easy to spot.

She sipped her coffee. What would she do when she saw him? From what she'd learned from Sarks, it was doubtful if he was connected with the men who'd attacked the sub. He'd been living here on a beat-up trawler for three years. He hadn't just shown up on the radar when the sub appeared. Maybe he was a submarine groupie after all.

Or maybe he wasn't.

She'd make a decision and cross that bridge when she came to it. In the meantime, she could think of worse places to catch up on her work.

Her cell phone rang; she checked the caller ID screen. Bradworth again. She thought about answering, but decided against it. To hell with him.

She turned off the ringer.

S hit!" Bradworth slammed down the receiver and walked across his office. Next time he'd block his name and number, in case Hannah was intentionally deep-sixing him to the voice-mail graveyard.

The red flag had gone up when Congressman Preston's office requested the *Silent Thunder* media clippings, and a few discreet inquiries confirmed that Hannah and her sister-in-law were behind it.

Bradworth rubbed his temple. Things needed to be handled delicately, with finesse. He couldn't allow a couple of grief-stricken family members to unravel years of effort.

Even more troublesome was the preliminary lab report on Hannah's would-be abductors. The Agency medical examiners had worked through the night over the charred remains, and their findings scared the shit out of him.

Hannah, answer your goddamned phone.

SEVEN

That had to be him.

Hannah stiffened in her chair at the coffeehouse window as she saw the tall, dark-haired man making his way down the pier.

There was something very familiar about that silhouette she'd stared at in those many photographs. He wore black jeans and a corded cream-colored sweater. Standard-issue Rugged Man of the Sea, she thought.

He boarded the trawler and disappeared inside.

After ten minutes, he reemerged and walked back up the pier. He moved with confidence and masculine grace. She tried to get a good look at his face, but it was getting dark. Damn.

He went inside the saloon.

What now? She could follow and get a good look at him in the bar.

She cast a glance back at his boat.

Or there might be one way to put an end to this. If he was a journalist or submarine buff, she'd probably know after a quick glance inside the trawler.

She packed up her laptop and walked out of the coffee shop. The night had brought even more mist, and the pier's wood planks shimmered from the peach-colored overhead lights. A lone buoy rang in the distance.

She was shivering. Nerves? It wasn't every night that she indulged in criminal trespassing. Or it could be the cold; the temperature had dropped a good ten degrees since she'd been inside. She stopped in front of the trawler and stared at it for a long moment.

Don't think. Just do it.

She climbed over the transom and pulled open the hatch.

Inside.

Dark, smelling of lemon wax and coffee.

She raised her key ring xenon flashlight and shined it around the cramped living quarters. The area was used efficiently, with almost every inch of wall space covered with shelving and corkboards.

Cotton sheets were stretched tightly over a narrow mattress. A military bedroll, she noted. She could have bounced quarters off it.

She turned toward a series of navigational charts plastered across the front bulkhead. Typical Eastern Seaboard charts, available for sale at any bait and tackle shop in town. She moved closer to look for any indication of the boat's recent travels.

She went rigid. "My God."

The charts were far from typical. They were filled with the same odd symbols she'd seen on the bulkhead of the *Silent Thunder* that night Conner had been killed. Only these navigational symbols were written with a variety of colored grease pencils. They could be other symbols or copies of the ones taken from the submarine. Which meant—

Holy shit.

It meant she was in bad trouble. She had to get the hell out of here.

The hatch flew open!

She caught only a glimpse of cream-colored sweater stretched over broad shoulders before she instinctively barreled forward and tried to get past the man standing in the doorway.

"What the hell are—" He didn't finish the question as his arm flew out to stop her. "Stop struggling. You don't—"

He grunted as her fist connected with his stomach. "Damn you." He knocked her down, dove on top, and straddled her. His hands grasped her wrists and pinned them to the floor. "I've no compunction about beating up on women when they exhibit lethal tendencies. Just give me an excuse."

God, he was strong. She could feel the muscles of his thighs rock hard against her hips. She was a strong woman herself, and he was holding her still with no real effort. "Let me go." Jesus, that sounded as futile as that panicky rush she'd made at him. Stupid. Use your brains, dammit. "You won't hurt me. It would be dumb. Do you think I'd come here without letting someone know I was going to do it?"

"Indeed? And did they know you were going to try to burgle my poor vessel? Very poor judgment. I'd be within my rights to shoot an intruder."

He did have a slight accent, but it wasn't Irish or Scottish. The accent was the same as the Russian naval officers she'd worked with. "I wasn't going to rob you. I just wanted to have a look around." Christ, she felt helpless. She couldn't stand being held down like this. Go on the attack. "And I think you know that, Captain Danforth. I think you know who I am and why I'm here. Either call the police and have me arrested for trespassing, or get the hell off me so we can talk."

He was silent and then chuckled. "May I point out you probably wouldn't be in this position if you'd indicated you wanted conversation earlier, Ms. Bryson? I'm the one who was assaulted. I was only defending myself."

He *did* know who she was and was making no attempt to hide it. "And how was I to know what you'd do? I've been attacked every time I've turned around lately. Maybe you had something to do with that too."

"And maybe I didn't."

"Then tell me why the hell you have those damn scribblings on that navigational map."

She could feel him tense against her. "You're in a very vulnerable position to discuss the matter."

"That's right, I've nothing to lose. You'd know I saw them anyway. If you're going to kill me, you'll kill me. If you're not one of those bastards who killed Conner, I'm going to keep after you until I get answers."

He hesitated and then swung off her and stood up. "Then by all means, I must let you get your breath before you start interrogating me."

She felt a rush of relief. God, she'd been scared. "I don't know if I can get my breath." She flinched as she sat up. "I think you cracked a rib."

He shook his head. "No, I only bruised you."

"You seem very sure of that." She ignored the hand he offered and got to her feet. "You must indulge in this kind of violence frequently."

"Enough to be able to gauge the damage." He turned and moved across the cabin. "While you, on the other hand, were miserably inept."

"You took me by surprise. I acted on impulse and didn't mean to—" She was defending herself, she realized in disgust. "I hate violence, and I don't need to make excuses for not being good at it. There's too much—" She stopped. He had turned on the light and she got her first good look at him. A shock of dark hair generously flicked with gray, blue eyes lined at the corners from squinting into the sun, high broad cheekbones. Not a classically handsome man, by any means. Yet it was difficult to look away from that face.

"Acting on impulse is foolish. One must always make excuses for being foolish." He opened the cabinet and took down a bottle. "Would you like a drink? You look like you could use one."

"No, I don't want a drink." She stared at him in frustration. He was perfectly calm, almost offhand, and it bugged the hell out of her. "I want to know about those symbols."

"They're navigational symbols as you guessed. Samsovian school." He poured himself a whiskey. "A bit esoteric but hardly criminal."

"But it's criminal if you kill to get your hands on them."

"True." He gestured to the map. "But if you study them I'm sure you'll realize they're not the same ones on the bulkhead of the *Silent Thunder.* Go ahead, take a look." He sat down in a chair at the desk. "And you'll see I'm just a poor fisherman charting my path."

She made a rude noise and heard him laugh as she crossed to stare at the map.

She was too upset to concentrate enough to bring up the full memory of those markings on the bulkhead, but now that she studied the map, she could see that they weren't the same. He was right, dammit. Similar but not the same. She turned to face him. "It's different. But that doesn't mean—" She wearily shook her head. "I don't know what the hell it means. I just know that you're probably as crooked as everyone else, and I want to know why you were following the *Silent Thunder* from port to port."

"Admiration for an exceptional vessel?"

"Damn you."

His smile faded. "I believe that sounded a bit quavery. You do need a drink. But I'll give you coffee instead." He turned to the galley. "Wait on deck while I make it. You'll feel safer than down here with me."

"I don't want coffee."

"But you want answers, and you've found out just enough to be troublesome to me. That might induce me to give you what you want."

"Or it might induce you to permanently remove the source of the trouble."

"I could have done that anytime since you barged onto my boat." He opened the coffee tin. "Wait on deck."

She hesitated, staring at his back. She didn't like orders, and he had been entirely too much in control of the situation. But refusing a possible breakthrough to make a token protest would have been brainless.

She turned and headed for the hatch.

She was sitting on the deck, her arms linked around her knees, when he came out of the cabin ten minutes later. "You took a long time."

"I thought you needed it." He handed her the mug of coffee. "Black. That's how you take it, right?"

"How do you know that?"

"It's not exactly classified information." He sat down opposite her and leaned against the rail. "I guess I must have picked it up somewhere along the way."

"Along the way to where? From where? And why should you know anything about me?"

"We have a mutual acquaintance." He lifted his glass to his lips. "And I have a boundless curiosity."

"Drop this enigmatic crap. Am I supposed to guess what the hell you're talking about?"

"Enigmatic crap," he repeated. "Interesting phrase. It brings up a rather bizarre vision." He held up his hand as she opened her lips. "But I've no desire to indulge in that kind of pretentious bullshit. Life's too short, and by nature I'm basically a simple man."

She studied him. His words had the ring of truth, but she'd judge him to be nowhere near simple. "Yeah, sure."

He chuckled. "You're right. I own to being convoluted on occasion, but that's by choice, not by instinct. Sometimes it's necessary."

"Like it was necessary to follow *Silent Thunder* from port to port."

"Exactly." He sipped his whiskey. "And like it was necessary for you to try your hand at burglary."

"I wasn't going to steal anything. I just had to be sure—I had to eliminate possibilities and I thought I might—" She was defending herself again. She wouldn't put it past him to have manipulated her into that posture. All the time she had been talking to him, she'd been aware of the easy confidence, the presence, and the sense of power he emitted. "There was a chance that you might be a reporter or someone else completely innocent."

"I haven't been innocent since I was nine years old. But reporters are seldom completely innocent either. I might be—"

"A reporter who's familiar with those Samsovian coordinates? A reporter who knew coordinates were scribbled on the bulkhead even though it wasn't public knowledge? A reporter who's lived on this boat for at least the last three years? A reporter who knows I drink black coffee?"

He was silent a moment. "You've been asking questions. Young Sarks?"

"He was helpful."

"I imagine he was. He likes the pretty ladies."

"And he says they like you."

"Of course, they do. Most women have tender hearts." He smiled mockingly. "And I'm obviously a pitifully lonely man. All I have to do with my life is follow an old submarine around."

There was nothing pitiful about this man. If women were drawn to him, it was because of the mature strength and confidence he exuded. "You're joking. But I know it was you following the sub. Why?"

He didn't answer.

"Dammit, you said that you'd give me what I want. I do know enough to make it difficult for you. I'll go to every newspaper in town, I'll talk to the police. I'll go to Congressman Preston and let him swing his weight around. I'll follow you and dog your footsteps until you—"

His phone rang.

"Pardon me for interrupting this fascinating oratory. I'll be right with you." He answered the phone and listened. "Yes, you're right, she probably did learn too much for comfort from those media files. I'll take care of it right away. As a matter of fact, she's sitting four feet away from me right now." He listened again. "Stop sputtering. I've no intention of disposing of her. Though your clumsiness almost succeeded in doing that several times. If you'd stopped her before she got to this point, I might have left it in your hands. Now she's mine, Bradworth." He hung up.

She inhaled sharply. "Bradworth?"

"Drink your coffee. It will get cold."

"Screw the coffee. You're working with Bradworth?"

"No, but we're working toward a common goal on parallel paths." He tilted his head consideringly. "Maybe."

"Then you're with the U.S. government?"

"No."

"The Russian government?"

"Absolutely not." He got to his feet. "I believe it may be a good idea for us to up anchor and take a little voyage down the coast if you want to talk. Bradworth may be nervous and send someone to check to make sure I haven't dropped you overboard."

"How can I be sure you won't?"

"Get off and walk away." He started the engine. "It's up to you."

But he knew she wouldn't do it, she realized in frustration. She could see it in his expression, the confidence in the way he moved. He was totally in control of himself and his whole damn world.

"I'm out of here. In another minute you won't have a choice," he said. "Make up your mind."

"Shut up." She got to her feet. "I'm not going anywhere, and you know it. Get going, you arrogant son of a bitch."

Twenty minutes later he anchored at a cove down the coast and turned to face her. "Here we are. Deserted. Dark. Lonely. Just the place for me to ply my fiendish way with you."

"Is that supposed to intimidate me? You sound more like a rapist than a murderer."

He snapped his fingers. "Foiled again. It's the nuances of the English language. There are far too many subtleties."

"And you're neither English nor American, are you?" She stared skeptically at him. "Henry Danforth?"

"That's what my driver's license says."

"Papers can be easily forged. Particularly by someone with connections with government agencies."

"You believe Bradworth furnished me with them?"

"Did he?"

"Yes." He opened the door of the hatch. "As well as quite a few other identities. I'm a man of a thousand passports. Well, maybe not a thousand but certainly several. Danish, French, Italian . . ."

"But you're Russian."

"Oh, yes. I have a Russian passport too."

"Under what name?"

"Nicolas Kirov."

"And is that your true name?"

"Of course not." He started down the steps. "You might as well come down and let me freshen your coffee. It's chilly out here, and the security blanket factor's gone for you."

She followed him. "You're not going to tell me your real name?"

"I didn't say that." He crossed the cabin and poured coffee into two mugs. "I'll probably have to share a few items of information with you. But I'm a private man, and you mustn't expect a bonanza to pour forth in a glorious waterfall."

"I already know Bradworth is our mutual acquaintance. But I can't see him sharing information about the way I drink my coffee."

"No, it wasn't in your dossier. But I spent a little time observing you and probably stored it away. I don't have a photographic memory like you, but I've trained myself to remember details." He handed her the coffee. "You like everything plain and straightforward. Your job, your relationships . . . your coffee."

"Observing me? What the hell were you doing watching me?"

"You were working on the *Silent Thunder,*" he said simply. "I had to keep an eye on you."

"Why?"

"It was possible you'd stumble across something you weren't meant to find. I had to be there."

"To save Conner and me?"

He didn't answer.

"You bastard. You and Bradworth were sitting there waiting for something to happen, waiting for them to come. Isn't that true?"

He was silent a moment. "Bradworth set up the job with the museum. He thought it was worth the risk to get a qualified expert down there to take the sub apart. He thought I was wrong about the sub being followed. He could have been right."

"Followed by whom?"

"Pavski." He sat down and sipped his coffee. "Very ugly, very criminal, and very desirous of finding that map scrawled on the bulkhead."

"Why?"

"It would lead him to a payload that would set him up in a kingly fashion for the rest of his life."

"Buried treasure?"

"In a manner of speaking."

"What kind of treasure?"

He shrugged. "Not the kind you found on the *Titanic*." He smiled. "By the way, I admired your work there. I understand that those tiny submersibles of yours were able to show us four times more of the interior bow section than any previous expedition. And I was fascinated by those digital 3-D virtual models that your data made possible. You're the best. That's why I recommended you to Bradworth."

"Damn you, I wish you'd been run over by a truck before you opened your mouth. Conner would still be alive."

His smile faded. "I can't deny it. If I'd let Bradworth bring in his naval engineers, they would have been dead instead of your brother. I never meant it to happen. I hoped it wouldn't."

"Hope?" She stared at him incredulously. "What good is hope? Why didn't you *do* something?"

"I warned Bradworth. I tried to make sure—" He shrugged. "But you're right. I'm guilty. Bradworth is guilty. Good intentions are never enough. You have a perfect right to detest us."

"You're damn right I do." She was shaking with rage. "Conner was a good man in the prime of his life. He deserved to live."

He nodded. "He seemed to be a fine man, and I could tell you were very close."

"By your spying on us."

"Yes." He turned away. "You're upset. I'll take you back to the dock and drop you off."

"The hell you will." Her hands clenched into fists. "I'm not going anywhere until you tell me how I can get my hands on this Pavski."

"I don't know."

"Dammit, you have to know something about him. You knew he was following the sub."

"I suspected it."

"Why?"

"One of his associates was seen in Helsinki."

"If you know where this associate is, then you can locate Pavski."

He shook his head.

"Why not?"

"Unfortunately, his associate is quite dead."

Frustration seethed through her. "Dammit. Dammit. Dammit."

"We'll talk more later. Here's my cell phone number." He scrawled the number on the back of a napkin and headed for the hatch. "I'll give Bradworth a chance to get the benefit of his share of the venom you're shooting at me. I'll call and tell him to meet you at the dock."

She crammed the napkin in her pocket. "I don't want to talk to Bradworth. Do you think I trust him either? He's told me nothing but lies since I met him."

"But you know he works for your government. Therefore, he's accountable."

"And you're not accountable?"

He didn't answer. "Come back and see me after you've talked to him and had time to absorb and adjust."

"To the little you've told me?"

"It's enough for now."

"The devil it is. It's *nothing*. And you won't even tell me your name."

"I'll tell you if it will make you feel better." He opened the door. "Dimitri Ivanov."

Ivanov.

She stared at the door after it closed behind him.

The name was familiar. She had heard it or read it . . .

Ivanov.

Bradworth was standing on the dock when they reached Gloucester. "This was a mistake," he said as he helped Hannah from the boat. "You should have discussed this with me before you came here."

She pulled away from him. "So that you could lie or talk me out of it?"

"So that I could keep you from running unnecessary risks." He glanced at Kirov. "You were wise to bring her back and turn her over to us. We won't tolerate your—"

"I'm not turning her over to you," Kirov said. "I told you she was mine, and nothing has changed. All I'm doing is letting her vent some anger and try to get a few answers from a source she has at least a minimal trust in. But I'm not letting you drown her in red tape or get her killed because you're inept. You had your chance." He turned to Hannah. "I'll be here until tomorrow night if you want to see me." He went down the hatch.

"Son of a bitch." Bradworth was staring after him. "Bastard."

He was afraid of Kirov, Hannah realized in shock. It was there in his expression—anger and frustration and fear.

"I'm sure he is," Hannah said as she turned away and strode down the pier. "And so are you, Bradworth. Let's get out of here. I'm going back to Boston. Follow me and meet me at my condo."

"I'll have one of my men drive your car back. We can talk on the way."

"I don't want to be in the same car with you for that long."

"I can understand your resentment, but I only did my duty as I saw—"

"You can't understand. Damn your duty. Damn you." She opened the driver's door of her car. "Meet me at my condo."

He hesitated, then as she started her car, he turned and hurried toward his vehicle.

Draw a deep breath. She had to get to Boston, and she didn't want to pile up against a tree because she was so angry she couldn't see straight. That would be a victory for those bastards who'd killed Conner.

Pavski. She had a name now. Not much more, but it was a start.

And she had another name.

Ivanov.

EIGHT

"Come in, Bradworth," she said curtly as she turned away from the door. "How much of it is true? Did this Pavski kill my brother?"

"We . . . suspect it."

"And you didn't tell me?"

"It's sensitive, classified information."

"Screw your classified information. Don't give me that. My brother is *dead*."

"I would have discussed it with you when I could."

When hell froze over, she thought bitterly. Go on to something else. "What do you know about Dimitri Ivanov?"

He went still. "What?" A multitude of expressions flitted over his face. "I beg your pardon?"

"Kirov. Ivanov. Whatever you want to call him."

"He told you—" He stopped and was silent a moment. "I wasn't expecting him to do that."

"Obviously." She went to the window and stared out into the darkness. "Why not?"

"What did he tell you?" he asked warily.

"His name. But he must have known I'd ask you questions about him. He knew I'd read those *Silent Thunder* dossiers, didn't he?"

"Yes."

"I thought so." Her lips twisted. "He was privy to everything that went on from the time we were hired. Right?"

"Yes."

"Dimitri Ivanov. Second officer on the *Silent Thunder*. Killed in an explosion at the Black Sea shipyard in 1994. He's very spry for a corpse."

"A veritable Frankenstein's monster," Bradworth said sarcastically. "I've often wished he'd meet the same fate."

"But you're clearly on the same team now."

"He doesn't think so. Ivanov's not a team player."

"And you hate his guts."

"I believe he's dangerous to the mission."

"And you hate his guts."

He shrugged. "I have a right to my opinion. I disapproved of recruiting him, and nothing that's happened since has altered my view. He's a wild card and too volatile for my taste."

"Recruited? You staged his death, and he defected?"

"He had information that was invaluable to us at the time, and he was willing to dedicate himself to further investigation."

"What kind of investigation?"

"During the period after the Cold War ceased, there were so many players in Moscow we didn't know whom to trust. Pavski was in a position of power and trying to climb higher on the ladder. He might have made it, but we thought it wise to remove him and his cohorts from the scene."

"Why?"

"He was from the old school and was eliminating his competition one by one."

"You mean he was killing them?"

He nodded. "Totally ruthless. We thought we might have another Stalin on our hands if he gained power. It was decided that he and his friends should disappear from the political scene."

"Oh, you were going to convince him to retire to the country?" she asked sarcastically.

"I'm trying to be honest with you."

"That's a first. And Ivanov was helping you make them 'disappear'?"

"He had the background. He had the motivation. It's not as if we forced him to defect and go after Pavski. He came to us with some information we could use to discredit Pavski, then offered us a deal."

She remembered her first impression of Kirov. "No, I doubt if you could force him to do anything."

"He's not invincible. It just wasn't worth our while."

"Then why are you afraid of him?"

He bristled. "I'm not afraid. You just have to be careful when you're dealing with that kind of volatility."

He was lying. "Why did he want to go after Pavski?"

He was silent a moment. "He blamed him for what happened to the captain on the *Silent Thunder*. Did you read the dossier on Ivanov?"

"Yes, but at the time I didn't pay much attention. I wasn't interested in anyone but the captain and the first mate."

"Ivanov grew up in Sevastopol. Strike a bell?"

She thought about it. "That's the town where Captain Vladzar retired."

"Where he supposedly retired. The details are sketchy, but the captain disappeared as soon as he made port in the *Silent Thunder*'s last voyage."

"You're saying he was killed?"

"We don't know. I'm saying he disappeared and was never heard from again. But Ivanov thinks he was murdered."

"Why?"

"Because they tried to kill Ivanov. That's why he went on the run and defected."

"Then how does he know that Captain Vladzar didn't just go on the run too?"

"He saw Pavski's goons take him off the sub. And he had contacts in Sevastopol who told him that the captain's reported 'retirement' never happened. He never showed up there. Ivanov waited six months on the run, one step ahead of the GRU before he contacted us. He wanted to be sure that there wasn't any way he could find to save the captain and get him out of Russia."

She frowned. "Who is this GRU?"

"Military equivalent of the KGB. They handled all military intelligence but their existence wasn't publicized by the government. They're Russia's largest intelligence agency and even commanded 25,000 Spetsnez troops in 1997. Very powerful, very nasty."

"And Ivanov was willing to risk his neck against an organization like that? Why?"

Bradworth paused before he said reluctantly, "Ivanov and Vladzar were related. That may have something to do with it."

"Related?"

"Ivanov was his stepbrother. The captain sponsored his entry at the naval academy and pulled strings to get him accepted as a junior officer on the *Silent Thunder*."

"Stepbrother . . . Gratitude and family feeling?"

"More likely he wanted revenge and was pissed off because his fine career went down the tubes with Captain Vladzar."

"You really do dislike him." She shrugged. "But you could be right. I'll have to find out."

Bradworth swore beneath his breath. "Didn't you learn anything tonight? He's a killer, an assassin, and he wouldn't give a damn if he had to snuff you out to get to Pavski. You'd be a fool if you don't stay away from him."

"Perhaps I'd be a fool if I did. If he wants Pavski that much, then I may need him."

"You don't need him. You have the United States government."

"Who decided they needed Ivanov themselves several years ago." She turned to face him. "Don't talk to me about trusting you or any other bureaucrat, Bradworth. I've no more faith in you than I do

Ivanov. And, at least with the Russian I'm dealing with someone who obviously doesn't give a damn about rules and red tape."

"Look, he doesn't care anything about you, and you're going to need protection. Pavski's calling out the big guns. I was trying to reach you to warn you."

"About what?"

"The men who attacked you at that gas station." He drew a computer-printed photograph from his pocket. "The lab was able to extract DNA from both men, and we've managed to ID one of them. His name was Anton Leonovsky. Familiar?"

She took the photograph. The picture was slightly blurry and shot from across a crowded restaurant, but it was clearly the man she'd last seen on fire next to the gas pumps. She shuddered. "I recognize him." She handed the photo back to Bradworth. "What do you know about Leonovsky?"

"An extremely lethal Russian assassin. We didn't even know he was in the country. Leonovsky was ex-KGB, then associated with some particularly vicious Mafia families in Kiev. More recently he was freelance. You're lucky to be alive. If Pavski sent that caliber of assassin after you, then you *need* me."

She shook her head.

"You can't believe anything Ivanov says. He's a murderer. He's as bad as Pavski."

"No," she said fiercely. "As far as I'm concerned, no one's as bad as the man who killed my brother. No one." She drew a deep breath, trying to control her anger. "Now get out of here. I can't look at you without remembering how you set Conner and me up."

"I thought we could protect you."

"But you didn't do it, did you?" she said wearily.

"How can I convince you that we need to be on the same team?"

"Tell me what Pavski thinks was so important on that sub that he was willing to kill to get it."

He shook his head. "I wish I could."

"Then get the hell out of here."

He hesitated and then headed for the door. "I'll be in touch. I'm not leaving you at the mercy of that son of a bitch."

"Mercy? You're joking." She turned her back on him. "I don't expect mercy from either one of you."

She heard him mutter something and then the sound of the door closing behind him.

Jesus, she felt raw and hurt and filled with searing anger.

Chess pieces. That's all she and Conner had been to all those bastards who'd circled the *Silent Thunder* like deadly predators. Bradworth and Ivanov and, most of all, Pavski. Damn them all to hell.

Chess pieces.

She was coming.

Kirov watched Hannah walk down the pier toward him. It was almost dawn, and the misty gray light made her figure appear ghostlike and without substance from a distance. As she drew nearer, he could see there was nothing of the phantom about her. Her stride was as purposeful as her expression.

She stopped as she caught sight of him sitting on the deck. "You were expecting me," she said flatly.

He nodded. "Actually, I thought you'd be here sooner. I was betting you'd come back as soon as you found out Bradworth was an exercise in futility. You're not one to waste time once a decision is made."

"And what decision did I make, Ivanov?"

"Call me Kirov. Both the CIA and I prefer the world think my alter ego is dead these many years. It's safer for me."

"What decision did I make, Kirov?"

"That I'm the lesser of two evils. You need help to get Pavski, and Bradworth isn't aggressive enough for you."

"And are you aggressive enough?"

He smiled. "Oh, yes. Ask Bradworth."

"I don't have to ask him. He's already volunteered your dubious credentials. He says you're an assassin."

"On occasion."

"That you only want to use me."

"I do want to use you."

"And that you'd kill me if I got between you and Pavski."

"Then you'd better not get between us."

"I've no intention of preventing you from killing Pavski. I'd hand you the gun."

"That's kind of you, but I don't like guns." He leaned back against the rail. "But I take it that you're extending a helping hand?"

"I want Pavski. I'm not going to take a chance on Bradworth's letting him slip through his fingers." She stared him directly in the eye. "You told Bradworth I was yours. I know it was part of the tug-of-war game that you two are playing, but I'll make it true. Everything I know and everything I am are at your disposal. You can help me. I can help you."

"To get Pavski."

"To get Pavski. What else?"

"And you're not heeding Bradworth's dire warnings?"

"I'm heeding them. I'm just not acting on them. Why should I? I don't trust him. I don't trust either of you. I'm not even sure that there is a Pavski or that he's responsible for Conner's death. As soon as I get back to Boston, I'm going to call the congressman and ask him to check out all the information he can gather on Pavski."

"Very wise."

"And about Dimitri Ivanov."

"Even wiser. I'm sorry, but I can't afford to twiddle my thumbs here until you check us out. I'm sailing in twenty minutes."

"You're not going to rush me."

"I'm not trying to rush you. Unfortunately, last night you were probably followed here by Pavski's men, and I can't run the risk of staying here until you make up your mind. I want Pavski, not his errand boys. Bradworth is probably having you watched, but be careful all the same." He rose to his feet and headed for the bridge. "You have my cell phone number. Call me, and I'll come to you."

She frowned. "Why are you in such a hurry now? Before you didn't think the danger was too great to wait until this evening."

"Yes, I did." He started the engine. "But you were worth waiting for. You're very valuable. I told you, Bradworth was right. I do want to use you." He backed away from the pier. "Call me . . ."

RASTADT, RUSSIA

Dananka parked his motorcycle next to the market on the outskirts of town. Christ, how could people live in such a depressing little shit hole? He had yet to see anyone under the age of seventy, and the houses were crumbling under their own weight. Another decade, and this pathetic little village could be a beautiful resort, Dananka thought. It couldn't happen soon enough.

He knew he stuck out like a sore thumb in places like this. He'd turn thirty on his next birthday, and he took good care of himself. He was young and strong, and any thoughts that he might be getting old were erased by a few minutes in this place. The town represented the Russia he hated, the disintegrating country that proudly hung on to its old-fashioned ideals even as they plunged the country deeper and deeper into the abyss.

He found the house and pushed the door buzzer. It didn't work. Naturally. He knocked on the door.

After a minute, an elderly man with gigantic black-framed glasses answered. His entire face seemed to squint. "Yes?"

Dananka flashed his most boyish smile. "Frederick Samsova?"

"Who are you?"

"I'm an admirer of yours, sir. It's such an honor to meet you."

Samsova stared at him suspiciously. "It is?"

"Yes. My name is Ilya Dananka. I'm in the naval academy at St. Petersburg, and you have a lot of fans there. May I come in?"

Samsova shrugged and swung the door open wide. "The place is a mess. I don't have many visitors."

"It looks fine." Dananka glanced around the depressing little shack, which was cluttered with newspapers, magazines, and several ship models in various stages of completion. "Just wait until my friends at the academy hear that I was in Frederick Samsova's house."

"I'm surprised you've even heard of me." Samsova pulled open the window blinds. The late-morning sun highlighted the dust on every surface. "They don't like talking about the old guard anymore. They wish we didn't exist."

"That's not true, at least not in your case. Many of the students have discovered your navigational system."

Samsova raised his eyebrows. "Really?"

"Oh, yes. It's totally brilliant. I'm surprised it's not being used everywhere."

"That was my hope, but I'm afraid political realities took precedence." His eyes sparkled with sudden eagerness. "Your classmates really know my work?"

"We all do. It hasn't been easy to research, because your texts aren't in the library anymore."

Samsova sighed. "Of course they aren't. It's a world that shuns complexity and embraces mediocrity."

"But I found a box of acetates that you used on the overhead projector in your classes. We borrowed a projector, and some of us get together twice a week in the basement and study your lessons." He smiled. "We've taken your name for our group. I hope you don't mind. We call ourselves the Samsovians."

Color filled the old man's pasty face. He smiled and gestured to a narrow bookshelf in his living room. "These are my texts and lesson plans. I might have some extras around here for you."

"That would be wonderful. Thank you so much." Dananka reached into his backpack and pulled out three eleven-by-fourteen prints. "We found this in a box in the archive room. It looks like your system, but we can't read it. Do you have any idea what it means?"

Samsova took the prints and angled them toward the sunlight. "Hmmm. Yes, it's my system. It's difficult to make out . . ." He held up the first print. "Points of origin, one primary, and two alternates. These are in the Western Hemisphere, in the North Atlantic."

"Are you sure?"

"Yes. We'll check the maps later." Samsova held up the second and third prints. "These go together. There are an unusual number of markers here. Far more than you'd need to get from Point A to Point B."

"What kind of markers?"

"All kinds. Physical, astronomical, compass readings. These are actually quite advanced. Only a very few of my students were taught to this extent."

"Tell me about the markers. To what do they correspond?"

He shrugged. "I've no idea. They don't appear to be complete."

"What about this mark at the bottom of the third photo? It's different, isn't it? What does it mean?"

Samsova frowned. "It's not Samsovian. I've never seen it before."

"Think. Make a guess." Dananka realized at once he'd made a mistake. His tone had been too harsh and demanding for the role he was playing.

Samsova's expression was suspicious again, closing him out. He could almost see him withdrawing. "I can't help you," Samsova said coldly. "This isn't a navigational map. It looks as if it was written on a wall or some other surface. It almost looks like . . ." He glanced up from the photo. "Who are you?"

"I told you. I'm a student at—"

"I heard you before. But who are you *really*? I may be a little past my prime, but I still have my wits about me, you condescending bastard." Samsova picked up the phone. "I believe I'll call the academy. I still know a few people there."

"There's no need to bother your friends." He smiled. "I confess. I'm not a student. Just one of your greatest fans."

"Lying pig." Samsova started to dial. "Get out of my house."

"Of course." He took a step closer. "I wouldn't think of abusing your hospitality. And you're right, you obviously can't help me. I'll have to see what I can glean from your books."

"You won't touch my books. Get out of—" Samsova stiffened, his eyes widening. "Wait, please. I—"

Dananka's palm drove upward under Samsova's nose and sent the broken bone fragments into his brain.

BOSTON

Y ou called?" Kirov bowed as Hannah opened the door of her condo. "The message you left on my voice mail was less than polite, but I'm still at your service."

"I didn't feel polite." She slammed the door as he came into the room. "I feel angry and frustrated, and I don't want you in my life."

His brows lifted. "Then why am I here?"

"You know why. I don't have anyone else."

"True. May I sit down?"

She nodded jerkily. "By all means, make yourself comfortable."

"I shall." He dropped down in the easy chair and glanced around. "This is a nice room. It looks like you. Clean and no-nonsense but enough color to keep it from being boring."

"I don't need an interior decorating critique."

"Just a comment." He leaned back in the chair. "It's just interesting. I realize you probably wouldn't bother yourself with designing your home. I'd wager you let it evolve around you over the years. Right?"

She didn't answer. He was far too perceptive. And damnably confident and at ease in her space. He effortlessly dominated the room. He was sitting in her chair, and it was suddenly as if it belonged to him. "Bradworth said Captain Vladzar was your stepbrother. Were you close?"

He nodded. "As close as a black sheep can be to the shepherd who tends the flocks. Sergai was quite a bit older than I, and he was always my idol." He grimaced. "Except when he rained his wrath down on my head when I got into trouble. That happened a lot during my misspent youth. He never understood the delights of decadence and lechery. He was too stern and upright, and I never appreciated what a solid foundation he gave me until I was older. He was always there to pull me out of trouble and set me on the right path."

"So you rode on his coattails to become second officer on his sub."

"You might say that." He met her gaze. "But I prefer to think that I earned my place by hard work and at least moderate intelligence. You can go only so far relying on influence. Sergai would never have tolerated any of his officers who weren't top-notch."

"Even a relative?"

"Particularly a relative. When I was accepted on the *Silent Thunder,* I promised myself I'd learn more, be more valuable to Sergai than any of his other officers."

"And did you?"

He nodded. "Of course. I was a complete pain in the ass to Sergai and everyone else who knew any skill that I didn't. I was going to be the fastest-rising officer in the Russian Navy. I was going to make Sergai proud of me."

"But that didn't happen."

He was silent a moment. "No, that didn't happen."

"Why not? What did happen on the *Silent Thunder?*"

He smiled faintly. "If I were Bradworth, I'd tell you it was classified."

"You're not Bradworth."

"So I'll tell you that I've no intention of confiding anything I don't find necessary to a woman who'd flay me alive if given the opportunity."

"Not until I'd wrung whatever use I could from you."

He chuckled. "I'm already feeling the squeeze. It's a little erotic."

"Bull."

"Not entirely." His smile faded. "But you didn't call me to find out my relationship with Sergai."

"You're wrong. You and Bradworth won't tell me anything else I need to know, so I have to try to judge your motives for tracking down Pavski. Revenge?"

He looked at her.

"Bradworth thinks you're pissed off because your career was deep-sixed."

"Maybe he's right. You'll have to decide for yourself. Did you call your Congressman Preston and ask him your questions?"

"Yes, he said he'd investigate you, but it would take time."

"Ah, the common answer of bureaucracy."

"He'll do his best. And I called a friend of mine in the Russian Navy and asked him to network with his friends and find out what he could."

"That might be more productive."

"But I can't wait for answers before I move. Who knows? Pavski might kill you, and I wouldn't have any leads at all."

"Unfortunate for you. Tragic for me."

"I don't care about you."

"That's obvious. Have you made a guess at why I want Pavski?"

"No." He'd seemed sincere when he talked about Vladzar, but he was an enigma to her. "It's too soon. I'll have to give myself a little time to probe."

"Heaven forbid." He paused. "Does that mean we're going to be best chums?"

"Bastard. How can I get Pavski?"

"By finding out what he wants and holding it out like a luscious carrot."

"He's got what he wants."

"Not everything. That navigational chart evidently wasn't complete. He needs more information, and he believes you have it."

"I don't."

"But he doesn't know that. And even if he couldn't get back on the sub to find any more plates, everyone who can read a magazine article is aware of that memory of yours. You might have seen something that could be forced out of you under pressure."

"I didn't see anything else." She frowned. "Could there be more charts on the *Silent Thunder*?"

"It's possible."

"Then I want to go back on board. Bradworth won't let me." She stared him in the eye. "Make it happen."

"Bradworth's already searching the sub."

"Make it happen."

He smiled. "Why do you think I can?"

"He's scared of you."

"All the more reason for him to balk. He resents me. Unless you want me to get radical."

She didn't want to question what he meant by that last sentence. "You want to know if there's anything important on that sub too. I think you'd prefer to find it yourself rather than have Bradworth's men do it."

"Quite true. But I walk a fine line with the CIA. I try not to antagonize a valuable source completely."

"If you don't want to manipulate him yourself, then tell me how to do it."

He was silent, thinking. She could almost see the wheels turning behind that intent expression. Then he smiled and leaned forward in the chair. "First, let's make a few phone calls."

Her phone rang forty-five minutes later.

"What the hell are you doing?" Bradworth said, when she picked up. "I just got a call from Peterson at the museum, and he was insistent as the devil that you be let back on the *Silent Thunder* to continue your work."

"Good."

"I told him to forget it."

"He won't forget it. I told him I'd sue him for breach of contract and have the story of Conner's murder on the *Silent Thunder* plastered on the front page of every newspaper in the country. Museums don't like bad publicity."

"You're bluffing. You don't want any publicity that might hurt your sister-in-law."

"I backed down when you threatened me with that before. But

Cathy and I are in sync with the fact that we may have to bite that particular bullet. We'll do what we have to do." He was cursing, and she interrupted, "And I hear that the CIA has to be careful of their image too. It takes so little to bring a CIA director before a congressional committee these days."

"Dammit, what do you think you're going to find? My people have been tearing the sub to pieces searching for answers."

"Then tell them to stop and let us have a shot."

He didn't speak for a moment. "Us?"

"Kirov is coming with me."

"The hell he is. I should have known he had his fine hand in this. No deal."

"He knows the sub. He might be able to help me."

"Help you get killed. I told you to stay—"

"He's coming with me. I'll be on the pier at eight tomorrow morning. I want my team's security clearances reactivated. Some may be with me tomorrow. Others may be back on board later in the week."

"Everyone's already left their offices for the day, and it will be difficult to get the necessary clearances."

"You're stalling. Cell phones are a wonderful thing, Bradworth. I'll be there at eight."

She waited.

It was a moment before he finally said, "I can't get papers for Kirov on this short notice. We can't risk them not being absolutely authentic. He's too valuable to us to run the risk of exposure."

"He's willing to run the risk."

"We've invested too much in him to—"

"He's coming with me. I'll furnish the ID for him. I promise you won't have a problem with it. Just pave the way."

"Aye, aye, Captain," he said sourly. He hung up.

"Pleasant," she muttered under her breath. She pocketed her phone and turned to Kirov. "We're in. You were almost the stumbling block. It seems you're too valuable to risk exposure."

"It's wonderful to be appreciated." He smiled. "You handled Bradworth very well, by the way. I was impressed."

For the first time she was aware of the magnetism young Sarks had mentioned. It shocked her that she would even notice, considering the tension between them. Yet that facet of Kirov was difficult to overlook when it was an integral part of his personality. She might not be able to overlook it, but she could certainly ignore it. She turned away. "Whatever. We should get on the road in the next hour."

"Why not now?"

"I have to call my sister-in-law, Cathy."

"And tell her everything?"

"I owe it to her."

"Do you owe her honesty at the price of her anxiety? Can she do anything but worry about you at this point?"

He was right. There was nothing worse than having to stay at home and fret about things you couldn't change. "You don't want her involved."

"No, the more people who know what we're doing, the greater the chance for problems. But I'll accept it if you insist."

She thought about it. Then she got out her phone and dialed Cathy's number. She was relieved when voice mail picked up.

"Cathy, Hannah. Henry Danforth proved to be a good lead. I'm following up on it. I managed to get back on the *Silent Thunder*, and I'm going to be there for a few days. Everything's fine. I'll contact you when I know something. Take care of yourself and the kids."

"Very good," Kirov said, when she hung up. "A brilliant job of avoiding lies."

"I hate lies. I'll tell Cathy the whole story as soon as I have anything concrete." She headed for her bedroom. "I'm going to pack my bag. I'll be with you in fifteen minutes."

NINE

In the parking lot adjacent to the *Silent Thunder* ramp, Hannah tossed a plastic card at Kirov, sitting in the passenger seat next to her. "You'll need this."

He picked it up and studied it. "What is it?"

"Your ticket onto the sub. If anyone asks, you're Lance King, my nuclear propulsion expert."

"He must weigh forty pounds more than I do."

"So you've been on the Atkins diet. No one looks that hard at the photo anyway. As long as the security people see you with me a few times, and the badge's bar code works, you're golden."

"No one here knows the real Lance King?"

"No. Lance's credentials were issued, but he never made it here before the project was disbanded. You'll be fine."

"If you say so." Kirov clipped the ID card to his jacket as he climbed out of the car.

It wasn't until they passed the security checkpoint and walked up the ramp to the *Silent Thunder*'s forward hatch that it hit her.

Conner.

Hannah stopped as pain tore through her.

"Are you all right?" Kirov asked quietly.

"Yes."

Kirov moved closer to her. "Do you want me to go inside first?"

For God's sake, get a grip. She pushed past him and started down the hatch. "We have work to do. Stop treating me like an invalid."

"By all means." He followed her down the hatch to the engineering deck, where they stopped to let their eyes grow accustomed to the dim illumination of the work lights.

Kirov sniffed. "Diesel fumes."

"That's the first thing Conner said." Another painful memory. She tried to smile. "I told him the Oscar IIs had poor ventilation."

Kirov made a face. "Believe me, it never felt as if the fumes were being ventilated at all. The few times we had to use the auxiliaries, it made most of the crew sick." He glanced around. "Well, everything seems to be in order here."

"Did you spend much time in this section?"

"More time than you'd think. I told you, it was my goal to be able to do each job on this vessel better than every crewman." He motioned ahead. "Shall we move to the control room?"

They walked down the main corridor, past the turbines and radio plates, until they reached the control room.

She switched on a light above the instrument plates. "Is it like
you remembered it?"

There was no reply. She turned to see Kirov standing in the en-
tranceway, staring silently. "Hello?"

"I'm sorry." He still didn't look away from the control plates. "I
never felt more . . . *whole* than I did in this room. I don't expect you
to understand." His hand touching the bulkhead was caressing.
"Magnificent," he said quietly. "There will never be another quite
like her. A machine with a soul."

"Now you sound like my brother. What is it about men and the
sea?"

Kirov smiled. "You people design and build these things, but
they're not truly finished until after they're put to sea. That's when
their true character comes out. I don't know how it gets there, but
believe me, it exists."

"Uh-huh. So what's the *Silent Thunder*'s character?"

"She's a noble soul. She's always at her best when you need her
most."

"Sentimental rubbish."

He shrugged. "Believe me, I've been on vessels where that wasn't
the case. But I'm telling you, maneuvers that were impossible for her
suddenly *became* possible when the chips were down, and the crew's
lives were at stake."

"You had a captain who knew what he was doing. Leadership

can usually sway the balance between the possible and the impossible. You said yourself Vladzar was extraordinary."

"You prefer to believe in a man rather than a ship?"

"Any day. And there are hundreds of variables that can affect performance. Speed, churn, shock waves from those mines you were probably dodging . . ."

Kirov smiled. "I'm afraid that I side with your brother on this issue. I suspect I would have liked him."

"I don't know if he would have liked you." Yet she had an idea that Conner and Kirov would have found a strong common ground. Strange when their characters were so different. "But I'm sure he would have loved teaming up with you to torment me. Where next?"

"The officers' quarters." He waved his hand. "After you."

She climbed the mate's ladder and stepped into the dark corridor that would take them to the Section 4 living quarters. A dim light shined from a hatch about thirty feet toward the bow. "This is where I first saw Vladzar's book with the Samsovian symbols."

He moved toward the bookcase across the cabin. "I'm surprised they're still here after all these years."

"They probably wouldn't be if the officer who brought the sub here hadn't fought the Russians who tried to strip the sub. And, who knows, maybe they didn't consider Vladzar's personal effects important."

"I did." His hand touched the spine of one the books. "I borrowed every one of these books from Sergai at one time or another. We all traded books during the missions."

"Are they all here?"

He studied the books. "Yes. Plus one."

"What do you mean?"

Kirov picked up a paperbound collection of Greek myths. "This wasn't Sergai's."

"One of the other officers?"

"Possibly." He looked around the cabin. "Otherwise, this compartment is just the way Sergai left it." Kirov slipped the book into his jacket pocket. "Let's go take a look at the rest of the ship. Which areas did you miss when you were working here?"

"The turbines, the galleys, and what's left of the reactor room." She preceded him. "Though if the rest of the sub is like the command center, we're not going to find anything. It looks like a tornado hit it. It's shameful. We were so careful putting everything back the way we found it."

"This cabin isn't so bad. But maybe they didn't get to it yet."

The rest of the ship was in as bad a shape as the command center. Plates and cutlery strewn all over the galley. Radio logs scattered in the communications section. Mattresses tossed over every bunk.

"It's terrible. I hate to see it like this," Hannah murmured. "As soon as the team gets here, we'll get it shipshape. This was Conner's last job, and he'd want it tied up and neat the way he liked it. He was proud of his work, and he was so excited about this damn sub. He thought it was beautiful."

"She is beautiful," Kirov said.

She shook her head. "Conner died here."

"The sub didn't kill him, Pavski did."

"I can't separate them right now."

"You can't blame every vessel for the deaths of the people who served on them. It's not logical."

"Screw logic."

He smiled. "Screw logic," he repeated. "Forgive my pragmatism. Remember, I'm only a poor sailor who had to earn his berth on the *Silent Thunder* by being able to reason and calculate. I find it odd that you can hate the sub and yet be horrified about its state of disrepair."

"Do you?" She turned away. "Too bad. I don't have to explain myself to you. We're on board. Let's get to work. There are at least two areas that Bradworth didn't manage to reduce to shambles."

"I'll take the turbine room." He began to roll up his sleeves. "You should be happy that I relegate myself to the depths. When is your team supposed to get back?"

"Probably not for a few days. I'll call them." She frowned as she watched him go down the passage. "Don't get impatient when you're searching. I don't want the team to have more mess than necessary to put back in order."

"I'm seldom impatient." He didn't turn around. "And if I find something, I'll be sure to let you know."

"Liar."

He laughed. "Then you'd better check up on me, hadn't you?" He disappeared down the stairs.

Find anything?" Hannah knelt beside Kirov's prone body near a large diesel fuel tank.

"Do you think I'd tell you? I'm a liar, remember?"

"How could I forget?" She crawled in beside him. "I drew a zero on the conning tower." She pulled on the panel of a pressure gauge. "How did you get this apart?"

"I told you I knew every job of every crewman. Vladzar took delight in making me crawl in here and run tests on these engines. It was claustrophobic and loud as hell."

"Why? It's a dirty job. After all, you were his stepbrother."

"That's why he did it. I wasn't to be spared. Sergai was always on the straight and narrow." He carefully lifted the plate and shined his flashlight into the interior. "Nothing." He put the plate back and screwed it in place and drew a deep breath. "Let's get out of here. This is a zero too, and I need some air."

"Evidently you still find it claustrophobic. I don't know how you passed the psychological tests that got you on this submarine."

He looked back at her. "I had Sergai to tell me the right answers, of course."

She shook her head. "You told me he was too straight and narrow."

His blue eyes were glinting with mischief as he grinned. "Caught. I stole them from the dean's office of the academy."

"Why would you even want to be on a sub if you suffered claustrophobia?"

"It wasn't an extreme case."

"What about the captain?"

"I think he suspected, but he never confronted me."

"Because he wanted you on the *Silent Thunder*."

"Yes, I think so. I hope so."

They walked forward three compartments and climbed the ladder to the conning tower. He stood there a moment breathing in the night air. "That's good."

He had admitted to weakness, but that very admission seemed a strength in this moment, she thought. It took an unusual man to accept his own faults with no excuses. And there was nothing weak about his appearance. His dark hair was tied back by a sweat-soaked bandanna, revealing the bold structure of his face. His sleeves were rolled up above his elbows, and his arms were corded with muscle. He looked tough and basic and vaguely primitive.

And . . . disturbing.

She tore her gaze away from him. "Yes, it is. It's hard to take a deep breath down there."

He cocked his head toward the scaffolding that bridged the gap between the conning tower and the museum's concrete walkway. "Then let's go to the café and get a cup of coffee. I promise I'll clean up in the restaurant washroom so I won't offend you."

She hesitated. Oh what the hell. A cup of coffee was no commitment, and she definitely needed to know more about Kirov. She had been surprised and intrigued by the glimpse of his past he had so casually confided. "You won't offend me. I'm as dirty and sweaty as you are." She smiled. "And I promise I'll use the washroom, too."

Kirov and the woman have left the sub," Agent Teague said when Bradworth picked up. "They've gone up to the café on the pier."

"Tell me about the body language. Chummy?"

"No. Kirov never changes, but I'd say she appears to be distancing herself."

Bradworth wished the hell she'd distance herself right off Kirov's radar. "Keep an eye on them."

"No problem. They're settled in a booth in the café. They don't seem to be anxious to go anywhere else."

"Don't assume anything with Kirov. He likes to run his own show. He'd like nothing better than to cut us out and go after Pavski on his own." He hung up the phone.

If Teague was right about Hannah's attitude, at least Kirov wasn't entirely having his own way with her. Not that he could be assured that coolness would remain intact. Kirov always used every weapon at his disposal, and he was good with women.

It would be okay. He just had to make sure that they were constantly under surveillance until he could remedy the situation.

That's good." Kirov set his cup down on the table and leaned back in the booth with a sigh of contentment. "It's amazing how comforting the small pleasures can be. When I was on the run before I defected, I didn't know whether I'd live through the next day, but whenever I'd get the chance to get a good meal or a shot of vodka or an excellent cup of coffee, it made everything okay for a while."

"Bradworth said you were searching for word of Vladzar."

He shrugged. "There was a chance he was alive. I kept hearing stories that he might be. It wasn't likely, but I had to try to find him."

"What made you give up?"

"I didn't. I still have contacts in Russia who will tell me if they hear anything." He lifted his cup to his lips. "But after the government toppled, and Pavski was put on the undesirable list, the odds were that Sergai would have surfaced if he was still alive."

"You must have cared for him if you risked your life by staying in Russia."

"He would have done the same for me. Family feeling is very strong among us Russians." He met her gaze. "And among you Americans. It's a trait we share. It's clear you loved your brother very much."

"Enough to resent the hell out of you and Bradworth playing games with our lives."

"And so you should. That was a terrible night." He looked down into his cup. "I tried to get to him and save him. I was too late. I had to make a choice."

She stiffened. "Choice?"

"More coffee?" He gestured to the waitress to refill the cups. "We should get back to the sub. I want to spend more time in the turbine room."

"Choice?" She stared at him as memories of that night rushed back to her.

Icy water. Drowning. Drowning.

Stop fighting me. I'm trying to help you.

She whispered. "You were the one who pulled me out of the water that night."

He shrugged. "You were unconscious. You would have drowned."

"So you let Conner die instead."

"I wasn't sure your brother would be killed. I knew you'd die. There are always choices to make in situations like that."

"You should have gone to Conner."

"Probably. I might have saved him and kept the plates from Pavski. Since I'm such a self-serving bastard, that choice amazed me later." He looked her in the eye. "But I didn't do it, and there's no going back."

She could feel the tears sting her eyes. "No, there's no going back."

"But we can move forward. Revenge is sweet. Take it from someone who knows."

Her lips twisted. "And you know that emotion very well, don't you? How many people have you killed, Kirov?"

"Not as many as Pavski."

"That's no answer."

"That's all you'll get from me." He threw some money on the table. "Let's get back to the sub. I want our search over before Pavski figures out how to bypass Bradworth's men to get to me."

"You believe he's watching us?"

"Of course. Bradworth and Pavski both. You're the magnet that draws all of us. Pavski evidently found the plates to be incomplete and thinks that wonderful memory of yours may give him something else to work with. Bradworth and I need you to draw him out in the open."

"Then why do you think Pavski wants to get to you as well as me?"

"Because I stand in the way." He stood up. "I've stood in his way for a long time, but I've never let him get this close before. When I decided to come to you, I put myself in the spotlight instead of in the shadows. It makes me more vulnerable."

She rose to her feet. "Then why did you do it?"

"Because you're more valuable to me right now than anonymity." He smiled. "Choices, again."

"Well, this particular choice may have been a bust. We're not finding anything on the *Silent Thunder*."

"We'll give it the rest of the night. Then we move on." He headed for the door of the café. "If one door closes, then you open another." He glanced at her. "If you choose to go along with me. It's up to you."

"You're damn right it is." She paused. "And what door do you plan on opening?"

"I have a few contacts who might help us locate Pavski. But we'll have to lose Bradworth. If you consider him a safety net, that's too bad. My friends aren't fond of the CIA."

She thought about it. "My experiences with Bradworth haven't been very reassuring. But if we're being watched by him as well as Pavski, how do you intend to do that? It's a very small town."

He smiled as he opened the door for her. "Then we'll just have to go to a bigger town, won't we? Will you have breakfast with me tomorrow morning?"

"What?"

"I've done a little research about the town since the *Silent Thunder* arrived here. I think you'll find a little restaurant called Mrs. Finley's Kitchen very interesting."

Y ou *lost* her?" Bradworth said between his teeth into the phone. "How in the hell did you lose her?"

Agent Teague stammered. "It was the restaurant. That Mrs. Finley's kitchen. I didn't know—I didn't read the back of the menu until later."

"What the hell are you talking about?"

"I stationed Willis at the back entrance and I watched the front. I thought that would be enough, but it—"

"How did they get away, dammit?"

"The restaurant has a secret underground exit that lets out in a shed about half a block away. It's been there since the Revolutionary War days."

Bradworth couldn't believe what he was hearing. "A secret exit."

"Not so secret, actually. There's a whole write-up about it on the back of the menu. I talked to the manager, and she says Ms. Bryson and Kirov went in back and asked to walk through it."

"How long has it been since they flew the coop?"

"Forty minutes. We're in the car now, scouting the area."

Forty minutes. Kirov would have a plan and an escape route, and forty minutes was more than enough time for him to implement it.

"Shit!"

W hat makes you think this friend of yours can help us?" Hannah asked Kirov as they walked down East 51st Street, past Lexington Avenue, and into a charming neighborhood of brownstones and small boutiques.

"Eugenia Voltar was one of the youngest and sharpest agents in the KGB's history." Kirov gaze was on the address on one of the buildings they were passing. "If anyone can help us, she can."

"KGB?"

He nodded. "However, she was never popular with the higher-ups there because she possessed the dangerous trait of speaking her mind. She was pushed out in the general downsizing, when the KGB became the FSB, and she eventually ended up here."

"She's a spy?"

"Not anymore. In the last few years, she's become quite wealthy by helping Western corporations move into Russia. She knows just which palms to grease to make anything happen." He cast a sideways glance at Hannah. "There was an arms trader I'd spent years searching for, and I finally found him with Eugenia's help."

"And what did you do when you found him?"

He didn't answer.

She hadn't really expected a reply. Kirov disclosed only what he chose to reveal about his life. In the past days she had found that sometimes he was surprisingly open, and at others he was completely uncommunicative. Just enough information to pique her curiosity and interest. Oh, yes, she couldn't deny the interest. He was a totally fascinating man, and every minute with him was a challenge. Yet she also was beginning to feel a strange sense of comfort and security when she was with him.

"Ah. Here we are." Kirov stopped. "318 East 51st Street. Nice place, don't you think?"

It was a converted brownstone with a fresh brick façade, red canopy, and a brass plaque that read CONNECTIONS INTERNATIONAL.

"Terrible name," Kirov said, as they climbed the short flight of stairs and rang the doorbell. "I told Eugenia she should have used more imagination. It sounds like a dating service."

A youthful female voice came from the speaker box. "Yes?"

Kirov looked up at a security camera and winked.

Laughter pealed from the speaker box. "Kirov, you devil. I knew you couldn't stay away. You're powerless to resist me, you know." The voice was an intriguing mixture of Russian and British accents.

"So you keep telling me, Eugenia. Are you going to buzz me in, or am I going to stand out here like a panhandler?"

"I'm still deciding. I'm offended that, after all these months, you finally choose to visit me with such a pretty young woman at your side. Tsk, tsk. Very bad form, Kirov."

"You know I only have eyes for you, my dear."

"Ah, *that's* the charming liar I know and love."

The door buzzed. Kirov opened it and held it open for Hannah as they entered the foyer.

Before they'd even closed the door behind them, a petite young woman flew down a flight of stairs and threw her arms around Kirov. "I can't believe it! I thought you were dead, or worse, married and living in the suburbs!" She drew back and checked his left hand. "You're not, are you?"

Kirov smiled and kissed her cheek. "You know me better than that." He motioned to Hannah. "Eugenia, this is—"

Before Kirov could finish the sentence, Eugenia threw her arms around Hannah as if they were long-lost friends. "So nice to meet you! You are—?"

"Hannah Bryson."

"Hannah!" Eugenia gave her another squeeze and frowned as she felt Hannah instinctively pull back. "Too much? Kirov keeps telling me I'm too demonstrative, but life's too short to curl up inside yourself like a snail. And any friend of Kirov's and all that . . . You *are* a friend?"

Hannah smiled. Eugenia's high spirits were contagious. Although Kirov indicated the woman had worked for the KGB more than a decade before, she couldn't be older than her late twenties or early thirties. She was a pretty, fair-skinned woman with shoulder-length brown hair and bright, lively dark eyes.

"Actually, we're more acquaintances than friends."

"Oh, then I take back the hug. But I like your honesty. Come along."

Kirov and Hannah followed Eugenia up the stairs to see that the entire second floor had been converted to a large, sleek office that looked as if it should have been the home base for the CEO of a Fortune 500 company.

"You like my office?" Eugenia said.

"It's beautiful," Hannah said, admiring the granite countertops, marble floor, and tall mahogany shelves.

"I hate it," Eugenia said. "It's not me at all. Too showy. But, if the head of a multibillion-dollar corporation is going to trust me to expand his company into Russia, he needs to see this to feel comfortable. I do most of my real work upstairs." Eugenia motioned for them to follow her. "We can talk up there."

They climbed another flight until they found themselves in a room about half the size of Eugenia's office. Hannah's initial impression was that they'd somehow stumbled upon a college dorm room. The walls were hot pink and decorated with posters of the Beatles, the Clash, and Bruce Springsteen. A Jimi Hendrix solo blared from the small stereo even though Hannah had heard no trace of it on the floor below.

Eugenia smiled proudly. "Much more personality, yes?"

Hannah nodded. "Yes. I like it."

Eugenia turned to Kirov. "I was most surprised to hear that the *Silent Thunder* lives. I thought it was sold for scrap and now part of thousands of poorly made Russian automobiles."

"No one was more surprised than I. Hannah is overseeing its modifications for the museum exhibit." He turned to Hannah. "I called Eugenia last night and brought her up to speed about the situation."

"It was very sad about your brother," Eugenia said. "I'm sorry for your sorrow. And I met Anton Leonovsky a few times, and I'm extremely happy to hear the bastard met such a horrible end."

"Then translate that happiness into action," Kirov said.

Eugenia smile faded. "Are you pushing, my friend? I don't like to be pushed."

For the first time Hannah saw the steel beneath that effervescent exterior. Tough. Very tough.

"Do you take me for a fool?" Kirov asked. "I'm not about to ruffle your feathers by taking you for granted."

Eugenia was silent for a moment, and then smiled. "I look gorgeous with ruffled feathers, and no one has a better right to take me for granted than you. What do you need from me?"

Kirov looked at Hannah. "Hit her now before she changes her mind."

"I need to know who killed my brother," Hannah said. "And I need to know where to find him."

"I have no crystal ball." Eugenia turned to Kirov. "I thought you said it was Pavski?"

"Hannah doesn't entirely trust my word on that."

"When you're such a straightforward, uncomplicated bastard?" She smiled at Hannah. "You're wise to doubt him if you have no proof. I certainly did at one time. But the chances are it's Pavski, or Kirov wouldn't be interested."

"Thanks for the unstinting recommendation," Kirov said dryly.

"I'd give you an unqualified recommendation in many circumstances, but not where Pavski is concerned." Her tone became businesslike. "If you want help, give me specifics."

"My source in Moscow told me that Pavski has sent out word that he's revving up for a big operation and needs extra manpower." He nodded at Hannah. "And her contribution to the drain on his manpower may make the recruiting even more urgent. He lost two more at that gas station." He paused. "And Pavski wanted something else that he didn't broadcast far and wide. He contacted a few old GRU contacts and asked to be sent certain records."

"What records?"

Kirov shrugged. "I don't know. I was lucky to get that much."

"And who is your Moscow source?" Eugenia asked.

"Blenoff."

"He's usually at least eighty percent accurate. It's probably worth acting on."

"I'm glad you don't think I'm spinning my wheels," he said dryly. "Since Pavski doesn't trust Americans, he's probably recruiting all his help from Russia."

"And?"

"You know the players, in Moscow and here, like no one else. If a Russian acquired a doctored passport to slip into the country, you'd be our best hope of finding out about it. I need to know who they are, how many, and who sent them."

"I'm surprised you don't want me to try to grab those GRU records," she said sarcastically.

"Considering you have such great contacts, I was considering it."

"I can try to find out what files they were, but that's the limit. The KGB and GRU were never good friends. Is that all?"

"A current street address would be nice."

"Of course." Eugenia shook her head. "Russia is a big country, and so is America. There's no way I can track the comings and goings of each and every—"

"Not each and every," Kirov said. "Probably ex-government men. Men who might want to slip into the country undetected. Maybe some with a naval background. You know the people who can facilitate that kind of thing, don't you? There can't be that many."

"You'd be surprised." She thought for a moment. "But there aren't many who can do it well enough to suit the likes of Pavski. I can look into it, but it's still no guarantee that I'll be able—"

"We don't expect guarantees. Just your best effort. I'll pay well, Eugenia. Do we have a deal?"

She wrinkled her nose at him. "A deal? No."

"But you said—"

"A deal, my dear Kirov, implies a mutually beneficial transaction. This is a favor. I want you to owe me for a change." She glanced at Hannah. "Don't worry, I'm very good. You will see."

"I'm sure I will," Hannah said. "Thank you."

A radiant smile lit Eugenia's face. "I think I like you. You're sincere. That's rare in this counterfeit world." She went to the carved table in the foyer and opened a black enamel box. "You may need a place to stay. Hotels are never safe. I own the brownstone at the end of the block and keep it available for clients. I don't want them invading my space." She tossed Kirov a set of keys. "If I have time after

I've contacted my sources, I'll come over tonight and have a drink with you." She grabbed a yellow legal pad and cranked up the music. "Now out of here, both of you. Dow-Corning wants to build a sixty-five-floor office building in the heart of Moscow, and I have to think of a way to make the Russian government pay for it."

TEN

"Interesting woman," Hannah said, as they walked down Eugenia's front stairs. "She's much younger than I imagined."

"She's older than she looks, but of course, she was only seventeen or eighteen when she started with the KGB. They were training her to be a swallow."

"Swallow?"

"An agent who specializes in obtaining information by sexual seduction. She decided that patriotism could only carry you so far and opted out."

"I'm glad she didn't let them use her like that. She seems very nice."

"She is. And she's a great person to have on your side. She truly has a good heart, but don't let that charming personality fool you. There are dozens of souls in the world who probably consider her the most intimidating person they've ever met."

Hannah nodded slowly. "I can believe that."

"That's good. I wouldn't want you to underestimate her. If there's a threat to her or someone she cares about, she won't hesitate to eliminate that threat. I've seen her in action, and she's very proficient."

"She said she owed you? Why?"

"Oh, I was able to get her out of a sticky situation once." He changed the subject. "Bradworth will know we're in New York, you know."

"How?"

"Shortly after we crossed the Triborough Bridge, your license plate was photographed and probably matched with an alert that he logged."

"Homeland Security at work."

"Another camera may have already caught us in the city. In any case, when we pass close to the U.N. or another landmark, they'll get another shot."

"Should we just leave my car in the lot?"

"No, I believe it's time to bring him into the picture again. I just didn't want him to zero in on Eugenia." Kirov pulled out his cell phone and punched a number. "Hello, Bradworth," he said into the phone. "You're not on your way to New York yet, are you?"

"New York? Why would I be there?"

"Come now," Kirov said. "Ms. Bryson and I are contemplating an early dinner in TriBeCa, and we would be delighted to have you join us. How are you doing on pinpointing our location?"

Bradworth cursed softly. "We got her car crossing Eighth Avenue, near Times Square, about half an hour ago. What are you doing in New York? And why the hell did you sneak away from here?"

"We needed a change of scene. We thought it would help Hannah clear her mind."

"You son of a bitch."

"You had your chance with her, now it's my turn."

"What are you doing? You have an obligation to keep us in the loop."

"That was never a condition of our agreement. I promised you results, not cooperation."

"Kirov—!"

"Good-bye, Bradworth. I'll be in touch soon." He hung up and turned to Hannah. "Now let's look over the guest quarters Eugenia offered us. I could use a shower and a meal without Bradworth or his men looking over our shoulders."

"No TriBeCa?"

"Definitely no TriBeCa."

N ice." Hannah gazed around the parlor of the brownstone. High ceilings, wonderful moldings, and the muted paisley cushions on the oversized couch and chairs looked very inviting. "How long do you think we'll be here before Eugenia comes up with the information?"

He shrugged. "It will take as long as it takes. She can't work miracles." He smiled. "Though she might deny that. Eugenia doesn't lack confidence."

"I could tell she was no shrinking violet." She started up the stairs. "But I'd rather deal with someone who believed in herself than a wimp. I'm going to go settle in and explore that shower you were talking about."

"I have a few calls to make and then I'll shower and check out the kitchen." He pulled out his phone and dropped down on the couch. "Relax. Take a nap."

"Not likely." She reached the top of the stairs and opened the first door. The bedroom had the same comfortable ambiance as the furniture downstairs, and there was a door that probably led to a bathroom. She threw her duffel on the bed.

A few minutes later she was stepping beneath the warm spray of the shower. God, it felt good. Some of the tension was flowing out of her. She had been on edge since the night she had met Kirov. Even in their more peaceful moments when they were working together, she had been acutely aware of both him and the bizarreness of the situation. But then everything in the world had taken on a nightmare strangeness when Conner had died.

And she couldn't live with that strangeness for much longer. She couldn't allow herself to go forward blindly over a cliff. Events had moved so quickly that she had been more accepting than she would ordinarily have been. She had let Kirov lead her to his friends, his turf, and she knew little more about him than the night she'd met him. She'd been swept along by that dynamic forcefulness and the hope that they could quickly put an end to Pavski.

It was time to stop, slow down, ask questions.

And Kirov had better be prepared to answer them.

heard from Eugenia." Kirov was taking a carafe of coffee off the stand when Hannah came into the small kitchen. "No luck yet. She's still putting out feelers." He studied her. "You look more rested. Though a little grim. Have you been brooding?"

"I've been thinking," she corrected.

"I thought you'd be analyzing the situation as soon as you had time to take a breath. It's an integral part of your character." He picked up the carafe and two cups. "There's a tiny courtyard out back. Let's go outside and drink coffee and look at the stars."

"I don't want to look at the stars."

"Then let's go outside so that I can look at the stars while you interrogate me." He was already heading for the door. "It will relax me. You might find me more accommodating if I'm communing with nature."

"Not likely." She followed him out into the courtyard. "Accommodating?"

"I can be accommodating when it suits me." He sat down at the mosaic bistro table and gestured for her to sit across from him. "And when it doesn't foul up my plans."

"I don't give a damn about your plans."

"Yes, you do, because now you're part of them." He filled up the cups and set the carafe down on the table. "And we have a joint objective. While you were analyzing our partnership, didn't you throw that into the mix?"

"That's the second time you used the word analyze."

"Does it bother you? I admire that about you. You have such a clear vision. You see all the nuts and bolts, and most of the time can come up with magnificently creative answers. You transform confusion into clarity." He smiled. "What a wonderful gift."

He meant it, she realized. "Conner used to say that I was closer to machines than I was to people."

He shook his head. "Machines are easier than people, and maybe you found it easier to concentrate on them after your child died."

She stiffened. "Your dossier on me must have been very detailed. My little boy died after only a few weeks."

"I didn't pay any attention to the personal stuff when I first got the report on you. It was after I started watching you at the sub that I went back and began to explore in depth."

"Why?"

"I felt I had to know you," he said simply.

"Again, why?"

"I wasn't sure." He smiled faintly. "Perhaps it was because I began to think of you in the same way I did *Silent Thunder*. It was most unsettling."

Her brows rose skeptically. "You thought I was like a submarine, and you still wanted to get to know me?"

"I've never thought of the sub with detachment. I've always had a personal feeling for her." He lifted his cup to his lips. "And, yes, I probed and dug to find everything I could about you. Your divorce, the loss of your baby. The death of a child can twist a person's soul. I'm sorry for your pain."

His tone was absolutely sincere, and she found herself asking him. "Do you have children?"

He shook his head.

"A wife?"

"My wife is dead." He lifted his cup to his lips. "Her name was Mira and she was . . . exceptional. I had her for seven years, and every one was a journey of discovery."

"Discovery?"

"We were nothing alike, but that only made it better. She was smart and funny, and she cut through the crap."

"That must mean she stood up to you. Did you argue?"

"Not much. I was away from home too much. Every minute we were together was too valuable to waste on arguments. About the only thing we argued about was the sub."

"What?"

"She said I loved it more than her."

"Did you?"

"Maybe at one time. I was obsessed. After she died I felt guilty, and that might mean I thought I hadn't given her all she needed from me." He met her eyes across the table. "But I did love her, Hannah."

Intimacy. She could hear the traffic on the streets beyond the courtyard walls, but she felt as if they were cocooned in this green oasis in the city. She didn't want to feel this intimate with Kirov. She had meant to confront him and had ended with learning that he was not invulnerable and feeling a sense of bonding at the loss that they'd both suffered. She tore her eyes from him and reached for her coffee cup. "I didn't mean to question you about your private life. It's none of my business."

"Turnabout is fair play. I was curious about you, and I invaded your privacy. You have a right to know something about me too."

It was an opening, and she had to grab for it. "Yes, I do. It's my right to know a hell of a lot more than I do right now. I'm sick of 'classified.' I want to know what you know."

"I thought that was where we were heading when you walked into the kitchen this evening."

"And you tried to distract me by bringing everything down to a personal level."

"No." He smiled. "I didn't need to do that. Everything has been on an intensely personal level between us since the moment we met. Haven't you noticed?"

She couldn't deny it. Fear, anger, frustration, and now pity had drawn them together in the most basic fashion. "I want to know about those plates on the sub."

He was silent a moment, then said, "Ten years ago much of the Atlantic fleet, including *Silent Thunder,* was engaged in military exercises in the North Sea. Then the fleet commander radioed Captain Vladzar and ordered him to break off the exercises. We were told to navigate the sub toward a remote atoll about four hundred miles south of the fleet."

"Why?"

"We didn't know," Kirov said. "Usually the fleet command would give us some indication why, but this time they were damnably cryptic.

We were all nervous about this, because we were carrying warheads with bacteriological agents that were notoriously difficult to contain. The sooner those capsules were off the sub, the better for all of us."

"Germs?"

His lips tightened. "Why are you so horrified? The U.S. has its own germ warfare program. It was just a nasty fact of life. Anyway, I assumed we were going to a testing range for them, but I soon found out I was wrong. We were on a recovery mission."

She frowned. "Recovering what?"

"One large capsule, sixteen feet long."

"A misplaced weapon?"

"No, the captain was being asked to endanger the lives of everyone on his ship for a treasure hunt."

"What?"

"Oh, it wasn't just any treasure. This was special. The treasure was seized from Czechoslovakia during the years of Soviet occupation. There were the requisite jewels and priceless statues, but there was one object there that made the cache truly priceless."

"What object?"

He leaned closer. "Have you ever heard of Czechoslovakia's Golden Cradle?"

She shook her head. "Should I have?"

"Most Eastern Europeans know the legend. Supposedly, a wise, mystical Czech princess in the second century A.D. tossed her son's golden cradle into the depths of the Vitava River, claiming that the country would emerge from chaos and reach greatness only after it reappeared. Both Princess Libushe and the story were thought to be mythology, only remotely linked with any kind of reality. Rather like the King Arthur legend."

"Are you telling me the cradle exists?"

"Yes, I've seen it."

"When?"

"Soviet engineers uncovered it during a construction project in the 1950s in the Vitava River. It's been authenticated. The cradle is almost two thousand years old, but it's beautiful to behold. There are markings on it that link it to Libushe's eldest son."

"That's amazing."

"Yes, it's something that many people would give anything to possess. Czech politicians, insurgents, tycoons, art collectors."

Hannah could imagine that to be true. Both the legend and the prophecy would make it even more valuable than the actual material was worth. She had run across that factor during the *Titanic* expedition and this treasure was even more mystical. "How did Pavski come into this?"

"Why, my dear, Igor Pavski was the fleet commander."

"What?"

"Did you think he was a common criminal? Oh, no, Pavski is totally brilliant and was one of the youngest officers ever to become commander of the fleet."

"And he'd risk losing that high office to go after the cradle?"

"He'd risk anything. Pavski had an obsession for obtaining the cradle from childhood. He had a general idea where the cache was located, and he spent months secretly directing resources to find it. It was under the pretense of finding an undetonated classified missile. After he found it, he redirected my vessel from the testing trials to launch a recovery operation. We brought it aboard without much trouble."

"When did you realize it wasn't a weapon?"

"Almost immediately, but most of the crew still didn't know. The captain was furious that we'd been forced to go hundreds of miles out of our way with an unstable bacteriological agent aboard—all for Pavski's personal quest. Captain Vladzar, the first officer, I, and a few other senior officers made a stand against him and we were promptly relieved of our commands and placed under arrest. Some Pavski loyalists had been transferred in just before the mission, so I suspect Pavski knew we wouldn't be happy. We were boarded, taken off the sub, and placed into the brig of a destroyer."

"Along with the treasure?"

"No, Pavski had other plans. He brought in a Captain Heiser to take command, and Heiser headed for coordinates that Pavski gave him. Heiser was brilliant at navigation and a computer genius, but his main qualification for Pavski was that he always obeyed without question." His lips twisted. "But the crewmen whom Pavski had brought on board with Heiser weren't familiar with bacteria containment, and they screwed up." He added bitterly, "Damn them to hell. The capsule drum was ruptured and the bacteria were released. The crew became infected."

"My God."

"Heiser radioed the fleet commander for assistance, but all ships in the area were ordered to stand down. They couldn't risk spreading the infection."

She shuddered at the thought. Alone and sick and no one to help them. "It reminds me of the *Kursk*."

"Yes," he said harshly. "And those were my men, my friends, on that sub. Their only crime was trusting their government and believing in their commanding officers. Then Heiser did something smart; he discharged the capsule and tried to use its location as a bargaining chip against the fleet commander. I have transcripts of the radio communications, and it was obvious that Pavski was trying to persuade Heiser to disclose where he'd hidden the cradle. Heiser wouldn't tell him. He was trying to leverage his knowledge for a rescue attempt that never came. The bacteriological agent did its work quickly, as it was designed to do. Everyone aboard was dead within twenty-four hours. The strain was engineered to die quickly without live hosts, so after a brief period of quarantine, the *Silent Thunder* was boarded and searched. None of the logs or journals or the captain's personal books gave any indication of where the cradle was hidden, and time ran out for Pavski. The outbreak of disease on the sub made the government very nervous. They were in the process of denying they had such weapons to the U.S. Solution: Cover up. *Silent Thunder* had to disappear quickly. They insisted the sub be immediately decommissioned and taken to the shipyards in Helsinki to be scrapped."

"Which would have happened if it hadn't been for a corrupt Russian bureaucrat."

"Yes, and our Fleet Commander Pavski scrambled to cover up his involvement in the crew's deaths. It was difficult to do. But fear and bribes can accomplish miracles. He kept his post and was soon busy climbing higher."

"With all those deaths at his door?"

"He had power. Anyway, in the intervening years, there was a persistent rumor that Heiser might have hidden the location of his prize somewhere on the *Silent Thunder*. It was based on something he said to his father on the radio in the last hours of his life. He quoted an obscure Polish writer, which people later traced to a poem in which the narrator hides the key to his treasure in the room where he lay dying. And at one point he told his father how he'd like to go back with him to the Rioni River, where they'd gone when he was a child. There were a few other references that might have been clues, but no one could make the connection. No one really thought that much of it, since the sub was thought to have been scrapped."

"But then it was rediscovered . . ."

Kirov nodded. "Then everything changed. I was skeptical that there was really any hidden treasure map, but I knew the mere possibility would draw the players out of the woodwork. I'd been looking for them for years, and this was finally my chance."

"Who are the players?"

"Pavski and his committee of vultures who killed the officers and crew of the *Silent Thunder*." His lips twisted. "I won't give you all the names. It would be a waste of time. Most of them are dead."

"I'm sure you've seen to that. How many are left?"

"Just one, but he's the central figure, Igor Pavski. He thinks he's indomitable. He almost proved it. He was well on his way to putting himself beyond my reach."

She remembered something Bradworth had said. "You went to

Bradworth and offered him information that would bring Pavski down. The deaths on the *Silent Thunder*?"

"Yes. Bradworth arranged for rumors to flood Moscow that caused Pavski's position to become too dangerous. He knew that if the full story was known, he'd be put before a firing squad. So he disappeared from view."

"And surfaced here."

"He'll do anything to get the cradle. He'd walk on the edge of hell for a chance at it. He's still well connected, and there are certainly an abundance of unemployed KGB and shore patrol officers who would gladly join him for a tiny sliver of that fortune."

"And kill Conner and me without a second thought." Her hands tightened on the cup. "Pavski *did* do it."

"You believe me?"

"Yes," she said unevenly. "I believe you. I don't think even you would have been able to concoct such an ugly, depressing story."

"You would have had to live through it to realize just how ugly it was."

"How many crewmen were on board the sub?"

"One hundred and four," Kirov said. "Ninety-two were under thirty years of age."

"Terrible," she whispered. "I can see how you'd want to make Pavski pay for their deaths."

"And your Conner means as much or more to you than those men do to me. I'm not downplaying your loss. A hundred men or a single loved individual, the pain can be the same."

"Yes, it can." She paused. "You said Pavski had an obsession about the cradle from childhood? Why?"

"He thinks the cradle was meant to herald his rise to glory. He believes he needs to reclaim it to reach his destiny."

"He believes the legend? Why?"

"Pavski is half-Russian, half-Czech. His mother belonged to a noble family and married into a family whose castle was located on the Vitava River. She claimed to be a descendent of the princess who threw the cradle into the river. I don't know if she was nuts or just trying to raise her social status among her peers, but she raised Pavski to think he had a special destiny. When he rose to power in the fleet, it confirmed that belief. All he needed was the cradle, and he could rule the world."

"Christ."

"And when he was forced to disappear from Moscow after the loss of the cradle, and rumors of his actions began to be circulated, it reinforced that belief. It seemed proof to him that he had to have it to succeed."

"It's crazy."

"No one said he was particularly stable." His lips tightened. "It takes a special madness to kill over a hundred men." He poured another cup of coffee. "Now, unless you have more questions for me, I think we should not discuss this any longer. It's better if I don't dwell on that time. I have a tendency to lose perspective and go a little berserk."

"One would never guess it. You're one of the coolest men I've ever met."

He shook his head. "Training," he added lightly. "Inside I'm a veritable seething volcano. Ask Bradworth."

"I make my own judgments."

He studied her expression. "And at the moment that judgment is leaning a little in my direction." He smiled. "Then suppose you make another judgment about what topping you want on your pizza. I'm about to call Domino's for dinner."

"I'm not very hungry."

"Neither am I. We're both emotionally strung-out, but we need to eat." He leaned back in his chair. "I'll hold off calling for another hour. And while we're waiting, we'll veer away and talk about pleasanter subjects."

"For instance?"

"You tell me about your *Titanic* expedition. I've read about it, but I want to hear your own version. There are always stories that never come to light."

"And what are you going to tell me?"

He thought about it. "I'll tell you about my wicked doings at the naval academy. It's much more amusing than my training on board the sub. I was kept firmly under control there."

"I can believe that. My impression of your captain is that he was strictly no-nonsense."

He tilted his head. "You say that almost with affection."

"I liked what I read about him. I liked his taste in books and music." Her smile faded. "Conner said I had a father fixation on him."

"Really? Actually, part of me was also drawn to that side of Sergai. Perhaps he was the man I wanted to be." He shook his head. "Though I would never have admitted it to him."

"And now it's too late."

"Yes." He shrugged. "Enough of this brooding. Talk to me about your expedition. Tell me about your submersible."

"Some people would say the *Titanic* wasn't exactly the most cheerful subject."

"I don't want to hear about a doomed ship. I want to hear about you. What you did, what you are. Tell me."

And she wanted to hear about him, she suddenly realized. What he had told her about the events that had led him here had only revealed the tip of the iceberg. Kirov had lived a life that was foreign to her, and yet his love of the sea and his ship struck an answering note within her. She wanted to stay here under the stars in this quiet place and think of something besides Pavski and the horror he had brought.

She lifted the cup to her lips. "When they contacted me and told me they needed me to design the submersible, I was over the moon. I'd been following the progress of the different expeditions, and I already had an idea about . . ."

How cozy you are." Eugenia smiled as she came through the courtyard doorway. "Forgive me for not ringing the bell. I wasn't going to wake you if you'd already gone to bed." She plopped down in a chair. "Pizza!" She took a piece and leaned back with a sigh. "I forgot to eat dinner. You kept me too busy, Kirov."

"Evidently not busy enough if you were going to let us sleep."

"I put out feelers. No answers yet." She nibbled at the pizza. "I decided I needed a break and I wanted to be among friends for a while. It's a rare pleasure."

"Bull. You have thousands of friends, Eugenia."

She made a face. "But very few who know and accept me for what I am." She shrugged. "And what I was. We're a pretty exclusive club, Kirov." She turned to Hannah. "And I think we could be friends. I've been reading up on you. You're a woman like me. We both take charge."

"You're right there," Kirov said.

"Hush," Eugenia said. "I'm talking to Hannah. In fact, this pizza is cold. Go heat it up for me."

"You want to get rid of me?"

Eugenia smiled. "You've got it, cha-cha."

He looked at Hannah.

"We wouldn't want her to eat cold pizza," Hannah said.

He took the plate. "Ten minutes."

"He'll be back in exactly ten minutes," Eugenia said. "It's that military mind-set."

"You seem to know him very well."

"Yes, as well as anyone can know him. When you've gone through what he has, it tends to make a person develop a shell." She grinned. "But I just light a fire under him and, poof, it goes up in flame."

"Fire? Are you lovers?"

"No. Though I've thought about it occasionally. He's a very sexy man."

"I didn't notice."

Eugenia gave her a skeptical glance. "You noticed. I'd judge that you're not one of those women who like pretty boys."

"Well, he's definitely not pretty."

"No, but he has a way of moving, a way of looking at you. Sometimes there's a stillness about him that's very erotic. Because you know there's so much more going on underneath. And watch his hands. They're a real turn-on."

Hannah's brows lifted. "Are you sure you're not lovers?"

Eugenia chuckled. "As I said, I've been tempted to try to lure him into my web, but we're both too intense. We'd probably destroy each other. Besides, we both need friends we can trust. That's rare in our circle. Sex would get in the way. No, we're definitely not lovers." Her eyes narrowed on Hannah's face. "Are you?"

"You're not listening. I told you, we're just acquaintances."

"That's what you told me. But when I came out here tonight, I thought I caught a glimpse of something more."

"What?"

"You looked . . . close. As if you'd been together for years."

Hannah felt a ripple of shock. "I'm afraid you have a vivid imagination."

"Maybe. But I'm very good at reading nuances. It was part of my job once."

"Then you must be slipping." She frowned. "Is that why you wanted to speak to me alone?"

"Partly. I wanted to make sure that I'd warned you to treat my friend well. Kirov wouldn't have understood that protectiveness for him in me. But I think you do."

"Warned? What would you do if I didn't treat your pet tiger with gentleness?"

Eugenia made a cutting motion across her throat. "But only in an extreme case. I'd give you a chance to explain first."

Hannah laughed. Eugenia was truly an original. "Well, I'm safe. Kirov doesn't give a damn about me."

"You're wrong. There's something there. I could see it."

Yes, there was something between them, Hannah thought. In the last hours she'd been aware that the bond had strengthened. She had learned he had a wry sense of humor, and the outrageous stories he'd told her of his years at the academy had given her a new view of Kirov. He was intelligent and stimulating, and he listened. He watched her expressions, and she felt as if he was intently interested in every word she'd said.

For God's sake, but that didn't mean anything more than they'd spent a few pleasant hours together.

"Ah, you're thinking about it," Eugenia said. "That's good."

"Why?"

"Because I don't want you to make a mistake."

"Because you'd hate to cut my throat?"

Eugenia nodded. "Absolutely."

Hannah laughed. "Did Kirov really save your life?"

"Oh, yes. And from a very unpleasant demise. I was dealing with an extremely nasty customer, and Kirov heard I was going to be chopped. He came in and saved the day."

"One of Pavski's people?"

"No, Kirov was on another job. He doesn't rely on the CIA for funds. It would compromise his freedom of choice. He takes assignments from other sources, and he's very much in demand."

"Doing what?"

"This and that."

"And his boat wasn't cheap. This and that must be very profitable."

"You're probing. Yes, Kirov doesn't always walk the straight and narrow. But he manages to stay out of the tar pits." Eugenia shook her head. "And that's all I'm going to say. I'm just grateful that he was there when I needed him. I'm more careful with whom I do business these days."

"Why do you run any risks at all? You're obviously smart and very talented."

"How clever of you to be that perceptive."

"You're dodging."

She shrugged. "I lived on the edge for many years. I got used to it. Every now and then I'm still tempted to dip my toe back in the mire." She glanced at the door through which Kirov had disappeared. "I sometimes wonder how he'll be when he manages to kill Pavski."

"He'll handle it."

She was silent a moment before she stirred. "Yes, of course." She looked at the coffee carafe. "Coffee with pizza? What are you thinking? I'll open a bottle of wine."

They were on their third bottle of wine when Eugenia received the call on her cell for which she was waiting.

She grabbed a pen from her bag and started writing on a napkin. "Got it. Many thanks." She hung up the phone and beamed at Kirov. "Am I not wonderful?"

"Are you?"

"Magnificent. Clever." She nodded. "And very well connected."

"And a tiny bit tipsy?" Hannah asked.

"On wine? Vodka was my mother's milk. I'm merely mellow. It was good drinking with friends. Usually, I have to be careful."

"Eugenia," Kirov said.

"I'm getting to it. I just wanted a bit of praise."

"You're fantastic. Now talk to me."

"There's an antiques dealer in Fairfield, Connecticut, who specializes in interesting imports. The type of imports that one obtains outside the twelve-mile territorial waters limit and brings in under the cover of night."

"Are we talking about narcotics?"

"No, nothing quite so distasteful. He buys jewelry, medallions, documents, and small trinkets with questionable ownership. Objects that may have been liberated from Eastern Bloc museums and government special collections in the past ten or fifteen years. His name is Boris Petrenko."

"Why would he interest me?"

"Because he also imports people. He arranges passage for Eastern Europeans who want to slip into the country undetected. He uses the same network that he does for his antiques. He picks them up and brings them in along with his purchases."

"Do you know him?"

"Not personally."

"Interesting. Why do you think he may be involved with Pavski?"

"According to my sources, he's been boasting about a very rich deal he made for himself. A last-minute job to bring in three very important visitors from Russia."

"Who?"

"I know I'm a miracle worker, but I'll need a bit more time for that one. I'll work on it. All I know is that he was boarded by the Coast Guard shortly before dawn Saturday, and the men slipped overboard several miles from shore."

"Did they make it?"

"Apparently. He received the balance of his payment Monday morning."

"How was he paid?"

"Can't help you." She poured herself another glass of wine. "Do your own work. His shop is at 1408 Post Road."

"The timing is certainly right," Hannah murmured.

"It's worth checking out."

"But not tonight," Eugenia said. "It's 2:00 A.M. Tomorrow morning is soon enough. His shop is closed, and unless you want to roust him from his bed . . . You don't even know that he's your man."

Kirov looked at Hannah. "Your choice."

She thought about it. "We'll be at his shop when it opens in the morning."

"Good," Eugenia said. "Because we have this perfectly wonderful bottle of wine to finish."

ELEVEN

"It's good to see them doing so well." Congressman Preston stared out the sliding glass door of Cathy's kitchen at Ronnie and Donna playing in the backyard with an assortment of *Star Wars* toys. "They're amazing kids."

"I'm lucky. Ronnie is taking charge of Donna. He keeps her busy. Heck, he tries to take charge of me, too." Cathy poured coffee into George's cup. "It's worse at night. At bedtime they're alone with their thoughts, and there's nothing to distract them." She stared blindly out the door. "I thought I was so tough, but I'm not. How can I help them when I can't even help myself? How does anyone recover from something like this, George?"

"I don't know," he said quietly. "But they will heal. And so will you."

"I know we will. It's just difficult to see that time right now." She sat down across from him at the kitchen table. "So what brings you here?"

"I wanted to see how you're doing."

"Uh-huh. You could have picked up the phone. So why are you here?"

"You don't think I'm sincere?"

"You're very sincere. But you're an extremely busy man, and you just saw me at your office a few days ago. What's up, George?"

He shrugged. "The CIA called me yesterday. A man named Bradworth."

"Why?"

"Because they weren't pleased about my information-gathering on *Silent Thunder*. Evidently it aroused some interest at Langley."

Her eyes widened. "Are you serious? What did you tell him?"

"The truth. I don't lie to U.S. intelligence agents. Particularly when he said your sister-in-law may be in danger. It seems she's associating with a man, Kirov, who may not be trustworthy."

She frowned. "I never heard of this Kirov. She called me a couple days ago and told me she was tracking down a lead. But Hannah wouldn't keep secrets from me if it concerned Conner's death. Bradworth told you this?"

"You know Bradworth?"

"I met him the day Conner died. Hannah doesn't trust him."

"Well, he's very concerned about her. He's afraid that this man might be using her for his own purposes."

"What purposes?"

"Search me. But if you talk to her, it might be wise to tell her to come home."

"Why didn't Bradworth come and talk to me himself about this?"

Preston didn't respond.

Cathy stared at him for a long moment as the realization hit. "He wanted *you* to talk to me."

"Cathy, I—"

"He thought it would carry more weight coming from someone I trusted."

"Okay, he *did* want me to talk to you. But I didn't argue with him. If your sister-in-law has even a possibility of being in danger, I thought you should know."

"So now I know." Cathy stood up. "Tell Bradworth you completed your errand. You can also tell him to talk to me directly from now on."

He made a face. "Believe me, I will."

"You'd better go."

"Cathy, if there's anything I—"

She made an impatient gesture to stop him. "George, I know you meant well, but I'm disappointed that you let anyone use you like this. It's going to take a little while to come to terms with it."

"No one used me. I did what I thought best, Cathy," he said gently.

She nodded jerkily. "I can't see that right now. I'll call you later, George."

"Do that." He got up to leave. "And think long and hard about leaving Hannah out on a limb like this."

She stared at the door as it closed behind him. She was bitterly disappointed in George. He'd always been totally up-front with her, and yet this time he'd let Bradworth convince him to be his errand boy. What the devil was happening?

And who the hell is this Kirov, Hannah?

ananka watched Congressman Preston leave Cathy Bryson's house and climb behind the wheel of his energy-efficient hybrid car. Good for a few thousand votes from the Sierra Club, he thought.

He'd been ordered to trail the congressman and watch for any sign of Hannah Bryson. What total bullshit. The bitch had gotten what she needed from Preston, and there was no reason to think she'd be back.

Perhaps this stakeout was punishment for his handling of the Samsova matter in Russia. Christ, Pavski never specified that Samsova was to be left *alive.* In Dananka's mind, the assignment was a major success. After all, they now possessed the charts and teaching materials from the old man.

His cell phone beeped.

"Where's Preston?" Pavski asked.

"He's leaving Cathy Bryson's place." Dananka hesitated. "Are you sure this surveillance is necessary? The chances of Hannah Bryson's meeting with the congressman again aren't that good."

"Don't worry, Dananka. Sometimes the obvious target isn't the true one. Don't let Preston out of your sight. I'll call you with further instructions."

Dananka smiled. "Understood."

No sign of Hannah Bryson," Teague said as he came into Bradworth's office. "And the agent doing surveillance at Cathy Bryson's home reports she hasn't shown up there."

"Damn." Not that it surprised him. Kirov wouldn't have let Hannah surface if he chose not to do it. He knew all the tricks. Which left Bradworth no option but to sit and twiddle his thumbs until the bastard decided to get in contact with him. He'd used Congressman Preston to intercede with Cathy Bryson once, but he doubted if he could get him to do it again. "Keep looking. I need that woman—"

His phone rang, and he started to ignore it. Then he saw it was Sordberg, the director. He picked up. "Bradworth."

"What the hell is happening?" Sordberg asked. "Have you screwed up, Bradworth?"

"I don't know what you're talking about."

"My assistant just got a phone call. Get the hell up here. We have to talk. You have some explaining to do."

There he is," Kirov said to Hannah.

A mustached man in his late fifties was unlocking the antique store's accordion-style security gate.

"Are you sure he's the one we're looking for?" Hannah asked.

Kirov nodded. "Boris Petrenko."

"How do you know?"

"I downloaded his driver's license photo to my laptop last night."

"Breaking into a secured Web site?"

"No, I had a friend who did that for me."

"You evidently have the ability to tap many people in many places for favors."

"Any objection?"

How could she object when she'd done the same thing to find Kirov? "No." She got out of the rental car. "Let's go."

Petrenko stared at Kirov and Hannah with a frown as they entered the shop. "I'm sorry, I'm not open yet." His brow wrinkled. "I thought I locked that door."

"You did." Kirov locked the glass door behind him. "We're here to inquire about some merchandise not on display. Your real merchandise is in the back room, isn't it? Or perhaps downstairs?"

He stiffened warily. "I don't know what you're talking about."

"Don't worry, Mr. Petrenko. I'm no customs agent. My name is Kirov." He gestured to Hannah. "Hannah Bryson. We just want some information."

Petrenko moved toward the main sales counter in the large, musty showroom. "I don't sell information. I've found that it's too hazardous to my health."

"Oh, I don't want you to sell it to me. I expect you to give it to me."

"And why would I do that?"

"Because it would be hazardous to your health *not* to do it." He added, "And please don't step any closer to that counter. You're making me nervous. You don't want that to happen."

Petrenko stopped short. "I really can't help you."

"You won't know that until you try."

Hannah stepped forward. "Mr. Petrenko, I can't tell you how important this is to us. Please help us."

Petrenko glanced at her and his expression softened. "I'd like to help you. But it's not—"

"We need to know about the three men you picked up last weekend," Kirov said. "Two questions: who were they and who hired you?"

Petrenko's gaze shifted from Hannah and narrowed on Kirov. "Who the hell are you?"

"No one who gives a damn about your midnight imports. However, if you don't help us, I won't hesitate to inform some people who do care. Believe me, U.S. Customs would be the least of your problems. Many countries are quite protective of their treasures, and they can be ruthless in dealing with individuals who appropriate them."

Petrenko hesitated.

"I'm not bluffing, Petrenko."

Petrenko muttered a curse. "I'll tell you what I know on one condition."

"And that is?"

"Tell me how you found me. If you found out about me, others might, too."

"No deal. But rest assured, my sources aren't available to just anyone. You'll probably be able to continue your operations for some time to come if you don't make another stupid mistake."

Petrenko shrugged. "It was worth a try. Not that I can help you much anyway."

"Try."

"I know very little about these people."

"You're lying."

"No. One of my usual suppliers contacted me a few days before a shipment was due. They asked if I'd bring in some human cargo. It more than paid for that evening's purchases, and a little extra besides."

"How were you paid?"

"In cash. Half was paid to me that evening, the remainder I found in an envelope on my car dashboard Monday morning."

"After your three passengers made it safely to shore."

Petrenko lifted his eyebrows in surprise. "You know that?"

"You were boarded by a Coast Guard cutter?"

Petrenko nodded. "Yes, but they only seemed to be looking for drugs or weapons. They let the dog sniff around for a while, then left."

"I'll need the name of your supplier."

"I'm afraid I can't—"

"He made the arrangements for those passengers. I'm not leaving here without his name."

Petrenko moistened his lips. "Please respect my position. I understood when you couldn't reveal your sources, and you must understand that I can't reveal mine."

"No choice."

Petrenko had turned pale, but he still shook his head.

Kirov glanced quickly at Hannah. "Go back to the car."

"Why?"

"Don't argue. This won't take long."

She looked at Petrenko. Jesus, he looked frightened. "What are you going to do?"

"Only what needs to be done." Kirov was staring at Petrenko. "The choice is entirely his."

"Please," the man gasped. "I can't do—"

"Go wait in the car," Kirov repeated to Hannah. "Or take a walk. Or go take a look at that charming old movie theater down the street. Whatever you do, I don't think you want to be here."

His voice was calm, almost expressionless, but Hannah could sense the restrained violence behind that coolness. "I'm not sure this is the way to—"

"You bet it's not." The voice came from the rear of the store.

Hannah whirled to see a fair-haired, teenage girl of maybe sixteen or seventeen with a gun aimed at Kirov's head.

Petrenko stiffened. "Anna! No."

The gun was wavering in the girl's trembling hand. "Move away from him."

Kirov didn't move.

"Anna, I'm fine," Petrenko said gently. "Go upstairs and lock the door."

Anna shook her head. "No way." She spoke to Kirov and Hannah. "Get the hell out of here, both of you."

Kirov slowly turned to face her. "You don't want to do this."

"The hell I don't."

"We didn't come here to hurt your father."

"Yeah, sure, I heard you. And he's not my father."

"Then who is he to you?"

"None of your goddamned business." She readjusted the gun in her hands. "I could blow your brains out, and nobody would blame me. I'd tell them that you broke in here and tried to rob us."

Kirov's brows lifted. "Rob you? With what? I don't even have a gun."

"Anna, we didn't come here to hurt him or anybody," Hannah said. "We just need to find out some things that are very important to me."

"I heard the whole thing. He said he couldn't help you, so go."

Kirov spoke softly. "We can't do that. I'm totally unarmed, but if you want to kill me, you'll just have to press that trigger."

"Anna," Petrenko said, "go get the briefcase."

Anna's eyes widened. "What?"

"The briefcase from the other night. From the boat."

She shook her head. "The others may come back for it."

"No one is coming for it. Go get the case, please."

She thought for a moment, then moved close to Petrenko. "Here. Hold the gun."

"Gladly."

Keeping the gun aimed at Kirov, she slowly handed it over to Petrenko. He turned and casually threw the weapon into a counter drawer.

"No!" Anna gazed at him in horror. "What are you doing?"

"Go get the case. Hurry along now."

Still keeping a wary eye on Kirov and Hannah, she slowly moved toward the back of the store.

"I hope there aren't any other guns back there," Hannah said.

"No. You must excuse my young friend's tempestuous nature. She's very protective."

"Like a pit bull," Hannah said.

Kirov smiled. "Yes, she's obviously a bit impulsive. You know, of course, she had the safety on."

Petrenko nodded. "She's protective but completely unversed in the use of firearms. I prefer that she remain in that ignorance. Violence can scar children."

"More than children," Kirov said. "What's in this case you sent her to fetch?"

"As you know, my passengers from the other night were forced to slip overboard a few miles from shore. One of them left behind a small satchel. Apparently it contained nothing of real value because I received a note with my money instructing me to destroy it."

"Which you obviously didn't do," Hannah said.

"I hadn't gotten around to it." He grimaced. "Okay, I thought it might prove valuable if they wanted it destroyed. I was considering my options."

"That case isn't going to buy you out. I still need the name of your contact," Kirov said.

"I was afraid you'd say that," Petrenko sighed.

"If I have to question him, I'll make sure that he thinks someone else tipped me."

"His name is Dan McClary. He works out of Cobh, Ireland."

Anna brought the black satchel from the back and placed it on the counter in front of Petrenko. "You said I could keep the iPod."

Petrenko shrugged. "It belongs to this gentleman now."

Anna looked at Kirov.

"Sorry," Kirov said.

Anna shook her head. "I should have shot you when I had the chance."

"Not over an iPod." Kirov picked up the briefcase. "This is a far happier solution for everyone, I assure you." He turned to Petrenko. "But if I find that you lied to me about McClary . . ."

"You'll know where to find me." Petrenko waved his arm around the store. "I've been here twelve years. This is my life, and I don't intend to abandon it."

"Sometimes life abandons you," Kirov said as he opened the door for Hannah. "Thank you, Petrenko." He glanced at the girl, who was still glaring at him. "Take good care of him. We all need someone to stand by us."

A t a rest stop on Highway 25, Hannah and Kirov stopped to examine the contents of the black satchel.

"I don't suppose there's any chance that this is the GRU information Pavski sent for," Hannah said as she opened the satchel.

"Not if Petrenko was ordered to destroy it."

That was what Hannah had reasoned. She held up a cylindrical object. "What's this?"

"A silencer for a .357 Magnum handgun. Petrenko's passengers obviously didn't come to sightsee." Kirov took the silencer and sniffed it. "It's been used."

"Recently?"

"Difficult to tell. There's nothing particularly silent about these things. It's not like the movies, where silenced handguns only make a slight whistling sound. It's more like a cannon being shot in the next room."

"Good to know for the next time I need to use one." She pulled out a well-read copy of *The London Times,* dated six days earlier.

Kirov glanced at the front page. "I'd say this paper was probably purchased somewhere else in Europe, maybe Ireland."

Hannah studied the page. "Are you looking at the price sticker?"

"Yes. It covers the newspaper's price, as you'd see with out-of-town newspapers. It's in euros, and much higher than you'd pay in London."

Hannah pulled out the Apple iPod portable music player. "And here's the MP3 player that Anna wanted so much. I think you enjoyed taking it from her."

"You're wrong. I never enjoy depriving women of things they desire. I'm much too primitive."

"Primitive?"

"From cave days man has instinctively provided for the female." He smiled as he unwound the earphones. "Or maybe it's not instinct but the knowledge that they'd be given what they want much more easily if they kept them happy." He put on the earphones and powered up the player. "She probably would have appreciated this terrible Euro-rap music far more than I do." He yanked the earphones and turned off the player.

Hannah reached into the satchel and pulled out an assortment of personal items with Russian-language packaging, including toothpaste, floss, shampoo, and condoms.

She tapped the pack of condoms. "Someone was planning on a busy stay here."

"You'd be amazed at the effect a Russian accent can have on young American women. It surprised me."

"I'm sure you used that as efficiently as you do everything else."

"I'd be disappointed if I thought I had to rely on anything so trivial," he said absently as he examined the iPod more closely.

He was right. His appeal was not surface shallow. He was totally adult, totally male, with a potent mixture of both the primitive he had mentioned and sophistication.

She lowered her eyes to the contents of the bag. "You don't have that much of an accent anyway."

"Nice jab. What else is in there?"

She pulled out a handheld GPS locator/mapping device, similar to the models used by hikers and campers. She switched it on. "Conner used one of these. He had the worst sense of direction known to man. If this was used to navigate the user to a specific destination, it may still be in the memory."

"Good thinking. What do you see?"

Hannah cycled through the options as she glanced through the menu screens. "Damn. A big fat nothing. All previous destinations have been deleted."

"Pavski has always been good at covering his tracks, and I'd expect the same from anyone he would hire." Kirov took the device. "Still, there's deleted and there's *deleted*. Just because the operating system doesn't recognize the data doesn't mean it isn't still in there somewhere."

"How can we tell?"

"I'll give it a once-over with my laptop. If that doesn't work, I have many friends in low places."

"Of course you do."

"Anything else?"

Hannah turned the bag upside down and shook it. "Nothing."

Kirov leaned back in the car seat and surveyed the objects on their laps. "Well, these should keep me busy this afternoon while I see what I can find out about this McClary fellow. We'll check into a motel and see what we can come up with."

Hannah nodded. "And I need to call Cathy back. She's left four messages on my voice mail."

W hat the hell are you doing?" Cathy asked curtly when she picked up the phone.

"I'm doing what we said we were going to do. I'm trying to find out what happened to Conner."

"I thought we were going to do it together."

"We are. It's just that it's gotten . . . complicated."

She was silent a moment. "Does complicated really mean dangerous?"

"Ronnie and Donna need you. You can't—"

"Don't tell me what I can or can't do, Hannah. Conner was my husband."

"I'm sorry."

"And who the devil is Kirov?"

Hannah went still. "How do you know about Kirov?"

"A United States congressman sat in my kitchen and told me, that's how. Your buddy Bradworth turned the screws on George to get him to talk to me. They said this man is using you to get what he wants, and he doesn't care if you get hurt or not."

Tell me something I *don't* know, Hannah thought. "Cathy, you have to trust me. I know what I'm doing."

"Who is this man?"

"He knows the people who killed Conner. He's been after them for a long time."

"Then why does he need you?"

"The *Silent Thunder* is at the center of it. I just don't know how yet."

"Hannah, he isn't who he says he is."

"What?"

"That's what George wanted me to tell you. George could see I wasn't hopping to do what he wanted, so he called me back this morning after talking to Bradworth and getting new ammunition. Bradworth said you think Kirov's real name is Ivanov?"

"Yes. That's not news, but I'm surprised—"

"Bradworth told George that his director received a phone call from an anonymous informant who said Ivanov was killed by Russian intelligence agents seven years ago."

Hannah took a long moment to absorb that before speaking. "Bradworth would have told me."

"He said the call came in this morning."

"Convenient. *Too* convenient. It's his way to smoke me out. He doesn't want me involved with Kirov."

"*I* don't want you involved in this, Hannah."

"I'm already involved. There's more going on here than Bradworth would ever tell us. I'm not going to come back until I find out everything."

"You really think he's lying?"

"I don't know. It would be an awfully big coincidence that they managed to uncover this about Kirov—make that *Ivanov*—at this particular time after working with him for years."

"But he said that—"

"Bradworth is CIA," Hannah cut in. "He could make black look white."

"We're about to find out. George says the CIA has sent a team to try to recover Ivanov's remains, but Bradworth's almost positive the man you're with is not who he says he is. Talk to him."

"I'm sure he can hear us now. Or he will, when this recording is played back for him."

Cathy was silent. "You think he bugged my line?"

"Yes. Good-bye, Cathy."

Hannah cut the connection. Shit.

She wanted to call Bradworth and grill the hell out of him, but she knew that was exactly what he wanted her to do. He clearly didn't want her working with Kirov, and he'd do or say anything to get his way.

But what if it was true that Ivanov was dead?

Bradworth wasn't above a convenient lie to get what he wanted, but neither was Kirov. Who the hell should she believe?

She slowly rose to her feet.

Well, there was one way to find out. Maybe it was time to put her freakish brain to work.

Her photographic memory had earned her a good deal of attention, dating back to her elementary-school days, when a terrified second-grade teacher was convinced she was channeling the spirits of U.S. soldiers killed in combat. Actually, she was merely showing off, scribbling entire pages from the *Letters from Vietnam* book she'd seen her father reading the previous evening.

While she always insisted that her talent was insignificant compared to the powers of creativity and reason, it had served her well over the years. If she got a good look at something, she could usually bring it back.

But no one realized it wasn't as easy as just snapping her fingers, she thought ruefully.

She walked over to the desk and sat in the narrow, straight-backed chair. She'd have to concentrate and let herself drift back to the night she arrived in Maine, allowing the sights, sounds, and smells wash over her.

No, that wasn't right. She'd examined the dossiers of the captain and first officer that first night sitting on the pier, but she hadn't glanced through the others until the next evening. She'd looked over the rest of the files while eating dinner alone at a diner down the street from the maritime museum. Conner had wanted to talk to Cathy and the kids while he was eating his sandwich, so he'd stayed at the sub.

She closed her eyes.

Picture the diner.

It was small, a dozen tables at the most. Blue-and-white-checkered curtains, hardwood floors, and suspended lighting fixtures with glass tulip bulbs at the ends. A small counter stood across from the door.

She'd sat at a table near the far side of the counter. The files were stacked in front of her, on the other side of her plates and plastic drinking glass. She'd lifted the files one at a time, glanced at the cover page, then put them down in a second pile.

See the names.

She couldn't. They weren't clear enough yet.

She'd heard burgers sizzling on the grill. The young cook cursed as hot grease spattered onto his arms.

She took a whiff of the fries cooking in the fryer. Damn, they smelled good.

See the names.

Andre Kolonchovsky. Tevye Soldonoff. Lucius Dannisaya . . .

It was working. Each file was more visible and detailed than the last.

Danique Relyea, Garen Totenkolpa, Poul Farenevla . . .

The diner's door opened and shut, ringing a tiny copper bell attached to the frame.

It had to be here somewhere.

Vladmir Yaltsin, Dimitri Ivanov . . .

Ivanov!

She stopped and pictured the file folder in her hands. Wrinkled manila, soft from wear.

Focus on the file page.

Perfect. Clear as day . . .

Dammit.

Cathy hung up the phone after twice trying to dial Hannah back and having it go to voice mail. Hannah must have turned off her phone. She'd probably realized that Cathy wouldn't give up on the argument.

"Mama, will you read me a story?"

"Not now, Donna, I have to—" She broke off as she raised her head and saw Donna standing in the doorway. She was carrying her favorite book of fairy tales, and she was actually looking tentative. Her Donna who was always a whirlwind of activity and confidence. She smiled. "Sure, that would be fun. Which one?"

" 'Beauty and the Beast.' " She came over to the couch and plopped down beside Cathy. "I like the beast better than the other princes. He's not boring."

"No, he's not." She pulled her into the curve of her arm and brushed the straight, fair hair back from her daughter's forehead. "Suppose we do it together? It's always better that way. You need to practice reading the story yourself."

"That's what I told her." Ronnie stood in the doorway, frowning. "She wasn't supposed to bother you. I told her I'd read it to her."

"I'm not bothering her," Donna said defensively. "She likes fairy tales. That's why I picked this book." She looked up at Cathy. "You do like it, don't you?"

"I like reading with you. It's one of my favorite things." Cathy held out her hand to Ronnie. "Come on and sit with us. I haven't had a chance to be with you today."

"I came to see you earlier." He moved toward her. "You were on the phone with Aunt Hannah."

How much had he heard? Probably enough to worry him. "She sends her love."

Ronnie looked at Donna, who was busily turning the pages of her book. "I want her to come home, Mom."

"So do I. But she'll be fine, Ronnie. She's very smart."

"The Beast," Donna prompted. "I'll read the first page."

"That will take you an hour," Ronnie said. "Let me do it."

"Will not," Donna said. "I'm good. Mama said so."

"She just wants to—" He stopped and then nodded. "Yeah. I noticed you were getting better yesterday when you were reading that Dora book."

"You did?" Donna's face lit with excitement. "Honest?"

"Honest." He dropped down on the floor at her feet. "Go ahead. Let me know if you have trouble with a word."

"I won't have trouble." Donna turned to the first chapter. "Mama, you just sit back and listen. I'll do the whole story. I told Ronnie this would make you happy."

Was that what this was all about? Good God, her five-year-old was administering therapy. The story made Donna happy, so she wanted to spread the joy? Cathy was touched. In the midst of sorrow, there was this sudden rainbow. "You were right." Cathy leaned back and her hand caressingly touched Ronnie's head as Donna turned the first page. "And that makes you very smart, young lady." She gazed down at the huge beast standing in the doorway of his castle. "He's pretty ugly, isn't he?"

"Beasts have to be ugly," Donna said matter-of-factly. "But that's okay, they always turn out to be princes in the end."

Only in fairy tales, Cathy thought. Hannah was dealing with a hideous reality right now and not letting her help. She was scared to death this Kirov would prove to be an uglier beast than the one in Donna's book.

And the finale of the story would bring not a happy but a deadly ending.

Hannah caught up with Kirov behind the motel, strolling in a surprisingly charming small Shakespeare Garden. Small plaques with quotes from the Bard were scattered among the lush, colorful flowers.

"I wouldn't have expected a garden like this behind an ordinary motel," she said.

"Beautiful flowers are a cheap way to dress up the ordinary."

"I never would have taken you for a botanist," Hannah said.

"I'm not." Kirov nodded toward one of the plaques. "I'm more interested in the Shakespeare quotes."

"Your stepbrother was a fan of Western literature. I guess that's something you shared."

"I suppose." He frowned. "But we certainly didn't share a love of mythology. I still don't know why there was a mythology book in his cabin. I did a few crude chemical tests on some of the pages last night, and I don't believe there are messages scribbled in invisible ink. That would have been too easy. Pavski had a chance to go through all those books before the Kremlin jerked the sub away from him and sent it to Finland. He obviously found nothing."

"Those are some of the most widely read stories in the history of the world. Maybe there's no special meaning to it at all."

"Possibly, but I knew all the men who might have occupied that cabin, and it doesn't seem like something that any of them would have cracked open. Strange."

"How well did you know them?"

He raised an eyebrow. "The crew? I tried to know them as well as I knew every piece of equipment on that sub."

"That's smart. I guess your life depended on each and every one of those people."

"More to the point, they were trusting their lives to me and their other officers. The least I could do is to try and get to know them."

"You knew some of them for a long time, didn't you? All the way back to the naval academy in St. Petersburg?"

"It was called Leningrad at the time, but yes. Some even earlier than that."

"Earlier?"

"I had known the assistant engineer since grade school."

Chalk one up for Kirov, Hannah thought. She'd read that engineer's mate Alexander Rotonoff had grown up in the same neighborhood as Ivanov.

"What was his name?"

"Alex Rotonoff. A good man, yet limited outside his narrow expertise."

Chalk up another one.

They rounded the corner and proceeded down another path. "If I remember your file correctly, your father was a sailor."

He smiled. "Your famous memory at work. Yes, my father loved the sea."

"And his father before him?'

"A wagon maker. My father and I insisted that our love of adventure came from my grandmother."

"Your father's first command was a supply vessel in the Aegean Sea, the *Danitelvia.*"

"Actually, that was his second. His first was another supply ship, the *Lettenski,* but his command only lasted about seventy-two hours. The ship developed engine problems and eventually had to be scuttled." He cocked an eyebrow at her. "I'm surprised you didn't know that, since I'm sure a copy of his service record was attached to mine. I suppose there's a limit to that memory of yours, eh?"

The bastard knew he was being tested, but she wasn't ready to make an issue of it yet. In any case, he'd passed with flying colors. If he was lying about being Ivanov, he'd certainly done his homework.

She shrugged. "What are we waiting for now?"

"I'm waiting to hear back on a few inquiries I've made about McClary, and my computer is downloading the contents of that GPS device as we speak. By the way, how did your call with Cathy go?"

"Fine."

"Was it?"

"Yes."

His gaze held her own, and it was obvious he didn't believe her. Either he was extremely perceptive, or she was a bad liar. Both, she decided.

He didn't push it. "Good," he said gently. "I know you're worried about her. Let's head back to my room. The GPS download should be finished anytime now."

TWELVE

Hannah's gaze narrowed on Kirov's laptop screen, which was now divided into two distinct sections. One window featured a graphic representation of a GPS device, the other was littered with blue and white icons.

Kirov pointed to the icons. "These are the various destination coordinates still lurking in the GPS unit's memory."

"How were you able to do this on such short notice?"

"The Internet is a wonderful thing. I downloaded a recovery utility that people use when they accidentally delete addresses they need."

He double-clicked an icon, and a map appeared on the on-screen GPS device. "This is the Docklands area of London."

"Whoever owned this has been to that address?"

"Most likely." Kirov pulled up on online telephone directory and keyed in the address. "Club Oasis" came up on the screen.

Hannah nodded in recognition. "That's a dance club."

"Frequent the place, do you?"

"Some of the guys in my crew have been there. It wasn't easy getting them back to work after a night in that place."

"Fairly innocuous," Kirov said. "And we already know this man has a fondness for European pop music."

Kirov turned his attention back to the destination icons. One by one, he clicked them and checked the locations against his online telephone directory.

After he was finished, Hannah checked the notes she had taken. "Fourteen locations, all in either England, Scotland, or Ireland. All public addresses—restaurants, pubs, dance clubs, a racquet club. On their own, they don't mean very much."

"I agree. Perhaps we should just give it a rest until I hear something back about McClary."

"Fine." Hannah picked up the digital music player and earphones.

"What do you want with that?"

"Maybe it'll help me get to know the person who owns it better." She headed for the adjoining door. "Besides, I might like it. Just because you don't like anything recorded since 1970 doesn't mean I don't."

Static. Shrill, earsplitting static.

Hannah sat bolt upright in her bed and yanked out the earphones. At first she thought it was nothing more than the opening refrain of a bit of obnoxious techno pop, but there was no way this could be considered music. She had been listening to the player for over an hour, and while the songs certainly weren't to her taste, she didn't detest them the way Kirov did.

This number was entirely another matter.

She checked out the tiny LCD screen and saw that the song was entitled "Waterbridge." She held the earphones up and still heard only static. She jumped to the next tune and heard guitars, synth drums, and heavily processed vocals, just like almost every other song on the player.

Back to "Waterbridge." More static.

Then, nothing.

She looked at the LCD screen again. It now read: INVALID FILE.

Invalid file.

She went rigid. Christ almighty.

She picked up the phone and punched Kirov's extension. "Get your laptop and bring it down to my room. Now."

"I'll be there in three minutes."

Two minutes later Hannah opened her door to Kirov's knock. He was carrying his laptop and cables. "What is it?"

"You can set up the laptop on my desk."

He crossed the room to the desk. "The iPod?"

Hannah nodded. "We were on the right track, but concentrating on the wrong device. Upload the song 'Waterbridge' into your laptop and tell me what you get."

Kirov uploaded the file and double-clicked it. An "invalid or unknown file" error message came up on the screen. "That's strange," he murmured. "It has an MP3 extension, which would indicate it's an audio file."

"But it's not," Hannah said. "It was given an MP3 extension so that it could be downloaded to the music player and appear in the directory. We need to rename it."

"Rename it to what?" Kirov said.

"I don't know. I'll just start trying extensions and see what works."

Hannah sat next to Kirov and tried several of the more common file extensions, assignable to popular word-processing and graphic file formats. None opened the file.

Until she tried the .wmv extension.

"It's opening," Kirov said as the Windows Media Player appeared on the screen.

The video was a crudely animated map that showed a set of co-ordinates that Hannah quickly identified as a point off the New England coast.

The "camera" then plunged underwater to show four red cylinders at a depth reading of 1625 feet.

"What the hell is that?" she asked. "Is that what Pavski has been looking for?"

"I don't think so," Kirov said. "If he really knew the location, he wouldn't be bothering with the *Silent Thunder,* you, your brother, and with reinforcements from the motherland. This has to be something else."

"Like what?"

"I don't know." He stared at the crudely rendered red cylinders. "Those *could* represent training torpedoes we used during military exercises."

"Why would they be on the bottom of the ocean?"

"Actually, they were made to float. But it's possible that there's something placed inside to weigh them down."

"Do you think these may have been ejected from the *Silent Thunder*?" Hannah leaned back in her chair. "Something that can point the way to what they're looking for? Maybe what we want isn't on the sub at all."

The video repeated on the screen, and Kirov jotted down the co-ordinates. "Who knows? But if Pavski had this information over a week ago, he's probably recovered them by now."

Hannah studied the animatic as the underwater plunge repeated. "Maybe not. If this depth is correct, it would take some expensive equipment and a lot of expertise to do that. We might still have a chance."

"How? Unless you're willing to involve Bradworth and the resources of the U.S. government—"

"No way."

"You're thinking. I can see the wheels go round." He leaned back in his chair, and a small smile curved his lips. "It's a lovely thing to behold. How are we going to do this, Hannah?"

"Experts and expensive equipment," Hannah said. "In case you're forgetting, I *am* an expert. And as far as resources go, I have a few connections of my own."

By sundown, Hannah and Kirov were on a forty-foot rented fishing boat, heading toward the research vessel *Aurora* 125 miles off the Virginia coast. Kirov manned the wheel while Hannah stood beside him staring ahead at the 225-foot craft.

"Do you really think this is going to work?" Kirov asked.

"Who knows? If it doesn't, we'll try something else," Hannah said. "Captain Tanbury is a good guy, but he may be at the mercy of the researchers aboard. He says they're studying brine shrimp populations."

"Brine shrimp? You mean sea monkeys?"

Hannah chuckled. "Excellent pop culture reference. Did they advertise them on the back of comic books in Russia, too?"

"Not that I know of, but I've seen the packages in your country's souvenir shops, especially in coastal towns. It's ridiculous. Next they'll be packaging *algae* and selling it to children as pets."

"In any case, this is our best hope. My only other options are either too far away or too closely tied to military interests." She waved back at a man in a bright red shirt who was waving at her from the stern. "There's Tanbury now. I'm afraid you'll have to pretend to be a member of my crew again."

Kirov shrugged. "I'm getting used to being your lackey. As long as I don't catch you enjoying it too much."

"No promises," Hannah said, as they pulled alongside the *Aurora* and tossed mooring lines to the waiting deckhands.

A rope ladder flew over the side, and Captain Tanbury's round red face appeared above the railing. "Ahoy, Hannah Bryson. Have you come to rescue me?"

Hannah smiled as she and Kirov climbed the ladder. "Rescue you from what?"

"A life of indentured servitude to a bunch of eggheads. Oh, wait." He clapped his head in mock distress. "What am I thinking? You're no good to me. You're an egghead, too!"

"You were damn grateful I was an egghead when I was working with you." They high-fived each other as she climbed aboard.

Tanbury was a bear of a man in his early fifties, with thick red hair both on top and curling out of the neckline of his T-shirt. He gestured down to Kirov. "Who's your friend?"

"Another egghead. Captain Earl Tanbury, meet Nicholas Kirov."

Kirov climbed aboard and shook hands with Tanbury. "Delighted to meet you, Captain Tanbury."

"At least, an egghead with manners. A lot of these scientists think I'm such a redneck that they don't bother with the niceties." Tanbury gestured for them to walk with him down the deck. "I was happy to get your call, Hannah, but I'm guessing this isn't just a social visit."

She nodded. "I need to talk to you about a mutual friend of ours."

"Who?" he asked warily.

"*LISA.*"

Tanbury smiled. "A subject near and dear to my heart. Would you like to see her?"

"Very much."

"This way." Tanbury led them to the ship's stern, where a two-man submersible was suspended on a winch. "There she is. *LISA*—Lateral Intake Submersible Application. She still works as well as she did the day you left her with us."

Hannah ran her hand caressingly across *LISA*'s white hull. It was one of her first major contracts, one that had paved the way for many high-profile projects that followed. The egg-shaped underwater craft featured fore-and-aft observation ports and two pairs of finely articulated robotic hands extending from the front of the vessel, tilting downward almost as if poised to play the next movement of a piano concerto.

"Looks good," Hannah said. "You've been taking good care of it."

"*Her*," Tanbury corrected. "We've been taking good care of *her*."

Hannah smiled. "Of course."

"And she's been taking good care of us. She gets a little prickly when you try to overwork her, but overall she's a good gal."

Kirov turned toward her with lifted brows. "See?"

"Men and the sea . . ." Hannah murmured.

Tanbury chuckled. "Aw, I'm just trying to get under your skin. I know how you feel about this stuff. Seriously, though, she's as reliable as any submersible I've ever known. There may be newer ones out there with more bells and whistles, but she's a great little performer. The institute has a mile-long list of research groups waiting to lease this boat, and *LISA* is a big reason why. You did good, Hannah."

"Glad to hear it," Hannah said. "Because I have a big favor to ask, Tanbury."

"Shoot."

"I want to borrow *LISA* for a day."

Tanbury smile faded. "I'd call that a damn big favor."

"It gets bigger. I can't tell you why I need it, and no one off this ship can know I have it."

Tanbury shook his head. "I have people from the institute on board who expect to use it all day tomorrow."

"I wouldn't ask if it wasn't important to me. I *need* this, Tanbury."

He studied her expression. "Yeah, I can see it means a lot to you. Can't it wait a day or two? Maybe I can work it."

She shook her head.

"Tough." He thought for a moment. "Let me put on my bullshit hat for a second. What if I tell them you had concerns about the structural safety of the pod and needed to take it away to conduct some tests? That will satisfy the people on board. But after that, when word gets back to the institute and manufacturer . . ."

"I'll handle it. Stick by your story, and I'll take the heat."

"You'll have to." He grimaced. "Because this is the kind of caper I could lose my job over."

"I appreciate it. You won't lose your job. I'll make sure of that."

"I trust you. There's not many people in this world I'd trust with my livelihood, but you're one of them, Hannah." He walked to the side and stared down at their rented boat. "You won't get far trying to take *LISA* with *that*."

"We'll do an underwater tow from the stern. The winch will support it."

"I guess so, as long as the weather holds." He turned back. "Jesus, Hannah, a woman with your connections should be able to just pick up the phone and—"

"You're the only connection that will do me any good right now, Tanbury."

He sighed. "How did I get so lucky? Oh well, we're about to have dinner. Care to join us?"

"The sooner we leave, the sooner we'll have your submersible back to you," Kirov said.

"In that case, cancel the dinner invite. I'll get my crew out here to put *LISA* in the water."

I t took Tanbury's crew ninety minutes to replace *LISA*'s depleted power cells and attach it to the rental boat's winch. Soon after dark, Hannah and Kirov were under way, heading toward the co-ordinates indicated in the digital video file.

Kirov scribbled on the chart he had spread out on the interior cabin's dining table. "Perfect. We should make it there just before dawn."

Hannah looked at the Samsovian symbols on the map. "Sometime you'll have to teach me this system of yours. Is it really that good?"

"It's very elegant, very clean, and utterly confusing to those who don't take the time to understand it completely." He smiled. "I think it made us feel like we were members of an exclusive club. But snob appeal aside, it takes me back to a different time."

"What time?"

"When I was in the academy, the world was a simpler place. Or at least it appeared to be. We had a country we could be proud of, and we believed our navy was second to none."

"It's a fine navy," Hannah said.

"Don't believe the propaganda. There were fine people in it, and

I'd trust my life to almost any of them. But do you know how much of the time U.S. military vessels are at sea? Sixty-five percent of the time. Do you how much of the time Russian boats are out there? Only fifteen percent, all due to mechanical and efficiency problems. Our average was a bit better in my day, but not much."

"It's a country in upheaval."

"There needed to be upheaval. It took me a while to realize it was necessary, but the reality set in soon enough." His lips twisted. "It was forced on me at the point of an AK-47. So here I am drowning in reality and trying to make clarity out of the chaos of my life."

"By killing everyone who caused that chaos."

He smiled. "Trust you to simplify and rid me of any false rationalizations. You're right, of course. You're a very unusual woman, Hannah. It didn't surprise me that Tanbury was willing to trust you with his daily bread." He held her gaze. "I'm beginning to think I'd trust you with much more."

Christ, she couldn't look away from him. She felt . . . She finally managed to tear her gaze away from his. Crazy. Block it. Hannah quickly glanced at the rearview video monitor and saw the wake of *LISA*'s antenna as it cut through the water. "You don't think the video file we found is showing us the location of the capsule?"

"It wouldn't make sense. Pavski obviously has a copy of the video. Otherwise, he would have wanted that music player. We know that it's at least five days old. Why would he have bothered with the *Silent Thunder,* Conner, or you? As I said, this might be something else, perhaps Heiser's clue. Of course, Pavski may have already beaten us to it."

Hannah stared into the darkness that lay ahead. "If that's true, he could even be there now."

Hannah's eyes opened. It took her only a moment to realize that the boat's sudden downshifting had wakened her.

"Good morning," Kirov said. "Please return your seatbacks and tray tables to their normal and upright position."

"Are we there?"

"Just another few hundred yards. No sign of Pavski or anyone else."

Hannah pulled off the jacket that Kirov had draped across her while she was sleeping. It was still dark outside save for a sliver of orange on the eastern horizon. She quickly looked up at the rearview monitor, which now displayed a green-tinted "night-vision" mode.

"Don't worry, *LISA* is safe and sound. I've been keeping an eye on her." Kirov throttled down the engine and idled through the water. "Okay, this is about where we need to be. It's your show now."

Hannah glanced at the sea around them. The seas were calm, and there wasn't a light to be seen anywhere. "Let's get on that winch and raise *LISA* four feet. That will give us access to the top hatch."

"Aye aye."

While Kirov moved to the stern and activated the power winch, Hannah slipped on the jacket and zipped up. As chilly as it was on the water's surface, she knew it would be much colder a mile and a half below.

Kirov stepped onto *LISA*'s upper hull and rotated the wheel lock until he could pull open its narrow hatch. "Ladies first?"

"Ladies only."

He stiffened. "What are you talking about? I'm going with you."

"The hell you are."

"It's a two-man craft. I'm not going to stay up here while you—"

"Yes, you are. As brilliantly designed as *LISA* may be, things can and do go wrong. I never dive without a support team on the surface."

"I'm your support team?"

"Unless you think you can pilot *LISA* better than I can."

"You know I can't."

"Hello, support team."

"Shit."

Hannah reached into the pod, pulled out a four-foot rod, and handed it to Kirov. "This is an amplified underwater telescoping antenna. Attach it to the side of the boat and extend it all the way down. If you connect it to the boat's main radio, we should be able to keep in touch most of the way down."

"Will I be able to see?"

"Nope. For that we'd need a mile and a half of fiber-optic cable. I give great description, though."

"Terrific."

"Give me a few minutes to power up and run diagnostics. After that, you can disengage the winch."

"I'm not happy about this, Hannah."

"And I wouldn't be happy if something went wrong, and I didn't have a support team to rescue me." Hannah settled into the right-hand pilot seat, flipped the power switches, and initiated the diagnostic routine. While she waited, she listened to the familiar purr of *LISA* coming to life. The last time she was in there, Conner was her point man on the surface, making sure the company engineers didn't suddenly change the test conditions. He'd always been there to watch her back.

But Kirov was here. Kirov would watch.

After the "all clear" lights appeared, Hannah looked outside to see that Kirov had successfully mounted the underwater antenna. She gave him the thumbs-up.

He picked up the radio microphone and spoke into it. "Last chance for a little companionship."

She slipped on her headset and angled the microphone over her mouth. "Just close the damned hatch."

He slammed the hatch shut and locked it.

As she buckled herself in, she heard him releasing the winch hook. After a few moments, *LISA* was free in the water and slowly dipping beneath the waves.

Kirov's voice came over the radio a few seconds later. "Support team to *LISA*, do you read?"

"Loud and clear, support team. I'm glad you've finally accepted your place in the world."

"I didn't say that. I just wanted to feed your ego. What's your depth?"

She checked the readout. "Eighty-five feet and falling free."

"ETA?"

"About ninety minutes. Know any good drinking songs?"

"Too many. I take requests, you know."

"Maybe I'll save them for the trip back up."

"As you wish. Support team out."

Hannah settled back in the bucket seat and felt her body relax for the first time in days. Why did this experience always bring her so much peace? Many people went nuts in those tiny pods, but she always found serenity once the surface sounds faded, and the last traces of sunlight disappeared. The ocean was hers.

She checked the onboard CD player. Howard Hanson's Second Symphony, which for some reason was a favorite of researchers on deep dives. Dark and foreboding, but ultimately triumphant. Why not? She hit play and let the orchestra take her to the ocean floor.

Eighty minutes later, traces of sediment floated in front of her running lights. She spoke into the microphone. "Kirov, can you read?"

No answer.

"Kirov?

"Yes, my dear. Nice to hear from you. I thought you'd fallen asleep down there."

"I was starting to think the same about you. I'm glad the underwater antenna is working so well. We usually need a lifeline to communicate with someone this far down. I'm nearing the floor."

"Do you see anything?"

"Not yet. Sonar shows me about sixty feet from the bottom. I'm about to hit the high beams."

Hannah turned on the high-wattage navigation lights, which cast an intense aura of illumination around *LISA*'s hull. After a few moments, she saw waves of silt on the ocean floor, almost like tiny sand dunes.

"I've arrived. I'm about a quarter of a mile north-northwest of the target site."

"Keep your eyes open. We don't know how precise their coordinates are. If it was dropped from the surface, it could have drifted."

"Tell me about it." She thought of the two halves of the *Titanic,* which went under at the same spot but ended up almost a mile apart on the bottom. "I'm going in."

She gripped the control stick and piloted *LISA* six feet over the ocean floor, moving slowly so as not to kick up too much silt. "Visibility's good. I'm nearing the target zone. Still no sign of anything unusual."

Christ, he hated this, Kirov thought.

He knew what it was like down there. He wanted to be in that pod with her.

No, he wanted to be in that pod instead of her.

Okay, keep his voice calm and casual. She didn't need to know he was in a panic. Support meant emotional as well as physical and mental. She was alone down there and doing her job. If even a hint of the terror he was feeling crept into his demeanor, then that claustrophobic pod could seem like a coffin to her.

"Do you see anything?"

"I'll tell you when I do. Don't be impatient. Wait. I see something. I'm moving in for a closer look."

Kirov was so focused on Hannah's voice from the radio that the sound of his satellite phone ringing startled him. It was in the cabin connected to its charger/antenna unit.

Should he answer or let it ring? He strode into the cabin to check the ID box.

Eugenia.

THIRTEEN

Hannah's eyes narrowed on the four large red canisters. Clustered together on the ocean floor, they measured four feet long and twelve inches in diameter. To her surprise, they rested precisely where the video file had indicated they would be. Either they had been placed there by a sub, or there was a built-in beacon that had relayed precise GPS coordinates after the canisters settled to the bottom.

Hannah slipped her hands into the glovelike controllers that operated the mechanical hands outside the pod. She flexed her fingers and watched the steel fingers outside mimic every movement. Although she had specified the device in many of her designs, she never ceased to be amazed by the finely articulated robotic hands. Television news stories often gave her the credit for the hand probes, but she took great pains to give proper credit to their brilliant young designer, a kinesiology professor from Cornell.

"Hannah, stop. Don't go any closer!" Kirov's voice was tense.
Hannah froze. "Why?"

"I just heard from Eugenia. Pavski may have *wanted* us to have that satchel."

"What?"

"She found out that Petrenko didn't pick up anyone last weekend because he wasn't even in the country. He was at an estate auction in Paris from Saturday to Monday. It was a setup. A trap. No one is closing in on the boat, so it must be down there. The canisters."

"Then what the hell am I looking at?"

"What do you see?"

"Four cylinders. They appear to be welded together. There's no silt on them, so they haven't been here for long. There's no way the *Silent Thunder* deposited them here six years ago."

"Are they missiles?"

"No, not like in the video, but they are red. They're less than three yards from me."

"Don't do anything."

"After all this time and effort, we're just going to pack up and take *LISA* home?"

"It could be a trap. Pavski may have *wanted* us to find those cylinders."

"You really believe that? If I hadn't thought to look at the files in that music player—"

"*I* would have thought of it. I would have eventually gone

through everything. And Pavski knows that. The information had to be hidden well enough that we wouldn't suspect a trap."

"You're giving him a lot of credit."

"He's earned it, believe me. A lot of people have died underestimating Pavski."

She stared at the cylinders. "It's so damned frustrating. They're right in front of me."

"It's not worth it, Hannah. It might be a booby trap."

"I won't go any closer. Let me at least do a sweep with the radio and sonar sensors."

Kirov paused for a long moment. "Okay, but be careful. And whatever you do, don't touch it."

She grasped a tiny joystick on the main console and focused the secondary parabolic antenna toward the canisters. She wished she were in one of her other pods, designed for salvage missions rather than the study of natural phenomena. *LISA*'s options were limited in this type of operation.

Hannah switched on the scanner to determine if the canisters were emanating radio waves. After a few seconds, the scanner's scope lit up with a rhythmic visual pattern. "Okay, I'm getting a low-frequency pulse. Probably the GPS locator signal."

"Fine. Now get out of there."

"Not yet. I'm bouncing sonar off them, and there appears to be some dense mass there. They're not hollow."

"I never thought they were. Happy now?"

"Just another few seconds." She steered *LISA* over the canisters to give her sensors a clearer shot. "Okay, I'm getting some magnetic readings."

"How intense?"

"Strong . . . and suddenly getting stronger." She watched the readout. "The magnetic readings are going through the roof."

"Hannah, you may have triggered an explosive device. Get the hell out of there!"

Hannah hit the ballast control. "I'm on my way."

The pod didn't move.

What in the hell?

Clang.

A heavy metallic sound echoed in the small pod, and *LISA* listed hard to the right. Hannah looked out the observation window.

The canisters were gone.

Their imprint was all that was left on the ocean floor.

"Hannah?" Kirov shouted.

"Christ!" She struggled with the controls. "I must have activated an electromagnet in those cylinders. It's attached itself to *LISA.*"

"Shake it off. Now!"

"I'm working on it!" She thrust the pod forward, skipping along the sea bottom. Each impact shook the pod with bone-numbing force.

Come on, *LISA*, hold together . . .

The canisters scraped along the hull, but remained affixed to *LISA*'s underside.

Shit.

She punched the ballast control and rocketed upward. The canisters shook against the intense pressure.

"Hurry," Kirov said. "Pavski doesn't believe in long trigger sequences."

The entire pod shook. Sweat ran down Hannah's face, and her nose suddenly dripped cold and wet.

Blood. From the sudden pressure change, she realized.

"Hannah . . . !"

"The cylinders aren't budging. I can't shake them!"

"Don't give up. *Try.*"

She tasted the blood in her mouth. Christ almighty.

A massive rock formation suddenly filled her front window. She pulled the control stick and spun clear.

A near miss. She'd seen it on the sonar on the way down, but thought she was farther away from—

Wait a second.

She eased off the ballast control and slowed her ascent. No time to figure all the angles on this one. She swung back and charged toward the formation.

Was she out of her mind?

No doubt. A six-inch piloting error would slam her against a rock wall.

But any port in a storm . . .

She gunned the engines, hurtling faster toward the craggy formation.

Study the features, pick the best spot . . .

At the last instant, she tilted forty-five degrees to the port side and skimmed over the formation, ramming the cylinders against its sheer face. She accelerated and pulled the auxiliary ballast tank release lever. Compressed air blasted from the pod's back-side, further repelling the magnetized cylinders while *LISA* sped away.

She was free!

No time to celebrate, she thought. Keep moving.

Hannah pushed the engine harder. "Come on, baby. Give me some distance."

Her rearview screen suddenly lit up with a white, intense light that cast an eerily beautiful glow over the area. The underwater formation was now part of a majestic mountain range, stretching as far as Hannah could see.

The shock wave hit a moment later.

The pod violently rocked and tilted on its axis, spinning out of control as the power flickered on and off. Hannah gritted her teeth and closed her eyes as a dull roar overtook *LISA*.

She felt the bomb's explosive force in the hull, the equipment plates, in her bones and teeth.

No way in hell could *LISA* withstand this kind of force.

Then, finally, it stopped.

Total silence, except for the high-pitched whine of the emergency lamps.

Hannah opened her eyes and was startled when *LISA*'s power systems suddenly came back online.

She checked the diagnostic readings. All critical systems functioning normally.

She took a deep breath and smiled. "Good girl."

Two hours later Hannah sat in the rental boat's main cabin, holding a mask to her face and slowly breathing the pure oxygen needed to treat the ill effects of her rapid ascension . . .

Kirov turned from the wheel. "How are you feeling? Still faint?"

"A little. Funny thing about hyperbaric chambers. There's never one around when you need one."

"Do you want me to radio for a helicopter?"

"You'd really do that? It would be pretty hard to hide from Bradworth after drawing that kind of attention."

"I'd find a way."

"No need. It's not that severe. I was careful coming up."

"We should be back at the *Aurora* by nightfall. I spoke to Captain Tanbury during your ascent, and he says no one is giving him trouble about *LISA*'s absence yet."

"Good." Hannah pulled a blanket tight around her. "You're right about Pavski—it's not wise to underestimate him. He almost killed me down there."

"*I'm* the one he wants dead. Remember, if you hadn't been so stubborn, I would have been with you."

"If you'd been with me, we'd both be dead. The only reason I was able to maneuver with that bomb weighing me down was that *LISA* was a man short."

"Stop being reasonable. I'm not in the mood for logic." Kirov sat down next to her. "I'm mad as hell."

"At me?"

"Yes, you should have gotten out of there." He scowled. "No, I'm mad at myself. I should have seen it coming."

"Why? How could you? I sure as hell didn't."

"I know Pavski. After all these years, I should know how his mind works. He obviously knows how *mine* works."

Hannah studied him. "When this is over, after Pavski is dead, what will you do then?"

"You think my entire existence has been defined by a thirst for revenge? Once I lay down this last piece of the puzzle, my life will have no meaning?"

"It crossed my mind."

"Not true. Just the opposite, in fact."

"How do you mean?"

"My life will have meaning only after Pavski is gone. Until then, I have to stay in limbo."

"In limbo?"

"Yes. Caught between my old life and the new life to come."

"It's a long time to be in limbo."

"For a while I was dead inside, and then I began to come alive again. There are all kinds of pleasures to be had in this world. There are good people as well as evil, new worlds to be discovered if you have the eyes to see them. Companionship and sex." He shrugged. "Perhaps even love. Though that's the grand prize and not to be taken for granted."

"I don't believe you take anything for granted."

"I did once. I'll never do it again." He reached over and pulled the blanket closer around her. "You've probably never looked uglier in your life. Your nose is swollen, your eyes are bloodshot, and you're white as a sheet."

"Thanks. Do you want to make me feel worse?"

"No, I just wanted you to know that it doesn't make any difference." He gently brushed a scraggly tendril of hair away from her cheek. "Everything you are still shines out of you. You're like *Silent Thunder*. All the strength and the grace and the spirit. No matter how beat-up you get, no matter how much punishment you take, nothing can take that away." He leaned forward and brushed his lips across her forehead. "And I'm sorry I risked you because I didn't think far enough ahead."

She didn't know what to say. She was feeling . . . "That's the second time you compared me to *Silent Thunder*," she said unevenly. "I'm not a sub, dammit. Conner used to tell me that I identified more with machines, but he never said I was like one."

"Perhaps because he never reached that final empathy that some men have with ships and the sea. Close but not quite there." His hand dropped away from her cheek. "From what you told me he was very much involved in the human race."

Her cheek felt strange, sensitive, now that he was no longer touching it. "Yes, he was that." She felt too close to him, too . . . intimate. She straightened. Get back to business. "What's next, Kirov?"

"After we return *LISA,* we need to pay another visit to our favorite antiques dealer. Petrenko was obviously instructed by someone to give us that satchel, so there may be some coercion in order to find out what he knows."

"Just don't ask me to wait in the car again. After what I've been through this morning, I'd like to see him get anything you can dish out."

"As you wish." Kirov nodded. "By the way, I could hear you in the pod even when you couldn't hear me."

"So?"

"You were on quite friendly terms with *LISA* down there. 'Give me some distance, baby.' 'Good girl.' Is that any way to speak to an inanimate object?"

"It's just . . . slang."

"It was more than that. *LISA* surprised you, didn't she?"

"Yes. She's—*It's* very well constructed."

"And well designed."

Hannah bowed her head with mock modesty. "Well, now that you mention it . . ."

"But there's more there, and you know it."

"You mean a soul."

"Yes, and when the chips were down, even *you* felt it. I guess there are no atheists in foxholes, eh? Had you ever called a vessel 'she' in your life?"

Hannah sighed. There was no use arguing with him. "I'm sure I've slipped once or twice."

He smiled. "There's hope for you yet, Hannah Bryson."

The call from Pavksi had finally come.

After days of trailing Congressman Preston, Dananka had received his instructions. It wasn't what he had expected, but in this business, he'd learned to expect the unexpected.

Preston was a full block ahead of him.

There was obviously more to Preston than met the eye, or Pavski's orders wouldn't have been so urgent. What had seemed to be a fool's errand suddenly became much more interesting.

Preston disappeared in the shadows. Shit. Where did he go?

Dananka walked faster, keeping his eyes peeled for any sign of the congressman.

Preston finally stepped from the shadows, walking back toward him.

"Preston?"

Preston stopped. "Yes?"

"I'm Dananka. I was told you were expecting me."

"Unfortunately."

"No time like the present." Dananka reached into his pocket and pulled out a velour-covered ring box.

Preston tensed. "What's that?"

"Well, I'm not asking you to marry me." He opened the ring box to display a tiny wireless microphone. "You know what to do with this?"

"Pavski explained it to me. There's an adhesive backing, and I'm to put it somewhere in Cathy Bryson's living room."

"Correct. Behind a picture frame, maybe on the underside of a lampshade. Just like in the movies."

Preston took the box and closed it.

Dananka handed him a disposable cell phone. "He'll call you tomorrow morning at 9:30 A.M. Be sure this is turned on." Dananka smiled maliciously. "Would you care to tell me what Pavski has on you?"

"I would not." Preston turned and strode away from him. "Good night, Mr. Dananka."

evice delivered," Dananka told Pavski when he picked up the phone. "And so was the message."

"Good," Pavski said absently, and hung up the phone. He spread the photos from the Danzyl delivery out on the desk in front of him. He had gone through these photos after Heiser's father's death, but he hadn't remembered there were so many of them. There were at least forty or fifty ranging from childhood to the professor's senior years. The GRU had taken them out of the family albums at Pavski's request after Heiser's death on the sub. He'd thought there might be a clue among them after he'd been cheated of interrogating the old man. He'd studied these photos for hours all those years ago, but he'd found nothing.

Or maybe he had found something and not realized it. That symbol on the plate had not been Samsovian but it had been damnably familiar. He had seen it somewhere . . .

He'd gone through over thirty photos when he found it. He froze in his chair.

A photo of Heiser smiling into the camera. He was outside in the sunlight and behind him . . .

Yes.

FAIRFIELD, CONNECTICUT

A yellow crime scene police tape now stretched in front of Petrenko's antiques store.

"Not an encouraging sign," Kirov said. "We may have difficulty getting answers to those questions."

"Pavski?"

"We'll have to see, won't we?"

Hannah peered through the front windows. "Nothing looks as though it's been disturbed."

"Let's check in back. Most of these shops have living quarters over the store."

In the rear of the store a wooden stairway led up to a second-floor apartment over the store.

"It seems this shop is no exception." Hannah climbed the steps and knocked on the weathered oak door.

No answer.

Kirov glanced around and produced his lockpick.

Hannah used her body to try to shield him from view. "This isn't a good idea. It's a crime scene. What if a policeman—"

"The store is a crime scene. Not the apartment."

"You're quibbling."

"Yes." He bent over the door. "And breaking and entering is small stuff compared to what Petrenko tried to help do to us. Get a little perspective."

A young female voice called from below. "You don't have to break in. I'll unlock it for you."

Anna, the teenager who had held the gun on them only two days earlier, stood at the bottom of the stairs. She carried a bag of groceries in one hand, a set of keys in the other.

"What happened, Anna?" Hannah asked.

Anna didn't speak as she trudged upstairs and unlocked the door. "Petrenko's dead, that's what happened." She threw open the door and walked inside.

"How?" Hannah said.

"Two bullets in the head. I found him behind the main counter yesterday afternoon when I came home. The police think it was a robbery."

"What do *you* think?" Kirov asked.

"It wasn't a fucking robbery." Anna deposited the contents of her grocery bag into an already-stuffed knapsack on the floor. "The cash register was emptied, but we never had much money in there. It's a check and credit card business. There were a pair of twenty-five hundred dollar vases right next to the register, and they were untouched."

"I'm sorry," Hannah said. "You said that he wasn't your father. How was he related to you?"

"He wasn't."

"Boyfriend?" Kirov said.

She made a face. "Please. He was my *mother's* boyfriend. Two years ago, my mom got a new guy, and she left us both. I didn't have any other family, so Petrenko let me stay with him."

"That was nice of him," Hannah said gently.

"Yeah." For the first time, Hannah saw genuine emotion creep from behind Anna's tough veneer. "He didn't have to do that. He was a nice guy. You know, until that time I never liked him. He was just another one of mom's guys."

"Do the police have any suspects?"

"I told the police about the two of you."

Kirov's lips twisted. "Of course."

"I had to do it. But I told them that I didn't think you were involved. Petrenko pretended to be afraid of you, but he wasn't really. I could tell." She shrugged. "I was always worried about something like this happening. He dealt with nasty people. He was into some bad stuff. Smuggling antiques, smuggling people."

"But not last weekend," Kirov said.

She shook her head. "No, but somebody paid him a lot of money to make sure you got that bag."

"We know that now," Hannah said. "Can you give us any idea who?"

"No. Petrenko didn't even tell me about it until after you left here. Here I was ready to blow your heads off, and he'd actually been *waiting* for you to show up. Someone must have made the arrangements with him after he got back from Paris on Monday." She frowned. "Are you detectives or something?"

"Or something." Hannah glanced at Anna's duffel bag. "Where are you going?"

"A long way from here."

"Where?"

"Don't know."

"Honey, you just can't—"

"Why not? I'm only four months away from my eighteenth birthday, and I'd rather not spend that time trying to break free of Protective Services," Anna said. She zipped the duffel closed. "I'll be fine. I've already been accepted at Cal Arts for the fall semester. If I'm careful, I'll be able to get by on student loans and tuition grants."

Kirov handed her a thick fold of bills. "Until then, this might help you get where you're going."

She pocketed the bills without counting them. "If you thought I'd refuse this, you thought wrong. Everybody needs help sometime. I'll just pass it along when it's my turn." She nodded as she headed for the door. "Thanks."

She stopped, hesitating at the door. "Look, there was another package."

"What?" Kirov said. "Along with the satchel?"

"No, it was brought in the night before Petrenko was killed. It was a rush job. Someone came to the shop to pick it up."

"Have you any idea what was in it?"

She shook her head. "But Petrenko did. He opened it and looked through it before he turned it over. I was thinking maybe he shouldn't have done that."

"It wasn't smart. Chances were the package had a security seal to tell if it had been tampered with. He might have signed his death warrant."

"He was nervous. You scared him. He didn't want to have that happen again."

"You don't know anything about the contents?"

"It was from Moscow. There was an official-type paper on top and other papers and letters, photos and stuff underneath." She frowned, thinking. "And there was a name stamped on the folder. I caught a glimpse of it but I only caught a few letters before Petrenko shoved it back in the package."

"Can you remember?"

"It was Russian. Petrenko was teaching me but it was damn hard. H, E, I . . ." She shook her head. "That's it. Does it help?"

"It helps," Kirov said.

"I'm glad." She opened the door. "Good luck to you. And if that good luck means catching up with the guy who killed Petrenko, I hope you score big."

Hannah turned to Kirov as the door shut behind Anna. "The information packet your source in Moscow said Pavski was expecting? Heiser?"

"Probably."

"Which Heiser? Captain Heiser or his father?"

"I'd bet he wanted more background on Heiser's father. Heiser was trying to tell his father about the location of the cradle. Everything was aimed at him."

"But Pavski has the plates. What does he need with info about Heiser's father?"

"I've no idea. I find it curious that it was a rush job. That means he did send for it after he had the plates. That may mean he saw something on the plates that he wanted to verify."

"What?"

He shrugged. "But if Pavski wanted in-depth information about Heiser, then I believe we should have it too." He reached for his phone. "I'll fax Eugenia all the information we've gathered plus the transcript of Heiser's conversation with his father. Let's see what she can come up with."

After they left Petrenko's shop, Hannah and Kirov drove to a coffeehouse in nearby Bridgeport, where they sat on the patio and studied printouts of the sonar readings Hannah had made from *LISA*. The pages almost resembled X-rays, offering red-tinted views of the cylinders and the tight clumps of mass within them.

Hannah found it difficult to concentrate on the pages. She was haunted by her last sight of Anna, duffel slung over her shoulder and all alone in the world. So strong, yet so sad. Hannah had always been independent, but she'd never lacked loving family support. Every kid should be entitled to that security. It should be written on a human bill of rights.

Kirov was frowning down at the readout. "You know, I think your experience with that explosive device on the ocean floor could be of use to us."

Hannah snapped to attention. "How?"

"If we knew who built it, we might be able to track him to Pavski."

"Well, I don't recall seeing a name and address engraved on the damned thing."

"No, but we now know that the device had some unique characteristics." He pointed to one of the canisters. "Pavski and I both knew a man named Dane Niler, who was probably the best underwater demolitions expert in the Russian Navy. Twenty years ago, he designed a series of mines that are still used in every ocean on the planet."

Hannah looked closer at the scan. "You think this is his work?"

"It's a strong possibility. I hear he's been doing a lot of work for South American drug lords in the past few years. They hide their shipments in underwater containers to throw off the drug-sniffing dogs, and Dane secures them with his booby traps. I'm told many of them are damn ingenious."

"Ingenious like a bomb that suddenly turns into an electromagnet and clamps itself to the target?"

"It seems like something Dane would create. I've never known him to work with Pavski, but there's a first time for everything."

"So how does that help us?"

"Dane is a mercenary. Even if Pavski is paying him, he's still looking for his next job."

Hannah nodded. "So if a lucrative offer suddenly floated in his direction, he might surface."

"Exactly."

"But how are you going to float such an offer if you don't know where he is?"

Kirov reached again for his phone. "Where there's Eugenia, there's a way."

"Aren't you putting a lot of pressure on her?"

"Checking the GRU package is going to be dicey. Finding Niler should be fairly easy for her." He started to dial. "Besides, Eugenia thrives on pressure . . ."

Yes." Eugenia's voice was uncharacteristically subdued as she answered the phone.

"What's wrong?" Kirov said. "Are you all right?"

She hesitated before replying. "Yes. You know, just very busy these days. What do you need?"

"I need some information on Dane Niler."

"Last I heard, he was working out of Florida somewhere. What do you want with him?"

"He might be working with Pavski now. I need you to find out."

"My usual sources have been compromised, Kirov. Pavski obviously knows they've been working on your behalf." She paused. "I also have excellent reason to believe he knows I've been helping you."

"I know, Eugenia. I never meant this to happen." He paused. "I'm sorry, but you'll need to find a way to insulate yourself from this. Petrenko was murdered yesterday, so Pavski might be taking extra pains to cover his tracks."

"I understand. I'll call you when I hear something."

"Be very careful, Eugenia."

"I always am, Kirov. I always am."

Eugenia cut the connection and dropped down on the stairs

leading up from her office ground floor. Christ, she felt limp. She was actually shaking.

She stared into the foyer at the dead man lying gazing blindly up at the ceiling. Blood drained from the four tightly clustered bullet wounds in his torso. His twitching right hand still clutched the .38 handgun he'd pulled on her after she'd opened the door for his supposed delivery. She hadn't expected to be this shaken at killing a man. The years of being away from the KGB must have taken their toll. She was softer now. And she liked being softer, dammit. She liked her life, and she liked not having to put down pigs like that man in foyer.

But you couldn't ignore what you are, any more than what you were. There was always someone knocking on your door to remind you.

She leaned against the railing and closed her eyes. She'd have to move soon. That body had to disappear if she was to keep this good life intact. No problem. She had contacts who could take care of it.

Not yet. She would give herself a few more minutes.

Be careful, Kirov had said.

"Yes, my friend," she whispered wearily as she put her Walther P99 semiautomatic on the stair next to the cordless telephone. "I'm always a very careful girl."

FOURTEEN

CIA Agent Bruce Fahey climbed the snowy hill overlooking greater Koriazhma, an industrial town that boasted one of Russia's largest paper mills. He'd been warned that the mill's odors could be overpowering, but the subzero temperature now dampened most of the smells. Biting winds roared down the hillside.

"It's somewhere around here, isn't it?" The CIA trainee, Cal Wilkes, who was struggling behind him, was short of breath, and his nose was cherry red from the cold.

"It's on the other side of the hill," Fahey said impatiently. "Didn't you read the packet?"

"Uh, yeah," Wilkes said. "I guess I just got turned around."

The kid was never going to develop the stuff to become a field agent, Fahey thought. At least, he was also accompanied by two Russian operatives who might be of some help.

Maybe.

The Russians were ostensibly there to provide assistance, but he knew their primary purpose was similar to his own: to find out if Dimitri Ivanov, the man Kirov claimed to be, was actually dead. If Bradworth's source was correct, the answer was less than a hundred yards away.

Fahey had worked in Russia for the past two decades, long enough to see the end of the Cold War era. As far as he knew, the Russians now "assisting" him had tried to uncover his identity and kill him several times during his many undercover assignments. He wasn't naïve enough to believe that they still wouldn't eliminate him if the political winds shifted only slightly.

"It's pretty cold, isn't it?" the kid asked. "You don't seem to feel it."

"I feel it."

The kid had been alternating between making inane comments and pumping him for stories about the good old days, Fahey thought, like so many other WASPy recruits who found themselves increasingly irrelevant in an agency that now prized brown skin and knowledge of Middle Eastern dialects. Poor bastard. He'd be lucky if he wound up with an agency research job in an archive basement somewhere.

They reached the hill's summit and walked down the other side, stepping carefully to avoid the slick patches of ice. Fahey pointed to the remains of a wooden gazebo. "Okay, it should be ten yards west of there."

One of the Russians turned on a metal detector and passed the disc-shaped sensor over the designated area. The small speaker buzzed, indicating the presence of metal at the site. Fahey kicked the area, and his heel made a hollow thumping sound on the earth.

"This is it. There used to be a house over there, and this was the vegetable cellar. Let's go."

The Russians handed Fahey and Wilkes a pair of shovels, and the four men uncovered a four-inch layer of dirt and snow that obscured the varnished wooden doors. The metal hinges and latch were almost rusted through.

"Help me with this," Fahey said.

The four men pulled on the right door, and the wood and metalwork crumbled as they tossed it aside.

Fahey pulled out his flashlight and shined it downward.

The kid's eyes narrowed as squinted down into the cellar. "Holy shit," he whispered.

lorida is a big state," Hannah said, as their rental car entered the ramp that would take them onto I-85 South. "Shouldn't we have some idea where we're headed?"

"I have the utmost faith in Eugenia."

"And that means?"

"By the time we hit the state line, we should have all the information we need."

"A jet would get us there a lot faster." They had taken a jet only as far as Atlanta and picked up the rental car at the airport.

"But not as safely. I took the risk of the flight out of Boston, but I didn't have time to get you ID that would keep your name off the transportation grid. An airport visual recognition scanner could still bring our trip to an abrupt halt."

Hannah nodded. "I guess you're right. I wouldn't put it past Bradworth to transmit our photos to every law enforcement database in the country."

"I can guarantee it, but we should be safe here on the road. It's a long drive, but if we take turns, we'll be there in less than a day. The highways are this country's last bastion of anonymity, and the driver's license and credit card I used shouldn't raise any red flags with the rental car company."

"You have all the bases covered."

He shrugged. "I've been doing this for a long time."

Hannah watched him for a long moment. "Have you ever thought of giving up?"

"Never."

"When will it be enough?"

"When Pavski is dead, and not a moment before. When will it be enough for you?"

"I don't know. Sometimes I think it would be worse for him to just rot in prison for the rest of his life. Sometimes I just want to blow his head off. At the moment, I'm leaning toward decapitating the bastard."

"That's good, because Pavski wouldn't rot in prison no matter what Bradworth promises you. Pavski is too valuable to them. He has immense, albeit dated, knowledge of the Russian Atlantic Fleet and command protocols. And he knows where all the bodies are buried in the present Russian bureaucracy. If we turn him over to Bradworth, Pavski will probably become the permanent resident of a government-run resort with his own private beach. To earn it, he would provide assistance to U.S. intelligence whenever a situation developed."

"Sounds like a pretty sweet deal."

"It is. He's sipping piña coladas, and you have a lifetime of remembering how your brother looked that night in the sub."

Sudden rage flared in her. "Stop it. You don't need to do that."

"Do what?"

"Stoke the fires by reminding me of Conner." Hannah's voice shook with anger. "It's okay that we're using each other to get what we want here, but it's not okay for you to use Conner. Understood?"

Kirov paused a long moment before nodding. "Understood. May I just say I didn't mean to use him? Sometimes manipulation comes a little too easy to me. Forgive me."

And this wasn't manipulation. Kirov meant what he was saying. She could feel the anger ebbing away. She tried to hold on to it. "Is that supposed to disarm me?"

He smiled. "I hope so."

And it had disarmed her, dammit.

LANGLEY, VIRGINIA

Bradworth picked up his telephone. "Fahey, where are you?"

"I'm at the site on my satellite phone. Your source was correct. There are skeletal human remains in the vegetable cellar. Adult male."

"Is there enough material to extract DNA?"

"There should be. We're almost finished packing it up."

"Good. What about size?"

"I measured the fibula, and the height calculations jibe with Ivanov. This man was about six-foot-one. We'll know more once we get it into a lab. By the way, do we know where we're headed with it yet?"

"One of our specialists is already on his way to Moscow. We'll be using the facilities at the Burdenko Military Hospital there. We found an uncle of Ivanov's, and he's given us a blood sample so that we can compare DNA."

"Good. We'll have the skeleton there by this afternoon." Fahey's voice lowered. "Bradworth, his skeleton was hacked to pieces by a barrage of bullets. Somebody *really* didn't like this guy."

VALDOSTA, GEORGIA
6:15 A.M.

Kirov's cell phone ring broke the silence as Hannah drove past a marker on I-75 informing her that the Florida state line was only forty-four miles away.

Kirov put the phone on speaker mode. "You're up early, Eugenia."

"Actually, not that early for me. I'm in Moscow."

"What?"

"I have to be done with this mess you brought on me. It's become dangerous to my business and my health."

"You can opt out."

"No, I can't. But I can handle it myself. My contacts are good, but I'm better." She went on brusquely, "There are two GRU operatives who are known to sell information and services to the highest bidder. Salvak and Danzyl. I'm betting on Danzyl. From what I've learned, he worked closely with Pavski before he was sent packing from Moscow."

"And can we get him to sell information to you?"

"I don't think so. And if I tap Salvak, Danzyl may hear about it and make things difficult for me. I'm having to walk very carefully. I may have to find another way." She changed the subject. "And I didn't forget about Dane. I've just been a little busy. Your bomb maker is working in Florida. Panama City. He should be fairly easy to find."

"Well, unless you were able to come up with a street address—"

"9860 South Thomas Drive."

Kirov frowned. "Eugenia, how were you able to—"

"The Yellow Pages. Brilliant, yes?"

"Are you positive it's him?"

"No doubt. It's the address of his bar."

"They all know him there?"

"They should. He owns it."

He shot Hannah a glance. "You're not serious."

"He's actually in semiretirement from the bomb-making business. As far as I can tell, he won't work for terrorists or mobsters, which keeps him off high-priority U.S. watch lists. If you're hoping to draw him out by promising employment, it might not work. He does quite well by selling tall, colorful drinks on the beach."

"What's the name of the bar?"

"You're really going to like this. It's called 'TNT.' "

A few hours later Kirov lowered his high-powered binoculars and handed them to Hannah. "See it?" he asked.

Hannah scanned the beachfront bars until she found TNT. The colorful sign featured a graphic stick of dynamite traced in neon lighting. She shook her head. "Subtle." She smiled. "And amusing. He obviously has a sense of humor."

"I'm sure he gets a good chuckle every time he looks at it."

"Maybe he's not who we're searching for. It doesn't look like he needs Pavski's money."

"It may not be the cash. He's always considered himself an artist. He likes money as much as the next man, but I'm sure he still jumps at the chance to create new and better designs for his explosive devices. Especially if a lucrative offer came from someone he knows and trusts."

"Like Pavski?"

"Yes."

"Or you?"

"If he did the job for Pavksi, I'm not sure what he's been told about me. We can't just go stumbling in there. We have to have information."

"And how do we get that?"

"It's an electronic world. We'll try that first. But he's very smart. We have to have a hook."

"You know what he's like. What kind of a hook? What buttons can we push?"

"His ego, his conviction that he's the Michelangelo of explosives, his passion for good-looking women, his love of the good life." He took the binoculars from her. "Come on, we'll check into a hotel and clean up and plan strategy."

They found a decent Best Western Hotel located on the beach. Two hours later they had showered, rested, and met in the coffee shop on the lanai for dinner.

"The fish looks good," Kirov said as he handed her the menu. "Fish is almost always a safe bet on the coast. The competition for the tourist dollar is a guarantee."

Hannah nodded. "Order for me. I don't care. Anything."

"You're trusting me to make a decision?"

She smiled faintly. "I figured you couldn't mess up too badly on a menu choice."

"I'm flattered." He gestured to the waitress and ordered quickly before turning back to Hannah. "Did you get a nap?"

"No, I got a business call, and I had to take it."

"Business?"

"I do have a life apart from *Silent Thunder*. The sub was supposed to only be a fill-in job." She waited until the waitress filled her wineglass, then said, "I'm going to the Canary Islands and help with the exploration of Marinth. It's an underwater city that some people think may be Atlantis."

"I've read about it. The security surrounding it is cast-iron. Skeptic that I am, I wondered if that security was hiding a bogus discovery."

"It's not bogus. It's the real thing. I've seen some of the artifacts they've pulled up." She took a sip of wine and leaned forward, eagerness surging through her as she thought about it. "I don't know if it's Atlantis, but the city is ancient. It's going to be exciting. I can't wait."

"It's good to see you excited." He was studying her expression. "I haven't had the opportunity since we came together. Were you like this with the *Titanic*?"

She shook her head. "We knew too much about it going in. Marinth is different. It's a whole new world to explore." She chuckled. "You said something like that to me, remember? That there were new worlds to discover. Well, Marinth is one of them. Scholarly tablets and ancient inventions and fabulous treasures. Who knows what we'll find?"

"Who indeed?" He was cradling his glass of wine in his hands, rolling it back and forth. "A true adventure."

Hannah found herself fascinated by that lazy, almost sensual movement. The crystal seemed fragile, infinitely breakable in those big hands, and his rubbing fingertips were light but oddly rhythmic.

Watch his hands.

Eugenia had said those words when she'd been describing Kirov's sexuality. Hannah could see what she meant. That restrained, rhythmic delicacy made one wonder how it would feel to be intimately touched by—

"But treasures?" Kirov asked. "I didn't think you'd be impressed by treasures. You didn't seem interested in the Golden Cradle itself. Yet the cradle is probably as ancient as your Marinth."

"I'm interested." She forced herself to look away from him and bring her mind back to the subject at hand. "But it's hard to think of the cradle without thinking of all the death and pain it's caused. I'm sure your sub's crew and Conner were only the latest in a long history."

"You're probably right."

"But you don't make the connection?"

"Not once the first pain passed. Look at all the treasures we lust after. The Amber Rooms, the Holy Grail, the Ark of the Covenant. They dazzle us and draw us like beacons. The cradle is incredibly beautiful, but it's an object. Most treasures are created by man and, therefore, coveted by man. Men are violent creatures and will grab what they covet. That's why treasures must be guarded."

"How philosophical."

"I'm a realist." He met her eyes. "If I was taught anything at all by the Golden Cradle, it was to hold on to what I value and not ever let go."

She felt heat surge through her. She looked down into the wine in her glass. "Providing you live long enough."

He laughed. "There is that. Ah, here comes our food. Do you want to discuss Dane over dinner or wait until later?"

"We'd better discuss him now. After dinner I have something to do."

His brows lifted. "Really? What?"

She smiled at the waitress as she set her salad before her. "I have to go shopping."

Good morning, pretty lady." The bartender smiled at Hannah as she stepped off the sand and took a seat at the long bamboo bar. It was 11:15 A.M., and she was TNT's only customer.

She adjusted the flower-print skirt and bikini top. She wasn't comfortable in this outfit, but it had definite male appeal, and distraction was the name of the game. "Good morning. Am I your first customer of the day?"

"Yep."

No trace of a Russian accent, she noticed. The man was good-looking and had a beautiful bronze tan and unruly golden hair. No different than a thousand other beach bums she'd known. "Maybe it's too early for a drink?"

"Wrong. If that was the case, I would've slept in." He poured himself a shot of Bacardi and downed it. "You're on the Florida coast, honey. It's always time for a drink."

She smiled. "Okay, you talked me into it. Start me with one of those shots."

"Now you're talking." He poured the Bacardi and pushed the glass over to her.

She swallowed the shot. "Is this your place?"

He nodded. "You like it?"

"Very much. My name is Hannah."

"Nice to meet you. I'm Dane. Everyone around here calls me

Great Dane." His eyes were twinkling as he saw her brows raise. "I know. I know. But believe me when I say that it's nothing I expect or encourage."

Dane Niler in the flesh. This smiling, attractive man might have built the bomb that almost killed her, she realized. "I like the name of your bar, Dane. TNT. How did you come up with it?"

"I like surprises."

"Nothing more surprising than a stick of dynamite going off, I guess."

"Well, if you want to be literal about it. But since I'm a pretentious son of a bitch, I happen to like metaphors. When people sit at my bar, I want them to blow up all their inhibitions, all their preconceived notions, and start from a new place. Take a vacation from themselves, you know?"

"Interesting. It sounds like something I need to do."

"Then you've come to the right place. What brings you to Panama City? You're not from here, are you?"

"It shows?"

"Afraid so."

"You're obviously a student of human nature. Why don't *you* tell me what I'm doing here?"

"Oh, I figure you're in town for a conference. You looked at the schedule, and this morning's sessions were a little on the dry side, so you decided to log a little beach time."

"Wow."

"Impressed?"

"Dane, you couldn't be more wrong."

He smiled. "Okay, so I'm a lousy student of human nature." He held up the Bacardi bottle. "Another?"

"Sure."

He poured her another shot. "Normally, I'd go right to the second possibility—you're tagging along with your husband, and *he's* the one here on a conference. He's in a Hyatt ballroom learning about new actuarial analysis techniques, and you're trying to find ways to fill your days."

"You don't think that's the case?"

"Nah. A woman like you doesn't tag along with anybody. People tag along with *you*." He smiled. "Am I getting warm?"

"Warmer." She glanced at a small black-and-white monitor behind Dane. It offered a view of the bar's parking lot, where a single car, a Nissan Z-98, was parked. Kirov crouched next to the car, working on the lock.

Dane chuckled. "Warmer, huh? Okay. How about this: It's been years since you've taken a vacation, and your company's human resources department insisted that you take off for a couple of weeks. But now that you're here, all you can do is think about work."

"That's depressing. You've got me totally pegged. And here I thought I was a unique and fascinating individual."

"We all get lucky sometimes." He shifted position, as if about to turn toward the monitor.

Hannah quickly leaned closer to him. "I'd say you're an *excellent* student of human nature, Dane. How does your wife manage you?"

He turned back toward her. "I'm not married. Life's too short for the ties that bind. There are too many gorgeous ladies that need my attention."

She shot a quick glance at the monitor. Kirov was in the car's front seat, rifling through the glove compartment.

"I'm sure you give it to them."

"Another drink?"

"Not yet."

He refilled her glass anyway. "On the house."

"How can I possibly drink this? There are at least thirty other bars along this beach I need to visit by tonight."

"You'd only be wasting your time. You're already sitting at the best place in town."

Hannah laughed and stole another glance at the monitor. Kirov was gone.

She drank the shot, slipped off the stool, and tossed a twenty onto the bar. "I might come back and give you my verdict at the end of the night. Will you still be here?"

"I'll make sure that I am. I close at 1:00 A.M."

She gave him a brilliant smile. "Have a nice day, Dane."

He's gorgeous," Hannah said five minutes later, when Kirov opened the car door for her. "He's like something out of *Baywatch,* only better."

"I forgot to tell you what a charmer he is." His lips tightened. "You're definitely mellow."

"Trust me, if I'm a little woozy, it's not because of his charm. I just downed three rum shots in the space of five minutes."

"I'm surprised you're still on your feet."

She shrugged. "I've had practice keeping up with hard-drinking sailors. So what did you find out?"

"Not much. I found the auto registration, but he used the bar as his address. There were receipts indicating that he often eats drive-through fast food on the way home after work. There was a gym bag with workout clothes in the backseat."

"Which he probably wears to work off all that fast food. Nothing else?"

"No. It was always a long shot, but there was no DayRunner, PDA, or anything that could lead us to Pavski. There was a luggage tag on the gym bag that had Dane's name and phone number. I might be able to use it to get a home address."

"Even if it's unlisted?"

He shrugged. "Eugenia has made me a bit paranoid, so I'd like to stay away from my usual contacts if I can."

"So what are we going to do?"

Kirov turned the wheel sharply and pulled into a convenience store parking lot. "Wait here."

Before she could reply, Kirov jumped out of the car and walked quickly to a pay phone. He thumbed through the Yellow Pages telephone directory, deposited some coins, and made a call. She watched as he repeated the process several times, then finally hung up and climbed back into the car.

"What was that about?"

Kirov scribbled something down on a scratch pad. "It was about getting Dane Niler's address."

"Who gave you that?"

"Papa John's Pizza."

Hannah thought about it for a moment. "You called every pizza place in the vicinity of those other fast-food restaurants . . ."

"Exactly. When one orders a pizza delivery, the first thing the store does is ask for a phone number. That pulls up the customer address in their database, which the order taker reads aloud to confirm. I only had to call three other restaurants before I found one that Niler had previously ordered from." He handed her the pad. "Let's map this through the GPS device."

"Are we going to break in?"

"Hell, no. Believe me, we don't want to go in there. Think about it. Niler is one of the world's leading experts in explosive booby traps, and he could have a most lethal idea of what constitutes a home security system."

"Then I'm surprised you were willing to break into his car."

"It was a risk, but people in Niler's profession don't usually like to drive around town in cars packed with explosive materials. Too dangerous. A little fender bender could blow him to Kingdom Come." Kirov shrugged. "I might have to resort to bare-knuckled diplomacy to find out if he knows anything."

"There may be another way."

"How?"

"I think he and I have a date tonight."

"What?"

"I told him I'd meet him at closing time."

"Five minutes alone with him, and you—"

"I didn't really think I'd go. I was flirting with him, trying to keep his eyes off the security monitor, and I said I might drop by at closing time—1:00 A.M. He said he'd be there."

"Sounds like a date to me," he said grimly.

"I'll go back to his place with him, get the lay of the land, and see what kind of booby traps he may have in place. If I get a chance, I'll check his caller ID logs on his home and cell phones. Anything else I should look for?"

"This isn't a good idea. When you decided you wanted to play vamp to distract him, I didn't like it, but I went along. The risk wasn't that great. But this is different."

"Vamp? I wasn't trying to vamp him. You said he liked women, and I knew I could keep his attention for five or ten minutes. If I was Cinderella's ugly stepsister, I could have done that."

"But not as well. I'd bet you bowled Niler over."

"He's not that easy. The beach is crawling with women who want to sample an episode with a passing ship in the night."

"But not one who looks like she thinks as well as she fucks."

The rawness of that curt sentence stunned her for a moment. "I'm going to do it, Kirov. You can be my backup."

"Your support team again?" he said sourly.

"We'll use the speakerphone function on your cell. I'll keep it on me, and you can listen to every word."

"It's still a risk. He may be Mr. Charisma, but I assure you, he's smart, and he can be very dangerous."

"I can do this, Kirov. It might get us one step closer to Pavski."

He was silent. "I'm not going to talk you out of it, am I?"

"No," she repeated. "What else should I look for in there?"

Kirov said curtly, "Computer passwords."

FIFTEEN

"What do you know? The pretty lady returns." Niler smiled at her, leaning on the counter. "A dream come true."

Hannah stepped off the sand and glanced around the empty bar. "Does anyone but me ever come in here?"

"Slow day, so-so evening. The place pretty much cleared out after midnight. I might have closed early if I hadn't thought you might be back."

"Pretty sure of yourself, aren't you?"

"I could but hope." He smiled. "Okay, I'm pretty damned sure of myself."

"I like an honest man."

He started lifting the barstools and placing them on the bar. "How was your day?"

"Nice."

"Now that you've had a chance to check out the competition, you must realize there's no place on the beach better than TNT."

"Well, most had more customers than you. Have you considered ninety-nine-cent chicken wings?"

"This is a real bar. I don't need that stuff. And to be fair, you've only come to my place at odd hours."

"True."

He leaned close to her. "And even if the place is empty, you have to admit that the bartender lends it a certain charm."

"I came back, didn't I?"

He nodded. "I'm glad you did. What do you feel like doing?"

"A drink might be nice. After that, I'll leave it up to you."

"Perfect. Let me close up before some unwelcome straggler wanders in."

He unfastened a coil of nylon rope at a support post and lowered the canvas awning until it covered the front of the bar. He repeated the action on both sides, completely enclosing the seating area. "Alone at last."

The canvas folds of fabric brushed the pocket of her skirt, where Kirov's cell phone transmitted to him on the street outside.

Niler reached behind the bar and picked up something Hannah couldn't see. "A guy came in here tonight selling handmade jewelry. Most of it was seashell-and-bead crap, but he had a necklace that made me think of you."

"Did you get his number?"

"Nah. I bought it for you."

"You *are* sure of yourself, aren't you?"

He gave her a puckish grin. "Well, if you hadn't shown up I'd probably have just given it to another pretty tourist this weekend."

"I have no doubt."

"It's a necklace. Turn around. Let me put it on you. Though I have to warn you, there's just a chance that I want to get my hands on you."

"You're moving a little fast." But Hannah turned and lifted her hair, allowing him to fasten the necklace around her neck. Niler's hands felt warm and coarse on her skin as he carefully positioned it.

"There. Perfect." He reached over the bar, picked up a small mirror, and handed it to her. "I hope you like it."

"I'm sure I will." She angled the mirror toward her throat. She inhaled sharply. "Oh, my God!"

Six paper-covered blocks and a tiny radio receiver.

She turned on him. "What the hell?"

"It's a low-power explosive device." He stepped back and showed her a small remote control. "I push this button, and your goddamn head flies off."

Hannah instinctively reached for the necklace.

"Don't do it!"

She stopped and let her hands fall to her sides. "Are you some kind of psycho?"

"Not at all. I'm just not very good with guns. I'm a rotten shot, and I always have been." He raised the remote. "This is more my speed. You have half a dozen cubes of HMX-based explosives around your neck. In the trade, we call them bullion cubes. It's enough to lop off your head, but light enough to leave me and my bar intact. I'll be open for business tomorrow, no problem. The question is, will *you* be open for business?"

Hannah felt the perspiration beading her face. "Why in the hell are you doing this?"

"*You're* the one who needs to explain. Who are you?"

"My name is Hannah Bryson. I'm a marine architect."

"Bullshit."

"It's the truth."

"Who broke into my car while you were chatting me up this morning?"

Hannah stiffened.

"Yeah, I know about that. I have a hard disk recorder hooked up to my security camera. Later in the day I noticed that my car alarm was off, and I *never* forget to set it when I get here. So I scanned the disk back and caught your friend. You were the only customer during my first hour of business, and my car was broken into during the five minutes you were here. You expect me to believe it was just a coincidence?"

"We didn't take anything."

"I would've been less worried if you had. What were you looking for?"

Hannah didn't reply.

He raised the remote and said with cold precision. "*I repeat. What were you looking for?*"

Kirov's voice called from outside. "That's enough, Niler. I'll tell you everything you need to know."

Niler turned toward the tarp. "Who's that?"

"The man who broke into your car," Hannah said. "I think you need to talk to him."

"Are you a cop? A Fed?"

Kirov said something in Russian that Hannah couldn't understand.

Niler turned toward Hannah. "Now, I have to say, I wasn't expecting that. Okay, lift up the awning and crawl under."

The awning pulled away, and Kirov appeared from underneath. "Still up to your old tricks, I see, Niler."

"Never old, always fresh and new. Keep your distance." Niler gestured to the remote. "I believe we have some things to sort out."

"So I see." Kirov walked toward Hannah. "Are you all right?"

She nodded.

Kirov turned toward Niler. "What do you say we take off that dreadful necklace? You used to have much better taste, Niler."

"She had a problem with it too. I have a quick way to oblige both of you."

"It would be unfortunate if someone at the next bar changed television channels or made a cell phone call that accidentally set off this device," Kirov said. "Can't we be civilized about this?"

Niler shook his head. "You know my work better than that. The charge won't go until I push this button."

"Of course. The Great Dane never makes mistakes."

"Too bad I can't say the same about you. What are you calling yourself these days?"

"Kirov."

"And what the hell are you doing here?"

Kirov took Hannah's hand and squeezed it reassuringly. "We've recently encountered another one of your devices, Niler. Four red cylinders at extreme underwater depth—does that ring a bell?"

Niler smiled. "If you really encountered it, you're lucky to be standing here."

"I know Pavski commissioned it from you. He meant it for me."

"I'm not a terrorist."

"I never said you were."

"I only build sentry devices, to protect personal property."

"Like this necklace around Hannah's neck?"

Niler shrugged. "That's to protect *me*."

"Fair enough. But believe me when I say you're the last person on earth I'd want to see harmed. I want Pavski, and you're my best hope of finding him."

"That's what this is all about? Pavski?"

Kirov nodded. "I can make it worth your while to help us."

"I always protect the confidentiality of my clients."

"Very honorable, especially from a man who earns a great deal of his income from South American drug lords."

"I won't dignify that with a response."

"I wouldn't, either. Those are people you don't want to cross. If they somehow got the impression you're less than discreet . . ."

"Are you threatening me? Because if you are . . . ?" Niler raised the remote.

"Enough of that. Trigger the explosive, and I'll kill you before the smoke clears."

"That won't help her."

"Nor you, and I won't be any closer to finding Pavski. We all lose. Instead, why don't we pursue an option in which we all win?"

Niler was silent, studying her. "What do you have in mind?"

"Help us find Pavski. Tell us what you know about his plans, his contact information, anything you have. As I said, we'll make it worth your while."

Niler smiled. "I imagine there must be a lot of people who would like to find Pavski."

"Almost as many people who would like to find me."

Niler gestured to Hannah. "Does she know who you are?"

"She has her own reasons for wanting Pavski. He used your bomb as a weapon against us. He lured us to it. I don't believe that was your intent."

"It wasn't. I told you, I'm not a terrorist."

"Will you help us?"

Niler stared at them.

"The necklace, Niler."

He didn't move for a full minute, then finally walked across the room and unfastened the necklace from around Hannah's neck.

She rubbed her throat as if a crushing weight had been lifted from it. Only then did she realize how much she'd been trembling. Jesus, she'd been scared.

"Well?" Kirov asked.

Niler disengaged the necklace's small radio receiver and placed it inside a cigar box behind the bar. He smiled. "There's a possibility I may have good news for you."

Bradworth rolled over in bed and grabbed the cell phone from his night table. "Bradworth."

"It's Fahey. I realize it's late there, but I knew you'd want to hear this."

"What have you got?"

"We just finished the DNA work on that skeleton. It's definitely Ivanov."

"Christ, I was afraid of that."

"Your buddy Kirov is an imposter. Dimitri Ivanov hasn't walked the earth in over five years."

If Bradworth hadn't been fully awake before, he was now. "You're absolutely positive?"

"They matched it with DNA they took from Ivanov's uncle. The certainty level is something like six billion to one. I'd go to Vegas with odds a lot worse than that."

"How are the Russians reacting?"

"They're understandably curious about who Kirov really is. I'm sure you'll be hearing about it from your Russian contacts."

"No doubt. Damn."

"You've been working with Kirov for years. You don't have any idea who you've been dealing with?"

"I'm working with the analysts on a list of possibilities."

"No idea, huh?"

"Good-bye, Fahey." Bradworth cut the connection. Snide son of a bitch.

Better get used to it, he thought. The guys at the Agency were going to have a field day with this one. The director had already ordered a review of all operations in which Kirov had been involved, and with this final piece of evidence, the scrutiny would only intensify.

This was how careers were destroyed, Bradworth realized. Kirov was his responsibility, and he was going to catch hell all the way up the chain of command. Though at the moment that didn't matter as much as he thought it would.

What mattered was Hannah Bryson. She was still out there with this Kirov or whoever the hell he was, and it might just cost her life.

"Talk to us, Niler," Hannah said.

Hannah, Kirov, and Niler sat on the beach a few yards from the TNT Bar, facing the waves as they crashed ashore.

Niler sipped a mai tai from a tall sports bottle. "You sure I can't make either of you something?"

"We're fine." Hannah repeated through set teeth, "Talk, Niler."

"Relax, relax. I've been working all day, and I need to unwind."

"Sorry, but it's hard to unwind when I've just had a bomb strapped to my throat."

"A tall coco loco would fix you right up."

"Niler," Kirov said.

"Okay, okay. I should be seeing Pavski soon."

"Where?" Kirov asked.

"At a location to be determined. He's hired me to create another explosive device. I'll see him when he takes delivery of it. I'm supposed to finish it no later than this weekend, but he said he could meet me earlier if I finished it before then."

"What's the purpose of this device?"

"Actually, it's several devices. It's to provide protection for a fifty-square-yard area on the ocean floor. It's supposed to be rated at fifteen hundred feet."

Hannah and Kirov shared a glance. "Do you think he's found it?" she asked.

"No, but he's obviously making plans to protect it if he finds the location before we do."

"Hey." Niler's eyes were glittering with curiosity. "What are we talking about here?"

Hannah turned back. "Pavski didn't tell you?"

"No. I don't *want* to know what most of my clients are involved with, but it must be something special if Pavski and you guys are involved." Niler grimaced. "Shit. I don't think I've been charging enough."

"Probably not," Kirov said. "But if you work with us, perhaps we can make it up to you."

"I'm not saying I will or won't, but there's something I need to find out from you."

"By all means."

Niler paused to put his thoughts into words. For the first time, Hannah noticed the slightest trace of a Russian accent in his speech.

"For years, I've heard rumors about what happened to the crew of the *Silent Thunder*. Pavski's name comes up in most of the stories."

"And?"

"I knew men on that sub," Niler continued soberly. "I suppose a good many Russian sailors had a friend or a relative on the *Thunder*. But you of all people would know what really happened."

"Oh, I do," Kirov said.

"If half of what I've heard is true, then I would have no problem giving you Pavski. So that's the first condition of our deal: I want to know the truth about what happened."

"Fair enough." Kirov leaned back in the sand, gazing out at the surf. "We were carrying bacteriological weapons on the *Silent Thunder*. We didn't like it, but we had our orders. And then we got the order to . . ."

ane Niler was finishing a telephone conversation when Hannah and Kirov came into the bar the next afternoon. He cut the connection and smiled. "Hi. Fix you a drink?"

"No, thanks," Hannah said. "Have you spoken to Pavski yet?"

"Just got off the phone with Koppel, one of his lieutenants. I think I mean that literally—you know how he likes those ex-military types. Anyway, we're set for the Bay County Farmers Market Sunday morning at eleven."

Kirov nodded. "Pavski will be there himself?"

"That's what I've been led to believe, but no guarantees. He does like to inspect the merchandise himself before he lets go of cash. But

I do expect payment whether he makes the trip or not. In any case, you'll have a lead that should take you right back to him."

"Fair enough," Kirov said. "But I'll give you a bonus if you'll come through with two other items. First, I want you to set up a call with Pavski before the delivery date. Not one of his lieutenants, himself. I want to verify you're dealing with him."

"You don't trust me?" He shrugged. "It will be hard to do without tipping my hand, but I'll manage. Pavski doesn't usually deal with the peasants except during the initial negotiations. And the second?"

"I want to see the device you're making for Pavski."

Hannah was just as surprised as Niler appeared to be. "Why?" she asked.

"I just want to see what Pavski is up to," Kirov said.

Niler smiled. "I can tell you all you need to know about it right here, over a tall Pineapple Fizz."

"I don't want to hear about it. I want to see the device."

"Not much to see yet. I've always been a last-minute kind of guy, you know?"

"I'll understand."

Niler switched on his stereo system, flooding the bar with Caribbean island music. He shrugged. "If that's what it takes to make you happy, we'll go tonight after dark."

"Why not before?"

Niler smiled as two bikini-clad women strolled into the bar. "It's better if no one sees me coming or going. I've got a pretty good spot, and I don't want anyone stumbling onto it. Nine o'clock." He turned and headed toward the two women. "You look hot, pretty ladies. I have just the drink that will fix you up."

You're joking, right?" Kirov shouted above the roaring surf.

Hannah, Kirov, and Niler aimed their flashlights ahead as they half walked, half slid down a sandy embankment to a narrow strip of shoreline. They were on a lonely stretch about forty minutes' drive from Niler's bar.

"Nope," Niler said. "This used to be a nice little beach, but Hurricane Opal took most of it away a few years ago. There was a set of stairs on that embankment, but they're gone too. That's good for me, because it keeps people away."

"Maybe it should have kept you away," Hannah said.

"Nah." Niler aimed his flashlight ahead at a small dilapidated structure. "That's an old snack stand. One of my old girlfriends used to get hot dogs and boiled peanuts from there when she was a kid. Anyway, I own it now."

"The bomb maker's lair," Kirov said.

"It's out of the way, and I can test fuses and detonators on the beach without causing a fuss."

Kirov chuckled. "Pity the poor passerby who tries to duck inside for some shelter from the elements."

Niler produced a large key ring. "It's securely locked. Someone would need a crowbar to get inside."

"Meaning that they would deserve to get blown to bits by your booby traps?" Hannah said.

"Damned straight," Niler said. He raised a tiny car alarm remote much like the one he'd used against Hannah the previous night. A doorbell-like tone sounded inside the structure. He raised a second remote, and a second tone sounded. Niler unlocked the door and threw it open wide. "Ladies first."

Hannah smiled. "This is one place I'd rather you lead the way."

"Still a little shell-shocked from the necklace I gave you, are you?" Niler strode through the door and turned on the overhead fluorescent lights.

"Wow," Hannah murmured. Niler's workshop resembled a laboratory clean room, bearing no resemblance to the weather-beaten shack outside. Bright fluorescent light flooded every nook and cranny of the windowless, almost antiseptic room, and an equipment-laden workbench dominated three of the four walls.

Niler smiled. "You expected a grimy little toolshed?"

"I don't know what I expected, but this wasn't it."

"Building bombs isn't like fixing lawn mowers. It's an exact science, or at least it should be." He pointed to four steel platters on the workbench. "There's the current project."

Kirov inspected the gray platters, which were approximately four inches thick and eighteen inches in diameter. "You're building these for Pavski?"

"You've got it. There will be a total of eight for a total covered area of fifty square feet. They'll be spaced just close enough together that one detonation will trigger the one next to it, which in turn will detonate the next in line, and so on."

"A ring of destruction," Kirov said. "So whatever they're protecting will be totally destroyed?"

Niler gave him a sour look. "Do you see a sign around here that says 'amateur bomb maker at work'? You must really enjoy insulting me."

Kirov turned to Hannah. "Artists are so sensitive about their work, aren't they?"

"Artist is right," Niler said. "And for that you've just won your way back into my good graces." He gestured toward the discs. "There's still a protected area of about twenty square feet. The main purpose of my devices is to protect, not destroy."

"Twenty square feet," Kirov said. "That seems small for the cargo were looking for."

Niler shrugged. "That's what Pavski needed. Maybe he wants this for something else."

"It doesn't matter," Kirov said. "It's Pavski we want, not the objects."

Niler smiled. "It wouldn't exactly suck if you got both, now would it? Money makes the world go round. Speaking of which, we need to have a chat about logistics."

"What do you mean?" Hannah asked.

"I don't know what you have planned for Pavski and friends, but you'll need to wait until my business with him is done."

"After you've handed off these devices?" Hannah said.

"And after I've received my money and gotten the hell out of your way."

"We'll try not to blow your deal." Kirov smiled. "No pun intended."

"It's not just the money. If it gets out that I've ratted out one of my clients, it might make my other customers . . . nervous."

"Understood," Kirov said. "I don't suppose you'd want to get on the bad side of a South American drug lord."

"Damn straight." Niler nodded. "You screw this up for me, I'll make damned sure *you're* on his bad side, too."

SIXTEEN

Hannah watched Niler pass them in his Z-98 and disappear down Highway 98.

"What did you think?" Hannah asked Kirov.

"I'm pretty well versed in the art of demolitions, and Niler clearly knows what he's doing. I still can't get past the small size of the protected area. The treasure occupied a good part of the forward hold of the *Silent Thunder,* which as you know is well over twenty square feet."

"Maybe it's not the treasure he wants to guard. Maybe it's a clue to the location, like we thought those canisters might be."

"Possibly." Kirov nodded to a roadside diner up ahead. "That looks like a four-star establishment. Are you in the mood for a gourmet meal?"

"Sure. Greasy hamburgers are just what I need after looking at lethal weapons."

He pulled into the parking lot. "I might spring for a steak."

"I'll take the hamburger." She got out of the car. "There's nothing fancy about my palate. My ex-husband used to say that I was very lacking in that department."

"That's the first time you mentioned your husband." He opened the glass door for her. "I gather he's totally out of the picture?"

"Totally." She slid into a red leather booth, picked up a menu, and handed him one. "But my relationship isn't one that I'd discuss with you, Kirov. It's personal."

"There's personal and there's *personal.*" He looked down at the menu. "I'd never ask you to talk about the child you lost. But ex-husbands are fair game."

"Why would you want me to talk about either one?"

He grimaced. "You're right. I've changed my mind. I don't want to hear anything about such a stupid bastard." He smiled. "It would tell me nothing about who you are now. We all change according to our experiences, and you've gone through a lot since you were with him."

The death of her child, the murder of Conner. "Yes, I have." She looked him in the eye. "And did the death of your wife change who you are?"

"Turnabout?" He shrugged. "Yes, I changed."

"How did she die?"

"Pavski."

She went still. "What?"

"She was sucked down in the morass after *Silent Thunder* was taken over. Pavski had staked out my home and was trying to use her to capture me after I escaped. For years we had a special code word.

Whenever one of us used it in a telephone call, telegraph message, or e-mail, we knew to pack up and immediately proceed to a pre-arranged rendezvous spot. Those were uncertain times, and many officers had such arrangements with their loved ones." Kirov stared out the window for a long moment. "I called Mira with the code, but she never showed. I heard later that she was murdered by Pavski's men when she tried to escape from him and get to me."

"Jesus, I'm sorry."

"So was I."

"Does Bradworth know about your wife?"

"No; I needed him and his resources. If Bradworth knew that Pavski killed Mira, he'd know the chances were zilch I'd leave him alive long enough to turn him over to them. He's doubtful with what he knows about me now. He would have frozen me out."

"Like he tried to do to me."

"To his credit he was probably concerned for your well-being. On one hand you have Pavski, whose only concern is extracting information you have about the sub and those plates. On the other hand there's me, who obviously has no problem using you as bait in order to trap Pavski. I think Bradworth was trying to protect you as long as it didn't get in his way."

"You didn't mention your wife's death when you told me about the death of all those seamen on the sub."

His lips twisted. "And Mira would have said that it was characteristic that I told you about them and not her."

"Because she always thought you put the sub before her?"

"It was a joke, but maybe she really felt like that." He wearily shook his head. "I don't know. But that wasn't the reason I didn't tell you Pavski killed her. You'd suffered the loss of your brother. I didn't want you to think I was trying to identify with that loss."

"And you don't think the death of a hundred and three seamen wouldn't cause me to identify? You said they were a personal loss to you. Were you telling the truth?"

"God, yes. Every one of those men were like family." He met her eyes. "But they weren't my family. There's a fine difference."

"I still don't see why you—" She stopped, studying him. "Were you, by any chance, being honorable?"

"Perish the thought."

She smiled. "I think you were. How funny."

"It's not funny." He scowled. "Okay, perhaps I had a soft moment and wanted not to influence you unduly, but honor isn't the word. Honor doesn't fit me anymore. It would be like wearing squeaky shoes."

"Squeak. Squeak."

"I believe I need a diversion." He waved to the waitress across the room. "I think I'll feed you. And after your meal I have a favor to ask."

She stiffened. "Ask it now."

He shook his head. "When we get back to the hotel. After I've plied you with greasy hamburgers and strong coffee."

Congressman George Preston sat in his Prius, staring at the disposable mobile phone that thug had given him on the street the other night. How in the hell had he gotten to this point?

One mistake twenty years ago. One bad night, and now it had come back to bite him in the ass. He couldn't believe he was still paying for it. It wasn't fair. He had spent all those years serving his country. Now he was sitting here, in terror of his whole life going down the tube.

It mustn't happen. He couldn't let it happen.

He pressed the speed dial button on the phone.

"Your damn bug's in place," he said curtly when Pavski answered. "Now back off. Leave Cathy alone and leave me alone."

"I'll leave Cathy Bryson alone if I don't have to use her or the children. It's a matter of need. But you're on the hook until I get what I want, Congressman. There's always a price to pay, Preston."

"And I'm willing to pay it. Hell, I'm evidently willing for everyone else to pay it too. But no violence, Pavski."

"What will be, will be. I have to have Hannah Bryson."

"There's no reason. I told you that she doesn't know anything. Bradworth assured me that she didn't know anything more, and she told him she wouldn't be able to remember the carvings on the plate. She was too traumatized by her brother's death."

"I believe you. I'm working on another angle now, and I may not need her input about the plates. But I do still have another agenda. Kirov. He's been a thorn pricking me, and he's getting nearer all the time. I can't have him getting in my way right now. There's no way I can get close to him. He's too experienced at playing hide-and-seek after all these years. But he's been working hand in glove with Hannah Bryson. I may be able to use her to trap him."

"Bait?"

"No, Kirov would just let me kill her." He paused, and when he spoke again his tone was malicious. "But you've just demonstrated how easy it is to persuade someone to betray a compatriot if the price is right. If I give Hannah Bryson a choice, I think I'll have no trouble getting what I want."

"No violence. I won't permit it."

"Stop bluffing, Preston. You'll weigh your career against an anonymous favor, and you'll close your eyes and bite the bullet." He hung up on him.

What a son of a bitch.

Preston pressed the disconnect. Pavski had treated him with an ugly arrogance that had made him feel pitifully ineffectual. Was he right? Would he look away and bite the bullet?

Christ, and was the fact that he was considering it already sending him halfway down that path?

Preston had been ridiculously easy to manipulate, Pavski thought. He'd been surprised how quickly he had caved. But then he was a politician, and politicians were always afraid of damage to their image. So much for the Frank Capra mystique.

His phone rang, and he glanced at the ID.

Danzyl. Excitement surged through him.

"Do you have it?" he demanded as he answered the phone.

"No." Danzyl hesitated. "It's extremely difficult. I believe we should renegotiate."

He stiffened. "Are you holding me up for more money?"

"I'm a poor man, Pavski."

"But you're alive. You won't remain that way long if you don't fulfill our bargain."

"I got those files for you. Even that was a risk. People are very cautious about dealing with you these days. What you did to the *Silent Thunder* left a certain taint." He paused. "But I asked myself why you'd dig up all of this again. It's not safe. You're a smart man, and you should leave it behind you. There are too many people who suspect you of the murder of all those men. But you can't resist. You don't care. That means it must be the Golden Cradle. Am I correct?"

"You're supposed to give *me* information."

"It has to be the cradle. I remember how furious you were with us when Heiser's father was killed before you could get to him. You'd do anything to get it."

"Yes, I would. That should cause you to be more careful in try-ing to gouge me, Danzyl."

"Fair is fair. I'm not asking for a percentage, just a little more money to pay the rent."

"How much more?"

"Double."

"Done."

He was silent. "No argument?"

"Oh, I'll give you a big argument if you don't come through. And for that money you'll have to do more than research. I want an-swers now. Get your ass moving." He hung up.

Slimy bastard. Danzyl had surprised him. He had thought he was a drone like Koppel. Smarter, more lethal, but not capable of facing up to him. It didn't matter. After he got what he needed from Danzyl, he'd remove him from the scene in the most painful manner possible.

It has to be the cradle. You'd do anything to get it.

Very perceptive, Danzyl.

He could remember his mother taking him to the Vitaka River and sitting there with him while she told him about the cradle and how he must reclaim it for the family.

"You're the one the legend talks about, Igor," she would whisper as she stroked his hair. "When I married your father, I had no love for him. He wanted my body, and I wanted his name. And I knew he would give me a special child. I *felt* it. Someday you'll claim the cradle, and everyone will know how wonderful you are. Then you'll make me a queen, won't you? All these people here think I'm not good enough, but you'll show them."

He would nod in agreement, but even then he'd scarcely been aware of her ambitions. He'd been lost in the dreams of glory of what he was to become.

What he was still to become.

His mother would never realize her ambitions. She had died before he had become fleet commander. He had barely noticed her death and been too busy to go to the funeral. He was starting to make plans to go after the cradle.

And then came the disaster on the *Silent Thunder* that had almost brought him down.

But it had only been a temporary setback, and he had been strong enough to put it behind him. Now all he needed was the cradle, and he'd be able to start his climb again. Nothing could stop him.

He got up and moved across the room to stand before the plates. He reached out and touched the unidentified symbol with his fingertips, tracing the cross within the circle. It felt curiously warm beneath his touch. Was it a sign? "I'll have it soon, Heiser," he murmured. "You and your clever tricks are nothing. You can't keep it from me much longer. Just a few days more . . ."

May I come in?" Kirov asked as they stopped in front of Hannah's door. "I promise I won't keep you long."

A quickie? Where had that thought come from, Hannah wondered as she unlocked the door. Any favor Kirov wanted from her would not involve sex. "I'd bust your head if you just walked away without telling me what you want." She unlocked her door. "I hate a tease."

"So do I." He followed her into the room. "I'd never tease you, Hannah. It's not in my dour nature. Unless you told me that you— Never mind." He turned on the light. "It's late, and I want your head clear." He went over to the desk, drew out several sheets of hotel stationery, and jotted down a series of Samsovian symbols.

"What are you writing?"

"I'm providing some lunar coordinates that will give some information as to the time of year. This should match closely to the sub's final voyage six years ago." He slid a sheaf of stationery over to her. "The favor."

"What?"

"Will you write down everything you can remember from those bulkhead plates. Can you do that for me?"

She had known it was coming. She was surprised he hadn't asked before. "Why do you need it?"

"I have to be certain that Pavski doesn't have all the plates. We're assuming he doesn't by his actions, but maybe he's not certain himself. He's no expert. I have to know if there's another plate floating around out there."

She moistened her lips. "It won't be easy. I can't just call it up like a computer file. I need to concentrate to bring back the sights, sounds, smells, the feelings of that night."

"The night your brother died."

"It's not an experience I'm eager to revisit," she said unevenly.

"Will you do it?"

No, she wanted to tell him. Hell, no. She could feel her stomach clench at the thought. Okay, get over it. She'd been a coward for too long. It was time to brace herself and face that night and all its horror.

She didn't reply for a moment, then nodded jerkily. "Yeah, I'll do it." She sat down on the couch and placed the sheet of stationery on the coffee table in front of her. "Let's get it over with."

He handed her his pencil and several sheets of paper. "Anything else?"

"Just be quiet." She rested her hands on the desk and closed her eyes. She breathed slowly and deeply, trying to release the tension that had consumed her in the past several days. Ever since that awful night . . .

Can you come over here for a moment, Hannah?

Conner's voice.

Not quite, she realized. It sounded lower and more hollow. Was she already forgetting what he sounded like?

Can you come over here for a moment, Hannah? I've found something . . . weird.

Better. That was Conner. He'd called out to her as she was squinting through her camera viewfinder. At what? The recessed area behind the antiquated submarine navigational computer, she remembered. She could see the cracked insulation on the wires . . .

In a minute, she'd told him. She snapped another picture before turning to face him.

He wore the gray sweater, jeans, brown tennis shoes, and the cologne he wore whenever they were on or near the ocean. He liked the way that the salt air interacted with it.

Conner, in his last moments on earth.

Christ.

What is it? She snapped another picture.

There's another metal plate bolted to this surface metal.

She looked at the plate but saw nothing engraved on its surface.

Damn.

She and Conner unscrewed the last two bolts. She'd teased him and he'd smiled.

God, Conner . . .

She rested the plate on the floor. The work lights hit it and—

Pay dirt.

She froze the image in her mind and scribbled furiously on the piece of stationery in front of her.

"Incredible," Kirov murmured.

"Shut up."

She wrote faster, as if the image in her mind might evaporate at any moment.

Triangle, straight line, triangle, circle . . .

She filled the entire page with symbols she didn't understand. She reached the bottom, tossed it aside, and started another.

Wavy line, rectangle with three circles inside . . .

Finished.

The image disappeared as the movie in her mind continued. She looked from the plate to Conner's bewildered expression.

So what do we do with it? Turn it over to the museum? Conner placed the other two plates on the floor.

As they caught the light, she could read most of the markings on the other two plates. She mentally froze the images and scribbled quickly, filling three more sheets of stationery.

She finally threw down the pencil. "That's all. It's all I can make out."

Kirov gently brushed her cheek, wiping away the tears she hadn't realized were there. "Thank you, Hannah."

She couldn't bear the gentleness. She was too near breaking. She leaned forward to pick up the pages. "So what do these tell you?"

He studied the coordinates. "That *Silent Thunder* spent some time in or near the Black Sea." He frowned as he pointed at a symbol at the end of the third plate. "This symbol isn't Samsovian. I don't recognize it." He looked up at her. "And the final piece appears to be missing. Are you sure there wasn't more?"

"Not that I saw." Her eyes widened. "You thought that if I went over what happened that night, I might remember something else?" She shook her head, and said shakily, "Sorry to disappoint you. I can't remember something that wasn't there. All I could tell you was what happened that night. And none of it was good, damn you."

"I had to know."

"I know. I know." She looked away from him. "I didn't do it for you. We have to find that cradle before Pavski does. He killed Conner to get it. I won't let that bastard get his hands on it. I would have done it anyway."

"But you wouldn't have done it now, when the pain is still so fresh."

"Maybe not." She wiped her cheeks with the backs of her hand. Why couldn't she keep these damn tears from flowing? "But I did it. Are you happy?"

"No." He said haltingly, "I'm hurting because you're hurting. I didn't expect this. I don't like it."

"Tough."

"I . . . want to make it right."

"You can't make me stop hurting. It was my choice. I knew what would happen when I tried to pull up those memories."

"And so did I. I made you open the past and remember." He paused. "Would it help if I let you do the same to me?"

Her gaze swung back to him. "What?"

"I can't relive it, the way I made you do, but I'll answer anything you ask of me."

She stared at him warily. "Anything?"

"Anything."

"You're not Ivanov, are you?"

He slowly shook his head. "It's pretty obvious you suspected that. Bradworth?"

"He warned Cathy you were probably lying to all of us. That the real Ivanov was dead."

"It took him a long time to find that out." He grimaced. "It's inconvenient that he managed to put it together at this particular time. Did he tell you who I am?"

"I don't think he knows." She stared him in the eye. "Who are you?"

"My name is Andre Kocineyv."

"And?"

"I was captain of *Silent Thunder*."

She shook her head.

"You don't believe me?"

"I've seen pictures of the captain. I've seen his file."

"Complete fabrications."

She made a rude sound.

He smiled. "You're not making this easy for me. I'm baring my soul, and you're being very disrespectful."

"This is the fourth identity you've come up with since I met you. You remind me of that old Cary Grant movie where he played a CIA man who changed identities every other scene. What do you do? Pick them out of a hat? This one is completely bizarre."

"As you know, the Russian Navy has always been fond of re-naming its submarines in order to hide the true numbers and location of its fleet. They also took great pains to hide the identities of their senior commanders. I understand the U.S. Navy does the same thing."

Hannah slowly nodded. "I know the U.S. fighter pilots' identities are often kept secret."

"Of course. Otherwise, a country's enemies could cripple it with just a few strike teams to assassinate the most critical personnel. Vladzar was a name that was on the *Silent Thunder* command logs for years, but he never existed. I'm surprised they bothered to create a biography and history for him, but that may have been a late addition for the benefit of your museumgoers. The last thing they'd want to reveal is that the sub's real commander left in such disgrace."

"In disgrace?"

"Everything else I told you is the truth. But Pavski had the GRU on my heels from the moment I escaped. I managed to stage my death in a boating accident trying to escape the Shore Patrol in Belarus." He made a face. "Naturally, my body was never recovered."

"Ivanov," she prompted.

"I wanted to try to get my stepbrother out of Russia and tracked him down. He was wounded by GRU agents while we were on the run and later died. Later I took his identity. I don't know how the hell they found out that the real Ivanov was dead." His gaze narrowed. "Or maybe I do. Pavski may have tipped them. It would make sense that he'd want to stir up as much trouble for me with the CIA as he could."

"He knows who you are?"

"He didn't know right away, but I did a good job of cleaving my way through a number of his associates and goon squad. He might have gotten a description of me at some point and put two and two together. He probably did. I'm good, but I'm not the invisible man." He smiled. "And I'm sorry I'm not the father figure you imagined."

There was no one who looked less phantomlike than the man standing before her, and he was definitely not fatherly. "It's true? You're not bullshitting me?"

"I'm not bullshitting." He looked down at the navigational drawings. "You gave to me. I gave to you." He turned to leave. "Good night, Hannah."

"Wait." She paused. "All those books in the cabin. They were your books, right? That wasn't a lie."

"They were my books." He lifted his brows. "Why?"

"I just wondered. Good night, Kirov."

He didn't move, his gaze on her face. "Ah, you're still trying to identify me with the type of captain you wanted to command *Silent Thunder*."

"Perhaps. I found a photo of a woman in one of those books. Mira?"

He nodded. "She gave me a new photo every time I put to sea. She said if I was going to go off with her greatest rival, she needed to show me a face of infinite variety."

"She was beautiful."

"Inside and out. I didn't deserve her." He opened the door. "And for an arrogant bastard like me to admit that is a tribute in itself."

She sat there staring thoughtfully at the door after it had closed behind him. He probably was as arrogant as he claimed. Command required a certain amount of ego and arrogance, and Kirov would have been a great leader. He had drive and intelligence and the ability to make smart decisions quickly.

And his ego hadn't gotten in the way when she'd designated him to support status on the *LISA,* she remembered. He hadn't liked it, but he'd accepted the best course and stepped down.

It was strange thinking of him as captain of that sub. She had a sudden memory of the expression on his face as he stood in the control room. Passion. Nostalgia. Power. Hell, perhaps his wife had a right to be jealous of *Silent Thunder.*

And she shouldn't be sitting here analyzing the mystery of Kirov. The evening had been exhausting and emotional, and she had learned more about the man than she wanted to know. She needed to keep him at a distance, and it would be difficult to do that now that she was beginning to realize how he thought, what made him tick. She stood up and moved toward the bathroom. A shower and then bed. Call Cathy?

No, she had phoned her before they had started for Florida, and it was better to call with a *fait accompli* than a progress report. Of course, she could tell her about Niler's pretty necklace, and that would really freak her out.

Just go to bed and forget Kirov and Cathy and everything else for a few hours, she thought wearily. Being with Kirov was like living in an exotic third-world country where nothing was comfortable or predictable. Just when she thought she was on solid ground, he pulled the rug out from under her as he had tonight.

But tomorrow, she'd be cool and steady and ready for anything he had in store for her.

Tomorrow . . .

haven't found out anything yet, Kirov," Eugenia said when she answered the call Kirov made when he got back to his room. "Don't bother me."

"I'm not nagging. I'm going to send you a picture on my phone. I'm circling the symbol I want you to trace. The rest are navigational symbols."

"And this one isn't?"

"No. I'm not sure what it is yet."

"And I'm supposed to find out." Eugenia sighed. "Now I'm a decoder?"

"At least try to point me in the right direction. No news?"

"I managed to find out that Pavski's contact in the GRU is Danzyl. He's clever, money-hungry, and lethal. He's looking for a statue."

"Statue?"

"I thought it was pretty weird. But that's what he's been researching in his computer. I tapped it, and so far he's coming up with nothing. I'm wondering if maybe Pavski found a picture of Heiser in front of a statue. What do you think?"

"It's possible."

"It's my best guess so far. This afternoon Danzyl went to Heiser's old apartment building. No statue."

"The symbol will reach you a few minutes after I hang up." He paused. "We're running out of time."

"Okay. Okay. I'll work on it." She paused. "It's strange being here this time, Kirov. Lately, when I've come to Moscow, it's been as a high-powered businesswoman. This time I feel . . . déjà vu." She chuckled. "Of course, I have been here before and doing these same things. But it seems like another life. At first, I was a little uneasy."

"And now?"

"I'm beginning to like it. It's exhilarating. I thought I was done with the old life, but there's something about walking on the edge . . ."

"Not too close to the edge, Eugenia."

"Never. I like living too much." She added briskly, "Now hang up, and I'll study your pretty little symbol. It probably only takes a keen eye and a brilliant mind like mine to make sense of it."

Kirov smiled as he hung up the phone. Eugenia would probably be up half the night puzzling over the symbol once she saw it. She was curious as a cat.

His smile faded as he looked down at the piece of stationery. He half expected there to be tears on the paper. Hannah's tears.

Stop brooding. He'd done what he'd had to do, dammit. Now get the symbol to Eugenia and try to make the reason for those tears have meaning.

PANAMA CITY
9:00 P.M.

've logged my fair share of time in car backseats along these beaches." Niler smiled. "I far prefer that activity to doing this."

"Taking a phone call from a mass murderer?" Hannah asked. "I'd say anything would be preferable."

They were sitting in the rental car on a lonely stretch of beach as Kirov tested the connection between Niler's cell phone and the three-way splitter he had bought at Radio Shack that afternoon. Niler sat in back, setting up the proxy server connection on Kirov's laptop. He wore a telephone headset, while Kirov and Hannah sat in front wearing simple stereo headphones.

"Remember, Pavski said he *may* call," Niler said. "Koppel wouldn't give me any guarantees."

"For your sake, I hope he comes through," Kirov said.

"Was that a threat?"

"Only in an economic sense. The bonus I promised you is riding on it."

"No guarantees." Niler leaned back in his seat. "And I should tell you that I may be moving away after we conclude our business this weekend. You can count me out."

"You're closing the TNT bar?" Hannah asked.

"I'll sell it. I get offers all the time. You wouldn't believe how many uptight Wall Street moguls dream of retiring and running their own beachfront party bar."

"Why are you leaving?" Kirov asked.

"I need to get back under the radar. When you two run across one of my bombs and know right where to find me, that tells me something. I've been having a good time here, but it's only a matter of time before my luck will run out. I'm going to disappear into the sunset. Don't you think I—" Niler's cell phone suddenly blared Queen's "Another One Bites the Dust."

"You might want to try a new ringtone," Hannah suggested dryly.

"Shhh." Niler checked the laptop display screen. "I think this may be him. Are we ready?"

Hannah and Kirov adjusted their headphones and nodded.

Niler pushed the TALK button. "Speak to me."

"You're the one who insisted on this conversation," the caller said impatiently. "Perhaps *you* should speak to *me*."

Russian accent, sharp, precise enunciation. Pavski. The knowledge that he was on the other end of the line made Hannah's chest tighten. She glanced at Kirov.

His grim expression confirmed it.

"I've had a few problems lately," Niler said. "A few seconds- and thirds-in-command have been placing orders without their bosses' okay, and I've had trouble collecting payments."

"How foolish," Pavski said. "It's not a good idea to anger someone in your profession."

"I took care of the problem. Anyway, I recognize your voice. Your package will be ready this weekend."

"No, I want it tomorrow."

"Tomorrow?"

"Yes. I'm on my way there now. Same plan, same place, just a different day."

"But your devices aren't ready."

"Make them ready."

Niler was clearly flustered. "It's—It's not that simple. Your man said—"

"Forget what he said. You're talking to me now. That's what you wanted, isn't it? To hear it from me?"

"Yes, but I—"

"Is the deal on or off? Because if you can't deliver, I need to make other arrangements."

Niler paused. "I can deliver."

"Good."

"It might help if I knew what you're trying to protect."

Silence. "It's not like you to ask so many questions."

"Different objects have different properties," Niler said. "Some materials are better able to absorb shock waves than others. It would be helpful for me to know—"

"It's nonexplosive, nonflammable material. Do your best."

"I always do."

"Good. See you tomorrow."

Click.

Niler switched off the phone.

Hannah threw off her headphones. "Tomorrow?"

"I'm really not surprised," Kirov said. "Pavski likes to keep the people around him slightly off-balance. It's his way of assuring that he always has the upper hand."

"There's another explanation," Hannah said. "He's already found the stash, and he's in a hurry to get your sentry bombs in place to protect it."

"In any case, this moves things up a few days." Kirov turned to Niler. "Can you be ready?"

He shrugged. "Looks like I'll have to be, doesn't it?"

"Do you need anything from us?"

Niler smiled. "I saw the looks on both of your faces when his voice came through. When you finally lay eyes on him, all I'll need is a chance to get the hell out of your way."

SEVENTEEN

Blood.

Gray sweater.

Conner!

Hannah sat up straight in bed, sweating, panting.

Dear God.

Just a nightmare. No, more than that. It had been a reliving of that night in every detail.

Pain.

She got out of bed and went into the bathroom and drank a glass of water.

Conner.

Why was the shock and pain hitting her like this tonight? She'd managed to keep it at bay after the first few nights.

Because tomorrow she might be facing his murderer.

And she might be killing a man.

Don't think about it. What had to be done would be done.

But she couldn't go back to bed yet and risk another nightmare.

She pulled on her jeans and a shirt and headed for the door. She'd walk on the beach and try to exhaust herself enough to sleep without dreams.

The moon was bright and the surf was gentle.

Conner had never liked a quiet surf. He'd always been excited by crashing waves.

Walk fast.

Try not to think.

"Hannah."

Kirov. She stopped and turned to watch him coming toward her. "I don't want company, Kirov."

He studied her expression. "I can see that. You're getting it anyway."

She turned and walked away. "How did you get here?"

"I was coming back to my room, and I saw you leave."

"It's the middle of the night. What were you doing?"

"Maybe I was taking a midnight stroll too." He paused. "Nerves?"

She nodded jerkily. "I'll be okay."

"I know you will." He walked beside her in silence for a few moments. "You can change your mind."

"I'm not changing my mind." She walked faster. "I had a dream about Conner tonight. It was just like that night and he was— There's no way I could back out."

"I guess not. Just thought I'd offer."

She glanced at him. "Do you have nightmares, Kirov? I'd think you would."

"Because of the men I've killed?" He shook his head. "Only about the Pavski killed. I used to dream every night about my crewmen dying on the sub, wondering where I was, and reaching their hands out to me and begging me to die with them."

She shuddered. "Horrible."

"It was probably born of guilt. A captain is responsible for his crew and his ship. He should be with them to the end."

"You couldn't be there."

"My mind knows that. My emotions aren't at all reasonable. I've been trained to duty since childhood." He stopped. "Could we sit down? I'm tired of running a marathon. Tomorrow may be a taxing day."

"I told you not to come—" She shrugged and sat down on the sand. She linked her arms around her knees and stared out at the surf. "Do you think he'll come?"

He dropped down beside her. "Pavski? I don't know. There's a fair chance. It's worth a shot."

"What if he doesn't?"

"Maybe try to snag the man who delivers the cash. We'll play it by ear."

"Just like that? I don't believe this is something I want to be extemporaneous about."

"Then walk away."

"Stop saying that." Her hands clenched into fists. "If he doesn't come to us, we have to go after the cradle. That will draw him to us."

"No doubt. It's his beacon in the night."

"Then let's light it and lead him to hell. Tell me what I have to know to find it."

"If I knew that, I'd have found it already."

"You were interested in that mythology book."

"Because it wasn't mine. That means it could be Heiser's. Anything to do with Heiser is crucial."

"You said that the only clue could be the conversation between Heiser and his father."

"And that the area Heiser mentioned visiting with his father as a child was searched by everyone. Pavski, included."

"What about you?"

He nodded. "Me, too. Nothing."

"Maybe you missed something in the conversation with his father."

He shook his head. "I have the transcript if you'd like to read it."

"What about Heiser's father? Surely you talked to him?"

"No, I was on the run. It was nine months before I could get to Moscow to see him. By that time he was dead."

"How?"

He shrugged. "Pavski or the GRU. He was shot in a train station near his town. He was probably trying to run away. The poor bastard was no match for them. He was a professor of literature, for God's sake. But evidently he was killed before he was forced to tell what he knew, or Pavski would have the cradle."

Another death to be laid at the door of the cradle, she thought bitterly. "What about the contents of that package that Petrenko gave Pavski?"

"I haven't heard from Eugenia yet on it. She hasn't had much time since she got to Moscow. She'll get there."

"It's like chasing a will-o'-the-wisp," she said in frustration. "We don't know anything."

"And that's why we're not counting on finding it. Much better to go after Pavski directly."

She nodded. "I guess so. It's just that I want to be *sure.*"

"And you like to be in control, and there's nothing certain about anything we're doing."

She nodded ruefully. "You probably feel the same way."

"But I've had to develop patience over the years. This meeting tomorrow is as close as I've come to getting him. So I'm not nearly as discouraged as you are. One step at a time, Hannah."

But every step was like walking on barbed wire. "I could use a few giant steps."

"I know." His hand reached out to cover her own. "I wish I could give them to you."

She looked down at his big hand enveloping hers. Her hand was not small, and more capable than attractive, yet it seemed fragile and very womanly in his grasp. She *felt* womanly. Her palm was suddenly ultrasensitive, and she could feel a tingling moving up her wrist and arm.

Jesus. Her chest was suddenly tight, and her breathing was becoming rapid, shallow. The pulse was pounding erratically in the hollow of her throat. What an idiotic response. For God's sake, he was just holding her hand.

She jerked her hand away. She tried to remember what he had

been saying. "You're doing the best you can." She got to her feet. "It's just that I'm not at all patient." She started back toward the hotel. "I'm going to go back to the hotel and try to get to sleep. Coming?"

"No." He stayed where he sat on the sand. "I'll watch until you get safely back in your room from here. Lock your door."

"I always do."

She glanced back at him when she reached the hotel. His body language was relaxed and yet she was still aware of the alertness and strength that characterized his every movement.

Sometimes there's a stillness about him that's very erotic.

Eugenia again. Dammit, she didn't need to remember Eugenia's words about the explosiveness that lay beneath that deceptive stillness. She was entirely too aware of everything about Kirov.

He made a shooing motion as if to whisk her into her hotel room.

Bossy bastard.

She deliberately slowed her pace until she reached her door. Then she turned and gave him the finger.

Kirov chuckled with amusement as he watched the door close behind Hannah.

That last irreverent gesture was just what he would have expected from Hannah, and she never disappointed. In spite of her frustration and nervousness about tomorrow she still remained strong and intelligent and driven. What an amazing woman.

His smile faded as his gaze shifted back to the surf. He needed this time alone with the sea. It always brought him peace and clarity of mind. From the time he was a boy, he had come to the sea with his sorrows and his triumphs. The sea had tempered his arrogance and given him a sense of his own mortality. And, yet, it had created a web of power and challenge that could never be matched by any other experience. The sea had become his servant and his master, his lover and his enemy.

And being captain of the *Silent Thunder* had made him feel like a god from Olympus. Surrounded by power and able to loose lightning bolts.

Mythology, again.

Forget mythology, forget the cradle.

Just enjoy these moments of peace and rebirth before the chaos begins again.

BOSTON
3:35 A.M.

Get up, Ronnie." Cathy tried to keep the fear from her voice. "Get up, honey."

"Mom?" Ronnie sat up in bed and rubbed his eyes. "It's still dark."

"We have to leave." She came into his room and took his gym bag out of the closet. "Please don't ask questions. Just get your sister out of bed and come back here. Don't scare her. Tell her it's a game we're playing. I thought it would be less frightening for her if you were the one who woke her."

"Game? What kind of—" He stopped as he saw her face. "What's wrong?"

"No questions. We'll talk later." She forced a smile. "Just do what I tell you, okay?"

He didn't speak for a minute. "Okay." Then he swung his feet to the floor. "What kind of game?" he repeated. "Should I keep her quiet?"

"If you can."

"I can do it. She'll think it's fun." He headed for the door. "I'll think of something."

Bless him.

She quickly finished packing his gym bag and ran to the window.

The street below was empty.

They weren't coming yet.

Or were they?

Headlights were spearing the darkness as a car turned the corner two blocks down.

Her heart leaped in her chest.

Oh, God.

She whirled, ran out of the room and down the hall to Donna's room. She'd whisk them out the basement door and maybe . . .

Christ, this couldn't be happening. Not to her kids.

"I'm trying to keep them safe, Conner," she whispered. "Help me . . ."

BAY COUNTY FARMERS MARKET

t's crowded for a weekday," Hannah commented, as she and Kirov pulled into the parking lot adjacent to the dozens of open-air stalls lining Atlantic Avenue. The area was mobbed with shoppers, each perusing the vendors' selections of fresh fruits and vegetables.

"Do you think Pavski's here yet?"

"I don't see him." Kirov shrugged. "But then again, I wouldn't. He won't show himself until he has to." His gaze was darting around the market, assessing every building, every car, every person, every square inch of the area.

Hannah watched him. "This obviously isn't a new experience for you."

"Finding myself in the same place with someone who wants to kill me as much as I want to kill him?" He smiled slightly. "Oh, I've been in this position a few times before."

"I haven't," Hannah said.

"Is it bothering you? If you want a reason beside revenge, you can add survival. Pavski has no compunction about killing anyone who stands in his way. You fill that bill nicely."

"Revenge is reason enough."

"I agree." Kirov pointed to Niler's Z-98, parked a hundred yards away at a lighthouse-themed restaurant. "There's Niler. I promised to let him finish his transaction before moving in. We'll leave just *before* Pavski and block his exit onto the main road. You stay in the car." Kirov opened his jacket to reveal an automatic handgun. "I'll do the rest."

This was real. She was actually going to help kill a man.

"If something happens to me, don't wait," Kirov said. "Get behind the wheel and take off. Call Bradworth as soon as you can."

"You mean if he kills you." Hannah's voice was shaking. "Bullshit. He's already taken years from you. If he takes what's left, he wins. Don't you dare be stupid enough to let him do that."

He smiled. "I'll make every attempt to keep myself from making that much of an ass of myself."

Niler spotted Kirov and Hannah across the parking lot, sitting in the front seat of their rental car.

Cool people, he thought regretfully. He respected Kirov, and he was beginning to have a yen for Hannah Bryson. Too bad their time together had come to an end.

His cell phone rang, and he answered. "Yo."

"I have a visual confirmation on Kirov and the woman. You may proceed."

Niler glanced around. Where the hell was the spotter calling from? The upper tower of the restaurant, perhaps?

The man spoke again. "Any questions?"

"No questions."

"Then take care of it."

"Will do."

Niler cut the connection.

He wasn't looking forward to this.

He lifted the tiny remote and stared at it. One press, one squeeze, and twenty-four ounces of plastique would incinerate Kirov and Hannah's car, and their lives would come to an end.

Shit.

He stared across the parking lot at Kirov and Hannah. When they woke up that morning, they had no idea that every activity would be their last. Their last cup of coffee. Their last shower. Their last meal.

He hated this. It was better to pass the devices to someone else and let them do what they wanted. He was an artist, not a killer.

Christ.

He fingered the remote. If he didn't do it, Pavski's men would come down and finish them off anyway.

Fucking Pavski. The bastard didn't even bother to show up himself.

Get it over with. He spoke under his breath, "Three . . . two . . . one."

He pushed the button.

*W*hroom.

The explosion rocked the entire parking lot, blowing out the windows of the restaurant and dozens of nearby cars.

Hannah gasped at the sight of Niler's vehicle flipping over and landing on its roof, instantly transformed into half a dozen piles of burning, twisted metal.

She stared in shock at the spot where Niler had sat only seconds before. "My God . . ."

Kirov started the engine and peeled out of the parking space.

Hannah whirled toward him. "What are you doing?"

"Getting away while we still can."

"But Niler is . . ."

"Dead. Blown to smithereens."

She felt sick. She shook her head dazedly. "What the hell happened?"

"Niler made that bomb. He meant it for us."

"What?"

Kirov checked the rearview. "I found it fastened to the underside of our car last night. I merely put it back where it belonged. If Niler hadn't tried to detonate it, he'd be alive and well."

"He just tried to kill us?"

"Surprised?"

Before Hannah could answer, the rear window shattered.

"Get down!" Kirov pushed her head forward. He slouched in his seat and glanced at the side mirror. "Two men in a black Lexus behind us." He muttered a curse. "I don't think either them is Pavski. That would have been too lucky."

He fished into his pocket and produced a key-chain remote identical to the one Niler had brandished in his bar the other night. "Here, take this."

Hannah grabbed the remote. "What's this for?"

Two more bullets hit their car and punctured the trunk.

Kirov accelerated as they neared the parking lot's exit. "Right before we get to the road, we'll cross a small wooden bridge. I need you to watch behind us and press the red button just as that car crosses it. Understand?"

She couldn't answer.

"As soon as you see the Lexus's front two wheels on the bridge. And only if there's no one else nearby. Okay?"

Hannah stared at the remote. She understood perfectly, and it wasn't okay. Push the button, kill two men behind her.

"If you can't stomach it, let me know now."

Hannah took a deep breath. She grasped the remote. "No. Keep your eyes on the road."

"Are you sure?"

A bullet whistled between them and cracked the front windshield.

Hannah glanced at the entrance ahead. "Is that the bridge you're talking about?"

"Yes."

"Okay." She glanced behind her. "They're closing. Put some more distance between us."

Kirov accelerated, and Hannah's eyes searched on either side for any bystanders. All clear so far.

They roared across the tiny bridge, rattling its wood slats beneath their tires. Hannah watched her side-view mirror. A man leaned out of the passenger side of the Lexus, snapping together what appeared to be an Uzi.

Christ. Better not screw this up.

Kirov spun out of the parking lot and headed toward the main road. "Ready?"

Hannah concentrated on the mirror. As the Lexus approached the bridge, its passenger aimed the Uzi. The next moment the car was on the bridge.

Hannah pressed the button.

A violent explosion took out the bridge and car, spraying wood and metal in every direction.

"Perfect!" Kirov hit the steering wheel with his palm.

Hannah turned from the burning rubble and let her hands fall into her lap.

"It wasn't perfect. It was lousy." Hannah felt sick to her stomach, unsure what was bothering her more: killing those two men, seeing Niler die, or just knowing that such an amusing, personable man had been so willing to kill her and Kirov. Any way she cut it, it had been a rotten sixty seconds. She took a deep breath. "And you need to explain to me what just happened."

"Not now." His gaze raked her face. "You need a little time to absorb this before I hit you with anything else. I'll put a little distance between us and Panama City, then we'll talk."

"I don't need—" Maybe she did need the space he'd mentioned. She was still shaking, and her mind was in chaos from the shock. She leaned back in the seat and folded her hands tightly on her lap. "Thirty minutes," she said curtly. "No longer."

Twenty-five minutes later he pulled into the parking lot of a Radisson Suites Inn and got out of the car. "Wait here. I'll get us rooms, and then we'll talk."

"Why can't we talk—"

He'd disappeared into the hotel before she could complete the sentence.

He was back in five minutes and opening her door. "I'm over your deadline, but I figured you'd like a little privacy, with the security of walls around you."

"Will those walls do any good? Will there be more of Pavski's men coming after us? Are we safe here?"

"I wouldn't have stopped if I hadn't thought we'd be okay. The walls are a comfort factor. I think you need it." He unlocked the hotel room. "Go and sit down. I'll get you a cup of coffee."

"You will not. I'm not an invalid." She ignored the easy chair and sat down in the chair at the desk. She needed the firm, upright structure of the piece of furniture. She needed structure, period. "But I'm bewildered and scared and sick to my stomach. I need answers."

"And you'll get them." He sat down on the stool at the coffee bar. "All you have to do is ask."

"When did you find the explosives under our car?"

"Last night. Actually, I've been checking every day since we made contact with Niler. I never completely trusted him."

"What gave him away?"

"Nothing. Actually, I liked him. I've just learned it's best not to trust anyone completely. After you fell asleep last night, I went down and found that he'd planted it on the undercarriage of our car. I recognized his work and simply returned it to him."

"Under *his* car," Hannah said. "Weren't you worried it would go off while you were moving it around?"

"It was a concern, but any car bomb is designed to withstand a lot of jostling until it's detonated. I saw the radio receiver and knew that he built it to be triggered remotely."

"You didn't tell me. So when you say that you've learned not to trust anyone completely, that obviously includes me."

"That's not true."

"Of course it is. Why didn't you tell me any of this last night? Or this morning?"

"I thought you wouldn't approve of my method of dealing with the problem."

She looked at him in disbelief. "Dealing with the problem. You mean blowing Niler to bits?"

"I know you liked him. I knew if I kept you out of the loop, there would be less guilt for you later."

"How thoughtful."

"Look, Niler blew himself up. He literally engineered his own fate. I'm guessing that he called Pavski soon after we met. He probably extracted a tidy sum in exchange for handing us over."

"And those devices he told us he was making for Pavski?"

"They were probably for one of his drug clients."

A trap. A trap from the very beginning. "Why couldn't he have just blown us up before?"

"He could have. I think Pavski just wanted positive confirmation with his own people present. He thought he'd killed me on two previous occasions." He frowned. "Dammit, I'd hoped that Pavski would come himself."

"Maybe he had other fish to fry. The cradle?"

"I don't know. I don't like it. Last night's call from Pavski was pure radio theater. I actually would have been less suspicious if Pavski hadn't agreed to the phone call. As I've said, he likes to insulate himself."

"Where did you get the explosives?"

"I paid a visit to Niler's workshop last night."

She stared at him incredulously. "That was stupid. You could have been killed. How did you get past his security systems?"

Kirov showed her a black box about the size of a cigarette pack. "I had this in my pocket when we went there with him. It's a radio-frequency code reader. When he deactivated the system, this box caught and recorded the frequencies from his remote. That's the reason I wanted to go out there. I thought that his tools of the trade might come in handy for us."

"You suspected him even then?"

He shrugged. "That's the world I live in, Hannah. Do you want me to apologize for not negotiating with you every step of the way?"

"Yes. I don't like to be left in the dark."

"Okay, I apologize. But I'd probably do the same thing tomorrow. This isn't you, and I like it that way."

"*What* isn't me?"

"The guns, the bombs, the killing. This isn't who you are."

"It's not you, either. At least it didn't used to be."

"You're wrong. I was raised to be a warrior."

"Being an officer on a sub isn't the same as blowing up cars. Before you went on the run, had you ever used a gun against someone? Had you ever killed a man?"

He shook his head.

"Our experiences make us who we are," she repeated the words he had once said to her.

"Then you've just lost your argument. I don't want you to become who I am." Kirov went silent for a moment. "I saw the look on your face when I talked about killing Pavski, and you knew it was actually going to happen."

"That was just because—"

"It was because you're human," he interrupted. "It's how you *should* feel. You might want to kill Pavski, but doing it in cold blood made you back away. I felt that way once, but I don't now. I don't want you to lose that piece of yourself. I want to shield you from as much of this as I can."

"It's not your job to protect me."

"No, it's my pleasure and my privilege," he said soberly. "And I'm not going to let you take that away from me."

"Kirov . . ." She shook her head. Part of her was frustrated and indignant, and part of her was experiencing a kind of emotional meltdown. How often had she been feeling this dichotomy of feeling for Kirov lately? Best to shy away from the personal while she was feeling this vulnerable. "What happens now?"

"We regroup and take a look at where we are and where we're going. Things have changed."

"What do you mean?"

"Pavski no longer needs you alive. He knew you'd be in that car with me. It doesn't matter to him anymore. I've been thinking about it ever since I found Niler's bomb. It bothered me because it shows that Pavski no longer believes you have any information that can help him. He might have an informant with the CIA, he might have decided we wouldn't be wasting time with the antique dealer or Niler if we had any knowledge he was lacking. Or he may have gotten another lead on the cradle from the GRU file he got. You were our best opportunity of drawing Pavski out, and it's gone."

"Then we'd better look for another opportunity."

"That's what I'm doing. On the other hand, we have Bradworth and the CIA. Aside from my feeling that they'd be much too lenient with Pavski, I think he has some informants in the Agency. I don't like to trust them with information that Pavski could use against me."

"So?"

"It's time we turned our disadvantages into advantages."

"How?"

"That's what we have to decide." His brows lifted. "I'm open to suggestions."

And she had nothing to suggest. Everything was moving too fast, and she had to digest what Kirov had told her before she could think clearly. She shook her head. "Believe me, I won't be shy about giving you input when I come up with something."

He smiled. "No, there's nothing shy about you. It promises well for other aspects of our relationship." Before she could answer, he stood up. "In the meantime, I'll give you breathing room." He headed for the door. "I'm right next door to you. If you want to talk, knock on my door. I'll order takeout and deliver your supper at six. Okay?"

"Okay."

He looked over his shoulder. "And don't dwell on this. It won't do any good. It's over." He grimaced. "That's no good. Wrong thing to say." He whirled, crossed the room, and fell to his knees in front of her. "Do what you have to do. Feel what you have to feel." He held her gaze with his own. "But what's happened hasn't changed what you are. If I could take it away, I'd do it in a heartbeat. I can't do that." His hand reached up and gently touched her cheek. "And I'm too much of a bastard to wish that you'd never come into my life. All I can do is tell you that I'll shoulder every burden you'll let me. I'll fight for you. I'll give you comfort." His finger traced the line of her upper lip. "I'll give you anything you want from me. Is that enough?"

He was barely touching her, and her chest was tight, and the intensity in the room was thick and charged. Charged with what? She knew he was trying to comfort her, and the comfort was there. Yet there was also the disturbing element that seemed always to be between them now.

He shook his head as he got to his feet. "It's kind of mixed up, isn't it?" He turned and strode toward the door. "My intentions were good. It just didn't turn out the way I—"

The door closed behind him.

She slowly got to her feet and moved across to the picture window overlooking the sun-baked beach.

Another beach.

Most of her adult life had been spent either on beaches like this one or on the oceans of the world. She would have been contented and happy to have spent the rest of her days doing the same job with the same people. Even thirty days ago she would never have dreamed that she would be thrown into this chaos.

She had killed two men today. She had watched a man whom she'd found amusing and likable die because he'd tried to kill her and Kirov. And she had taken another involuntary step closer to Kirov in the midst of all that turmoil.

Mixed up? Yes, her life, and her responses were on a par with the confusion of every minute of this day. She'd just have to ride it out until all the madness was over.

And when the hell would that be? she wondered wearily. She'd thought they were on their way to getting Pavski when they'd found Niler. Instead, they'd barely escaped with their lives and were back to square one. Kirov might not be discouraged, but she was tired of treading water. She needed to see—

Her cell phone rang.

Kirov?

She took the phone out of her pocket and looked at the caller ID.

She stiffened. A chill went through her.

Conner Bryson.

EIGHTEEN

"The operation was a bust in Panama City," Koppel said as he hung up the phone. "The local news is reporting two car explosions within fifteen minutes of each other."

"Then it can't be a bust," Pavski said. "One of those cars must be Kirov's."

Koppel shook his head. "One vehicle was driven by 'popular bar owner Dane Niler.'"

Pavski muttered a curse. "And the other?"

"We think it's our men. They were in pursuit of a vehicle that resembled the rental car Niler said Kirov was driving."

"Verify."

Koppel nodded and started to dial again.

Pavski barely listened to the conversation as he tried to control the anger surging through him. He had thought he had Kirov, but he had slipped away again. He was beginning to understand why his men had referred to Kirov as a ghost.

Damn him to hell. He needed Kirov out of his life once and for all. He might be getting a call from Danzyl any minute, and he couldn't chance Kirov getting in his way.

Koppel hung up. "I can't raise either of our men in Panama City."

Confirmed.

Shit.

"What do we do?" Koppel asked.

"Well, we don't sit around looking helpless and asking stupid questions." Pavski thought about it. "Did you do as I asked you and accessed Kirov's phone?"

"Yes, we went through Bradworth's phone as you told me. But we can't trace Kirov. He must be using relays."

"I didn't expect to trace it. I want to talk to him."

"Why?"

Because it was time. Because he was tired of playing cat and mouse. Because he couldn't bear for Kirov to think he'd made a fool of him. "Just get him on the phone for me."

No identifier on the ID box.

Kirov hesitated, and then picked up the call on the fourth ring.

"You missed me again, Captain. I'd think you'd grow discouraged. Or should I call you Kirov? Yes, I think I will. The proud captain of *Silent Thunder* has faded into ineffectual nothingness."

He went still. "Pavski?" Of course, it was Pavski. "And you missed me. You're gradually losing all your support. Pretty soon you'll have to stiffen your backbone and face me."

"I don't have to confront a man who will be dead in days. It's very fitting you took the name of a dead man. It's only a matter of time until you join Ivanov."

"Were you the one who tipped Bradworth?"

"Of course. I've suspected you were still alive for the last year. The descriptions I received of the 'ghost' fit you far better than Ivanov. The FSB started investigating after hearing rumors three years ago from people in the village who claimed they had seen a wounded man who had died and was buried there. The description bore a resemblance to Ivanov but it wasn't worthwhile for the FSB to pursue it on their limited budget. I thought I'd let Bradworth confirm it."

"I hate to disappoint you, but you didn't cause much trouble for me. I was already distancing myself from Bradworth."

"It will keep you from going to him for help when I have time to go after you."

"Oh, and what was Niler's attempt? Admit it. You screwed up, Pavski."

Silence. "Enjoy your gloating. I'm the one who will end up on top. No one can keep me from—"

"You're a criminal and a mass murderer. You have no destiny but the same one as Stalin and Attila the Hun. You're going down, Pavski. And I'm going to be the one to do it."

"Such passion. I remember that about you. My officers said that you nearly went berserk when you heard about the deaths of your crew." He added softly, "I did that to you. I killed them. I killed your wife. I hurt you. I destroyed your life. I enjoy thinking about it. I wanted you to know that."

"Is that why you phoned me?"

"Perhaps. And to tell you that sending Eugenia Voltar to Moscow was an exercise in futility. She's going to find nothing. No one is going to talk to her. If they do, it will be too late. I'll already have all I need."

"We'll see. Eugenia is a remarkable woman. She can be very persuasive." He paused. "And I wouldn't think about taking her out if I were you. She's very competent, and you might lose another man."

"She's going to die. I'd already decided that she could become an obstacle. I *will* find the cradle."

"Only in your dreams."

"You'll see. Or maybe you won't. Unless you're looking up from hell. You still have Hannah Bryson with you. Don't you find her in the way?"

"No."

"I do." He hung up.

Kirov slowly hung up the phone. The rage was still searing through him. Christ, he was actually shaking with anger. Control. He and Pavski hadn't spoken since that last day on the *Silent Thunder*. Pavski had meant to remind him of that day of horror and failure, when he had been taken prisoner and Pavski reigned supreme.

Block it out. Go over the conversation. Could he pull anything of value out of it?

Yes, there was the information that he knew Eugenia was in Moscow and pursuing the goal Pavski had set for Danzyl. Other than that, boasting, threats, and malice.

And that last threat was to Hannah.

Okay, his cell phone couldn't be traced. He was sure they hadn't been followed. No need to be worried.

Screw it. He was worried. He had to see her, touch her.

He headed for the door.

She was gone.

Fear iced through him as Kirov looked around the empty suite.

Keep calm. It could still be okay, he told himself as he checked out the room. Hannah had been upset when he'd left her a few hours ago. She could have gone for a walk or downstairs for a drink.

Yeah, sure. And taken her suitcase with her.

No note. No phone call.

Pavski?

Dammit, he'd been sure they hadn't been followed.

He moved toward the door. Go downstairs, check with the desk, and ask questions.

Christ, he was scared.

Keep calm. He'd find her.

He dialed Eugenia as he was striding down the hall toward the elevator. He had to warn her that any cover she might have thought she had was blown. He had enough to worry about here without having to fly to Moscow to try to keep Eugenia alive.

ugenia's cell phone vibrated in her pocket. She stepped deeper into the vestibule of the bakery, pulled out her phone, and flipped it open. "It's a bad time, Kirov."

"Pavski knows you're in Moscow to try to get information."

"Of course, he does. It was bound to be noised about when I started approaching people."

"He knows, and you're a target. I don't want *you* taking chances."

"That's the name of the game. You don't get anywhere if you—" She suddenly realized that Kirov's tone was oddly tense. "What's wrong? Problems?"

"I don't know. Maybe. But I'll take care of it."

And he wasn't going to confide in her, she realized. "I'm sure you will." She went back to the business at hand. "I decided right away it was going to take too long to get the same information as Danzyl. I'm taking a shortcut."

"What kind of shortcut?"

"I tapped both Danzyl's cell phone and his computer. That way anything he finds out and tells Pavski, I'll find out. So hang up. I may be missing something. I think he's on a trail."

"Where are you?"

"Outside the university where Heiser taught. He took a path around the Lit building toward the rear campus. I'm going to follow him." She hung up.

Move carefully, casually, and hope that Danzyl was so involved that he wouldn't spot her on his heels.

She shouldn't have worried. Danzyl was standing before a statue of an old bearded man draped in a toga that dominated the garden. He was squatting and taking a picture of the inscription on the base.

She faded behind a tree and waited.

Danzyl was pulling out his phone and dialing. "I have it. I'm sending you the picture. Yes, it has the symbol but I can't—Judge for yourself. I think there may be another one." He flinched as he listened to the reply. "Of course, I'll check it out." He muttered a curse as he hung up. He took one more picture and turned away from the statue. A moment later he was striding away.

She waited until he was around the side of the building before she moved toward the statue.

The statue was old, mortar crumbling, and the execution of the old man was only mediocre. The figure had his arm raised and he seemed to be fighting off two small, female, birdlike—creatures.

She looked at the inscription.

Look not for riches on the surface of life.

Below it was the numeral letter one.

And below that was the symbol Kirov had faxed her.

Yes.

She took a photo on her phone and sent it to Kirov. A minute later, when she was hurrying after Danzyl, she phoned Kirov back. "Who's the old man in the statue?"

"Probably someone in Greek mythology. I'll look it up."

"I'll do that myself. I thought you might know. That numeral one might mean this statue is one of two or three or whatever." She frowned. "Danzyl thought so too. I might have to move very fast from now on. Does the inscription mean anything to you?"

"No."

"I'll hit the computer and see if I can bring up anything. I'll be in touch." She hung up. She could either tag along with Danzyl or spend the time researching. She would bet Danzyl was going back to the GRU office and doing the same thing. She'd rather rely on herself than bugging antiquated GRU computer files and Internet connections. She sat down on a bench and reached for her computer. "Okay," she murmured. "What do we know? That symbol—a cross within a circle. Heiser tells his father he wants to go back to the Rioni River, where he visited as a child. A statue set down in the middle of a garden at a university in Moscow. Old. Greek mythology. Let's see what we can do with it . . ."

BOSTON
COPLEY PLACE MALL

What the devil is happening, Cathy?" Hannah asked as she sat down beside her on the bench outside the Gap. "That telephone call scared the life out of me."

"I couldn't talk long. I tried to be careful, but I don't know how many bugs they have on me." Cathy grimaced. "Isn't it crazy? I sound completely paranoid, don't I?" She added soberly, "I wish I was paranoid. The alternative sucks."

"Why are we meeting in a mall? Why couldn't I come to your house?"

"Because that's what they want. Where's Kirov?"

"You told me not to bring him. I took a cab to the airport the minute I hung up."

"Good." She stood up. "Come on, let's walk. I don't have much time."

"Why not?" She fell into step with her. "For God's sake, what's happening?"

"That slimeball, Pavski, wants you very badly. He wants Kirov's head, and he thinks he can manipulate you to get it for him. He planted a bug in my living room to see if he could trace you. It's a good thing you haven't been in touch lately." She shot her a glance. "Though I was ready to murder you myself when I thought you were leaving me out of the loop."

"Things were . . . difficult."

"Tell me about it. They haven't been too good here either."

"How do you know he planted a bug?"

"George Preston told me he did it." Her lips twisted. "It was George who did the dirty work."

Hannah stared at her in shock. "What? Why?"

"Pavski had a hold over George. The NSA created a go-to list several years ago, and George's name was on it."

"Go-to list?"

"A blackmail list. When a prominent figure got into trouble that might mean damage to his image, the NSA stepped in and did a cover-up. But that also meant they could go to that person when they needed help in any area. When he first came to Washington, George was drinking and in a car accident that seriously injured a bystander. It could have ruined his career. The NSA stepped in and took care of everything and sent George on his way."

"And the NSA gave this info to Pavski?"

"No, four years ago the computer go-to list was stolen from the NSA data banks by a geek named Thomas Carwell. He now lives in a palace in Iran and sells information to the highest bidder. Anyone with the money can get whatever information they need."

"And Pavski wanted to get a hold over us and found George Preston on the list."

"That's what George told me."

"Christ."

"But Pavski read George wrong. George went along with him until he could figure out what to do, but when the chips were down, he told me what was happening." Her voice was uneven. "Pavski was talking about taking my kids. George couldn't stand the thought of anything happening to them."

"The kids?" she whispered.

"Pavski told George that he'd be doing me a favor by persuading me to get you to come out of hiding. He said that he wouldn't have to move on the kids if he got his hands on you."

Hannah felt sick. "Ronnie and Donna? Jesus, no wonder you're scared."

"And mad as hell." Cathy's lips set. "How dare that mad dog threaten my kids?"

"You were right to call me back. I'll deal with it."

"I've already dealt with it. Did you think I'd draw you back here to offer him a trade? I may be as ferocious as a mother bear with her cubs, but I wouldn't do that to you." Her lips tightened. "He killed my Conner. He wants to hurt my kids. We have to take him down."

"The kids come first. How have you dealt with it?"

"I packed them up and sent them to stay with a good friend of mine, Miriam Frey. I told her what was happening, and she agreed to help. God, do I owe her." She added bitterly, "Sweet Jesus, if you could have seen me smuggling the kids out of the house the night George told me about this mess. I was jumping at every shadow. He was sure the house was watched, and he didn't know how long I had before Pavski would act. I had to get them away from me somewhere they'd be safe. But I don't think anyone saw me take the kids out of the house to Miriam's place."

"Pavski will find them, Cathy."

"Do you think I'm stupid? I know that. George has hired body-guards to set up security around the house. But we have to stop Pavski before it gets that far."

Hannah was silent a moment. "You're trusting George Preston a good deal."

"And you're afraid he's still playing ball with Pavski?" She shook her head. "He's not trying to trick me. I believe him, Hannah. He didn't have to tell me anything. He could have just stepped back and let it happen."

Hannah nodded. "My suspicious nature. Nothing seems to be what it seems now."

"That's why I called you on Conner's cell phone. The authorities gave it to me with his personal effects. I wasn't sure I wasn't being monitored by Pavski or Bradworth or whoever. No one would monitor a dead man's phone."

"Very smart. But you almost gave me a heart attack."

"I had to let you know what was happening. We don't have much time to get Pavski. I want my kids home and safe."

"They will be." She reached out and squeezed her shoulder. "Nothing will happen to them."

"You're damn right it won't." Her hands clenched into fists. "I *hate* not being able to be with them. It's driving me crazy." She drew a deep breath. "I have to get going. I made sure I wasn't being followed, but I'm not taking any chances. If you want to get in touch, call me on Conner's phone." She turned away. "And you'd better get in touch with me. We have to do something to put an end to this." She glanced back over her shoulder. "Be careful, Hannah. Keep safe."

"I will. Take care of yourself." She watched Cathy move swiftly toward the escalator. Cathy's shoulders were square but rigid with tension, and she was clearly having to use all her strength to hold herself together. And why not? she thought in frustration. A man who would threaten children was outside both Cathy's and her experience.

But not out of Kirov's. Kirov knew the nature of the beast.

He would come if she called him.

And if she called him, she would be doing exactly what Pavski wanted her to do. He wanted Kirov dead, and she would be bringing him out into the open and setting him up. She couldn't do it.

The children. Innocent. Helpless. Prey.

Jesus.

She reached for her telephone.

Kirov picked up on the second ring.

"Goddamn you."

"Hello to you, too."

"Where are you?"

"I'm in Boston." She steadied her voice. "Pavski is setting up a trap for you. Well, you and me. But I seem to be of minor importance at the moment."

"Not to me. Why the hell didn't you wait and talk to me instead of bolting?"

"Cathy asked me not to—I'll tell you later." She paused. "If you choose to come."

"I'm on my way. When I tracked your cab to the airport, I figured you'd be on your way to your sister-in-law. She was the only one who could make you jump and run. And you wouldn't answer your cell phone, dammit. Where can I reach you once I land in Boston? You're staying away from your condo, right?"

"Right. I'm at Copley Place Mall. I'll meet you at the Chili's Restaurant. Call me when you get in."

"If you'll answer your phone," he growled.

"I'll answer my phone." She hung up.

Kirov was blazing angry.

Hannah instinctively tensed, readying for battle, as she watched him walk in the restaurant door. She'd been prepared for irritation, not thunderclouds and lightning. She'd never seen Kirov angry before.

"Talk to me." He sat down across from her. "Tell me why you walked out of that hotel without a word to me. Didn't it occur to you that I might think something was just a little amiss?"

"I promised Cathy I wouldn't tell you or anyone else that I was coming here."

"I would have thought you'd be able to trust me by now."

"Don't be an ass. She was scared, and she wouldn't have asked it if it hadn't been important to her." She met his gaze. "And she has a right to be scared. If she didn't, I wouldn't have called you. I don't like the idea of asking you to come and risk Pavski—" She drew a deep breath. "But I did ask you, and now I have to deal with it. So just shut up and let me—" Her hand clenched on her coffee cup. "It's the kids, Kirov."

He went still. "Cathy's children?"

She nodded jerkily. "And Cathy is trying to work through it but she's scared. *I'm* scared."

"Does Pavski have them?"

"No, Cathy says they're safe for the time being. I don't know if she's right. It sounds to me as if—"

"Start at the beginning. How do you expect me to sift through all that guilt and nail biting you're throwing at me?" Kirov interrupted as he motioned for the waitress to fill her cup. "And stop worrying until there's something to worry about. We'll work it out."

His bluntness was oddly more comforting than gentleness would have been. He was working, thinking, cutting through all the chaff.

She lifted the cup to her lips. "I don't bite my nails." She smiled slightly. "And I won't feel any guilt at all if you keep on barking at me." She quickly filled him in on what Cathy had told her and ended with her primary concern, "How far do you think we can trust George Preston?"

"I have no idea." He grimaced. "That's not the answer you wanted to hear. It's the best I can do. On the surface it seems as if he's now playing it straight. On the other hand, it could be some elaborate double dealing."

"He has control of the kids. He arranged for bodyguards for them. Which means he could call them off if he's the one paying their salary."

"Then it behooves us to make sure that there's other protection."

"You can't go near them. That's what Pavski wants."

"Then I'll make sure not to give it to him." He stared her in the eye. "Trust me. I won't let anything happen to those children, Hannah."

Warmth moved through her, and for the first time since she'd met Cathy today, the panic subsided. "I do trust you. That's why I called you." Her lips twisted. "Even though I knew it was going to put you at risk."

"Guilt?" He smiled. "Now, let me think how I can use that."

"I'm the one who is using you. Now, how can we safeguard the kids?"

"I'm working on it." He looked down into his coffee. "Except for the children, this may not be an entirely bad thing."

"I can't see how it could get much worse."

"Pavski's getting ready to set a trap. When you're concentrating on capturing the enemy, it takes the focus away from a possible trap laid for you."

"And how are we going to trap Pavski?"

"By using his trap against him." He was frowning. "But the bait has to be too tasty to resist. He has a possibility of getting the information about how to find the cradle from Danzyl in Moscow. He may want me dead, but he wants the cradle more." He thought about it. "We'll have to use the *Silent Thunder*. If we can lure him to the sub, he'll be out in the open, and we can get him."

"He'd never risk going down that hatch."

"We may get to him before he leaves the dock. All we need is to bring him out in the open. Even if he's on the pier, I have a chance at him. Guns aren't my weapons of choice but I'm a very good shot."

"I imagine you are," she said absently as she thought about it. "It would be risky." But hope was beginning to stir within her. "We can turn this mess around?"

He smiled. "And upside down. If we work it right."

"How do we do it?"

"We pull in all the help we can get from both solid and questionable sources." He reached for his phone. "And we start with a few telephone calls . . ."

She shook her head. "What would you do without that cell phone?"

"Perish the thought." He made a face. "I don't even like to think about it."

Kirov received a call from Eugenia four hours later. "I've *got* it, Kirov. It's all coming together."

"What have you got?" He put the phone on speaker for Hannah.

"There *were* two statues given to Russia by the Greek government in 1937," she said. "It was supposed to be a gesture of enduring friendship."

"What does the other statue look like?"

"No photos. It's not here in Moscow. Evidently we're lucky it was even entered into the historical art archives. It wasn't an important art object. But since it was Greek, I searched the Greek art Web sites. I went after the symbol first and hit a bonanza. It's the identifying mark used by sculptors in an artist colony near Athens. They've been signing their work with it since 1924." She paused. "And the figure is supposed to be Phineas and the Harpies. According to mythology, Phineas was saved from the harpies by Jason and the Argonauts. He was grateful and told Jason where to find the Golden Fleece. But Jason had to travel to Midia in Thrace to ask Phineas."

"So?"

"According to the transcript of Heiser's last conversation with his father, he mentions taking his father to the Rioni River when he came back."

"Eugenia, a hell of a lot of intelligence manpower was spent in that area because of that one casual reference. Including mine. It was wasted effort."

"Because you weren't looking at it the right way. You weren't tracing a link with mythology. The people in that area claim that the Golden Fleece was based on fact."

"Fact?"

"For centuries the farmers in that area would wash their sheep fleeces in that river and others to catch the gold washed down from upstream deposits. That's where Jason supposedly found his Golden Fleece."

"And you think the second statue is there?"

"Maybe. There's a chance. But I'm betting on Midia. I think Heiser was mentioning the Rioni River to give his father a frame of reference to think Golden Fleece. Midia was once the city of Salmydessus in ancient Thrace. Jason had to go there to get the answer to his quest. Everything centers around Phineas and the place he lived." Eugenia was speaking quickly, her voice vibrating with excitement. "Don't you see? What other city would be such a likely candidate to get that second statue? I can't find any reference to Midia's receiving it, but I'd bet I'll find it there." She added, "I'm on my way now. I'll call the artist colony in Athens and see if they have a record of where the second statue went, but I'm not waiting for an answer. Danzyl is sharp. He'll figure all this out too. I have to get there before he does. I'll call you when I find it." She hung up.

Hannah shook her head. "Damn, she's good. But it's still a long shot."

"Eugenia doesn't think so." Kirov smiled. "And she has excellent instincts."

"Well, her instincts are telling her that Danzyl could beat her to the punch." She shivered. "And you said Pavski has already told him to remove her as an obstacle."

"That won't be easy to do. And I couldn't stop her now if I tried. Didn't you hear her voice? She's alert, excited, on the hunt."

Yes, Hannah had detected all of those emotions in Eugenia's tone. She had never heard her sound more vibrantly alive.

She just hoped she'd stay alive.

God, he was bored.

Dananka pressed the surveillance receiver firmly against his ear. He hated this kind of wait and watch bullshit. His talent lay in other directions. Someone else should have been assigned to do this crap job of monitoring Cathy Bryson's incoming calls. All he'd been getting was PTA meeting junk and bereavement calls telling her what a great guy her husband had been.

Another call.

He looked down at his ID box. No ID.

Telemarketer?

"Cathy?"

"My God, Hannah. Why haven't you called me before? I've been worried sick. Are you okay?"

Dananka sat up straight in the seat. Fucking jackpot.

"As okay as I can be considering."

"Considering what?"

"Let's skip it. How are you and the kids?"

"Fine. I'm a little on edge, so I sent the kids to Miriam Frey's for a couple days. Ronnie's best friend is her son, Bobby." She paused. "Hannah, you have to let George help you. This Kirov is bad news."

"Tell me about it," Hannah said grimly. "He doesn't care whether I live or die as long as he gets that other plate."

"What other plate? You told me Pavski had stolen everything you found."

"It was safer for you that way."

"Hannah, damn you."

"It wasn't actually etched on those plates. Evidently Heiser had run out of time or was interrupted or was getting sicker and had to go to his cabin to etch those final coordinates on a plate. I found it behind the desk in the captain's quarters when I went back with Kirov."

"Then give it to Bradworth."

"Not possible. I threw it overboard."

"What?"

"Don't act so shocked. I don't trust Bradworth, and I don't trust Kirov. I wasn't going to let either one of them have it. What if they decided to forget about Pavski and walk away? I can remember and reconstruct the plate if I have to do it."

"And Kirov knows about the plate?"

"He was on the sub when I found it. He was mad as hell when he saw me toss it into the sea. He's been coercing me to do the reconstruction since he saw me drop it overboard. I told him I'd re-create that plate if he gave me Pavski's head." She paused. "But my time's running out. Kirov would as soon break my neck as look at me."

"Give him the plate. Then we'll call Bradworth to rein him in."

"Like hell I will. I'm not giving Kirov anything. He could have saved Conner and didn't do it," Hannah said. "He's on his way back to the sub to see if he can do some scuba diving and resurrect it."

"Is that possible?"

"How do I know? Probably. The seas are relatively quiet in the harbor, and the depth isn't extreme. But at least he's off my back. With any luck, Pavski will stick a shark spear in him. I don't give a damn about the plate." She added wearily, "The only thing that matters to me are you and the kids. The reason I called you is to tell you that I want you to sit tight and be careful. There's no telling what Kirov will do if he doesn't find that plate. He believes he can draw out Pavski with the damn thing."

"Can he?"

"Maybe. I'm flying up this afternoon to check and see if he's managed to find it."

"Call me back," Cathy said. "I worry about you, blast it."

"I'll call when I can." Hannah Bryson hung up.

Dananka was already busily working at his board verifying the number and model of her cell phone. After 9/11 the FCC required all carriers to have the ability to trace calls on cell phones to a hundred meters or less. That meant every cell phone had a built-in GPS that could be tapped given the right circumstances. He sent a tracer to check the nearest tower, and then initiated the access-tracking map device. Two minutes later he had her pinpointed on the map.

"Got you, bitch."

He reached for his phone and called Pavski.

Hannah turned to Kirov. "What do you think?"

"If Pavski's man isn't a complete amateur, he has your phone tagged and will be able to follow you to hell and back." Kirov smiled. "Or preferably just to hell. End of story." He stood aside for her to board the helicopter. "If not, you'll have to make another phone call."

"I stayed on the phone as long as you told me."

"And were suitably insulting." He motioned for the pilot to start the engine. "Was the release of all that suppressed hostility satisfying?"

She shot him a sidewise glance. "Perhaps."

"Well, let's hope you were convincing."

"Do you think Pavski will go for it?"

"Good chance. He has a chance to kill me and get the plate. Or as an alternate, he has a chance to scoop you up and force you to recreate the plate. As far as he's concerned, it's all good." He glanced at his watch. "We should be in Rock Bay Harbor in an hour. My bet is Pavski will be hot on our heels."

The signal on her phone indicates she's heading north," Dananka said. "She's going to the sub. What do I do? Follow her in the helicopter?"

Pavski thought about it. Excitement was tearing through him. Jesus, it was all coming together. He'd known that Cathy Bryson would be the key. "No, you stay here. I'll take Koppel and the two new men, Lepin and Norzalk. I have something else for you to do."

"What?"

"We may have to have leverage if I don't find that plate. Go after the children." He rose to his feet. "And I need at least one of them alive, Dananka."

"Only one?"

"Use your own judgment. I wouldn't mind you showing Hannah Bryson what to expect if she doesn't cooperate." He hung up and moved toward the door.

The Golden Cradle was shimmering in the distance, but it was getting nearer and nearer.

Almost in his hands, almost here . . .

NINETEEN

Where the hell was that statue? Eugenia wondered impatiently. It had to be here. She'd gotten vague directions from the head of the artist colony in Athens, but his information had been entered in their directory in 1937, and the statue could have crumbled into dust in that time. No, the torn and faded brochure she'd picked up on the porch of the tourist agency had listed it as the gem of their historical collection.

Some gem, she thought. This tiny park in the middle of town that was supposed to house the tribute to the Argonauts was deserted and overgrown. She doubted if anyone came here anymore, including passing tourists. One look at this tangle of brush, and they would pass on to greener pastures, or maybe that more welcoming coffeehouse down the street.

She shone the beam of her flashlight around the area in front of her. More overgrown brush and low-hanging branches. How could she find the damn—

There it was!

A glimpse of gray stone in the depths of green foliage in the path to the left.

She moved forward eagerly. No, not smart. She cautiously slowed her pace. This park might not be as deserted as it seemed. Danzyl might have made the connection too.

She played the beam around the surrounding area as she went toward the statue.

No sign of anyone.

No movement in the brush.

No sound . . .

Okay, but that didn't mean Danzyl might not be on her heels. Take the picture and get out.

She shined the flashlight on the statue. Jason with his arm raised in triumph, holding the Golden Fleece.

She took the picture and lowered the beam to the base. The same symbol that was on the other statue and another inscription. She took the picture of it and moved closer to get a better shot.

A rustle in the bushes to the left . . .

She dove forward and hit the ground rolling.

A bullet struck the ground next to her.

Jesus, she was a sitting duck.

She rolled behind the statue and got to her knees.

The stone splintered as a bullet struck the statue beside her head.

But she had a fix on where the bullet came from now.

Don't move, you son of bitch, she entreated silently. Just let me get one shot before you come in for the kill.

Another shot. From the same direction.

Yes!

She sprayed the area with a barrage of four bullets.

She waited.

No return fire.

Had she gotten him? Or was it a trick?

She waited.

Okay, go in and see for yourself.

She carefully moved to the other side of the statue and dove into the brush.

She lay there, breathing shallowly, listening.

Nothing.

She scouted around the underbrush toward the bush from where the gunfire had come.

Blood, dark and gleaming in the moonlight as it ran from behind the bush toward the path.

But blood didn't always mean dead.

But this time it did.

Danzyl was lying on his side with a bullet in his temple and another in his throat.

Lucky. Those had been lucky shots.

But how lucky had she been? Had Danzyl been here before she had arrived, or had he come right behind her? One way to tell.

She searched his pocket and pulled out his picture cell phone.

She searched his cell phone memory.

"Shit!"

Photo transmitted.

BOSTON

7:32 P.M.

According to the information Dananka was able to pull out of his computer, Miriam Frey was divorced, in her early forties, and lived alone with her son in a two-story house in a small subdivision twenty minutes from Cathy Bryson's home. Neither she nor her ex-husband had ever registered a firearm. Perfect.

He could already see how this would play out. The maternal instinct would destroy this woman. She would neglect her own safety for that of two children who weren't even hers. He'd seen it happen too many times. It would be a simple matter to dispatch her, scoop up the kids, and get the hell away. In and out in less than ten minutes.

He parked beside the detached garage and crept toward the back windows. A TV blared from the living room. He peered inside and saw a children's cartoon playing on the screen.

But no Miriam Frey, no kids.

He looked up at the second floor. Two lights upstairs—a bedroom and bath, he guessed. Bedtime for the kiddies?

He checked the back door. Locked, and he spotted a cheap alarm system wiring the door. It took him a few more minutes disabling it.

He was in the house.

He pulled out his automatic and moved quietly through the kitchen.

Thump.

Thump.

It came from upstairs. He cocked his head, listening.

Thump.

He smiled. I'm on my way, young ones . . .

He slowly climbed the stairs.

Thump.

Running water in the bathroom. Ah, of course. Bath time.

The thumping came from the same place.

He moved down the hallway to the open door of the bathroom.

The bathtub water was running, but the small room was empty. He stepped closer to the tub.

Thump. Thump.

He finally saw the noise's source. A battery operated floating duck, repeatedly ramming itself against the tub's inner wall.

No one here. They must all be in the bedroom.

He turned toward the doorway.

Thump. Thump.

Those two sounded . . . different.

Pain. He went cold and couldn't move. His breath left him. His gun slipped from his numb fingers.

What the hell?

He glanced down. Two red stains were spreading across his chest.

The door of the linen closet swung wide. A man stood there

holding a smoking gun equipped with a silencer. Bradworth. It was Bradworth. He smiled. "One last wish for a happy afterlife?"

Dananka's last memory was the flash as he raised the muzzle and the dull sound that came with it.

Thump.

Good riddance.

Bradworth ran down the steps to the basement.

"It's all right, Preston," he said as he reached the bottom of the stairs. "Except for the cleanup. How are the kids?"

He nodded at the two children, who were huddled over a game table with Miriam Frey. "Playing checkers and complaining because there's no TV down here." He paused. "I'm sorry you had to be involved, Bradworth."

"I didn't do it for you. I did it for Kirov. He made me a deal." He looked at the kids. "And for them. I've got a couple kids myself that I don't get to see near enough. The helpless have more rights than the rest of us. I have no problem killing filth who go after children." He turned to go back upstairs. "I'm calling a mop-up squad and telling them to get out here and get rid of that body. It's not something the kids should see."

"Could I help?" Preston asked. "It would be good to do something besides act as babysitter."

He gave him a cool glance. "I was wondering whether I should let you do that. But I wouldn't have found you here yourself mounting guard if you were a Judas. You'd have wanted clean hands."

"I didn't like the idea of sending away those guards."

"If he'd seen we had security, it would have tipped him, and he would have called Pavski. This way we had only one scumbag to eliminate. No problem."

His lips twisted as he looked down at his hands. "Clean hands. Instead, I let you get yours dirty."

"It doesn't matter. Vermin have to be smashed." He shrugged as he started up the stairs. "And this time I got to be Superman, saving the world. That's not half-bad."

Kirov's phone rang as they were getting in the rental car waiting at the small airport at Rock Bay Harbor.

He glanced at the ID. "Bradworth." He listened for a moment. "Thanks, Bradworth. No, I won't tell you what I'm doing. Yes, I know I owe you. I'm sure you're not going to let me forget it." He hung up and turned to Hannah. "Pavski sent one of his goons after the kids, but they're safe now. He said Preston turned out to be legitimate."

"Good." She added, "And if Pavski heard where the kids were being kept, then he must have bought the telephone call to Cathy. He knows where we're headed. He'll take the bait."

"I can hear him snapping now . . ." Kirov murmured as he started the car.

The phone rang again when he was only a block away from the airport. Eugenia. This time he put it on speaker.

"I've sent you a photo of the second statue," Eugenia said

quickly. "It was a statue of Jason holding high the fleece. On the base it had the same symbol and the inscription read. *Journey forth but always seek within to find the true treasure.*" She paused. "I'm sorry, but I didn't get Danzyl in time. He transmitted a photo of the statue to Pavski. He probably has it now. How bad could it be? That one line doesn't seem to mean much."

"I don't know. Don't worry. Get the hell out of there. You've done your job." He hung up the phone. "Let's just hope that picture doesn't trigger anything for Pavski. We don't want him distracted."

"I don't see how it could." She frowned. "Let's see. The line on the first statue was *Look not for riches on the surface of life.* On the second *Journey forth, but always seek within to find the true treasure.* Eugenia was right, it's not much to work with. I can't see how Heiser could think his father would . . ." She trailed off. "My God."

Kirov glanced sharply at her. "What?"

"Where are my charts I made of those plates?"

"In my duffel in the backseat. Why?"

She was on her knees and grabbing the duffel. "I need to look at them." She unzipped the duffel and rummaged until she found the tube of rolled-up stationery. "I think I may—" She broke off as she saw something in the bottom of the duffel. "Dynamite?"

He shrugged. "You can never tell when you might want to toss a few sticks at the undesirable elements we seem to be encountering."

"Where did you get it?" She answered her own question. "Niler's place. You certainly didn't limit yourself to what you needed in Florida. You must have snagged all he had."

"I figured he wouldn't need it. Though I had to use a private jet to avoid security." He changed the subject. "Why do you need the charts?"

"I need to check the third plate for the destination. Could it be close to Midia?"

"Yes. Somewhere near the Turkish-Bulgarian coast."

"That used to be Thrace, didn't it?"

He nodded.

"Then it could be . . ." Excitement was mounting, growing with every second. "Look, in the legend, the Argonauts had to travel to Thrace for Phineas to tell them how to get the treasure. On the back of those bulkhead plates, Heiser's coordinates lead to what used to be Thrace. What if that's where we need to go to get the location of this treasure, too? But in this case, it's the *Silent Thunder* that will tell us."

His eyes were narrowed on her face. "Go on."

"Think about it. Heiser was a computer genius, and you said he was a master of that navigation system. It's not too far-fetched to think that he may have buried some lines of code in there to display a message that reveals itself only when triggered by a specific event."

Kirov nodded slowly. "An event like the sub's compass registering the set of coordinates noted on the bulkhead plates?"

She nodded. "The *Argo* had to go to Midia to find the Golden Fleece. Heiser leaves a map next to *Silent Thunder*'s navigational computer that leads to the exact same place." She drew a deep breath. "But he wasn't sure his father would get it. His father wasn't a sailor, he was a professor of literature. He didn't think the same way. So he dredged up those memories from his childhood to let him know that those plates weren't the answer. He was to journey forth, but he had to look within for the answer."

"Within the navigation computer."

"I think I'm right, Kirov," she said eagerly. "I think I can find it."

"If we have time." He grimaced. "I could have wished we'd figured this out before we deliberately set Pavski to follow us to the sub."

"Just get me there. I'll pull out the information, and we can make sure Pavski can't get into the computer. We can't take a chance on that happening. What if there's a screwup? What if he somehow manages to get away? You said he'd done it before." Her hands clenched. "Maybe we'll get lucky. Maybe he won't figure it out."

"You did. All you needed was that final clue to nudge you. Pavski's very smart. He has the plates. He has the inscription Danzyl sent. He's been thinking of nothing but a way to get that cradle all his life. We'd have to be damn lucky."

"I won't let him get his hands on it, Kirov," she said fiercely. "Not for a second. He killed my brother to get it. He's not going to have it."

"We've set it up so that he thinks he has a good reason to go after us now. If he knows the final answer is definitely in that computer, nothing will stop him."

"Then that's even better. Get me there, let me take it out of the computer. Just give me a little time."

Kirov stepped on the accelerator. "I'll give you what time I can. After that we do what we planned. We go after Pavski."

The navigation computer.

Pavski inhaled sharply as he continued to gaze down at the photo of the statue he'd received on the helicopter ten minutes ago.

It could be what the quote meant.

It *was* what the quote meant. He felt it in his bones.

And if there was no fourth plate, then Kirov was luring him to the sub as a trap.

It didn't matter.

The *Silent Thunder* was now exactly where Pavski wanted to be. Nothing on earth or hell would keep him off that sub. He'd been planning on a certain amount of caution in his approach. No longer. He'd blast anyone who tried to stop him to hell.

The cradle was there, waiting for him.

No sign of Pavski." Hannah looked up and down the pier as she jumped out of the car. "I was afraid he might beat us here."

"He can't be far behind." Kirov was beside her by the time they reached the blue iron gate that now cordoned off the submarine exhibit's loading ramp.

A ruddy-faced guard held up his hands. "Whoa there. Let's stop and—"

"I'm Hannah Bryson." She shoved her ID badge toward him. "Has anyone else been here yet today?"

"Uh, no." He frowned. "Ms. Bryson, I didn't know you were scheduled to—"

"Change of plans. Are you the only guard on duty?"

"No. James is taking a walk-around in the museum."

"Give me the key to the gate leading to the gangplank." Kirov took two walkie-talkies from the security station next to him and tossed one to Hannah. "Hurry."

The guard handed the key to him. "I could unlock it for—"

"No, I'm keeping the key." Kirov unlocked the gate, pushed Hannah through, and locked it behind them. "Get that other guard over here. The two of you take cover and radio us if anyone else comes and tries to board the sub."

"Take cover? Sir, we're armed. No one is getting on the sub who we don't *want* to get on."

"There may be a lot of firepower coming this way," Hannah said. "Get help and take cover, dammit. Don't make yourself an easy target."

The guard spoke into his walkie-talkie. "James, I need you at the *Silent Thunder* loading ramp ASAP."

"Copy that. I'm on my way."

"The aft hatch, Hannah," Kirov said curtly as he ran toward the sub. A moment later they were moving through the narrow C-Deck corridor, past the galley, and finally to the control room.

Kirov stared at the dark instrument plates. "There's no power." He glanced around. "But the lights are on."

Hannah nodded. "We tapped an AC landline to power the illumination and ventilation systems, and we dropped a few outlets so we could use our tools." She switched on a small color monitor that relayed a security-camera image from the conning tower. "I was hoping that they'd managed to power the other systems by now."

"Well, they haven't. We're literally dead in the water."

"Not for long." Hannah moved quickly toward the corridor. "I'll start the diesel engine. That will generate the power we need."

"Is there fuel?"

"The tanks were almost full when it arrived."

"Hurry." His gaze lifted to the video monitor focusing on the pier. "I'll keep an eye on things here."

Hannah ran the length of the sub until she reached an iron ladder that took her two floors below to the engineering room. She passed the empty compartments that once housed the twin nuclear reactors, then finally stepped in front of the auxiliary power panel.

She flipped the conductor and ignition switches. A low rumbling shook the sub. After another moment, sharp diesel fumes wafted up to her.

She grabbed the red boot handle and pushed it upward, activating the main power generator.

The engineering plates lit up!

"All systems go, Hannah," Kirov called. "The navigational computer is booting up."

She breathed a sigh of relief. "Thank God. I'm on my way back."

Hannah ran into the control room. "Is the navigational computer online yet?"

"It's still booting up. Remember, this system probably has only a tenth of the power as a child's modern PlayStation console." Kirov stiffened as he glanced at the security monitor. "He's here."

"What?"

"Pavski."

Hannah looked up to see a van roaring through the museum parking lot. The guard stood at his post, but his gun was drawn and at his side.

"That fool," Kirov muttered. "I told him—" He spoke into the walkie-talkie. "Take cover, dammit."

No answer from the guard.

The van bore down on the guard, showing no sign of slowing down.

"It's too late," Kirov said.

They watched, speechless, as the guard raised his gun. Before he could fire a single shot, the van struck him. His lifeless body crumpled against the fence.

Hannah looked away. Christ almighty.

"Are all hatches secured?" Kirov asked.

"My God . . ."

"I need you *here,* Hannah. Are the hatches secured?"

She nodded. "Yes."

Kirov turned back to the monitor. Four men jumped from the van and rushed toward the iron gate that led to the sub's gangplank. "Pavski and three others." He asked curtly, "Do you really think you can trick this computer into believing the *Silent Thunder* has traveled to the coordinates on those plates?"

Hannah turned to the navigation panel. "Yes, but it's going to take time."

"We don't have time."

Hannah glanced at the monitor. One of Pavski's men had fired up a blowtorch and was using it on the gate.

Kirov pulled out his automatic and checked the magazine. "He'll be through that gate in two minutes and through the hatch five minutes after that."

"There's got to be a way that—" Hannah glanced desperately around the control panel. "Maybe we can—" Her mind was racing. She stiffened as a thought came to her. Crazy.

Not so crazy. But, Jesus, could it work?

Kirov's gaze was narrowed on her face. "What?"

"Let's take her out."

Kirov went still. "By *out,* you mean . . ."

"Out. Out to sea. It'll buy me the time I need with the computer."

"This is a fifteen-thousand-ton attack submarine. You think that just the two of us can—"

"Yes!" She punched the security-camera switch, which offered a view of the bow, the exterior fence, at the harbor beyond. "You take the conn, and I'll man the engine room. We'll head straight out with as much power as we can. No turns, no dives, nothing fancy. Then we'll work on the navigational computer."

"You know Pavski will come after us."

"I'm counting on it." She smiled into his eyes. "Aren't you?"

He nodded slowly. "One last mission . . ."

"We can do it."

"Once more into the breach, old girl?" Kirov said softly as he glanced around the command room.

The commander was back, Hannah thought. She could almost feel the authority, the dynamic force, the love for the sub that had driven him all those years ago. She cleared her throat. "When you say 'old girl,' you'd better be talking to the sub."

He didn't answer.

"She deserves one last voyage. Doesn't she, Captain?"

Kirov nodded. "Aye. She deserves it."

"Watch out!"

Pavski pulled Koppel down as the second guard's bullets pinged against the iron gate. Pavski whirled around with his AK-47, but one of his other men blew the guard away before he could even line up his shot.

Koppel shrugged off Pavski's hands and swung the blowtorch away from his midsection. "Be careful, dammit. You almost roasted my nuts off." He adjusted his goggles and continued cutting through the gate.

The *Silent Thunder*'s diesel engines rumbled louder. The water off its stern churned and foamed.

Koppel froze and looked up. "What the hell's happening?"

Pavski began to curse in disbelief.

The steel cables snapped, whipping ferociously around Pavski and the men on the pier.

The iron mooring posts exploded from the concrete.

Then, as if awakening from a long slumber, the *Silent Thunder* groaned and slowly moved toward the fence separating it from the harbor.

TWENTY

Christ, they'd done it. They'd done it. They'd *done* it!

The movement was lumbering and sluggish, but the sub was actually moving, Hannah realized thankfully.

"Get up here, Hannah," Kirov called. "You can't do anything down there now that we've got the engines started."

She was already on her way. A moment later she entered the engine room to see Kirov watching the monitor as the *Silent Thunder* drew close to the museum fence.

She tensed as the sub drew closer.

Closer.

Then suddenly the *Silent Thunder* was on top of the fence.

The sub plowed over the fence without the slightest bit of resistance!

"Hallelujah," she murmured.

Too soon. Alarm sirens sounded deep within the submarine.

Kirov turned toward her. "What the hell is that?"

"The museum must have installed an alarm after what happened to Conner. It's probably tied to the same power cells as the cameras and work lights."

Kirov ran to the periscope, flipped down the handles and peered into the eyepiece. "We should clear the harbor with no problem, but our maneuverability is extremely limited. You'd better get what you need from the navigational computer in a hurry."

She turned to the computer. "Are we almost finished booting up?"

"Another minute or so."

Hurry.

Be ready.

She quickly pulled open a drawer in the command center, looked inside, and moved to the next one. Find it.

Please let it be in the next drawer. No luck. It wasn't in the next one or the drawer after that.

Kirov frowned. "What the devil are you doing?"

"I have to find it . . ."

"What are you looking for?"

Thank heavens. There it was.

She finally pulled a package of Beeman's chewing gum from the drawer. "Conner always kept a supply stashed wherever he was working."

"Funny time to get a craving."

"Can't stand the stuff." She unwrapped several sticks and shoved them into her mouth.

"Well, that clears things up." He turned toward the computer. "Whatever you plan to do, you'd better start doing it."

She picked up a stool and swung it toward a small speaker mounted over the hatch. She struck it repeatedly until the speaker housing splintered and the coil dangled from the bulkhead, gripped the magnet in her hands, and yanked it free. "Keep your radio on. I'm heading up."

Pavski turned the steering wheel and spun into the marina parking lot two miles south of the maritime museum. He glanced at the harbor, where the *Silent Thunder*'s conning tower receded into the distance.

Koppel peered though his binoculars. "They're heading straight out to sea. If they manage to submerge . . ."

"They won't. They don't have the equipment or manpower to pull that off. It's a miracle they managed to get it out there." He leaped from the van and ran to the gangway, his gaze frantically scanning the marina for the right boat.

Slow-as-molasses sailboats, pleasure craft, and houseboats.

Nothing fast enough, he realized with frustration. He needed power and speed and enough space for him and his men. Not these pussy—

Wait a second.

There, only twenty yards in front of him, a narrow-beam power-boat stood at the ready.

Perfect.

H annah climbed the narrow conning tower tube, holding the magnets she had torn from three different speakers on the way up.

Diesel fumes. Thick, nauseating.

The alarm sirens pounded her brain.

Keep steady . . .

She adjusted her headset. "Support team, do you read me?"

Kirov responded. "May I point out that I'm the one standing on the bridge? Now *you're* the support team."

"I stand corrected. Is the navigational computer receiving magnetic compass readings from the repeaters?"

"Affirmative."

She climbed up the ladder until she found herself facing the sub's magnetic compass module. Surrounded by metal coils to shield it from stray magnetic forces of the hull, this compass was generally only used early in the sub's voyages. The more accurate gyroscopic compass took several hours to calibrate itself after powering up. This was the only game in town.

One of her first recommendations had been to remove the compass and place it in the exhibit building, where it could be more easily seen by museumgoers. Thank goodness the crew hadn't gotten to it yet.

Hooking one foot around the railing for balance, she leaned forward and placed several magnets on its metallic face.

"The readings are fluctuating," Kirov said.

"Good. Longitude or latitude?"

"Both, but mostly longitude."

Hannah shifted a magnet down an inch. "This will be like cracking a safe. I'm going to move the magnets around until we get to forty-one-point-five degrees longitude. Understand?"

"Yes. We're way off right now—about eighty-five degrees north."

Hannah moved the magnets left. "How about now?"

"Better. Seventy-two degrees."

Hannah continued to move the magnet as Kirov called out: "Sixty-three . . . fifty-eight . . . fifty-one . . . forty-seven . . . forty-three . . . stop! You've got it."

Hannah tore off a piece of the chewing gum in her mouth. She affixed it to the magnet and stuck it to the compass housing. "Are we still okay?"

"It's drifting."

"That's because we're moving. I'll make more adjustments after I get the latitude. Ready?"

Kirov was silent for a moment. "Make it fast, Hannah. Pavski and his men have a boat. They're approaching from the stern."

The salt water sprayed Pavski's face as the powerboat neared the *Silent Thunder*. He pointed to the conning tower. "Watch up there," he shouted over the engines. "If we're going to be fired on, it'll be from the tower."

Koppel turned from the wheel. "Where should we approach?"

"At the stern. There are cleats to tie off there. We'll climb on top, plant the charges, and blow the rear escape hatch. Got it?"

Koppel nodded, staring ahead at the dark leviathan cutting through the water. "It's amazing."

"What?"

"There's still life in that old sub. I didn't know she had it in her."

"It's a relic," Pavski said. "Just like Kirov."

Koppel eased back on the throttle as they pulled alongside the *Silent Thunder*'s massive tail fins. The sub's engine knocked and rattled, and the pungent smoke of burned diesel fuel wafted over them.

"Take the rope and snag one of those cleats."

It took two tries, but one of the sailors managed to do it.

"Good!" Pavski yelled over the engine. "Pull us closer."

A moment later they were bumping against the hull and tying off the rope.

Pavski picked up his two backpacks and tossed them onto the *Silent Thunder*'s topside deck.

"The three of you climb aboard," Koppel said. "I'll keep the boat steady."

Pavski shot him a cold glance. "I need you in there too, Koppel."

"After you're on, I'll cut the engines and climb aboard myself. Go!"

As they left the relatively calm waters of the harbor, Pavski and the others jumped from the boat and used a series of small crevices in the *Silent Thunder*'s rubbery acoustic coating to pull themselves up to the top deck. "Careful. The seas are getting rougher."

Koppel cut the powerboat's ignition and climbed up to join them. "Aren't the hatches stronger than the rest of the sub?" he shouted.

Pavski was already digging into his knapsack for the explosive charges. "Trust me, two of these charges on the devices on the rear hatch will put us face-to-face with Kirov in less than five minutes."

Hannah wiped the sweat from her eyes as she adjusted the magnets again. Dammit, she couldn't manipulate the compass to read the correct longitude and latitude simultaneously.

"Give it up," Kirov said over the radio. "It was always a long shot."

"*I* can't give it up. Pavski's not going to get that cradle. If I can just move it another few degrees . . ."

"We're out of time. Pavski and his men will be charging down the corridor at any moment. I have to be ready for them. I can't focus on this any longer."

"Keep your eyes on that monitor. Where's the compass at?"

"The longitude is still three degrees shy. Forget it."

"Please. Just another few seconds."

"We don't have any seconds to spare. You're through."

"What about now?"

"Hannah, stop it. We need to—"

Kirov's voice went silent.

Hannah held the magnets in place, not daring to breathe. "Hello?"

Kirov's voice finally broke the silence. "Good God."

Kirov stared at the navigational computer's amber screen. One moment, Hannah's generated 41.5 degrees longitude/112 degrees latitude had filled the screen, in the next an entirely different set of coordinates popped up: *32.4° E Longitude 44.1° N Latitude.*

Hannah, you're a goddamn miracle.

"We've got it!" he said into the microphone. "It looks like it's in the Black Sea. I'll write it down."

"Hurry. It may disappear once we drift off the coordinates."

He scribbled the figures on one of Hannah's discarded chewing gum wrappers. "Got it. Meet me in the forward torpedo room, Hannah."

"Why?"

"Change of plans. And if you get there before I do, get yourself into an MK10."

She was silent, but he could sense the shock that went through her.

"Do it, Hannah. No arguments. You're support, not command right now."

"MK10. Are you sure about this?"

"It's the only way. I'll see you down there."

Kirov turned back to the computer and kicked it repeatedly, smashing the console with his left heel. Sparks flew, and the monitor went dark.

MK10.

Dear God in heaven.

Hannah ran into the forward torpedo room, where the earsplitting alarm was even louder than it had been at the compass module. She opened a supply locker, where eight MK10 submarine escape-and-immersion suits hung. They probably hadn't been touched since a drill years before.

She knew that the British-made MK10s were standard-issue equipment in almost every submarine fleet in the world, but she hadn't been aware the Russians used them until her first visit aboard *Silent Thunder.* They had never been extensively used in crisis situations. The bulky, padded outfits were created for one purpose: for emergency deep sea escapes, commonly through a hatch. In extreme situations the wearer could climb into a firing tube and be shot out like a torpedo. It had always seemed to be an absurd notion to Hannah, since extreme depths would kill its wearer anyway, and in shallower waters there were far safer alternatives to evacuating a submarine.

Except maybe this time, this place.

She slid into the salt-encrusted suit and fastened the buckles at her waist, wrist, and ankles. If only Conner could see her now. He'd *love* this.

Kirov jumped through the hatch. "Hurry, Hannah. Put on the helmet and climb into the tube headfirst."

"What about Pavski?"

"Pavski will be taken care of."

She looked down to see that Kirov was holding his canvas bag, the one in which he'd carried Niler's explosives.

It was now empty.

She stared at Kirov as realization dawned. "You booby-trapped the sub."

"Yes."

"Where?"

"Where it will do the most damage."

"The aft fuel tanks?"

He nodded. "Being a museum piece wouldn't suit *Silent Thunder*. She'll like going down in a blaze of glory."

"How soon?"

"She only has a few more minutes to live."

"Like anyone who's still in here when those charges detonate."

Kirov motioned toward the open torpedo chamber. "Quickly. Pavski may already be inside the sub."

"We haven't tested the torpedo tubes. They may not even fire anymore. They might just fill with water and drown us."

"That's why you have to go first."

"Are you joking?"

"If there's a malfunction, I need to be here to pull you out." He took the helmet and opened the latches. "It looks like I'm only your support team once again."

"It's too risky. These things were finicky even in the best of circumstances."

"You'll be fine." He smiled. "Remember what I told you about the *Silent Thunder* having a soul?"

"You mean that bit about her coming through whenever you needed her most," she said unevenly.

"Yes. She's not about to let us down now."

"You'll be right behind me?"

"There's a trigger switch inside the tube. Once you're away, I'll go myself."

She stiffened as a sudden memory of the nightmares he had told her about came back to her. "You're lying."

"Hurry, Hannah."

"No." She stepped back. "You're planning to go down with your ship, you crazy Russian."

"There isn't time for this."

"This is insane. However you feel about the *Silent Thunder*'s so-called soul . . ."

"I didn't say I was—"

"You've served her well, Kirov," she said desperately. "Now let her go."

"We're out of time."

Kirov slammed her against the bulkhead and dropped the helmet over her head. As she struggled to break free, he fastened the latches.

"Thank you, Hannah." He leaned so close that his breath fogged her faceplate as he spoke. "Thank you for everything." He smiled gently. "*Pomni, ya vsegda ryadom.*"

He picked her up and pushed her into the open hatch of torpedo tube four.

"Kirov, come with me," she called frantically. "The same tube at the same time. Don't do this!"

The hatch slammed shut behind her.

Darkness.

Silence, except for the faint knocking of engines.

Damn him.

She heard, then felt, a trickle of cool salt water pouring into the chamber. Could the old pumps even pull this off?

The trickle became a stream, and the stream became a torrent. Water leaked through the suit's tattered seams. She became buoyant, floating in the center of the chamber.

The water climbed higher. She held her breath, trying to preserve the precious little oxygen her suit still held. The water ran cold against her cheek.

The moment of truth. She crossed her ankles, lowered her head, and folded her arms across her chest. She wished she'd inspected the tube. A piece of twisted metal or a bent plate in her path would tear her to shreds.

The Silent Thunder *is always at her best when you need her most.*

Hannah suddenly relaxed. Nestled in the *Silent Thunder*'s watery embrace, she somehow felt . . . protected. Cared for. Treasured.

Was the lack of oxygen making her loopy?

Probably.

Or maybe she was just an atheist in a foxhole.

A roar filled her ears, and thousands of pounds of pressure slammed her from behind.

Pavski, Koppel, Lepin, and Norzalk stood on the bridge, staring at the smoldering remains of the navigational computer.

"*Blin!*" Pavski swung the butt of his gun toward the console.

"Wait," Koppel said. "This means Kirov and Bryson must have the coordinates. All we have to do is find them, and . . ."

Koppel fell silent as they felt a distinct vibration and heard the release of enormous pressure from the sub's hold.

"It's the torpedo chamber," Pavski said.

Koppel eyes widened. "The escape suits. They're getting away?"

Pavski ran for the hatch. "Or we were meant to *think* they are. Kirov is a driven man. He wouldn't give up this chance to take me out."

They moved down the narrow midship stairwell to the engineering level, where the engine noise was almost deafening. He motioned for Lepin and Norzalk to proceed down the starboard service corridor. They nodded and disappeared through the narrow hatch.

Pavski turned and stared down the main passageway. "I know you're here, Captain!"

No reply.

He and Koppel crept down the passageway with their guns at the ready. "You couldn't come this close to me without wanting to finish the job. Not when I'm standing in the gangway of this stinking monstrosity you love so much."

No response.

They were now in the mechanical section. The engine noise and diesel stench were overpowering.

"Here I am, Kirov. Your chance at last. Come and get me."

He heard Koppel whimper behind him. Stupid coward.

"Pavski," Koppel muttered.

Pavski gave him an impatient glance, then stiffened as he saw the terrified expression on Koppel's face. He slowly turned his head, and his gaze followed Koppel's to the fuel tanks.

Pack after pack of plastic explosives, mounted on either side of the fuel tanks.

The triggering mechanism flashed red and emitted a high-pitched whine.

Hannah tilted her head back and clawed for the surface, writhing and spinning in the water like a towel in a washing machine. But which way was up? The direction seemed to change every second.

She'd never felt anything like this before; it was like . . .

Like being shot out of a freaking torpedo tube.

She finally broke the surface. She fumbled for the latches, lifted off her helmet, and tossed it into the water. Air!

There was a deep, metallic rumbling behind her. She turned to look at the sub.

The charges erupted deep within the *Silent Thunder,* their intensity magnified and spread by the massive fuel reserves. The back third of the submarine buckled, heaved, and tore open from the sheer explosive force.

Kirov!

More explosions, throwing spires of flame high into the sky. *Silent Thunder* listed hard to starboard as oil in the water caught fire around its superstructure.

She couldn't take her eyes off it.

In the next few minutes, the ruptured hull took on water, pulling the sub down by its stern. Pockets of air exploded to the surface. The burning, twisting metal groaned like a wounded whale. The anguished sounds continued as the *Silent Thunder* plunged beneath the waves, leaving a massive field of debris and burning oil in its wake.

Hannah trod water, stunned.

Kirov and the *Silent Thunder.* Gone.

"Goddamn you," she whispered, tears running down her face. "Goddamned men and the sea. There's no sense to you."

A white craft in the distance headed straight for her. Probably a Coast Guard cutter. Hard to steal a 560-foot Russian submarine without somebody taking notice, she thought.

She turned back to the debris field. Kirov had probably thought it was fitting for him to die with the sub he loved so much. And maybe it was.

To hell with that.

It was just one more tragic loss. She'd had enough tragedy. She didn't want Kirov to—

Something was moving, bobbing slightly out of sync with the rest of the floating debris. It almost looked like . . .

She swam past the pools of burning oil, a task made difficult by the sheer bulk of her suit. As she drew closer, she momentarily lost sight of the object.

Had she just imagined it?

No. There it was, less than ten feet in front of her.

The helmet of an MK10 suit.

"Kirov!"

No response.

She pushed herself forward, grabbed the suit's padding, and spun it around.

It *was* Kirov.

Unconscious? Dead?

She unlatched his helmet, yanked it off, and splashed water in his face. "Wake up. You come back to me, Kirov. Do you hear me?"

He couldn't die. Not now.

"Kirov!" She slapped his face as hard as she could.

He opened his eyes. "That hurt."

Relief surged through her. "Can you move? Wiggle your toes."

He nodded. "I'm fine. You?"

"Yes."

"Any sign of Pavski?"

"No. He's gone."

He glanced at the debris and burning oil. "And so is the *Silent Thunder*."

"Yes. I was afraid you were—"

"The thought occurred to me. After all, there is a certain tradition and obligation."

"Bullshit."

He smiled. "That's what I thought. *Silent Thunder* would want me to survive. She's saved me too many times for me not to realize that."

"You cut it close."

"I had to make sure Pavski was inside the sub. The charge went off just as I ejected."

"Then you're lucky to be alive."

"Lucky." He thought about it. "Do you know, I'm feeling very lucky at this moment. Would you like me to tell you why?"

She felt a warm surge of feeling as she looked at him.

"No." She tore her eyes away from him and glanced at the Coast Guard cutter, which was almost upon them. "Save it. That officer on the bridge looks pretty grim. We may need all the luck we can get in the next few hours."

EPILOGUE

"There it is," Hannah murmured as she stood on the top deck watching the eight-foot oval black capsule being lifted by a crane from the sea. "Right where Heiser said it would be."

"Good thing for you." Bradworth gave her a sour glance. "If you'd been wrong, you'd have been in pretty hot water with my superiors. The only reason they let you off the hook for blowing that sub is the deal you and Kirov made to give them the location."

"But we weren't wrong," Kirov said. "And you'll be able to make some pretty fancy deals yourself when you contact the Czechs and Russians. They'll be falling over each other to do you favors."

Bradworth shrugged. "The company thought Pavski would have been a much more valuable prize."

"What did *you* think?" Hannah asked.

Bradworth was silent as they watched the crane swing the capsule toward the deck near them. "I think Pavski is exactly where he deserved to be. That's strictly off the record, of course."

"Of course."

It was grudging approval, but in the three weeks since the destruction of the *Silent Thunder,* Bradworth had been surly but marginally supportive. That was all they could hope for from him considering how much flack he was taking. There had been grueling sessions of debriefing and interrogations, and the only weapon they'd had to survive was the cradle that was being carefully set on the deck.

And when weighed against the gratitude she felt for what he'd done to save Cathy's children, she had no problem with that surliness.

Bradworth glanced back at Hannah. "I understand that the maritime museum is already in negotiations to purchase another decommissioned Russian sub."

Hannah shrugged. "I talked to some friends. The Logan Foundation is giving them a very generous grant. I told them I'd donate my services if they— It's down! Come on, Kirov." She hurried over to the spot where the capsule had come to rest, steered gently into place by eight waiting sailors.

Several large bulletin boards were set up nearby, covered with photos to serve as a visual reference for the items that might make up the treasure. Two officers and three historians with bulky notebooks were standing ready to document the find.

"Easy." Kirov's gaze was on her face. "Anticipation sometimes leads to disappointment."

"Don't give me that morose Slavic bullshit. I have a right to be excited, and I'm going to run with it."

Kirov smiled. "By all means. And I'll enjoy every minute of watching you."

A young sailor with a tool kit began work on the corroded iron latches, chipping away at them with a small hammer and chisel. He worked through the latches in just a few minutes, and when he was finished, two other sailors helped pry open the capsule.

They separated the two halves to reveal thick pads of black felt padding. They lifted out the largest of the pads and carefully unwrapped it.

It was like a nesting box, Hannah thought, with each layer giving away to another, smaller package. Finally, under the eighth layer, she saw a glint of gold.

She stepped closer.

"*Kolybel*," Kirov said quietly.

The Golden Cradle of Princess Libushe's firstborn was less than eight feet in front of Hannah. She didn't even have to look at the visual references to know they'd found the real thing.

Gleaming in the sunlight, it was simply stunning. The craftsmanship was clean and elegant, and the sides—inside and out—featured intricate patterns that could only be the work of a master. The bejeweled rockers caught the light and bathed the onlookers in an ethereal rainbow glow.

"The paintings don't do it justice," Kirov said.

Hannah shook her head, unable to look away. "No painting could." She reached out a tentative hand. It felt . . . solid. Well, what had she expected? That it would vanish or crumble when she touched it? "Conner would have loved it," she said softly. "It would dazzle him . . ."

"It will dazzle millions once it's in a museum," Kirov said. "And you were responsible for saving it for them."

"Why are you making me out to be noble? That's crap." She turned away from the cradle and moved over to the rail. "I didn't do it for humanity. I did it to keep Pavski from getting his filthy hands on it. I wasn't going to let him have his dream even for a second."

He chuckled. "I can always count on you for blunt honesty. But I watched your expression when you saw the cradle. Perhaps it wasn't as enthralled as when you examined a fine piece of machinery, but there was a hint of bedazzlement in you too."

"Of course there was. I appreciate both beauty and antiquities. I told you I'm not like one of your submarines."

"But you are." His smile faded. "Smart and sleek and with all the thrust and heart that any captain could ever want."

She couldn't breathe. "Jesus, are you propositioning me?"

"No. I promise you'll know when I do that. But it doesn't hurt to make a few opening moves to let you become accustomed to the idea. After a few months at Marinth, I'll get serious."

Her eyes widened. "Marinth?"

"I need something to occupy my time while I decide what path to take. I contacted your employers at Marinth and told them how valuable I'd be to them during the recovery operation."

"They hired you?"

"I can be very persuasive."

God knows, she knew that was true. "It's my job. I won't let you get in my way."

He smiled. "We'll take turns being the support team. That way it will be less damaging to our egos. We can work it out."

She felt a warm surge of feeling as she looked at him. "Maybe we can. Do you think it will be worthwhile to try?"

"Oh, yes. Most definitely."

The sun was stroking his dark hair with light, and the expression in his eyes . . .

She suddenly wanted to reach out and touch him.

Christ, in front of Bradworth and a shipload of sailors?

She glanced away from him. "It could be difficult. I didn't like it when you slammed me into that torpedo tube."

"It was necessary. I didn't like it when you socked me in the jaw when we were in the water."

"It was necessary." She had a sudden thought. "You said something in Russian right before you crammed me in that tube. What was it?"

"Pomni, ya vsegda ryadom." His brows lifted. "If you were curious, I'm surprised you didn't look it up before this." Then he shook his head. "No, you started backpedaling even before you hit the water. You didn't want to know. I'm encouraged that you're asking now."

"Stop analyzing and tell me what it means."

"Remember, I'll always be with you," he said softly.

She felt a wave of joy and warmth so intense it almost overwhelmed her. Too intense. Don't lose control. "How completely sappy," she said unsteadily.

"What do you expect? I'm Russian. We're not afraid of being sappy when the occasion calls for it. It's you Americans who are embarrassed by sentiment." He smiled into her eyes. "Sappy can be both fitting and wonderful. Admit it."

"I don't have to ad—" Oh, what the devil. The sun was bright, treasures were being found, and perhaps another was right before her on the horizon. She smiled luminously back at him and nodded. "Okay, I admit it. Absolutely wonderful . . ."